ALIEN CONTACT

The viewing room was crowded. Everyone wanted to see what was overhead: the sun. Random conversations started up throughout the room and then died away.

And then the gray hole rose above the lunar horizon, and all conversation died. Breathing stopped. Thought stopped.

It was properly named: a disk like that of the rising sun, but glowing only with a faint gray light.

Its motion was visible against the moon's horizon. As it rose in the lunar sky, it seemed to grow smaller.

And then the gray hole disappeared. It simply vanished. The sky was filled with stars, like any normal night sky seen from the far side of the moon.

But there was no more sun.

DAVID DVORKIN

CENTRAL HEAT

ACE BOOKS, NEW YORK

This book is an Ace original edition,
and has never been previously published.

CENTRAL HEAT

An Ace Book/published by arrangement with
the author

PRINTING HISTORY
Ace edition/November 1988

ISBN: 0-441-09859-2

Ace Books are published by The Berkley Publishing Group,
200 Madison Avenue, New York, New York 10016.
The name "ACE" and the "A" logo
are trademarks belonging to Charter Communications, Inc.

PRINTED IN THE UNITED STATES OF AMERICA

10 9 8 7 6 5 4 3 2 1

CENTRAL HEAT

2008–2009

"Well, what did they have to say?"

Horwith snorted. "They told me there's a team of experts on the way over from Mendeleev to have a look. We're to 'cooperate fully.' "

"So much for letting us handle it ourselves."

"Yeah. We're not real scientists; we don't count." Honesty forced him to add grudgingly, "Of course, Battani is at Mendeleev, and he's part of the team that's coming here. I suppose he knows a lot more about this junk than we do." The white arm of his surface suit gestured clumsily toward the stacks of electronic gear before which he and Glen Alenian were seated. He let his arm drift down again in the gentle gravity. It bumped the side of the boulder he was leaning against.

Beneath their feet was the bare, barren, beautiful surface of the moon. The helter-skelter piles of equipment—some of it in smooth metal casings, some exposed like jury-rigged laboratory equipment, and all bound together by a bewildering rat's nest of wiring—was exposed to the vacuum. Its only protection came from the huge boulders which sheltered it on three sides, forming a cul-de-sac, and the flimsy metal roof fastened to the tops of the boulders. Sunlight was thus kept off the equipment, and it was adequately protected from meteorites, but since it required a very hard vacuum to operate, the enclosure was not sealed and pressurized. Horwith, used as he was to working in uncomfortable surroundings, nonetheless hated the necessity of spending all of his shift in his awkward surface suit.

Alenian said soothingly, "It's probably a good idea, then. Battani more or less invented T-band, didn't he?"

"Discovered." Horwith made the correction automatically. "Oh, I guess I don't mind too much. It gets boring sitting out here with nothing to do but monitor the equipment; the company'll be

3

welcome. But they'd better not get any ideas about moving the stuff over to Mendeleev and using their own people to run it."

Alenian laughed at the idea. "NASA would fight that tooth and nail."

"Also," Horwith added thoughtfully, "we could make the argument that we don't know how well it would operate that close to the big antennas at Mendeleev. We really don't know enough yet about how prone T-band is to interference." He pushed himself away from the boulder. "Well, they should be here any minute. I'll go look for them."

He stepped out from the shelter into the brilliant sunlight, sliding the dark, highly reflective sunscreen down over his visor. He stood still and scanned the sky, but all he could see was the usual wild blaze of stars, unblinking and many-colored. If anything was moving among them, it was invisible to him. Presumably, the vehicle bringing the team of experts from Mendeleev would be flying low, in which case it would slip over the horizon only minutes before arriving.

Nearby stood the rover that had brought him and Alenian here from their nearby base at the beginning of their shift. Behind him was the sun, small and blinding white, impossible to look at even through his sunscreen. It was low now, near the uneven horizon, casting his shadow long before him along the moon's rolling surface. Even further behind him, he knew, but beyond the horizon, was the lovely blue-white ball of Earth. He had spent months on this tour of duty. It would be Paradise to get back to a place where he could go outside a building without first squeezing into a space ship with arms and legs. He hated the moon.

The Mendeleev surface shuttle appeared suddenly over the lunar horizon, unsettling Horwith even though he had been expecting it to come into view in just that way. It arrowed toward him, no more than twenty meters above the surface, slowing as it passed over the rover.

The shuttle was a long, slender vehicle that flew with its long axis parallel to the ground. Small rocket nozzles were spaced evenly along the bottom, and small, round windows lined the side facing Horwith. He felt a surge of jealousy and resentment.

Budget-conscious NASA restricted its personnel to the rovers, wire-frame vehicles descended with little change from the lunar rovers originally built for the Apollo missions of forty years earlier. The rovers were cramped and uncomfortable, notoriously short on springs or shock absorbers. If driven too fast, they showered their occupants with lunar dust. They were powered by banks of batteries that had to be regularly recharged from sunlight and which seemed to require such recharging at least twice as frequently as the manual claimed they did—and which seemed to choose to go permanently dead just when their crews would be faced with long and exhausting walks back to base.

The Mendeleev shuttle stopped quite some distance away from Horwith. It hovered, sank toward the ground, then hovered again about three meters above it. Horwith could feel the vibration through his boots. A cloud of dust arose, completely obscuring the vehicle. Then the vibration coming to him through the ground stopped, and almost immediately the dust fell back down; in an instant, all was clear again. The shuttle rested upon four metal legs, one at each corner, each bent outward in the middle, so that it looked like a giant insect, some creatures of the vacuum that had landed temporarily upon the moon for its own obscure purposes.

Beneath the shuttle a cage appeared, descending slowly toward the surface. As the elevator reached the bottom and stopped, the four surface-suited figures in it shuffled about uncertainly, and at last plucked up their courage enough to leave it. They struggled across the surface toward the waiting figure of Horwith, who felt flushed with superiority at their clumsiness. He knew the type. They might spend years working on the moon and yet never go outside a building, out to the true surface, except in an emergency. They might never put on a surface suit, spending their time in office buildings that, except for the gravity, might as well be on Earth. *They* might as well be on Earth, he thought scornfully, forgetting the hatred for the moon and the longing to be home he had felt only minutes before.

Horwith tongued his suit radio on and uttered the appropriate greetings, then led the four newcomers back to the shelter where Alenian still sat monitoring the behavior of the T-band receiver.

The four from Mendeleev took over the pile of equipment immediately. They asked the two NASA men a few questions, but with so much open skepticism that Horwith could hardly prevent himself from asking them why they'd bothered to come, if they doubted the existence of the signal he and his partner had picked up.

Watching the four of them more closely, Horwith realized that only three of them were really dealing with the equipment. While his three companions examined the T-band receiver, their hands working with surgeon's skill even though encumbered by the gloves of their surface suits, the fourth man ignored the equipment itself but pored with total absorption over the records of the signal.

There was much for him to look at. Even though the signal had only been coming in for about two hours now, there was a substantial pile of hardcopy output. When the signal first caught Horwith and Alenian's attention, they had examined it in various ways, including audio and graphic representations, before making a report. Neither had been anxious to overreact to what might be a peculiarity of the electronics, rather than a genuine incoming signal. If it were real, it might be a discovery of immense importance. If it were merely an artifact of their experimental equipment, they could ruin their careers by sounding the alarm prematurely. So they had taken their time, and now Battani—Horwith guessed that the fourth man was he, even though none of them had deigned to introduce himself—had the records of their preliminary investigation to look over.

The suited figure put down the papers at last, straightened up, and stood still, as though lost in thought. After a few minutes, he walked over to the three men who were still examining the receiver and talked with them for a while. Horwith tongued his suit radio through the standard channels, trying to pick up their conversation, but all he could find was a meaningless gabble on one. Mendeleev had apparently added encoding/decoding equipment to its suits.

The fourth man left the group and came up to Horwith and Alenian. Still tuned to the same channel, Horwith now had no trouble understanding him: he had apparently turned off his encoder in order to speak to the *canaille*. "You are Mr. Horwith and Mr. Alenian? Good day, gentlemen. My name is Battani."

Horwith tapped Alenian three times on the shoulder, quickly and lightly, to indicate the proper channel in case he hadn't already found it by himself. "I'm Horwith." He raised a hand to show it was he who had spoken. Alenian mumbled something vague, and Horwith could hear the suppressed laughter in Alenian's voice.

They all had their sunvisors up, of course, and in the low-power electric light under the canopy, Horwith could see easily through Battani's faceplate, so he understood what had amused Alenian so.

Mendeleev bought its surface suits from NASA and was therefore stuck with two standard sizes, one designed for the average five-foot-ten-inch man, and the other for the average five-foot-five-inch woman. Battani must have been scarcely over five feet in height, and his eyes barely cleared the bottom of the faceplate. His was probably one of the suits designed for female surface workers, with minor modifications to the internal plumbing done by Mendeleev technicians. Perhaps they had also added height inside the boots for Battani's convenience, but if so, it had not been enough to really help. Not that they could have done much for him without making the suit impossible to use. Wearing the suit and working inside it must be an endless misery for him, Horwith realized.

Horwith felt a rush of sympathy for the man. He was six and a half feet tall himself and extremely thin, and it was something like torture to squeeze himself into his suit before his shift—and almost worse torture to unfold himself from it when his shift was over. A custom-made suit was supposedly on its way from Earth, but he'd been hearing that for months, and he suspected that his tour on the moon would be up well before it arrived. Men like him and Battani—too many *sigmas* away from *mu*—could expect no sympathy from Alenian, who was blessed with precisely average height and weight. "Dr. Battani—" he began.

"Please," Battani cut in, "call me Al."

"Okay. Al, then. Have you come to any conclusions about our signal?"

Battani laughed. "Obviously you think it's real. You should have called it 'the anomaly,' in the approved manner. However, I think you're right. I think it is a real signal and not just an electronic quirk."

"You *think*?" From Alenian. "Hell, I thought you were the guy who was supposed to know everything about T-band. Don't you *know* whether or not it's a signal?"

Battani sighed. "I've run into this misconception before, Mr. Alenian. I'm an astrophysicist; I know virtually nothing about electronics. T-band was an accidental by-product of something else, my work on a theoretical problem. The problem is still unsolved, by the way. But this," he pointed at the receiver, "this electronic realization of the theory—no, I don't understand it at all. However, those men do, and they seem to think the equipment is working just as it should. What you've picked up must be a real signal, coming from outside your receiver. I've been looking at the excellent preparatory investigation you two performed, and it's clear there is a significant pattern."

Alenian burst out, "A message, you mean! My God, it's a message from somewhere!"

"No, no, that's not what I said."

But the other two men weren't listening. "A message," Horwith whispered. "Christ, I wish we had a transmitter working already! We've got to respond somehow."

"You're being too hasty," Battani insisted. "I'd like to explain what I mean, but I'm sure you're impatient for us to get out of your hair, and I simply can't spend much longer in this space suit."

"Surface suit," Alenian said.

Ignoring his partner, Horwith answered Battani's objections. "It's true we're supposed to do quite a few more hours of testing, but I do think this takes precedence. Anyway, I was ordered to give you full cooperation, and if you think that includes giving us a lecture on T-band, how can NASA object?"

Battani laughed. "Jesuitical sophistry! I do have to get back, but you're welcome to come back to Mendeleev with us. We always have room for visitors there."

"Hey, wait a minute," Alenian said, his voice angry. "We can't just leave this equipment alone."

"I can order a couple of my men to stay behind and guard it," Battani said quickly.

"No, I don't think so." Alenian's voice was cold. "I'm sure NASA wouldn't approve of that at all."

"Then you stay here with it," Horwith snapped at him. Christ, what an asshole, he thought. "I'll go to Mendeleev. Gladly."

As he was gliding toward the Mendeleev shuttle with Battani and the three others a few minutes later, Horwith radioed, "So long, Glen. I'll be back at base before our next shift."

Alenian still sounded hostile. "See you later, Pole."

Horwith checked his stride for the barest instant and then walked steadily toward the shuttle. Battani had caught his reaction, however. Once the elevator had carried them up into the body of the shuttle and the locks had been sealed, so that they could take off their suits and talk directly rather than over radio, Battani said mildly, "Your friend called you Pole. I was told your first name is Clemmons."

"It is, but Pole is what most people here call me."

"Because they think your surname is Polish?"

"Partly." He longed to drop the subject.

Battani looked up at the remarkably tall, thin engineer. "I see. If you don't mind, I'd rather call you Clemmons."

Horwith smiled down at him.

Arriving at Mendeleev was anticlimactic. Horwith had been fascinated by the great multinational observatory from the moment its construction was first seriously suggested, almost ten years earlier. He had followed the press reports of the building of it within the great farside crater with intense interest (The Eye at the Back of the Moon, as the press called it), hoping that someday he would be able to get one of the rare and coveted non-scientific jobs there. To an extent, that hope had led to his going to work for NASA—only to discover that no NASA personnel were stationed at Mendeleev, that in fact there was a growing animosity between the aging space-agency management and the new, international upper echelon of the United Nations–sponsored organization formed solely to run the new observatory. And he had discovered that he hated life on the moon.

Still, the old dream had never quite died. At the very least, Horwith hoped that he would now get a chance to see the ring of mighty radio and optical telescopes sited along Mendeleev's rim, that the shuttle would pass close to at least one of them on its way in toward the administrative and residential buildings clustered together at the crater's center. That hope, too, was destined to be dashed.

They approached the crater rim flying only meters above the lunar surface, and they grounded between two other shuttles on the outside surface of the crater wall, on a terrace cut into the wall. At the last moment, just before landing, Horwith was able to look up and catch a glimpse, far above on the very rim of the crater, of a spiderweb gleaming in the sunlight, a spiderweb on a vast scale. Then even that was hidden by the dirt and rock of the wall of Mendeleev.

The party left the shuttle through a flexible tube that had attached itself to the shuttle hatch; it was provided with Earth-normal air pressure, so that they were able to leave their helmets off, which Horwith considered a blessing. The tube led them to a small building, the terminus of an elevator, which in turn took them down some distance into an underground tunnel. Here a railroad track stretched off into the well lit distance, and a small subway car, with room for no more than ten people, waited for them. They climbed aboard and were taken the rest of the way to the headquarters of the observatory.

"Anticlimactic, I know," Battani apologized. "A walk across the crater to the center is much more impressive. But this is much quicker, and for me it's a lot more comfortable."

"And for me," Horwith told him. "Sometimes, I really hate the moon. Walking outside here isn't like walking outside on Earth. I long for a place where you can go outside without having to stuff yourself into a cramped surface suit, where you can breathe because there's something there to breathe. Breezes and flowers and people."

One of the other men said, "And the girls in their summer dresses?"

Horwith grinned. "Yeah. That too."

Another man chimed in, "And breezes to lift up the dresses."

Battani grimaced. "Some things never change," he muttered, loud enough for only Horwith to hear him.

"Some things shouldn't," Horwith told him.

This leg of the trip ended at another elevator. They rose into sunshine, muted and pleasant. As he had imagined, the buildings at Mendeleev—all connected by surface tubes and underground tunnels—were as much like Earth-surface office buildings as possible. One could spend his entire tour of duty inside them, never stepping outside. Even the rare times an astronomer had to travel in person to one of the telescopes, Horwith was to learn, he could do so by subway and elevator, ending his trip in an airtight, sealed building at the telescope's base. Only the gravity and one other thing reminded the personnel at Mendeleev that they were on the moon and not on Earth—the silent, still, sterile landscape seen through the myriad windows.

Battani led the way down a maze of corridors to his office. This, too, was flooded with muted sunshine. A pleasant enough effect, but the office itself was minuscule, and it was crowded, a desk and a table covered with papers taking up most of the room. "Space is still at a premium here," Battani explained. "At least until our new building is ready, which won't be until sometime next spring. In the meantime, it's a good thing I'm not your size, or this coffin would seem even worse than it already does. Here."

He pushed some of the papers on the table aside carefully, clearing a small space for himself. He pulled himself up easily to a seat on the table and gestured to Horwith to take the swivel chair by the desk.

"Now, then, Clemmons. The guru of the mountaintop shall enlighten you."

"What I was getting at back there is this," Battani said. "It's true that what you picked up seems to be a signal of some sort, not produced inside your receiver, and it's also obviously not some sort of random stellar noise. The patterns you showed in those hardcopies simply can't be denied—even if you're the sort who tries to deny such things, as so many of my colleagues are. But that doesn't mean it's a message, a deliberate signal. Remember the pulsars."

"Sure. Who could forget them? A rock group, weren't they?"

Battani grinned. "No, but they *were* stars. Neutron stars. We're both too young to have been born when they were discovered and all the fuss started. That was"—he thought for a moment—"about forty years ago. Neutron stars had been predicted theoretically quite some time before, thirty years before, but no one had yet found one. Then radio astronomers in England found a radio source that was pulsing at them, throbbing, with a period, or cycle time, of about one and one third seconds.

"At first, they thought they must be picking up some man-made signal from Earth, just as we first thought your signal must come from inside your receiver itself. They even thought they might be tuned in on a signal from some other observatory! Finally, they were able to convince themselves that the signal was truly extraterrestrial. But it was so fast, and so remarkably regular! How, they asked themselves, could it possibly be natural? Eventually the connection was made with neutron stars. But for a long time, there was a spate of articles in the popular press all over the world, speculating madly about what these strange objects must be. The most popular idea was that they were navigation beacons for some interstellar civilization. Other pulsars had been found, with other cycle times, so that possibly you could determine your position during interstellar flight by identifying a few of them and determining the direction from you to them very accurately. Or you might be able to calculate your distance from them, based on signal strength, which would also give you your position in terms of a fixed-coordinate system."

"So you're saying we shouldn't get excited," Horwith said, feeling a strong sense of disappointment. "Even though there is a pattern, and it's so complex, it might just be a natural phenomenon."

"Exactly! But don't despair on that account. You may still have contributed to an astronomical discovery of incalculable importance. Remember the pulsars again! The astronomer who found the first one won a Nobel Prize for it, and, not coincidentally, what you've found may get me my Nobel. There's bound to be some recognition in it for you, as well," he added quickly.

Horwith sighed. "If it would persuade NASA to give me a promotion at last, I'd be happy. You know, when I was a kid, my greatest wish was to be an astronaut, but then someone told me I'd have to cut off my legs to even fit into the interplanetary vehicles they were designing—and then I'd be disqualified because NASA doesn't want any legless astronauts."

Battani shook his head. "It's strange what can destroy a dream." He shrugged, as if to drive the mood away. "I was about to explain that what you've found could just possibly be developed into a new area of astromony, an entirely new way of studying space. Conceivably, if that signal is being put out by a star, as pulsar signals are, we could now have a means of examining stars at the very edge of the Universe, and a way of studying the deep interiors of stars, and even a view into a black hole. And I mean *into* it—to the singularity itself."

"It's exciting," Horwith admitted, his disappointment fading only slightly, "but not as exciting to me as it must be to you. And not as exciting as a message from an alien civilization."

"Bah!" Battani jumped down from the desk and tried to pace about in the tiny space, able to glide only one energetic step in each direction. He waved his hands. Words flooded from him. "Alien civilizations, Clemmons! Nonsense! Unimportant! Nothing Man can devise, and nothing any aliens could devise, no matter how evolved they might be, could ever compare to the amazing things Nature has already experimented with out there. Neutron stars and black holes are just the start. And now, with T-band astronomy, we can really find them, really know what they are, how they work. What can aliens offer us to compete with that?''

"How to make a better mousetrap, maybe."

Battani stopped, brought up short in his enthusiasm. For a moment, he seemed angry, and then he relaxed and burst out into laughter directed at himself. "You're quite right! And they might also know how to make a T-band telescope."

"Okay. Now, why would your T-band telescope be such a great thing?"

"Aah, good!" Battani rubbed his hands together. "Just what I wanted: an excuse to lecture. First, do you know what the tunnelling effect is?"

"Vaguely. I know that tunnel junctions were very important in seventh-generation computer circuits."

Battani looked uneasy. "Let's stay away from that sort of thing. I have a mental block against it. I don't know a diode from a transistor."

"I guess not," Horwith laughed. "Okay, Professor. Treat me like I don't know anything at all, and you won't be far wrong."

"All right. First of all, you did have the right tunnel effect in mind. I know that much electronics, at least. That's electron tunnelling. It's a quantum mechanical phenomenon whereby an electron can cross a potential barrier without actually having to get over or through it. One moment it's on one side, and then presto! it's on the other."

Now Horwith looked uneasy. "This sounds slightly familiar. I think I heard it in college, but I have a mental block against it."

"You're in good company, then. Even Einstein never accepted quantum theory. 'God doesn't play dice with the Universe,' he said. We've made the dice a lot more complicated since his time; he'd probably dislike quantum mechanics even more now. Sometimes it seems like magic to me, even after all the years I've used it in my work. However, unlike magic, it works—does what it's supposed to. It's an adequate description of the Universe. The computers you mentioned work be— They do work, don't they?"

"Generally speaking."

"Good. They work because electron tunnelling exists and quantum mechanics gives us a good enough description of how it works."

"How about *why* it works?"

Battani waved his hand in dismissal. "Leave that to the philosophers and theologians. They're paid to waste their time. Now, here's why an electron can jump—or tunnel through—a barrier it doesn't really have the energy to get over. Imagine this wall is a potential barrier, even though a potential barrier doesn't really have to be something solid, a physical barrier. Oh, let's forget that detail," he said hastily, sensing confusion in his student. "My hand is the electron." He slapped his palm against the wall. "Obviously, it can't pass. I could make a hole in the wall, but the point is that the electron we're talking about doesn't have the energy to do that. In other words, my hand can't break a hole in this wall by itself.

"However, this is a misleading analogy, because my hand is a definite object, with well defined boundaries. When you get down to the super small level of the electron, matters are no longer so simple. You can think of an electron as being smeared in space. Instead of describing its position by, say, giving three coordinates, you have to speak in terms of probabilities—the probability that it will be at a given point at any one time."

"And that probability is derived from the wave function describing the electron," Horwith said. "It begins to come back to me from out of the dim and dusty past. However, I for one still believe that electrons and all those other particles are really hard-edged, definite, and solid. Like tiny ball bearings. Except duller: they're a dull gray."

"Philistine! Remember that your computers work, and that should count for something. You said they work, generally speaking. Well, when you speak about the position of an electron, you're also generally speaking, and speaking generally. Hmm, I may use that phrase in my Nobel acceptance speech. I'm sure it means something.

"Now, suppose my hand were like the electron, having a certain probability of being here, and a certain probability of being there, on the other side of the wall. A small probability, but greater than zero. So sometimes it's here. Most of the time. But every so often, it's there, on the other side. It has tunnelled through."

"Hot damn. I don't believe a word of it, but at least I understand it. Years ago, I couldn't get it at all. Now I see that it was just because my physics professor insisted on talking about electrons and potential barriers, instead of hands and walls."

Battani grinned. "Some teachers just don't know how to get things through the typical undergraduate's thick skull." His smile faded. "Now, T-band is an extrapolation of the tunnelling concept. I was trying to explain some observational anomalies, readings that indicated that some black holes give off too much energy. There should be a great deal radiating from their vicinity, such as X rays and gamma rays, given off by gas from their companion stars if they're in a binary system, as the gas falls into the black hole. The gas forms what's called an accretion disk, and there are many powerful radiation-producing effects going on in the disk. There are also quantum mechanical effects in which virtual particles and their antiparticles are produced at the black hole's event horizon, and that's equivalent to energy being given off. All of this energy is what we actually see. However, what was being observed couldn't be accounted for by those processes. It was clear to most people, including me, that something else must be under way.

"I tried to extrapolate the idea of electron tunnelling to come up with some way radiation trapped within the event horizon could appear outside it, purely by quantum mechanical means, in much the same way as an electron can suddenly appear on the far side of a potential barrier. . . ." His voice trailed off and he stood staring into space.

"And you succeeded?" Horwith prompted, unsure where this lecture was leading.

Battani hit the table lightly with his fist. "No!" he shouted. The mood passed away instantly. "I worked on it for almost five years, with absolutely no success. The anomaly is still just that, and"— he sighed—"I'm still as far as ever from fame and fortune."

"Ah, Ambition," Horwith said, "how many men have you gripped in your deadly embrace?"

"Me, for one," Battani said with a smile. "One good thing came of it all, however. Much of my work was done on a NASA grant, so the results were published as a NASA document and circulated to the agency. Someone there saw the potential of part of it. Apparently, without at all realizing it, I had laid the foundations for T-band technology. All this, you see, was just at the time when NASA was starting work on its interstellar probe project, and they were worried about how to handle the transmission problem. In spite of modern computer technology, there are still some old-fashioned engineers in your agency who insist on full ground control of probes whenever possible, just in case the devices get ideas of their own or run into problems their onboard computers can't handle."

"It's not just probes they treat that way," Horwith muttered. "Employees, too."

"Hmm. Well, the further the probe gets from Earth, the longer the delay in transmission time becomes, of course. Eventually, especially in the case of an interstellar probe, the time is too great for ground control from Earth to be practical. Unforeseen emergencies can always happen, so they want to be able to have engineers on the ground looking through the probe's eyes through TV cameras, able to make it respond quickly."

"And T-band is a form of instantaneous transmission. I've been told that, but not how it's possible for radio waves to go faster than the speed of light."

"They don't," said Battani, "not really. And they're not really radio waves. They are electromagnetic, but the frequency is far below what's usually considered the radio spectrum. Under the right conditions—which *I* thought should exist near a black hole's event horizon, although I must have been wrong—energy of the right frequency and the proper probability function will tunnel from one point to another. Think of distance and the speed of light as the potential barrier in this case. Or time, rather, since that's what really concerns us humans. In zero time, the energy front will tunnel from here to there, just as the electron tunnels through the barrier."

"Shit. You pulled a magic trick on me again, just when I thought I was following you. No, wait." He held up his hand. "Don't go over it again. I followed the words all right. Just give my brain a few days to catch up."

"I could show you the mathematics, but I'm not really sure that would help make it any clearer. We press on," Battani said, pointing upward as if to some far frontier. "Some electronics whizzes at NASA devised a way of creating the tunnelling effect at will. T-band, as they decided to call it." He grimaced in distaste. "They didn't ask my opinion on the name. Both transmitter and receiver have to operate in hard vacuum, so they set the receiver up here on the moon and set up the project you're part of to make sure it could operate for hours at a time without trouble. Presumably there will be backup receivers emplaced before the probe is launched. The only transmitter in existence is a low-power, experimental version in Houston, a version of the one that will fly. That's why we can be sure that what you received didn't come from a transmitter on Earth. I've been assured that no one else in the world has the ability to build one yet. And anyway, without the quantity of hard vacuum we have here, there's no practical way for anyone to build a transmitter with significant power."

"At last I think I see what you're hoping for," Horwith said. "You think the signal Glen and I picked up might be the radiation from a black hole you were after before?"

"Precisely! But there's a barrier standing in the way of proving that, or even of building a T-band telescope. The method doesn't provide a direction, a line of sight. The radiation tunnels from the transmitter and across a desired distance. The distance is proportional to the cube of the energy being emitted. So if you increase the power enough, the signal could show up at the end of the Universe, but it would be in the shape of a sphere. We can control that in the case of our probe, but a natural event, such as a black hole, would be putting out T-band signals over a vast range of intensities, so that the signals would tunnel to various distances in all directions, making the geometry problem intractable.''

Horwith thought for a moment. "At any one intensity, it would show up as a sphere, you said. It seems to me that all you'd need would be three points on the surface of the sphere. Noncollinear points, I mean. Draw the chords, the line segments connecting the points. You'd only need two of the chords. Then the perpendicular bisectors of those chords would intersect at the center of the sphere, giving you the location of the transmitter."

"Quite right," Battani nodded. "But practically speaking, it's much harder than that. First of all, given a signal, we have no way of deriving the intensity of the source signal from it, so we can't know if our three points are on the surface of the same sphere. Even if we do find a way of doing that, getting the three points will be difficult. We're talking about a very large sphere, because the black holes in question are on the order of a thousand light-years away, at least; that means the three points have to be very non-collinear indeed to do the trick. Points along the Earth's orbit wouldn't work. I think we'd have to send a receiver well out above the ecliptic to get the third point. You might try asking your superiors for money for a mission like that. I don't think relations between Mendeleev and NASA are warm enough right now for me to make such a suggestion through my channels. But you sound interested in the theoretical problem."

"I am," Horwith admitted. "I'd still prefer aliens, and maybe some sort of tunnelling method of transporting mass. I mean real mass, not just electrons, so that we could have instantaneous interstellar travel. But as second best, this sounds very interesting. I wish I had the brains to contribute something."

Battani hesitated, then said, "You underestimate yourself. Not all the work will be theoretical, and Mendeleev does lack practical engineers. This is a wonderful place to work. I don't normally offer jobs on such short acquaintance, but my intuition tells me that you could make a significant contribution. Would you like me to speak to Professor Larrieux? He's LOAM Director. He might be able to arrange something with NASA. Perhaps we can get you loaned to us or assigned here on an open-ended basis.''

Horwith needed no time to think about it. ''I'd love that, Al. I'd love to work here. That way, if there *are* aliens, I'll be the first to know, right?''

Battani chuckled. ''Hope springs eternal in the human beast. I hope you aren't disappointed with what you find out.''

Battani's influence (or perhaps it was the influence of Professor Larrieux) must have been of large caliber. Late the next morning, Horwith received word from his superiors at NASA Frontside that, while the T-band receiver would stay where it was and the test program would continue as before, he was being transferred to Mendeleev for an indefinite period, assigned to work under Battani.

He needed to return briefly to Frontside, to fetch some personal items and clean up the new payroll arrangement. He asked Battani if he could arrange for him to be taken by shuttle, since he had no other transportation.

''I'll see what I can do,'' Battani said. ''It does work out most inopportunely, though. When you arrived at the crater rim, did you happen to notice a large radio telescope just above us?''

''I did.''

''Well, it just so happens that there's a brilliant young astronomer on the staff here, a Dr. Thabanchu, who's been trying for months to get observing time for a pet project of hers, and the only time available started just before we got to Mendeleev Rim in the shuttle.''

''So?'' Horwith asked, puzzled.

''So our arrival and the elevator and then the subway starting off produced enough vibration to ruin all the work she was doing then. Or so she says. She now hates both my guts and yours. Why yours, I don't know, but Moira has a habit of blaming whoever's available when things go wrong. Anyway, last night she caught me in my office without warning. If I'd had warning, I'd have been sure not to be there. She bullied me into giving her another time slot, and I managed to squeeze her in today for a couple of hours. She's out there now, preparing, at Radio Three, which is the instrument she was using yesterday. In other words, it's the one directly above the elevator and shuttle terminal we used yesterday. That's also where the only available shuttle is right now. If I do it to her again . . ."

"So why not have the shuttle take off right now, before she begins her observations, and fly around the perimeter of the crater and land at some other terminal point, and then I'll go out to that one? You'll disturb someone else's observations, I suppose, but I gather that this Thabanchu woman is the one you're afraid of."

Battani stared at him for a moment in open admiration. "Brilliant! Of course! Trust an engineer, a man of action, to see the solution." His admiration gave way immediately to annoyance. "I am *not* afraid of Moira Thabanchu, Clemmons. It's just that she's considerably larger and stronger and shorter-tempered than I am, and I'm a sensible fellow."

"Sounds like an interesting woman. I'll get back as soon as I can, Al, so you'll have someone here to protect you."

If there was a reason it would be a pleasure to leave Frontside, that reason was Jim Dysan. Dysan was Horwith's immediate superior, a section chief with delusions of grandeur, despised by those beneath him and barely tolerated by those above. It was he who had insisted that Horwith return to base for instructions: he might have to buckle down to direct orders from above to assign Horwith to Mendeleev, but at least he could assert his power and authority this one last time. In fact, he had nothing to say to Horwith that he couldn't have radioed to him. Dysan specialized in such petty displays.

"So you're going to be working for that spick at Mendeleev, eh?"

Horwith knew better than to take the bait. "Looks like it, Jim." He's a spick? You're a prick. A dick. A hick. A . . . He couldn't think of anymore rhyming pejoratives.

Dysan leaned back in his chair, a very large, very plush executive swivel model that bore a non-accidental similarity to a throne. He was a grotesquely fat man. Even in one-sixth Earth gravity, his chair creaked and groaned in protest. He had added at least fifty kilograms since coming to the moon two years earlier. By now, it might be physically impossible for him to go back to Earth and endure full gravity again. "Yep, Horwith. A nice, soft assignment for you. Nothing to do but eat all that expensive food those guys can afford to bring up from Earth and grow fat and lazy. Right?"

Asshole. "I'll be working on a project over there, Jim."

"In charge of it?"

"That's how I understand it."

"Shee-it. So that explains why you're so eager for this. You'd never get to head a project here, not so long as I'm in charge. All right, get the hell out of here, you opportunist. You wanna know somethin'? At least I'm glad you won't have the garden to waste your time in anymore."

Horwith had expected to be glad to be leaving, to be able to clean out his small room at Frontside with no regrets, but the surprised himself with the affection he felt for the place. He was oppressed with a feeling that changes were coming for Frontside and Mendeleev just as they were for him, that he would never again see Frontside as it was now.

Most of all, he thought, he would miss the garden, that huge underground vault where a team of botanists conducted experiments in growing Earth plants in lunar soil, under lunar gravity, using sunlight piped down from the surface by means of optical fiber. It was supposed to be carefully isolated and controlled, but within the last year it had become common for the experimenters to allow favored NASA personnel to stroll about in it. It was a highly valued privilege, of great psychological value to men and women stationed for long periods on the sterile moon. Horwith was one of the privileged, and he had appreciated his favored treatment. He had come to love the garden.

On the other hand, there was another vault where a team of zoologists played their own scientific games with animals. That area was theoretically completely isolated from the rest of Frontside, but at least once a month the smell from it managed to circulate through the base airconditioning system to every nook and cranny. That smell was something Horwith would not miss at all.

It's a worthless experiment, he thought. It'll never serve any useful purpose. Animals on the moon, for God's sake! But the garden . . .

Horwith availed himself of his status one last time and spent hours wandering among the plants, in the cool, damp air, smelling the perfume of growth and life. He spent the hours of the trip back to Mendeleev not watching the cold, dry beauty of the sterile landscape outside the shuttle, but instead dreaming of the images of air and life of the garden. Something unique in the Universe, for all we know, he thought. Infinitely precious.

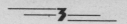

Battani welcomed him back enthusiastically. "I've been looking into the details of your background," he said. "All that hardware testing with NASA—perfect! My intuition was obviously correct. My young hardware geniuses are bubbling over with ideas about new T-band gadgetry, and I'll need someone with the right kind of administrative background and a good, broad view of the problem to keep them from wasting both their time and the observatory's money."

"And free you from all that so you can work on the theoretical aspects of your old problem and not have to bother any more with diodes and transistors?"

Battani grinned. "I've had that one explained to me. I won't make that particular mistake again. However, I won't promise not to embarrass you with some astrophysics jargon as soon as I get the chance."

Horwith grinned back. "I'm too easy a target. Pick on someone your own size."

Battani burst into loud laughter. "If there were any, I would."

"I meant, your own intellectual size."

"In all modesty, Clemmons, so did I." Battani held up his hand. "No, actually I didn't. I just wanted to see your face when I said that."

"By the way, you mentioned wasting the observatory's money. I'd always heard that Mendeleev had money coming out its, um, ears."

Battani grew serious. "That used to be the case, up until last year. This year's budget is tight. First time that's happened. Everyone's cutting back their contributions because of the troubles on Earth. The Russians and the Chinese, of course: they both want their money to buy arms and beef up the border between them. And that makes the Japanese and Americans both nervous, so they're withholding funds and spending the money on arms too. The Europeans are playing a waiting game. They also contend that they don't have as big a role at the observatory as other countries—that they're not getting as many staff positions as they ought to, in proportion to the funds they've provided."

"Is that true?"

"I don't know if it is or not!" Battani said angrily. "It doesn't matter to me. Professor Larrieux is French, I'm Italian, you're American, Moira Thabanchu is South African, and so on. We've got people here from practically every country on Earth. What difference does it make? We're not here to represent our countries! We're here as scientists and technicians, working together for knowledge. Astronomy has always prided itself on being the paradigm of pure knowledge, of the quest for the understanding of the Universe, untainted by political or commerical considerations. *That's* what we're all here for."

"Gosh, Al. How many days ago did you say you were born?"

Battani laughed. "The voice of cynical pragmatism. That's what I really need you here for: to remind me of the real world, eh?"

Horwith nodded. "It's a quarter of a million miles away, but the world is very much with us."

The United States Air Force's influence over NASA had been unconscionably large since January 20, 1981, and the Air Force insisted that the existence of the T-band transmitter and receiver and the signal the receiver had picked up be treated as military secrets. This made cooperation with Mendeleev extremely difficult, since the observatory was a United Nations facility, with a staff drawn from both sides of the Iron Curtain.

The expertise available at Mendeleev was undeniable. Perhaps the presence of Battani at Mendeleev had been the deciding factor, Horwith thought. And perhaps NASA had agreed to his transfer to Battani's team at least partially because the agency wanted to have one of its own men present. Was Horwith supposed to be a NASA spy within the observatory? No one had told him that that was one of his duties, and certainly he had no intention of adding it of his own accord.

NASA had insisted that only personnel from NATO countries, and even then only those who had security clearances, be allowed to work on the T-band project or even to know of its existence. The management at Mendeleev hadn't disagreed with this proviso; they hadn't actually agreed to it, either. Horwith suspected they intended simply to ignore it. In which case, every government in the world would know all about T-band in no time. That was a development quite acceptable to Clemmons Horwith.

The team at Mendeleev was varied and brilliant. That was to be expected, since only the best minds in the profession were chosen to fill the few available slots at the world's foremost observatory. They came in every age, shape, size, color, and temperament, but all were brilliant, including the army of technicians who maintained the array of telescopes along the rim of the crater.

Horwith had always been shy around women, largely because of his self-image as the ugly beanpole of his nickname. Here, where every woman he met must surely have an IQ at least fifty percent higher than his own, he was more reticent than ever. He retreated into his work, which he found increasingly satisfying, quite oblivious to the respect and high regard in which his subordinates held him. In that ocean of cranky, brilliant, undisciplined, and overly independent academics, he stood out as a rock of stability. Under his direction, and despite Battani's growing misgivings, a powerful T-band transmitter was being developed.

"You were supposed to keep them sensibly occupied," Battani fretted, "not encourage foolish fantasies about communication with aliens. Remember the Gospel According to Horwith: 'The world is too much with us.'"

"'Always with us,'" Horwith corrected him. "Here's another one: 'With money all things are possible.' So how's your theoretical work coming along? Have you solved the direction problem, or the matter of modelling the origin of the signals, or any of the other things we discussed?"

Battani grumbled to himself for a moment. "No," he admitted. "I've made almost no progress."

"Well, you won't win a Nobel that way, Al," Horwith smirked. "Whereas we should soon have a device capable of experimenting with, to explore different ideas about the direction to a transmitted signal and how the nature of the transmitter determines the nature of the signal."

"Do you know, Clemmons, that you are insufferable when you win an argument?"

"Frankly, it hasn't happened often enough yet to be a problem." But he didn't tell Battani that one of the bright young men now working under him was eating up huge chunks of time on the observatory's computers, trying to decode the incoming signal on the assumption that it *was* an artifact of intelligence.

The signal had paused occasionally, for a couple of days at a time, and then resumed. All in all, they had perhaps one hundred hours of it recorded. Surely this was enough for the computers to decode, if only some sort of key could be determined. Horwith could not understand the young man's ideas at all, his approach to the problem of deciphering the hypothetical alien language, but Hank Rawlinson had spent some years studying archaeology before discovering computers, and he assured Horwith that he faced a far easier task than the first translators of the languages of ancient Mesopotamia had faced.

"You mean they didn't speak Arabic?" Horwith had asked the young expert with feigned astonishment. Rawlinson had sneered quite openly and returned to his terminal. Horwith had permitted himself a smile.

The argument over whether the mysterious T-band signal was a natural phenomenon or the product of a civilization eventually drew in almost every astronomer on the observatory staff, and even most of the technicians and secretaries. It raged for months.

The majority of the professional staff sided with Battani, who held as firmly as ever to his position that the signal was caused by some as yet unknown natural process. He held to it even though neither he nor anyone else had as yet come up with a reasonable model that could account for the signal. It was the nonastronomers, like Horwith, who wanted the signal to be a message from an alien civilization. The telling point, when it came, seemed anticlimactic.

Horwith was outside, standing in a depression in Mendeleev Rim and watching the team working on the transmitter, when Hank Rawlinson tracked him down. The sun was setting with its usual majestic slowness, a normal, lengthy lunar sunset, throwing the ground and the suited figures into dramatic relief. Below, the plains stretching away from Mendeleev were already in darkness and had been for hours.

The surface suit hid Rawlinson's face and its bulky clumsiness robbed his gestures of nuance, but his excitement came through clearly over the radio. "I've got something! Come on!" He refused to say more.

What Rawlinson had was an odd display on the screen of his terminal. It was text—strings of letters, numbers, and punctuation marks—filling up the screen in ordered lines; but it was mostly gibberish. Here and there Horwith caught a word, and now and then two or three words in a row, but the rest was meaningless, little more to his eye than random nonsense. "What is it?" he asked, puzzled. "It doesn't mean anything to me."

"It's a beginning, that's what it is," Rawlinson said with obvious impatience. "It shows I've got at least part of the key." Realizing that his boss was still confused, he said, "This is the T-band signal after processing by my translation program. This is the first time I've gotten anything even halfway sensible out of it."

Pride at his accomplishment spilled out suddenly. "You see, basically what I've been doing is this. I figured that if it really is a message from one alien civilization to another, or just to anyone who might be listening, then there should be a frequently repeated section in it to identify the source and give some parameters about the signal and the language it's in. Sort of like station identification," he said, grinning. "I kept trying, and finally I did find a very short repeated segment. Not much to go on, but it's the only obvious candidate for what I just described. Okay, so now I tried using it. There are accepted ways of describing a language, giving its parameters, but I won't try to explain those to you." Horwith caught the condescension but chose to ignore it.

Rawlinson continued. "Of course, it was a slim chance that any of those ways would work on this alien language, since they're devised for what we speak on Earth, and at that mainly for the Indo-European languages, and of course it's an even slimmer chance that they'll come up with the same way of describing a language, but what else did I have? So I broke up the repeated segment of the signal into what seemed like byte-sized chunks"— he grinned at his own pun, but then hurried on when Horwith didn't respond—"and fed those into my program as the parameters. And of course I'm making a lot of assumptions to build up a primitive dictionary. I'd just about run out of permutations, too, when real words started showing up at last among the output."

"It could be coincidence, garbage that happens to form words. Like the monkeys and the typewriters and the books in the British Museum."

Rawlinson stiffened. "Of course that's possible," he snapped, "but unlikely. Have you ever thought about how long it would really take those monkeys to get anywhere? Fifty possible keys, more or less, for them to press for each character position. So even if they were limited to a single line of type, say eighty characters, that would still give them fifty to the eightieth possible combinations. I don't know how much that is offhand, but it's a hell of a lot of possible lines. Anyway, I'm not just seeing words; I'm seeing phrases." He pointed to a sequence his program had translated as "three orbits later."

Horwith felt himself in the grip of a growing excitement. "Hank, you pull this one off, and I'll personally buy you a trip back to Earth so that you can go to Kermanshah and study the Great Rock." He'd spent hours in the library looking for that allusion. Rawlinson's goggle-eyed stare filled Horwith with satisfaction. "Practically speaking, what next?"

"Uh, now it's just a matter of time, sir. Computer time, especially. But I'm on track now. Every run should come closer to a complete translation."

"Keep at it. I'd better tell Al about this."

* * *

He found Battani in his office, hunched over his desk, staring hopelessly at a blank sheet of paper. "Aah," Horwith said, "the theoretician alone in a room with pencil and paper, quietly changing Man's view of the Universe."

Battani sat back and growled something. He threw his pencil violently against the wall in front of him. With an obvious effort, he dredged up the good humor which had been steadily deserting him in recent weeks. "A blank paper and a blank mind never changed anything, my friend."

"Yes, well, perhaps what's needed is a different approach." He quickly outlined Rawlinson's breakthrough.

"My God!" Battani made as if to leap to his feet but caught his desk in time and held himself on the ground. "Clemmons, why didn't you tell me this before?"

"Because you're a furriner. With World War Three on its way, I have orders not to trust furriners. Also, you might have told us to stop. Frankly, this puts the kibosh on your Nobel, and I didn't know how you'd take that."

"Ah, yes, the Nobel." Battani sighed. "One can't have everything, to coin a cliché. It sounds to me as if it's young Rawlinson who deserves the Nobel for this. Why, it puts the archaeologists of the last century in the shade."

"Yeah. Mesopotamia and all that. I'm sure Rawlinson would agree with you if you asked him, which I hope you won't."

But Battani wasn't listening. "Dynamite, you know. It's tainted money, anyway." Suddenly his eyes shone with excitement. "And your people are building that transmitter right now," he said in a low tone filled with wonder. "When they're finished, we can use it and Rawlinson's program to—"

Horwith cut in, "To send a reply. It's a whole new ball game, Al. The world will never be the same again."

—————4—————

The new year came and went. It was now 2009, and the Millennium was nine years behind schedule—or eight, if one subscribed to the accuracy to which astronomers are wont—but no one at Mendeleev had any attention to spare for such matters. Nor did they spend as much time as Horwith might have expected discussing the deteriorating international situation on Earth. At Mendeleev, there was no international situation, and the calendar was irrelevant. What mattered, what overrode almost everything else, even the normal scientific functioning of the observatory, was the translated message scrolling constantly across Rawlinson's terminal screen and the transmitter now ready out at the Rim to send a reply.

Battani tapped a chart he had tacked to his wall. It was a depiction of the solar system, the scale distorted so that all the planets could be shown on it. Various points were marked along the Earth's orbit, with numbers written next to them. "I wouldn't use this for any real calculations, of course," Battani said apologetically. "It's a graphic tool to help me keep track of what we've learned so far, and also it's more pleasant to look at than a naked wall."

"But not more pleasant than a naked woman," Horwith said. "I've got a few pictures I could lend you instead."

Battani snorted. "We're here to discuss the glories of the Universe, not those of mammary glands. One of Rawlinson's parameters appears to denote signal strength. If that's so, well, you know what that means. It has changed during the last few months. From that I conclude that the aliens"—Horwith noticed that he used the word now without any hesitancy—"are broadcasting to whoever wants to listen and has the ability to decode their signal. And of course the ability to discover T-band in the first place. Selecting a few pairs of points such that the signal

31

strength matches up in each pair gives us a few chords, so that we can use the geometric method you mentioned some time ago to determine just where they are, with fair accuracy."

Horwith sat forward, filled with sudden tension. "You know? Where are they?"

"At a right ascension of fifteen hours, twenty minutes, and a declination of fifty-nine degrees. That's in the constellation Draco. And about thirteen thousand light-years away."

Horwith sat back, stunned. Suddenly it seemed real, converted by these numbers from a fantasy or an intellectual exercise into an actual alien civilization, far out there in the emptiness. "Thirteen thousand light-years," he muttered. "That's . . ." He tried to convert it into more familiar units.

"Real far," Battani finished, straight-faced. "We'll never meet face-to-face, but we should be able to talk ourselves blue in the face. Or whatever color they turn when they run out of oxygen. Or whatever they breathe."

"Jesus," Horwith whispered, stunned out of all flippancy. It was almost more than he could absorb at once. "Talk, you said?"

"Of course. You were the one who wanted to send a reply in the first place. How is the transmitter development coming?"

"Oh, it's been ready for a while, as far as my people can tell. We need a real test, though, not just the ability to transmit to our own receiver here on the moon. A real test—a receiver a significant distance away."

Battani laughed. "Thirteen thousand light-years is pretty significant. Why bother with tests? Some of the astronomers here have already put together something to send—if you and your circuitry whizzes have no objection."

"Is that wise? We've been running along full-tilt without NASA really knowing the details of what we're doing, and legally, they own the technology. I'm using it as a NASA employee, and Mendeleev is using and building it under a letter of agreement. You know, the letter doesn't cover sending a message to an alien civilization. It's really all intended for use by NASA for its interstellar probe."

"Does that mean you want to discuss any message first with

Frontside? And then with NASA headquarters in Washington, and then probably with your State Department and the Pentagon, before we can act?"

"Hell, no. NASA likes to take a vote among its centers before it makes a major decision, and you can bet Houston and JPL, at least, would scream their heads off and want to be given control of the whole thing." A further thought struck Horwith. "Not to mention the United Nations and your own Ministry of Defense and every other Ministry of Defense that knows what's going on up here."

"Which by now is probably all of them on Earth," Battani said.

"Then I say, 'Onward, into the Valley of Death.'" It was an inappropriate and unfortunate quotation. Both men suddenly shivered, and the air of lightheartedness vanished, replaced by a chill that might have come through the wall from the lunar vacuum beyond.

Rawlinson's program had been vastly improved through the combined efforts of many of his colleagues. It seemed to injure the young man's pride that others had taken a hand in the work, but Horwith had ordered him to cooperate with them. It was the end that counted, he had said firmly and loudly, not who contributed the most; the epochal contact with an alien civilization that would shape human history, rather than the identity of the man who first got the central idea. Rawlinson had been made to feel ashamed— no easy task—and all the others working for Horwith had grown all the more dedicated to him, all the more admiring.

The hours of transmission that had been faithfully recorded at the receiver proved, when translated by the improved version of Rawlinson's program, to be a rather tedious history of the aliens' civilization and an astonishingly detailed explanation of their ethical code. Even Battani, ever volatile, despaired at the translation and sank swiftly into gloom. "I had expected them to give us the keys to the Universe!" he complained to Horwith. "The answers to all the unanswered questions in astrophysics! The secret of interstellar flight! We know that's possible, since they refer to it obliquely. But all we get is hour after hour of history and politics and religion. Ancient dynasties, and something much like parliamentary speeches, and those damned religious epigrams! An endless list of those! One more explanation of what a Proper One is and how he should conduct his life, Clemmons, and I swear I shall explode!''

Horwith nodded. ''I've got to admit, it's a bit strong. You know, there are thousands of academics down on Earth who would kill to get their hands on this stuff. Think of all the papers they could churn out! Or all the desperate graduate students who would have dissertation subjects at last. Fresh fodder for the degree mill.''

''Bah!'' Battani waved his hand in a gesture that dismissed every university and college on the mother planet. ''We've got to get our message put together right away, translate it, and send it out. We'll include a list of things we want to know, if we can all agree on a reasonably short one. Force those creatures to take note of us and talk to us on a more concrete level.'' He stopped pacing at last and stood still, breathing heavily.

Horwith said thoughtfully, ''We'll have to convince them somehow that we're all Proper Ones, in order to keep their attention.'' But his friend did not appear to have heard.

When the message was finally sent, it included only a short list of the type of questions Battani had wanted the aliens to answer. Partly, this was a pragmatic decision: there was already a great deal to be sent, in order to satisfy the many factions in Mendeleev who had managed to get themselves involved, and many hours of transmission time would be necessary. In addition, however, Rawlinson had been reading the accumulating piles of translation over and over, and he believed he had detected a strong distaste on the aliens' part for those who asked for too much without giving even more in return: it was not what a Proper One would do. His use of that term elicited curses from Battani, but his argument carried weight with the majority.

The bulk of the message from mankind was modelled after those which had been sent aboard certain unmanned probes nearly two generations before. In those days, a series of interplanetary probes which had been expected to eventually escape from the

solar system had been provided with recordings, drawings, and
star charts which would, it was hoped, provide any aliens who
might discover the probes far from the sun, perhaps millions of
years later, a good idea of where Man lived, what he thought, and
how he conducted himself.

The T-band message to the aliens included recordings of waves
on a seashore, a baby crying, birds singing, and endless other
sounds of Nature. One young woman of a metaphysical bent had
added to it, typing laboriously at her terminal for hours every day,
a large chunk of the works of Teilhard de Chardin. "Chewing it all
up into little bits," Horwith had quipped to Battani, who certainly
did not get the weak joke. "Which was more than I was ever able
to do, when I passed through that phase in college."

"We shouldn't mislead them," Battani argued. "Let's show
them our less spiritual side." And so a short summary of the
political situation was added, including a description of the virtual
dismantling within the past year of the Soviet, Chinese, and
European space programs in the face of border tensions in Central
Europe and along the Russo-Chinese border. Even the American
space program supported almost no manned flight, with the
exception of NASA's one large and several small moon bases and
an Earth-orbiting space station, now manned by a skeleton crew
and used only to support the Earth-to-Earth-orbit and Earth-orbit-
to-moon shuttles. Mendeleev, in theory international, in fact
depended almost entirely now upon the American manned space
program to keep it going.

Reading a transcript of this portion of the message, Horwith
shook his head and said to Battani, "I never really thought about it
before now—how bad it's gotten. We're turning away from it all,
aren't we? Withdrawing to Earth so that we'll all be in one place
and we can blow ourselves up and be sure we haven't missed
anyone."

He sat up as a new thought struck him. "This message will
reach anyone at the same distance from us as the aliens we already
know about. Thirteen thousand light-years in all directions. What
if there's someone out there with interstellar flight who's very
aggressive? We're telling them how weak and disunited we are.

And," he added, thinking of the young woman typing in Teilhard de Chardin, "how softheaded. Ripe for the picking."

Battani shrugged. "At this rate, there won't be anything left of mankind for them to pick. The whole exercise may be futile."

But just in case it wasn't, Battani insisted on sending a complete transcription of a recent popular book on general science. Perhaps he shouldn't ask the aliens too many questions directly, he reasoned, but if he could show them the limitations of human knowledge, and if they were feeling in a generous mood . . . well, it certainly seemed to him that anyone deserving of the name "Proper One" ought to be willing to donate a generous amount of astrophysics to a hungry astronomer thirteen thousand light-years away.

Rawlinson's terminal had been permanently tied in to the receiver over the moon's horizon so that there would be one screen in the laboratory on which a translation of the signal was displayed as it came in. If Rawlinson was annoyed at losing the use of the terminal so conveniently near his desk and reference materials, he seemed to feel more than compensated for the loss by being the center of attention. He often made a very public fuss over the crowds gathered in front of the small screen, some of them reading aloud for the benefit of those at the back who couldn't see. But it was obvious to everyone that he scarcely minded being interrupted and kept from his work. He had always loved the spotlight and being given his due reward, and he felt that here, at last, was the very barest step in that direction.

As the day approached on which the human message was to be transmitted, the crowd increased, as if expecting an instantaneous response from the aliens. In fact, even speeded up—squirted out into space at many times normal human reading speed—the whole thing would take many hours to reach the end. But occasional announcements to this effect by Battani seemed to have no effect on his colleagues, who stood entranced before the silent terminal, as if expecting something, although none of them could have said what.

Once transmission was under way, Battani and Horwith

restrained themselves for as long as possible, to set a good example. But when the end of the transmission approached, they could hold back no longer, and they joined the crowd in front of the terminal. The murmurings and readings aloud from the screen had stopped, and the packed room was silent.

Horwith stood to one side. He could see the screen, though not well enough to see what was displayed on it. However, he had a telephone handset pressed to his cheek, keeping him in constant touch with both the technicians at the transmitter and the NASA team at the receiver, and the short cord of the telephone allowed him to get no closer to the terminal than this.

"Transmission has just ended," he announced to the room at large. He had spoken quietly, but in the tense silence his voice was a shock.

No more than a minute later, a blank line appeared at the bottom of the terminal screen, and then another, and then yet another. The lines filled with text scrolled silently upward, replaced by blank lines, until at last the text disappeared off the top of the screen and all was blank. The silence was complete, until someone said accusingly, "Rawlinson, your damned terminal's on the blink."

Horwith had been listening intently to the soft words in the telephone handset. "No," he said. "The receiver team says the signal switched abruptly to completely unmodulated. Now it's cut off. The receiver's working properly, but there's nothing more for it to pick up." Trying to break the tension, he said, "Maybe Teilhard de Chardin was more than they could take." But his words seemed to have no impact on the stunned faces around him. Of all the possible responses from the aliens he and Battani and the others had hypothesized, this one—total silence, no response at all—was the one they had not foreseen.

5

Six months had passed, and Horwith was beginning to wonder if NASA had forgotten him. Presumably not, since his paychecks continued to be deposited, at proper two-week intervals, in the branch bank at NASA's main lunar base. Every two weeks, Horwith found a secluded terminal, one where no one would be able to see how small his balance was, and accessed his account to make sure his paycheck had arrived. He assumed that his open-ended assignment to Mendeleev was still in effect, even though the end of the signal from Draco had also put an end to his contribution.

Horwith had spent the days since the cessation of the T-band signal patiently reading his way through the more elementary books in the observatory's library—or at least what passed for elementary books at Mendeleev. He was hoping to get rid of his automatic flinch reaction when the local scientists threw technical terms at him. All he had accomplished, though, he told himself gloomily, was to verify that the mental block he had first come up against in physics courses in college was still firmly in place. He had always suspected that that explained why his best work was managerial rather than technical. It was a bitter admission: he had always admired technically competent men and wanted to be one.

He was searching for one explanation in particular, and he had been unable to find a single reference to the mysterious term. Some days earlier, while eating alone in the observatory cafeteria, Horwith had overheard two staff astronomers at an adjacent table talking excitedly about the recently discovered "gray hole." Horwith was as familiar with the idea of a black hole as any other layman, for he'd read no end of popularized articles on the subject, and he had also read an old book about "white holes," an idea which had apparently lost adherents over the years. But he was sure he had never before heard of a "gray hole." What little

38

he could understand of the conversation, though, fascinated him (as did one of the two astronomers), and he decided to try to find out more about gray holes before exposing his ignorance to any of the professionals around him. There was certainly no overabundance of real work that he need feel guilty about slighting.

But the library was blank on the subject. "That new?" he muttered. Since the Mendeleev observatory had begun operations five years before, astronomy had been revolutionized yet again. The huge telescopes on the moon—optical, radio, radar, X-ray, and gamma-ray—unencumbered by atmosphere or man-made noise from Earth, had swept away old theories in a flood of new data, of measurements that could not be made before or could be made only in snatches from balloons or satellites or short-lived orbital flights. Some older, eminent astronomers had moaned in public that they couldn't keep up with the constantly changing picture of the Universe, a complaint which had never before aroused any sympathy in Horwith. Now, though, he felt chagrined that this gray hole was such a new discovery that the most recently published reference works in the library, and even the most recent issues of magazines, contained no mention of it. He would have to swallow his pride after all. At least there was one astronomer to whom he could admit ignorance without fear of ridicule.

Horwith found Battani in his office, as usual, hunched over a blank sheet of paper and looking unhappy. "Gosh, Al, sometimes I wonder what they pay you for."

Battani groaned. "Don't joke about it, my friend. I feel guilty enough already about making so little progress." Once the excitement of translating the alien message and sending a reply had finally died away, Battani had felt inspired to return to his old problem, the investigation that had produced T-band transmission as a by-product. He was finding, however, that the intervening years and professional advancement, and the technological success of T-band, had done nothing to make the old problem any more susceptible of solution. The anomaly was still an anomaly, and no one, including Alfredo Battani, had come up with a satisfying explanation of the excessive energy flow from the vicinity of certain black holes.

"Cheer yourself up with a lecture. Tell me all about gray holes."

"*Gray* holes?" Battani chuckled. "I suppose that's what you get when you combine black holes with white ones. It embarrasses me vastly to admit this, Clemmons, but I've never heard that term before. Are you sure someone hasn't been pulling your leg?"

"A delightful idea," Horwith said, thinking of one of the two astronomers. He told Battani about the conversation he had overheard in the cafeteria. "I don't know either of them, but you probably do. One was black and one was white. The two people, I mean."

Battani snorted. "Thank you. That narrows the field considerably. Next you'll say they both had foreign accents, just like everyone else in this place, including me. And you."

"Well, as a matter of fact, they did. And mine isn't foreign, it's Hoosier. The black astronomer was a woman." The truth was that Horwith would have had trouble describing the other astronomer; contrasted with his companion, the man had made almost no impression on him. "She was rather small, not much taller than you. And slender. Very beautiful, I thought. Very forceful and aggressive throughout the discussion. I got the impression the other guy was a bit afraid of her."

Battani smiled. "Add all of that up, and it fits only one woman here: Moira Thabanchu."

"So *that's* Moira Thabanchu! From the way you always speak about her, I expected her to be seven feet tall and breathing fire."

"She gets taller when you try to stand up to her," Battani assured him. "And she breathes fire. But I gather you didn't find her to be precisely a dragon, hmm?"

Horwith pointed at Battani's desk. "There's your phone. Call her up and find out about gray holes and stop grinning at me."

Battani punched in the number. "Shall I try to get you a date with her while I'm at it?"

Before Horwith could frame a reply, Battani's call was answered. "Moira? This is Alfredo Battani. One of my spies has just brought me an intriguing report about something called a gray hole. I'd like to know more." He listened silently for some time, then said, "I can understand your feelings, and I certainly have no intention of stealing anyone's thunder. You keep charge of the project and publish the results, and so on. You know, though, Moira, the Director and I are supposed to be kept informed of any new projects or any major new discoveries. We even have to approve new projects. That's all I'm really asking you—that you abide by the rules. . . ."

Again Battani listened without speaking, and this time the voice from the other end was loud enough for Horwith to hear it, although he couldn't make out the words. "Yes, Moira, in the cafeteria. If you want to keep secrets, you shouldn't discuss them in public places. And no one should be keeping secrets from me, anyway. Now, wait a minute. . . ." Again a pause. "Yes, that was him." Battani winced. "Yes, I know, but appearances can be misleading. He's a wonderful fellow once you get to know him." The loud voice from the other end of the line said a few more things, and then the telephone gave out a very loud bang as Moira Thabanchu disconnected with emphasis.

"Excellent!" Battani said brightly. "Something new. She's sending me copies of everything they have on this gray hole so far. And as you probably heard, I gave you a fine buildup, and Dr. Thabanchu's dying to meet you."

Horwith grimaced. "To kill me, it sounded like."

"Something like that," Battani agreed. "She's certainly a strong-willed woman with a large vocabulary."

There was a thump from the wall beside Battani's desk. "Already?" the astrophysicist said in surprise. "She works quickly." He leaned over his desk, opened a small door set into the wall, and took out a message tube. From it he extracted a thick sheaf of papers. "Hmm," he said, riffling through the stack. "You'd best give me an hour or two to digest this. Then I'll tell you what I know."

Horwith nodded and left, to wander disconsolately through the halls. What he ought to spend his life looking for, he told himself, was a tall, thin woman of average intelligence to whom he'd be acceptable. It was worse than foolish to indulge in fantasies about a beautiful woman of half his height and twice his brainpower.

"There's really not much in there," Battani said, gesturing toward the pile of paper Moira Thabanchu had sent him. "Most of it's a detailed description of the readings they've obtained and their arguments about it, blow by blow. I'll tell you the gist of it. Moira and the team who work under her have been doing precise measurements of Persephone's orbit, trying to determine which of the two most popular relativity theories is correct. Each theory predicts a slightly different interaction between the sun's gravitational field and the combined fields of Alpha and Proxima Centauri. Persephone is far out enough at this point along its orbit, and fortunately in the direction of the Centauri system, that Moira hoped the perturbations to its orbit might enable her to choose between the two theories.

"It seems that— I'm sorry." He waved his hand. "I'm getting badly off the track. The point is that a few days ago they processed a couple of weeks worth of data, and they thought that they saw far more perturbation than *either* theory predicts. It's still not much, by usual standards; it probably wouldn't even be detectable from Earth, given atmospheric and other noise effects in the instruments. However, Moira isn't the sort of woman to allow Nature to win, and she hates being puzzled. She got hold of a large collection of photographs of that part of the sky, taken over the last few months by a different team for an entirely different purpose, and started checking Persephone on all of them, doing old-fashioned manual orbit determination." He shook his head. "That woman thinks she's more accurate than a computer!" He shrugged eloquently. "She probably is. However, I'm smugly happy to say she made little progress. What did happen, though, was that she noticed, on a sequence of photos from two weeks ago, that the star Iota Draconis had, uh . . . disappeared."

"I gather that's not normal?"

"Of *course* not! One of Moira's staff suggested that it was due to some large, dark object some undetermined distance out, blocking the view, and that object is the source of Persephone's perturbations."

"Pretty big, then?"

Battani nodded. "There's no distance determination yet, of course, but it could be solar mass or more. Possible considerably more."

"A black hole?" Horwith felt the hair at the back of his neck prickling at his own suggestion. He laughed nervously. "You couldn't solve that black hole anomaly, so now one of them's coming to get you."

"No, not a black hole. For one thing, Iota Draconis wouldn't have disappeared. Because of refraction by a black hole's gravitational field, the star would have appeared to shift, or even to split into multiple duplicate images. In fact, such refraction would give us a way of determining mass and distance. I wonder if Moira's thought of looking for such duplicate images?" He reached for his telephone, then hesitated. "No, better not.

"Well, the day before yesterday, Radio One was able to lock onto a faint signal from the direction of Iota Draconis. Since then, it's been determined that it's very broad-spectrum noise, detectable at various points from X ray to infrared. Nothing in visible light yet, though, but she hasn't been able to free up any of the large optical telescopes to search for it. Someone came up with the name 'gray hole,' and that's what they were talking about in the cafeteria. Now you know just about as much as I or anyone else knows, except that you know it in English, while I know it in numbers."

Horwith nodded. "The advantage of being a genuwine scientist. Iota Draconis would be in the constellation Draco, right? I don't suppose the direction . . . ?"

I'm afraid so," Battani said unhappily. "Right ascension of fifteen hours, twenty minutes, declination of fifty-nine degrees. Approximately. If you want the precise figures, they're the same as the direction of our mysterious friends. Probably just a coincidence." He looked as though he didn't believe that at all.

"Probably." Horwith had a strange, empty feeling in his stomach.

"I suppose you'd have told me if there were any new messages from the aliens? Anything beyond those bursts of random noise over the last few weeks?" Battani said.

"Yes, of course I'd have told you. There's nothing else. Rawlinson's keeping track of it right now. Hoping the messages will start again, I suppose. He even told me yesterday that he'd figured it all out. The messages stopped before because the aliens had a malfunction with their transmitter, and the noise bursts have something to do with them repairing it, or maybe testing it before they start trying to transmit again. The kid's got optimism, I'll give him that. He'll alert me right away if anything comes in. You know, though, NASA's planning to close down the receiver in another few weeks, anyway. The testing period was supposed to be over by now. They'll probably want to reassign me to something productive while they're at it."

"We'll see what we can do about that," Battani said absent-mindedly. "About those static bursts—"

"Yes," Horwith nodded. "The timing. That had occurred to me. Give me Dr. Thabanchu's figures, and I'll check into it." He already had a strong conviction that he knew what he'd find, and he was both excited and frightened at the idea.

"This is all we have so far. I don't think it's enough to draw any conclusions." Horwith leaned back in his chair, his hands clasped behind his head. On the desk before him lay a single sheet of paper, divided into two halves by a vertical line. The right half was headed T-BAND, and the left, GRAY HOLE. Below the heading on the right was a column of numbers, the start and stop times of the bursts of T-band noise Rawlinson had been keeping track of during the preceding weeks. In almost every case, the time interval between start and stop was less than half a second. The most recent time listed was only two hours earlier, and in this case, there was as yet no stop time.

On the left-hand side of the paper, beneath the GRAY HOLE heading, only one number was written. This was the time, two weeks earlier, when Iota Draconis had disappeared. Horwith had found the number in the data sent by Moira Thabanchu; thus, to his mingled relief and disappointment, it had not been necessary for him to approach her for it.

He had placed this time opposite to the next to last figure on the right, to which it was closest in value. Even so, Moira Thabanchu's time was some hours later than Rawlinson's. "I guess I was intuitively expecting an exact matchup. The only time we have from Moira is off by hours from Rawlinson's times."

"But remember," Battani said, "that's when the phenomenon was first noticed. There just didn't happen to be any photographs taken earlier, say at the same time as that noise event."

"Taken here, you mean. What about on Earth?"

Battani shook his head. "No one's done any optical sky surveys on Earth to speak of since this observatory went into operation. What I would have expected would be amateurs noticing it and alerting the professionals. A star in a major constellation vanishing! But no professional would notice even that," he added with barely concealed venom. "The typical professional astronomer nowadays never looks at the real sky."

Horwith was tempted to ask Battani when he had last done so himself, but instead he said, "With the tensions on Earth now, and society going to pot, and everyone expecting the bombs to start falling any minute, maybe they're all a bit distracted. Speaking of which, you didn't notice this, did you?" He leaned forward and pointed at the last number in the right-hand column. "This latest burst of T-band noise is still going on—or was, when I got those numbers from Rawlinson a while ago. That's a lot longer than any of the others seem to have lasted."

"Of course I noticed it," Battani said, offended.

The telephone on Horwith's desk rang, and when he answered it, a voice that made his heart skip a beat asked for Battani. But then, *why would she be asking for me?* Wordlessly, he held the telephone receiver out to the other man.

"Hello? . . . Yes, Moira." Battani listened without saying anything more. After a while, he hung up, and his normally dark face was pale. "We may have a more significant matchup now. Come with me, and bring that sheet of paper along. You might want to forward all your calls to Moira's extension."

* * *

Battani led the way through what seemed to Horwith to be miles of corridors, into a section of the observatory he had never yet visited. He noticed with some surprise that the offices were considerably larger and plusher than Battani's. "Not a bad setup," he said quietly.

Battani grunted and just as quietly replied, "Our Director is always willing to do a lot for brilliant astronomers who are also female and beautiful. Speaking of whom . . ." He raised his voice. "Here we are, Moira."

She turned from the two men to whom she'd been talking. Her lovely face bore a far from welcoming expression. "Dr. Battani," she said, and Horwith thought her voice thrilling in spite of the open anger in it, "I called you in on this only because you've pulled rank and given me no choice. What is *he* doing here?"

Despite the tone and the words, Horwith found Moira Thabanchu more fascinating than ever. He had never heard an accent quite like hers; it was wonderful. He had never seen any woman whose beauty struck him physically quite the way hers did; it was wonderful. There was surely no woman on Earth, no other woman in space, no female being anywhere quite so—so—well, so *wonderful* as Moira Thabanchu.

"Clemmons Horwith is a colleague of ours," Battani said, his voice icy cool but his face betraying his anger. "He's probably one of the most important and well-informed workers here."

Horwith smiled and wanted to say soothingly to Battani that it was all right, that nothing mattered anymore, but Moira said harshly, in a voice that no one but Horwith considered lovely at that moment, "Horwith! You mean this man's not only your spy, the one who eavesdropped on my conversation, but he's also the one responsible for all those lost observations months ago?" She stepped toward Horwith, fury crackling from her.

Eat me alive! Horwith thought. Please!

"Moira!" Battani exploded. "For God's sake, grow up!" Surely no one had dared to say such a thing to Moira Thabanchu since her childhood. It had the effect, if not of calming her, then at least of banking the fires. "Now, then," Battani continued in a surprisingly normal tone, "tell Clemmons what you told me on the telephone before."

Stiffly, refusing to look at Horwith, retreating behind the protection of professionalism, Thabanchu said, "At five thirty-five this morning, our time, Iota Draconis reappeared. That is to say, the gray hole that was blocking it from us moved. We've had Radio One searching for the hole since then. They've just succeeded. It's inside the orbit of Jupiter already, moving inward, and accelerating. It seems to be moving in a straight line, as though other masses do not affect it, even though it perturbs them."

Horwith glanced down at the suddenly remembered paper he held. "Jesus! Five thirty-five, you said? Give me the exact number, if you've got it."

Moira's expression grew still angrier, but she responded in an even tone. "Five hours, thirty-five minutes, ten point six seconds, Greenwich Mean Time."

"Well?" Battani asked, impatient.

"Oh, it's the same. Exactly the same." Noticing the puzzlement on everyone else's face, Horwith explained, "The same as the time when the latest T-band noise began." Something else occurred to him. "I don't remember the distances, but wouldn't that object of yours have to be moving unbelievably fast to go from outside Pluto's orbit to inside Jupiter's in, um"—he glanced at his watch—"less than seven hours?"

Moira's hostility faded at this unexpected display of rudimentary intelligence on Horwith's part. "Almost seventy percent of light speed, in fact," she said, "if it were in the plane of the ecliptic. Considerably faster, since it's moving at an angle of seventy-seven degrees to the ecliptic. That puts it at three-point-three times light speed. But that's another thing that's puzzling us . . . Clemmons, is it?" He nodded, and she smiled at him, turning his knees to water. "Actually, Clemmons, it's scarcely moving at all, now, relatively speaking; it's on the order of kilometers per second. So it must have moved in even faster than I said, at many times light speed, and then . . . slowed down. Stopped." Her tone changed to one of absolute bewilderment, and

Horwith felt the urgent desire to put his arms about her and protect her from a harsh Universe.

One of her assistants, who had been listening to this conversation without speaking, now contributed his opinion. "As if it's under intelligent control."

Horwith recognized him as the man with whom Moira had been discussing the gray hole during breakfast in the cafeteria. Various ideas connected suddenly in Horwith's mind. "It tunnelled!" he shouted. "That's how it happened!"

He laughed at the bewildered faces around him. "The gray hole—it's a spaceship! From the aliens! That's why they stopped broadcasting as soon as we responded. They send out a mission, an embassy, as soon as they get a reply. Probably they can locate a T-band source easily, since they're so advanced. Gee, Al, maybe this is a group of evangelists, coming here to show us how to become Proper Ones."

Battani groaned loudly.

Horwith said, "Anyway, we know from their broadcasts that they have interstellar flight. We also know that's impossible, or not practical, anyway, from our point of view, because of distances and time and so on. The good old speed of light. But if their ships can tunnel, the way an electron does, the way T-band transmission does—"

"And just how do they manage that?" the man from the cafeteria asked sarcastically.

"Don't ask me, boss. I just test radios," Horwith snapped. "Ask the aliens, when they get here."

"Now, listen," Battani said soothingly, his expression thoughtful. "I think Clemmons has hit it. It's taken me a while to absorb it all, but I think I understand him now. That's always a problem with Clemmons," he added apologetically to Moira Thabanchu. "Sometimes, his intuitive leaps run so far ahead of me and of his own ability to describe them, that I have the Devil of a time keeping up with him." With those absurd words, spoken to a surprisingly credulous Moira, Battani won Horwith's lifelong gratitude.

"I think this is what Clemmons was about to explain," Battani went on. "Suppose the aliens do have . . . well, let's call it T-travel, since we seem to be stuck with such names. Suppose it to be a further development of T-band, or perhaps simply a related phenomenon. And suppose, as a consequence, that every time one of their ships performs a T-travel maneuver, every time it tunnels from one point to another, a great burst of T-band noise is produced, perhaps by the engines but more probably due to the tunnelling of a large mass. Clemmons, you have suggested an enormous, fertile new area of study for me!"

"Uh, you're welcome," Horwith said, unable to tell whether the gravity of Battani's voice was feigned and whether his eyes held a twinkle. He held up the sheet of paper. "We've been observing these T-band bursts over the last six weeks. Perhaps their ship can't tunnel the whole thirteen thousand light-years in one jump. Or perhaps there are navigational problems involved, so that they have to tunnel relatively short distances and then recalculate, like a mid-course correction. Anyway, let's say they did it in steps, then hung around beyond Persephone for a while, perhaps to make sure they were in the right place. Finally, they tunnelled in as far as was safe, say because of accuracy problems, and now they're coming our way, but maybe using more conventional travel."

"But they're not!" Moira said angrily, and now for the first time Horwith became aware of the impatience and annoyance that had returned to her face. "If you and Dr. Battani hadn't been jabbering away, I could have told you this some time ago. The gray hole is moving in a straight line, I said. Well, that line doesn't lead to Earth. It leads directly to the sun."

Trying hard to digest this, Horwith scarcely heard her next words. "Furthermore," she said, with a growing anger that was an imperfect mask to her fear, "with a mass at least as great as the sun's, if it *did* approach close to any planet, including the Earth, it would destroy that planet through tidal effects, or draw it into itself, or pull it out of the solar system with it as it left."

Somewhere in the background, a telephone had been ringing, ignored for some minutes. Finally, someone answered it and called out, "It's for you, Dr. Horwith."

Too numb to notice his suddenly acquired degree, Horwith walked to the telephone and took it. He listened, said, "Thanks," and hung up, and then he said to the room at large, "That was Rawlinson. He said the noise stopped a couple of minutes ago, and now there's a new message coming in, something translatable. He's got it on his screen now." He looked around until he spotted a terminal nearby. "Here. I'll slave this one to his."

Horwith hunched over the keyboard. He was still so preoccupied with what Moira had said that he had trouble remembering Rawlinson's access codes, and when he did dredge them up, his fingers were curiously clumsy and refused to obey him. But at last he succeeded, and the screen before him lit up with a copy of the display then on the screen of Rawlinson's terminal.

The alien message was a short one, this time—only twenty lines long, so that it didn't even fill up the standard twenty-five-line screen used on the terminals throughout the observatory. Thus there was no scrolling, no upward movement of the lines of text. Instead, the message stayed on the screen, perfectly still, while everyone in the room gathered around the terminal to read it. And as they did so, they stepped back wordlessly, as though the terminal had become something frightening and dangerous, and they exchanged with each other looks of astonishment and dismay.

6

Alfredo Battani walked to the podium, looking old and worn and smaller than ever. He nodded to the Director of the observatory, cleared his throat, and spoke.

"As you probably all know, we have been sending messages to the aliens constantly. I won't say we've been begging them to change their minds, but I will say that we haven't stood on our dignity. They have not replied. I'd even say that they've ignored us. We still have a week, so there's still a chance that they might respond. Of course, that's even assuming they can still control the gray hole: it's possible that it's fully autonomous once it leaves their world. At any rate, we are presuming that they could yet change their minds and not carry out their threat. But personally I don't think that will happen."

There was a stir from the audience filling the small auditorium, rustling movement and low, murmured conversations. Battani gave it a chance to die down and then said, "My personal conviction is that we have to plan right now on the assumption that what they told us in their last message is really going to happen. In that light, I'm asking all of you to forget whatever orders you may have received from your respective governments before you left Earth and to agree not to tell your people what the aliens said."

At this, the noises grew louder. There were a few shouted protests. Battani held up his hand. "What would we accomplish? We can't prevent the inevitable. What good would a few extra days of panic and riot accomplish? Those of you with families on Earth—well, you have my deepest sympathy. I have a daughter living in Milan. Three months ago, I became a grandfather for the first time. But we can't even think about ferrying our relatives up here. We're at our limit now, and the food supplies we already have are going to have to last as long as we can stretch them out. And I'm sure none of you wants to go back home now."

Horwith, listening from the audience, felt that Battani was doing a fairly good job of presenting his argument, but he wondered what the point of it all was. What difference would it make which course of action the observatory personnel agreed on? As Battani himself had pointed out, the aliens' action appeared to be irreversible. And, in that case, Mendeleev was as doomed as Earth. He forced his attention back to Battani. His friend was saying, "We might as well start thinking of ourselves as isolated up here. We are no longer Earthmen. We're . . . well, Lunarians, or whatever name you want to make up. That's all of us at this observatory, and all the men and women at the NASA bases on the moon."

Someone stood up in the audience and shouted, "What the hell are you talking about? We're all dead, anyway! We're not Lunarians! We're corpses!" All around him, Horwith saw nodding heads.

Battani held up his hand again and waited for a chance to talk. "Quietly, quietly," he said. "This is a small room. The answer to your objection is that we're still alive. Where there's life, there's hope, to coin a cliché. There are avenues to explore. We don't know what the NASA people might have developed. We need to find that out. And to do that, we need to be able to approach them with the suggestion that they, too, keep their silence about this message and that they align themselves with us."

Later, Horwith told Battani that he thought the astrophysicist displayed a surprising flair for politics. "But you know," he added, "I have my doubts too about how much good any of this is going to do. They went along with you, but so what? And can you really trust everyone here?"

"No, of course not. Of course I can't. I'm sure that as soon as the vote was taken and the meeting was over, various people headed for the nearest radios and tried to tell their governments and their families what's happening. I could almost tell you just which people they are, too."

"So what was the point of having the meeting and forcing a vote? Earth's going to know, anyway."

Battani grinned—his first sign of amusement in hours. "I said they'd *try* to radio Earth, not that they *would* radio Earth. Before the meeting, I bullied the Director into closing down all our outgoing links. We can still receive, but we can't send."

"There are unwholesome depths to you, Dr. Battani." But banter rang hollow now; it was a case of whistling past a graveyard—a very large graveyard. "What if some Earth government gets suspicious and sends out a ship?"

"It won't get here in time," Battani said bluntly. "Look. Normally it takes three days to make the trip. Add to that a few days for the decision to send it. By the time the ship arrives here, the truth will be there for everyone to see. Or not see. The government that sends the ship probably will no longer exist when the ship lands."

"All right. But what about the NASA Frontside base? I'm sure they're still in touch with Houston, and they could be ordered to take action any time. Maybe within the next couple of hours."

"You're assuming the NASA people know what we know. How would they, unless someone here told them? And no one can, because that radio link is down, too. For that matter, what good would it do any government to take action against us? We're not the enemy. Oh, I understand that at a time like this, unreason could take over completely. But within days, they'll all be collapsing. We only need to hold out that long."

"Wrong," Horwith said. "We need to hold out forever."

Battani grunted. "By the way, the radio link to Frontside can be reactivated in moments. We didn't disable it; we just put it under guard. The reason for that is that I want you to use it to contact your fellow employees and break the news to them and persuade them to do what we're doing."

Horwith thought of Jim Dysan. "You don't know what you're asking."

"I've heard all the harsh things you have to say about your colleagues over there. But they're intelligent people. They'll see our point."

"Yeah. Some of them even speak English."

"Well, you know, that's more than you can say for many of the astronomers here."

Clemmons smiled. "But the astronomers here who don't speak English at least speak some other language. I meant that the guys at the NASA base who don't speak English communicate in Gorilla, instead."

"Surely that's unfair."

"Okay, then. Chimpanzee. All right, all right: I *am* being unfair. Actually, there are some brilliant people over there, and I'm perfectly willing to go back and try to reach them. But the difference between NASA and Mendeleev is that over there the brilliant people aren't in control, and the men who *are* in control are under the thumb of their superiors on Earth."

"Have you noticed," Battani asked, "that we've both been referring to 'NASA' as if the term covered only the NASA personnel on the moon? As if they were already separated from Earth? That's your clue: we think that way, knowing what the aliens said, and once you tell the NASA people what was in that last message, your colleagues will start thinking in those terms, too. They will realize that they have no reason to care what their superiors on Earth say."

"I don't suppose 'Alfredo' translates as 'Pollyanna'?"

"I've heard that accusation before. It translates as plain old Alfred, I'm afraid. We Italians simply add an 'o' or an 'a' or an 'i' to the end of every word."

"I understand that makes life easy for your poets."

"We're *all* poets."

Once again, Horwith had the feeling that they were jointly whistling past a graveyard. "All right. I'll go. By shuttle, of course. If I took a rover, I wouldn't even get there before it no longer mattered. Which raises the question of whether it really *does* matter what we do. But I won't pursue that. I'll do it as a favor to you—the last favor I'll ever do you."

"Don't bet everything on that. Remember: 'The Universe is not only stranger than we imagine. It is stranger than we *can* imagine.'"

"The Gospel According to Battani?"

"No. Wish it were. You can go immediately, I hope?"

"Why not? Anyway, every second counts."

* * *

Dysan was surprised to see Horwith back. Horwith had the impression that his boss had put his existence out of his mind and was not pleased at being reminded of it. "What the Hell are you doing here?" he growled.

"A problem with the credit union," Horwith told him. "They wanted me to come in personally and straighten it out." He had decided on the way over from Mendeleev that it would be better to report to Dysan upon arrival and tell him something that would keep him pacified. Otherwise, if he discovered that Horwith was on the base without his having been notified, he would certainly grow suspicious and interfere.

Dysan shook his head. "Jeez, you guys are all such incompetents. They threatening to repossess your jockey shorts, or something? With the kind of money I pay you, you shouldn't be having problems. Why didn't they handle it by radio?"

"The link to Mendeleev is down." Horwith froze. If the link was down, how had the credit union contacted him in the first place? He held his breath, waiting for Dysan to ask him exactly that question and searching in vain for an answer to it.

But Dysan was too preoccupied with drawing comparisons that were flattering to him to see the inconsistency. "Yeah, so I heard." He sneered. "Those guys over there at that observatory are supposed to be so brilliant, and yet they can't even maintain a damned radio! What a bunch of gobblers."

To his own surprise, Horwith found that he didn't react to Dysan with his usual barely suppressed disgust and anger. It was the aliens' message, he supposed: Dysan simply didn't matter anymore. He extricated himself as quickly as he could and left the area.

Horwith took an elevator down three floors and made his way to the office of the person he had really come back to the base to see. This was Gilda Taves, a tall, beefy woman of indeterminate ethnic origin and uncertain disposition. She had made her way to her present position of Staff Scientist to the Director of the base more through her powers of intimidation than her competence, even though she was technically brilliant and could perhaps have gone just as far by relying on her technical ability. Horwith had always suspected that Gilda preferred intimidation as the route to success simply because she enjoyed it.

He had always had the impression that Gilda Taves was not a woman to be bound by orthodox scientific ideas. It hadn't taken him long to settle on her as the most likely to react favorably to Battani's ideas. In fact, he told himself, he ought to introduce the two of them. He suspected they were both sexually frustrated, and if it was true that physical opposites attract, then they certainly ought to be drawn to each other. The thought of the two of them in bed—huge Gilda and tiny Battani, as his imagination painted them—brought a smile to his face and then a surprising surge of vicarious arousal to his groin.

Great, he told himself. I'm about to enter Gilda's office to discuss with her the most important event in human history, and I'll have a hard on. What I need is to find my own opposite and get some attraction going. But he knew he had already found her: it was Moira Thabanchu. Unfortunately, the attraction was definitely on his side only, and moreover, there would be no time for anything to happen even if she had been attracted to him. He didn't think there would be time to introduce Battani and Taves, either, despite Battani's enigmatic hints about everything not being over yet.

On the positive side, such gloomy thoughts did away with his erection.

Fortunately, Gilda was in her office when he reached it. She looked surprised to see him. "Clemmons! I thought you were over at Mendeleev. The assignment over?"

He closed the door carefully behind him and shook his head. "I'll be going back there very soon. I just came here to see a couple of people. You, most of all." He sat down uninvited; Gilda was not the sort with whom one stood on ceremony.

Gilda's standard bookmark was a toothpick. She kept a jar full of them on her desk for that purpose and would become furious (an awesome sight) if an ignorant visitor misunderstood their function and dared to use one of them to pick his teeth. She took a toothpick from the jar now, put it in the document she was reading, closed it, and leaned back. "That sounds like you're either preparing to resign or commit suicide," she said in her unplaceable accent.

Horwith laughed. "Neither. Or both, in a manner of speaking. Read this." He took from his shirt pocket a folded-up sheet of paper and spread it out for her on her desk.

Gilda glanced over it quickly. Then she looked up at Horwith searchingly for a moment and read the paper again, more carefully. "I don't understand. What is this?"

"You know we picked up some T-band signals, Glen Alenian and I, when we were working out at the receiver?"

Gilda nodded. "And then you directed the building of a transmitter at Mendeleev. That was basically why you went over there. Also because they had a lot of political pull at the time."

"Right. Well, what you're not supposed to know yet is that we determined that the signal Glen and I received was a message from an alien civilization, and we managed to translate it."

Gilda nodded again. "I heard that." She grinned at his astonishment. "Never mind how. Those folks at Mendeleev aren't very good at cloak-and-dagger. But that's all I know."

Horwith gave her a quick summary of the nature of the messages that had been translated at Mendeleev. "Theologians and historians and anthropologists would have loved that stuff," he told her, "but it seemed to drive the astronomers crazy. They kept hoping for hard data, numbers, about physical phenomena, not reams of information about how Proper Ones behave and examples of great Proper Ones in alien history. I didn't know astronomers knew the words I've heard some of them use."

Gilda shrugged. "Even scientists are human, Clemmons."

"I never knew that! But we'll let it pass for the sake of argument. Anyway, we finally got the transmitter working and sent a long reply. We told them all about ourselves and our history and philosophy and so on. I guess we expected a pat on the head from them and a promise of foreign aid."

"And you got?"

"Nothing. They stopped transmitting. And then they did something entirely different." He told her about the gray hole.

"We figured out it must be from them, because of the T-band interference. It tunnels. At any rate, we thought at first it was a ship from them—you know, filled with ambassadors and scientists and so on. But then they sent us that message, the one I just gave you. And not a peep since then."

Gilda read the message again. "What more is there for them to say, after they've said this?"

She leaned back in her chair and stared at the calender on the wall beside her desk. January's picture was a beautiful snow-covered meadow in the Rockies, marred only by two brightly-dressed skiers racing across it. But it wasn't the picture she was looking at. "So how long do we have?"

"Until about the end of next week, according to their message. The gray hole is already inside the solar system, but it's travelling slowly now. The Mendeleev people are making their estimates based on its present speed, but of course they don't know if it'll slow down or speed up."

"Yes, of course." There was a pause again. Then Gilda said, "You've kept this quiet, though. Shouldn't the world know about it?"

"Do you think it would make any difference if the world did know? By the end of next week, it'll be as clear as . . . day. Why prolong the agony?"

"I don't know. It doesn't seem right to act like gods."

"Doomed gods. Ragnarok. Fimbulwinter. All that sort of stuff."

"You almost make what's about to happen sound romantic," Gilda said with a touch of anger. "I can guess why you came to me with the story, but tell me anyway."

"That was Battani's idea. He wants all the NASA people on the moon to keep the secret, too. We're all Lunarians now, he says."

"But we didn't know anything about this gray hole, anyway. You could have just kept us in the dark. So to speak."

Horwith nodded. "True. But next weekend, let's say, official-dom on Earth might very well give you orders to shut Mendeleev down or take it over or evacuate everyone there to Earth. Or everyone here, leaving us behind."

Gilda looked exasperated. "What difference would that make, anyway? Look at this message." She tapped the sheet of paper with her forefinger. "These aliens of yours . . . Well, it just seems pretty obvious to me that we can do whatever we want, and it won't make any difference."

"Yeah, well, I tend to agree with you. I think Battani is just going through the motions to make himself feel we're still in control of our destinies. However, he keeps saying mysterious things implying that he knows something the rest of us don't. He's very respected over there, you know. We're all playing along. For want of anything better to do, maybe."

Gilda stared into space for a long time. At last she grunted and said, "I suppose it makes as much sense as running around in circles and screaming. But you know, I have a family on Earth, in Dallas. . . ."

Horwith said gently, "A lot of people at Mendeleev have families on Earth, too. And a lot of people here. But if you're right, and Battani *is* just whistling in the dark and there's nothing we can do, then why make your family suffer any longer than necessary?"

Gilda shivered. "I could be with them," she said in a husky voice.

"But you couldn't save them. Maybe we have some sort of chance up here, but you know you can't bring your family up here. You can sacrifice yourself for nothing by going home. Or you can stay here, where you might be able to contribute something."

"That's a hell of a choice!"

Absurd clichés flitted through Horwith's mind as possible answers: "Life isn't fair." "You take what you get." But since he couldn't offer real comfort, he certainly didn't want to say anything that would have the same effect as deliberate cruelty. And he felt guilty that his reaction to what was about to happen was limited to concern for himself and a generalized, intellectually based compassion for the billions on Earth. His parents were both dead, his only sibling, an older brother, he had hated since both were boys, and he had never had a close friend. It was too easy for him to offer hackneyed and meaningless words of compassion to those who were in agony.

"All right," Gilda said at last, "I'll play along, too." There was another silence. Then she put her hand flat over the sheet of paper before her as if to hide the words it bore. "Christ!" she exploded. "What pompous, supercilious assholes they must be! What right do they have?"

"Someone at Mendeleev said that their message boils down to, 'You are slime, and you make us retch.'"

Gilda rubbed her eyes. "It wouldn't matter what they think of us, if they stopped there."

Horwith stood up. "I think I'd better move on. I wanted to talk to a couple of other people here, and time's getting short. I want to be back at Mendeleev as soon as I can." Because in a way, it suddenly occurred to him, he *did* have a family he wanted to be with now, a new family. It was a warming thought, but at the same time it made him feel all the more guilty: his family, such as it was, was here, and not on Earth going about its usual business in ignorance.

Gilda waved her hand dismissingly. "Go on, then. I'll speak to some people, too. We can probably pull it off. I'll call you up at Mendeleev and let you know. Um, let's say by Tuesday."

"Right. Goodbye."

For a strained moment, they both pondered the thought that this "goodbye" might never be followed by another "hello." Then Gilda said, "Goodbye, Clemmons," and the mood was broken, and Horwith left her office.

The curious thing, in Horwith's view, was how normal and everyday everything seemed for the first few days. People strolled or hurried along the corridors of Mendeleev, according to individual taste and circumstances, just as they always had. Meals continued in the cafeteria, seminars in the conference rooms, and work in the offices. Even social life seemed strangely unaffected. Thinking it over, Horwith wasn't sure what else he had expected to see, but he was sure this wasn't it.

More than once he heard people refer to the band on the *Titanic*, playing as the liner sank. There had been no room for the band on the lifeboats; whereas in this case, Horwith reflected, there *was* no lifeboat.

The mood began to shift after the weekend.

On Monday afternoon, the second of February, for the first time he noticed large numbers of people not working. At loose ends himself, Horwith roamed the observatory. Everywhere he went, even in normally deserted places, he found people. They were wandering aimlessly in the halls, filling the recreation rooms and park rooms, or standing at observation windows and staring silently out at the lunar surface.

He couldn't have called it goofing off, for there was no joy in it. They seemed distracted in some cases, stunned in others. Those he greeted as often as not didn't reply; he thought they hadn't even heard him, or perhaps lacked the energy to respond.

The situation was puzzling to Horwith. After an hour or two, he began to find it disturbing. It became frightening when he entered one long, narrow, dusty corridor that was used as a storage area and heard weeping. He followed the sound to a small space between two file cabinets.

Here he found Lonnie McClory, a young secretary who had once done some word processing for him. She was curled up in the small space, almost in a fetal position, crying steadily and shivering.

Horwith knelt down beside her. "Lonnie, what is it? What's the matter? Can I help you?" He had never heard of rape at Mendeleev, but it was the conclusion he jumped to. He tried to remember what one should do to help a rape victim.

Lonnie shook her head and curled up tighter. There were no police at Mendeleev, and not even the sort of security guards available at the NASA base. "Listen, Lonnie, let me help you to the infirmary. They can give you first aid there. Uh, who did this?"

She stopped crying and looked at him at last. "What?"

"Who did this to you?"

"Did what?" She was staring at him in puzzlement now, but she was no longer weeping or shaking, and Horwith felt that must be better for her. He hesitated to use the word "rape," though: might that not drive her back, upset her again? He settled for, "Who hurt you?"

"No one. No one hurt me. I'm okay. Go away. Leave me alone." Her mouth began to tremble.

"But . . . what's wrong?"

"I don't want it to happen! Go away!"

At last Horwith understood. She was weeping in terror of the rape that was yet to happen. After a moment's hesitation, he rose to his feet and left her weeping again, curled in her tiny refuge.

By Wednesday afternoon, everything was grinding to a halt. The high motivation and drive of these people, which had impressed Horwith so much and intimidated him, had evaporated since the weekend.

Battani was one of the very few people at Mendeleev still working. For a change, he was not using pencil and paper and brainpower; now he was spending hours at a computer terminal he'd had installed in his office. Moreover, his door was locked almost all the time—a message that was clear enough to Horwith.

Late on Sunday afternoon, Horwith was sitting in the cafeteria eating an early supper. He was virtually alone in the large room: normal biological schedules seemed to have lapsed along with all others. He was staring at his tray, chewing on his hurt at being excluded by Battani as he chewed on his food. Feeling hurt made him feel silly and adolescent, as though he were a kid whose best friend had suddenly abandoned him. At the same time, even while he lectured himself to be mature about the matter, he argued with himself that whatever Battani was doing wasn't really important; nothing was, now. Someone sat down beside him. Horwith made a vague gesture of greeting without looking up and continued with his thoughts.

"I didn't know you were ever without your shadow."

The words sank in slowly, and so did the voice. Horwith looked at his new companion in astonishment. "Dr. Thabanchu! I beg your pardon?"

"You should have done that when you first arrived," Moira

Thabanchu said. "That way, maybe I wouldn't have been so angry at you. Call me Moira, please."

"Uh, glad to. You said something about my shadow?" Horwith was amazed at his ability to speak so calmly and rationally in this woman's presence, for once. Perhaps it was because for the first time she looked friendly and not angry. Perhaps also it was because in this environment and seated next to him she looked so small and unintimidating.

"Your shadow. That's Dr. Battani. The two of you are always together. I've never had a chance before this to talk to you alone."

Had she ever really wanted to speak to him alone? It was a remarkable thought. "I've been alone at various times." Especially at night, but I'd better not say that.

Moira looked away from him in embarrassment and toyed with her food. "Oh, I know. The truth is that I've been very bitchy. Not just toward you but toward everyone I've ever worked with."

Horwith had no idea what was behind this intimacy on her part, this opening up toward him, but he didn't want to do anything to stop it. "Sometimes, it's very hard to behave the way you know you ought to," he said hesitantly, and then, warming to his theme, added, "Sometimes it's as if there's another personality taking over and forcing you to act in certain ways toward others, in spite of yourself."

Moira looked up at him gratefully. "Yes, exactly! That's the way it is with me all the time! You, too?"

"Well, no," Horwith admitted. "Or . . . yes. It's a matter of interpretation. In my case, my problem is that I can't make myself speak or act at all, even when I really want to and know what I want to say and do."

"You're talking about women, aren't you?"

"Well, yes. I have the same trouble with men also, but in that case it doesn't matter as much. With women, yes."

Moira nodded. "You're shy and inhibited and tongue-tied, and you hate it, and I'm nasty and cutting and overbearing, and I hate it. But we're both overcoming our problems now."

"I noticed. You're treating me like a human being. That's a change."

She laughed. "I've known from the start that you're human, Clemmons. See, I even know your name. I made a point of finding out."

"Why?" he asked bluntly. He refused to believe that this about-face was genuine; the suspicion was growing in him that she was setting him up for some particularly unpleasant trick. He couldn't imagine why she would do such a thing, but the alternative was too good to be true.

But at his change in tone, Moira looked hurt and vulnerable, and Horwith couldn't believe she was acting. "Because . . ." She struggled for a moment, and then said rapidly, "Because I was attracted to you as soon as I met you."

"Attracted! But the way you acted toward me . . . It doesn't make sense!"

"I know." Moira looked away again. "It's the way I am. It's that other personality you were talking about. But now . . ."

"Yes," Horwith said in a gentler tone, "now it's different. Why is that?"

Moira shrugged. "I don't know. It's what's about to happen, I suppose. I'm ashamed to admit it, but it's made me feel liberated. For the first time since I was a child, I don't have to worry about the future or what other people will think about me. I can forget about ambition. I can forget about everything. I can do what I want, for a change—whatever I want."

"And what do you want to do?"

Her voice lowered to a whisper. "I want you to come to my apartment with me right away." She looked up at him hopefully. "Unless you want to finish your food first."

"My—my what? Oh." He had forgotten the food was there. "To hell with that. Let's go." He grinned at Moira and she grinned back, and to Horwith life seemed to be beginning instead of ending.

Later that night, as they lay side by side in the subdued light, telling each other about their lives, Moira told him that she was married.

"Adrian. That's his name. He's still down there, teaching at

Wits University. We're separated. Legally, I mean, as well as by a quarter of a million of miles. He's white. The marriage was a real mistake. We were both too young to know what we were doing."

"You mean, there was a racial problem?"

Moira laughed. "No, not on our part. On my family's, yes. Adrian and I just aren't very well suited. And we disagree violently on politics. He's an anti-government radical, and I'm very conservative. I've made it, and I want to protect what I have; that's how he always described my attitude. Anyway, that's why I go by my maiden name. I feel sorry for him, in an abstract sort of way. Being down there next weekend, I mean. The fact is, though, that maybe that's why I feel so liberated. If not for the aliens, I could never have invited you here. I would never have even spoken to you, probably, except on business."

"Thank God for the aliens, then."

They lay together silently for a while, stroking each other softly, and then Horwith said, "I remember reading a novel once in which there was an earthquake. It was in ancient Crete. I remember: it was a novel about Theseus. Anyway, he was with a woman—would that be Medea?—and the earthquake started, and the two of them rip each other's clothes off and make love madly, over and over. I was a kid when I read that book; it really made an impression on me."

Moira giggled. "I'll bet."

"Well, my point is that since then I've read that behavior like that is common during great catastrophes. Probably Nature trying to ensure the survival of the species, or something. Anyway . . . I hope that's not what this is."

Moira pressed herself against him and hugged him. "It isn't."

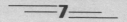

7

On Saturday morning, the tone of news broadcasts from Earth began to change.

A wide range of television and radio channels was available throughout Mendeleev, originating at various points on Earth. In Moira's apartment, where Horwith had formally moved his belongings on Monday morning, the comm set was always set to the channel carrying the broadcasts of the South African Broadcasting Company.

The music coming from the comm set ended and a news broadcast began. The first few items concerned domestic politics, which Horwith ignored even though Moira listened with absorbed interest. But then came something that caught his attention just as securely as hers was already caught.

"Astronomers at Stellenbosch University have reported," the announcer said in that accent that Horwith had at first considered very odd but had come in the last few days to think endearing, "that for the past two days they have been observing a curious new object within our solar system." He went on to describe the gray hole, adding that the Stellenbosch astronomers believed it was disturbing the orbits of both Jupiter and Saturn during its passage through the solar system. "This should not cause any alarm," the announcer added, "because it does not appear this object will in any way effect the Earth itself. The nature and origin of the object are still the subject of investigation. A statement from the government will be forthcoming by morning." Horwith realized suddenly that it was only noon in Cape Town.

"Whew!" Moira said. "The cat's out of the bag."

"Doesn't sound like it. They think it's harmless."

"Oh? How often does a government feel the need to issue a statement about a new astronomical phenomenon?"

Horwith admitted the point. "Would you mind too much if I

66

changed the station? It might be worth listening to the BBC, because it's morning in England, and then maybe to a U.S. network. Maybe not, since it's still the wee hours of the morning on the East Coast."

"Yes, but don't forget the major observatories in Hawaii. Isn't it yesterday evening there? Go ahead."

"Ycster—" He held up his hand. "Never mind explaining."

And so they were in time to hear almost identical announcements on the BBC and on all three major American commerical networks. "Sounds very coordinated to me," Horwith remarked.

"Yeah," Moira said, looking annoyed. "Coordinated with Mendeleev, in fact. I think your pal, Battani, has violated his own rules."

The night before the final day, they partied with their colleagues until the wee hours, and then Moira and Horwith went back to her apartment and partied for an hour or two more, in bed, but not very successfully because of the alcohol both had drunk, and then they fell into a stupefied sleep until Moira's comm set clicked on at seven A.M.

It was Battani's voice, alcoholically cheerful, against a background of laughter and noise: he obviously hadn't bothered with sleep. "Two hours to go, boys and girls! I knew you wouldn't want to miss it! Just enough time to finish up what you're doing, clean up, and have a nice, big breakfast. Remember: it's the most important meal of the day!"

"Fuck you," Horwith moaned.

Apparently, the comm set was sending as well as receiving, for the crowd behind Battani laughed, and Battani said, "Aah! Bed talk between lovers. Isn't it sweet?" The set clicked off.

Horwith groaned and rolled out of bed. Moira lay as if dead. He showered and then came back and tried to wake her up. It took some time, but eventually she got up and went off to shower as well.

It was while Moira was in the bathroom that part of what Battani had said struck Horwith, making him temporarily forget his hangover. "Two hours!" he said aloud. He looked at the clock. More like an hour and a half now.

Surely it wasn't real. Surely it had all been a dream. Moira was real; all of that was real. But the rest—no, that couldn't be. They had mistranslated the aliens' last message, misunderstood some crucial word or phrase. Then Moira emerged from the bathroom, sober and serious, and Horwith could no longer delude himself.

Moira glanced at the clock. "Too bad about last night," she said. "It should have been heavenly. That would have been more appropriate. Come on, Clemmons. Let's go get some breakfast."

"Most important meal of the day," he agreed.

"Most important day in history," Moira added. She turned on the comm set and clicked it to her favorite channel, the SABC. She was just in time for an announcement of an interesting astronomical event that would be visible at 9:12 A.M., Greenwich Mean Time. The announcer then gave the times for various areas of southern Africa, concluding with a cheery recommendation that the listener make an effort to be outside to watch at that time, if possible, because it would be a once-in-a-lifetime sight.

The cafeteria was a mess. It was littered with glasses, plates, food, spilled drinks, clothing, and here and there an individual or a couple—and one larger group—sleeping off the previous evening's manic phase. Various people drifted in for food while Moira and Horwith were there; all of them studiously ignored the intertwined sleeping figures. Horwith grinned suddenly. "Sedate, serious, sober scientists. Never have any fun."

Moira laughed. "We're human, too."

"Some of you are more than human," Horwith said, and kissed her cheek. "I'm terrified, but thank God I'll be with you." Moira smiled at him and squeezed his hand.

Yesterday's mood of fevered ebullience had dissipated entirely. Those eating around them were serious and sober enough now. Horwith and Moira finished their cereal and untoasted bread (there were no cooks working that morning) and set off for the largest of the viewing rooms. Others leaving the cafeteria drifted either in the same direction or toward the conference room Battani had mentioned.

The viewing room was crowded when they got there, but that only meant that Moira and Horwith couldn't see the surface of the moon beyond the windows. What Moira and Horwith and everyone else wanted to see was overhead: the sun.

Random conversations started up throughout the room and then died away: a burst of noise here, a second or two of overly loud laughter there, a murmuring somewhere else. The noise came and went across the large space like a wave running through the crowd, reaching the walls, and then reflecting back into the room again. It occurred to Horwith that it was odd that these people weren't at their posts, glued to television screens showing solar observations from the telescopes all along Mendeleev Rim. But then he thought, once again, Why bother? Why bother with anything, now? Would he be doing his work now, if he had any to do? he asked himself, and he answered, Of course not.

And then the gray hole rose above the lunar horizon, and all conversation died. Breathing stopped. Thought stopped.

It was properly named: a disk like that of the rising sun, but glowing only with a faint gray light that Horwith couldn't look at easily. The stars were visible around it. It was featureless: nothing like sunspots, no brightening toward the center or dimming toward the limb. It looked insubstantial, made of tissue paper and almost transparent. Surely a stiff breeze, if there were such a thing in space, would tear it apart and blow it away in ragged gray streamers. It was anticlimactic, disappointing, not heralded by any strange phenomena, nor bringing any with it.

Its motion was visible against the moon's horizon. As it rose in the lunar sky, it seemed to grow smaller. Horwith could still tell it was moving because it gradually eclipsed star after star, and other stars came into view behind it as it moved on. It rose further and further above the horizon, and the distance between it and the sun, at the zenith, lessened steadily.

Time no longer meant the changing of digits on a watch face; time was measured by the motion of the gray hole, by the angle between it and the sun, by the shrinking distance between it and the sun. In that sense, time passed steadily. It seemed to Horwith to take forever. After it was over, it seemed to him to have taken an instant.

The gray hole's leading edge touched the edge of the sun and then, unpausing, slid over it. Horwith could see that the gray hole was precisely the same size as the sun. "It's just like an eclipse," someone said, puzzled. "A lot faster," someone else said.

In minutes, the sun was entirely covered. The gray hole stopped moving. The stars around the sun, normally invisible, sprang into being. Outside the observatory, the hills and valleys of the moon were hidden in a darkness as deep as that of the lunar night. Only near the observatory buildings, where light shone out of the windows of viewing rooms, was the ground visible. Horwith strained his eyes, trying to see the fires of the sun through the substance of the gray hole, expecting that the gray hole was too insubstantial to shield the sun's fierce heat completely. But he could see nothing except the bland gray surface. "Where's the corona?" he heard Moira saying. "Why can't we see the corona?"

And then the gray hole disappeared. There was no fading, no change at all in its appearance; it simply vanished. The sky was filled with stars, like any normal night sky seen from the far side of the moon. But there was no sun.

8

"Antarctic outposts," Horwith said. "They're used to cold temperatures."

"Not that cold," Battani said. "Not even the Antarctic has ever experienced temperatures as low as Earth will within just a few weeks."

"And besides that," Moira pointed out, "they depend on civilization for food and fuel. Just as we do."

"They could grow food in hydroponic tanks," Horwith insisted. "They could use artificial lights."

"Run from diesel generators, I suppose?" Battani said.

"There's coal in the Antarctic."

"It's all a moot point, anyway," Battani said. "There's one overriding factor that you're not considering: the atmosphere."

"It'll be cold. So what?"

Battani shook his head. "It will be solid and liquid, not gas."

Horwith stared at him in disbelief. "The atmosphere?"

Moira said, "Hadn't you realized that, Clemmons? The gases of the Earth's atmosphere are gaseous—I mean, have been until now—because of the temperature, which is to say because of the heat of the sun. Take that away, and they'll start to precipitate out. They'll form layers on the surface of the Earth, with the gases with the highest freezing point at the bottom, I suppose. I'm not sure, but I'd guess it would end up being a layer a couple of miles thick. You'd have to have a space suit of some kind to even survive down there."

"And," Battani put in, "it would have to be a better space suit than anything we've ever had to build so far. Lower temperatures, more severe conditions even than those outside the observatory at night."

Horwith stared at both of them in horror. Until now, what was about to happen to the sun and the Earth had presented itself to him only in terms of darkness and severe cold, something along the lines of the worst winter night he had ever experienced. But now he realized that he had no experience that enabled him to understand what was about to happen on the surface of his home world. He forced himself to imagine houses, cars, animals, people all covered by a miles-thick blanket of snow, ice, and liquefied gases.

He looked around at the warm, well-lighted cafeteria. Now that Armageddon had passed and, anticlimactically, life at Mendeleev continued without immediate, visible threat, the cooks had come back to work. People sat at tables in small, quiet, peaceful groups, eating sandwiches or even full meals, drinking coffee, chatting with each other. It was all so normal as to be bizarre, considering the circumstances. But even more than that, the scene seemed unreal to Horwith because it was so bright and warm. Suddenly, the cold, dark surface of Earth was the reality to him; this, the surroundings he was really in, was the fantasy, the dream.

"Earth," he said. "What's happening down there? The temperatures must be dropping already. People will be freezing to death everywhere, even at the equator, in days."

"The equator," Battani said pedantically, "is now no different from any other spot on the surface of the planet."

"Even South Africa," Moira said quietly, her mind a quarter of a million miles away. "There aren't any warm places anymore."

"But all of this . . ." Horwith gestured at the room.

"Won't last," Battani said. "We rely on solar-generated electricity stored in batteries for about half our energy, you know. And we have a small fission reactor. We can shut down most of the base, move into the central area of it, and do all right for heat and warmth that way. The reactor could take care of us for a long time to come."

"But?" Horwith glanced at Moira, but she was still mentally back at her home, living through the deepening freeze with her relatives.

"But all our food comes from Earth. We usually have no more than a two-week supply of fresh food, with a few months' worth of emergency supplies which are frozen and vacuum stored. But sooner or later, we'll be down to a choice between suicide and cannibalism.''

And technology won't come to our rescue, either, Horwith realized. There isn't time for breakthroughs that big. He had heard through an acquaintance who worked for a defense contractor about the recent development of force fields. "Just like in science-fiction stories," his aquaintance had said. "But we can't make them big enough to do any good—like maybe to provide us with an antimissile shield over a city. We can make the field real dense and strong, but no more than a few metres across. And it doesn't look like that's ever going to change, according to the theory." If only that limitation weren't there, Horwith thought, the entire surface of Earth could be protected with one of the newly discovered force fields, and its heat kept in. Instead, the Earth's stored heat would steadily and unstoppably radiate away into space.

Horwith shivered. "I'm going to go watch the view of Earth for a while," he said. And listen to some radio broadcasts. He didn't explain that it was because he felt guilty at surviving for even a few extra months and even then dying in surroundings that would still be warm and lighted, while billions of people on Earth would be freezing to death in only days. Nor did he add that he felt the consequent need to tie himself to Earth and its last agonies by means of radio. However, Battani nodded as if he understood.

Moira snapped out of her reverie and stood up as Horwith did. "I'm coming with you," she said, and he understood that she feared being separated from him, as if the end could come at any time now, instead of months in the future.

Battani rose too. "One for all and all for one," he said. Alone of all of them, he seemed placid, almost content with what had happened.

In the West Wing of the observatory, the second-floor conference room was almost empty. Horwith suspected that the other residents of Mendeleev were withdrawing from reality, were pretending, or convincing themselves, that this little lunar world of theirs was all the world there was.

Of course, in a few days they would be correct. Nonetheless the attitude seemed dishonorable to Horwith; he felt, although he knew there was no logical support for the feeling, that it was his duty as a human being to be here, now, witnessing the death of the world that had given birth to his species.

Perhaps even that was not sufficiently honorable. Perhaps his real duty lay on the surface of the Earth itself, so that he could share in the death of the human race. There was still time to join Larrieux and his group. But he also knew that he lacked the physical courage necessary for that course. And there was Moira, who needed him here and with whom he wanted to stay until the last instant of his life.

One wall of the conference room was a giant television screen, normally used for showing astronomical views at seminars or meetings. Now it held a steady view of the turning Earth, as seen from Frontside. Of course, it wasn't the same view Horwith would have seen hours earlier. The familiar blue and brown sphere, partially covered with clouds and swirling weather patterns, high noon directly beneath the moon on this date, was gone. Now there was a black circular object blocking out the stars, and the only lights within the circle were those of cities.

Still, those lights seemed unchanged. It might have been any nighttime view of Earth from the moon, for example, as seen at the time of full moon, when the moon hung over the middle of the nighttime hemisphere. When the gray hole and the sun had vanished, it had been new moon from the Earth, and the sublunar point was in Africa. Now, hours later, the Americas lay below them.

The great cities along the Atlantic and Pacific coasts of both North and South America and along the Gulf Coast outlined the two continents perfectly. Cloud cover must have been almost absent, because Horwith could make out, at the top of the disk and distorted by perspective, the cities along the edges of the Great Lakes. It was so normal, he could, had he wanted to, have deceived himself into believing that if he watched for another day or two, he would see the right-hand edge of the circle begin to glow with the rising sun, and then, as the days passed, see the terminator creep across the Earth from right to left.

A murmuring voice intruded itself gradually upon Horwith's consciousness. He realized it came from a speaker high on one wall, just below the ceiling. Listening to it more carefully, he found that it was a broadcast from Earth. The accent was American, and the substance consisted entirely of government announcements. Horwith asked a man who had been in the room when he had entered if he knew exactly where the broadcast was coming from.

The man shrugged. "No way to tell. All U.S. stations are carrying the same thing. Commerical stuff is all off the air, and this is all there is, anywhere. We tried some stations in Europe and we got the equivalent sort of thing."

Horwith listened to the broadcast for a few minutes. It alternated among assurances that the situation was temporary, admissions that the government had no idea what had happened, pleas for calm, and instructions about centers being established for the control of food and fuel supplies. "All citizens are required to deliver any extra food, or gasoline, or wood in their possession to the nearest police or fire station. All local police and fire departments are now under direct personal control of the President, under authority of emergency legislation passed by both houses of Congress an hour ago and just signed into law by the President. Food and fuel will be rationed as needed. These steps are necessary so that the nation can emerge unharmed from this temporary crisis."

"My God, what idiocy," Battani said. " 'Temporary crisis,' indeed! Why don't they all give up and go home?"

"And what can they do when they get there? Commit suicide?" Horwith said.

Battani nodded. "It would be better than freezing."

Moira said dreamily, "I've always heard freezing to death is painless. You just get sleepy, and then you go to sleep and don't wake up."

"Good God," Horwith muttered. This is the way the world ends, he thought. Not with a whimper, after all, or with fire, but with ice.

The voice on the speaker spoke on, repeating its messages with minor variations. Hours must have passed, but the group watching the Earth from the conference room at Mendeleev and listening to the voice from the dying world were oblivious to the passage of time. Slowly, the city lights on the world below them diminished in brightness. They're saving their fuel, Horwith thought. But what difference will that make? What was the temperature down there now? He would have asked Moira or Battani for a guess, but he was afraid to speak: the silence was reverential; speaking would have been like chatting at a funeral.

From the light pattern, he decided that the Pacific coastline of the Americas was passing below them now, and soon they'd be over the Pacific Ocean itself. Except for major island chains, there'd be no lights for hours until the coastlines of Asia began to pass below them. It startled him to realize that, normally, he would have been able to see the sun reflected in the ocean, the brilliant sub-solar point. Subtly, he had already begun to accept the new situation as normal.

Before land passed out of sight, however, orange glows began to spread in various places. "Fire," someone said softly. "They're setting fires."

"Why?" Horwith asked. "For warmth?" No one answered him. For warmth, he thought. Or maybe it's social breakdown, riot. Or accidents, perhaps.

Shortly thereafter, the speaker on the wall went silent. Horwith assumed they had lost the last American station, or that the broadcasts had at last been shut down to save energy. But some time later—a half hour, three hours; Horwith had no idea—the speaker came to life again. There was a brief burst of music—"The Star-Spangled Banner"—and then a vigorous male voice announced the overthrow of the United States government and its replacement by a military council drawn from the three main services. The cause of the current crisis was known, the announcement proclaimed, and the new governing council was undertaking actions which would end it. The President and his cabinet and leading Congressional figures, along with senior officers in the armed forces, had disappeared from Washington but were being hunted and would be brought to justice for their incompetence in allowing the crisis to develop.

"Bizarre," Moira said. "Truly bizarre."

Some hours later, more lights appeared below them. Horwith couldn't make out coastlines by their help, partly because he had never been very strong on the geography of Asia and partly because there seemed to be a great deal of cloud cover over the hemisphere. Patches of bright light that must be cities vanished suddenly and then reappeared.

And then one of those patches of light exploded in a half-dozen brilliant flashes. Orange blazes sprang into being everywhere: the city was being consumed in fire. The electric lights of the city blinked out. The fires lit up the cloud cover and the rising columns of smoke from the explosions. More flashes glared among the ruins, and new firestorms erupted and blazed on the surface. Elsewhere, to the horizon to the west, the north, and the south, there were more flashes of brilliant light, and more fires.

Among the small group of observers in the conference room, there were exclamations, groans, mutterings, as if no one even realized he was speaking his thoughts aloud. Finally, Battani said bitterly, "They couldn't go quietly, the madmen! Someone had to push the button at the end."

Horwith thought, Not just ice, after all. Fire and ice.

Battani turned to leave, wearing a bitter expression. He paused, searching for words, and then murmured, "Don't do anything hasty, the two of you. No suicide pacts. Just wait."

My God, Horwith thought, what else is there to do? He couldn't imagine waiting until the people still alive on the moon were reduced to cannibalism, to hunting each other through the corridors of Mendeleev. But Moira was clinging to him, weeping against his shoulder, and he found himself full not only of tenderness toward her, but of protectiveness, too, of the need to guard her from any evil, including self-imposed evil.

2031—2082

9

Holroyd watched in horror, unable to tear his eyes from the screen. At first glance, the tiny figure struggling in the center of the screen might have been a fly, caught upon some reddish-white, glowing, slightly flickering surface. Then the camera zoomed in and the figure resolved into a man, squirming desperately on the frictionless, bowl-shaped surface of the force screen that suspended him above the hellfire of the magma.

Martinson's image expanded still more, and at the same time he looked up at the camera suspended above him, so that his face suddenly filled the screen. His eyes were wide, bulging, his face glistened with sweat. His lips moved, but whether with curses or pleas or recantations, Holroyd could not tell.

Alone in his small apartment, Holroyd said aloud, "For God's sake, get it over with!"

Martinson stopped moving, surrendering at last, and the camera drew back again to savor the image of the condemned man lying still in the very center of the force screen, its lowest point, his eyes closed, his shoulders heaving as he wept in despair. Only then did the executioner act.

A second force screen came into existence above the weeping man. It was invisible, ultimately transparent, but its presence was obvious from its effect. It was lowered until, as Holroyd and all his fellow Americans watched, Martinson was forced flat on his stomach, spread-eagled, squeezed between the two screens. He stayed that way for only a moment, too tightly held to move, perhaps too tightly held to breathe.

With the upper screen now strong enough to hold the magma by itself, the executioner cut the flow of energy to the lower screen, and it vanished. Liberated by that tiny amount, the magma blossomed upward until it hit the upper force screen. All Holroyd could see was how his cousin shrivelled in an instant, vaporized, was gone. The picture of the now empty, glowing magma surface persisted for a few seconds, the calm sun at the heart of the world, and then the television screen went blank.

To Holroyd's astonishment, Cathy was at work the next day. White-faced and thin-lipped, she sat at her console next to his, making fine adjustments, recording changes in heat flow, saying nothing. After more than an hour of this tense silence, Andrew could bear it no more. Eyes still on his console, he said softly, "Cathy, I'm sorry."

"Killer!"

Holroyd looked at her in shock. Tears were rolling down her cheeks, and yet her tightly clenched jaw did not betray even a quiver. She looked at him at last. "*You* murdered him, not the government!"

"No," he gasped, shaking his head, "no, I just—"

But she was gone, running down the long stone corridor. He waited almost another hour, hoping she'd return, and then reluctantly he called in an Operator Missing alarm. The consoles must always be manned; he feared he might have endangered his own freedom by waiting so long to report Cathy's absence. He was overwhelmed by the irrational feeling that he would never see her again.

The premonition was wrong in the sense that he saw her image again, on television. Three days after her disappearance, as he was eating his supper and idly watching the evening newscast, Andrew was surprised into full attention when Cathy's face appeared suddenly on the screen. He recognized the shot: it had been cropped from a picture of the three of them taken during an outing in California a couple of years earlier, before Cathy and Henry had decided to get married. Andrew shook his head as if to clear it of the memory and tried to force his attention to the rich baritone of the newscaster.

"According to the announcement from the Acting Secretary of Security, Cathy Martinson, the widow of the traitor Henry Martinson, whose execution was broadcast earlier this week, was seen prying the cover off an old ventilation duct in Chicago. The police warrant who saw her tried to stop her, but she eluded him and escaped into the duct. A note was later found at her quarters stating that she intended to carry out the plot for which her husband was executed. She is of course presumed dead."

Both of them dead! It seemed impossible. They had been a part—a major part—of his life ever since their childhood together, a part of his world, a constant part of the background; and now to have them both gone violently . . . The image of Henry's execution returned with frightful clarity, as it was to do again and again during the coming years. Another image came to him suddenly, this one purely imaginary: Cathy lying on the surface, on the frozen ground, her body permeated with ice, dead beneath the silent layers of snow. Pretty Cathy; eternally unchanging Cathy.

It was the very next morning that Andrew Holroyd's patriotism received its reward.

The red light on the corner of his console blinked at him, signifying a message from his supervisor. When he acknowledged, Clayton's voice boomed out, causing operators' heads to turn throughout the cavern. "Holroyd! Good work on that traitor last week. I've just got the papers confirming your promotion. W01, Holroyd, and there'll be more to come, you can bet. You're Warrant class, now, boy. Congratulations!" The red light winked off.

"But that wasn't what I wanted at all," Andrew whispered. "I was just trying to save him." But the thought intruded that now, at last, he would be able to move from his cramped apartment, that he could afford and would be allowed something better.

10

During the decades that followed, as he moved up the ladder, reaching the very top of the warrant category, moved to ever better quarters, married and raised a family, Andrew Holroyd did well at suppressing the memory of his cousin and his cousin's wife. He was blessed in not remembering his nightmares any better than most other men remember their dreams. Thus, often as he might awaken sweating in the middle of the night (despite the ever-constant temperature and low humidity of the caverns), he did not remember the fearful images that had fragmented his sleep: Henry consumed by magma; Cathy lying frozen on the surface of the Earth, buried beneath the miles-thick blanket of snow that had once been the gases of the atmosphere; one killed by the elemental heat of the Earth's core, the other by the unrelenting cold of sunless space.

Shrinking population had necessitated the abandoning of the laws against incest the first generation had brought underground with them. Andrew's son and daughter married each other, something readily accepted by their contemporaries but horrifying to the older generation such as Andrew and his wife. The young couple produced only one child of their own, a son named Jonathan.

To the urging of their parents that they have more children so that the survivors of mankind might have a future, the young people replied with the answer their generation gave to all suggestions involving the future: "Why bother?" Why bother making an effort, why bother fighting the inevitable? It was, after all, a *Götterdämmerung* world, a society with a terminal social disease, and they were a doomed species.

If not for the ancient urgings of Nature combined with the occasional, statistically inevitable failure of contraception, there might have been no babies born underground at all. It didn't take a genius or a statistician to predict that the day would come when there would be so few people of childbearing age that even the rare contraceptive failure would no longer be enough to ensure more babies, and at that time the final end of the human race would be assured.

But for now there were still children, and in particular there was still Jonathan.

"My grandson!" Andrew would sometimes say to himself in astonishment. How could he have a grandson? When he saw his face in the mirror, wrinkles and sagging jowls, it seemed to him that it must be someone else's face, as if some evil wizardry had stolen his youthful face and body and forced him into the body of some old man who was a stranger to him.

And yet he was only forty-nine! Surely he shouldn't look and feel this old. His parents hadn't, at the same age, as far as he could remember.

What had he accomplished in all that time? he wondered. He had reached WO3, which was more than respectable for a man whose parents had started out as mere bucks. From buck to noncom to warrant (and almost gentleman, at that) in two generations wasn't at all bad. There weren't too many other men Andrew knew who could boast the same sort of progress. Not that such progress would still be available: in the days of his parents' youth, there hadn't been the socially crippling differences in speech patterns between the classes that one encountered now. His parents' English had been excellent, and they had taught him to speak the same way. That had been of inestimable value in his career, he was sure (ignoring the betrayal of the Martinsons, still flagged in his personnel folder). He had impressed his superiors and progressed—all the way from E7 to WO3—while his onetime playmates had let their speech and behavior patterns deteriorate to the level of the bucks who surrounded them, and as a result many of them had slid down into the buck class themselves. Much of the difference might be propagated by the educational system, but that didn't mean that a man with the proper self-respect and self-discipline couldn't rise anyway. Andrew had. So he did have a lot to show for the years, professionally speaking. And he had a grandson as well. Admittedly, the boy was the offspring of incest; but he loved the child dearly nonetheless.

Andrew had big hopes for Jonathan. Even as a baby, he showed his high intelligence in many ways. Jonathan's two parents had managed to slip back a few grades, so that Andrew's daughter was a WO1, just barely hanging on to warrant classification, and his son was actually an E10, back to noncom! However, the law said that Jonathan could start off with his grandfather's classification if he wanted to—and why should he choose otherwise?—so there was a good chance that the boy would break the social barrier and become a gentleman.

Andrew felt warm thinking about that big day in the future. Jonathan would be pulling his parents and grandparents up with him, too.

Jonathan was sixteen, a sophomore in high school, the day he encountered his grandfather's name in a history textbook. The reference was vague, and Jonathan was intrigued by what little it said. He should have gone straight home to the apartment he shared with his parents. He could have taken his friends up on their invitation to join them in one of their mindless *fin de siècle* amusements. Instead, he commuted through the tunnels to visit his grandfather and ask for an explanation.

Andrew had been napping. The knocking at the door pulled him reluctant from the depths of sleep, and he was still feeling foggy and divorced from reality when he answered the door, oppressed by vague images of intense heat and cold. The confusion and annoyance vanished when he saw his grandson waiting impatiently in the hallway. "Johnny! I mean, Jonathan. This *is* a pleasant surprise. Come in. Do your parents know you're here? They'll be expecting you."

"Never mind them," the boy said briskly, stepping into the apartment. "I want you to explain something to me that I read in here." He held up his textbook, *The History of our Country*.

Andrew sat down on the wide couch in the center of the room and listened attentively, ready and eager to help his grandson with his schoolwork in any way he could.

Jonathan paced about the room, filled with too much energy, both physical and mental, to stay in one place. "It says in this book," he said, "that there were a lot of rebels and traitors in

America about forty years ago, and that you were a hero then. 'Instrumental in stopping the Martinsons,' it says here. But it doesn't say what you did, or even who the Martinsons were and that *they* did.''

Andrew sighed. "Sit down here next to me, Jonathan, and I'll try to explain. Sit down, I said. Don't be so impatient." He waited until the boy had reluctantly seated himself on a corner of the wide couch before he continued. "They would be your cousins, I suppose. And what I did was simple enough. I betrayed them. Unwittingly, I murdered both of them. But I was trying to save them. Both of them. I really was," he insisted. "Henry as well as Cathy."

Jonathan shook his head in bewilderment.

His grandfather said, "They still teach you in school about how the solar system used to be, don't they? Good. Well, somehow Henry had managed to convince himself that the official story about what had happened must be wrong. We'd all been told since childhood that when the sun went . . ." His voice trailed off and he stared into space, his expression dreamy.

"You know, Johnny, I can just vaguely remember the sun, I think. I was only two when it happened. No, almost three. I've always wondered whether it's a real memory or something my imagination manufactured from what my parents told me about it. I think it's real, though, because I can remember sand and water and waves. I remember someone holding me in the water, and everyone was laughing, and I was laughing, too. It must have been a family day at the beach. But the sun . . . A huge ball in the sky, so bright you couldn't even look right at it because it hurt your eyes. Not like the pictures and films we have of it. They're not quite right. They don't give the feeling, how it felt on your skin. I remember that." He smiled at the memory of heat and light and parental hands, lost in a world that was lost.

"Come on, Grampa." Jonathan's impatient voice, banishing memories. "Tell me about the Martinsons."

"Yes, of course. I'm sorry. You see, the government always told us that once the sun was gone, the planets would all have coasted off in different directions, along tangents. Not that anyone who's still alive stayed around to be sure. We all escaped down here. Maybe some scientists stayed up there to watch it all happen. They'd all be long dead, of course." *She is of course presumed dead*. Andrew shook his head again and forced himself to go on.

"Henry worked in the computer archives, processing the tapes that had been stored down here before, when this was a military installation. He was supposed to decide which tapes were still of use and which should be erased and reused. He told me he had found one which he almost scheduled for erasure before he had an idea." The old man grimaced. "If he had only had it erased, he would have survived." He stopped talking again, his face contorting with the pain of long-suppressed memories.

"Forget it," his grandson said roughly, with all the careless cruelty of adolescence. "He'd probably be dead by now, anyway."

Andrew chuckled, suddenly amused. "That's a thought. Yes, I'll try to remember that! Well, this tape was . . ." He frowned, searching for the word. "Ephemeral? Ephem-something. At any rate, it was a detailed list of the positions and velocities of all the planets—when the sun was there, of course." Henry Martinson lying on the force screen, sweating, staring up through the television camera at him. "Uh, well,"—he licked his lips—"the tape was only a year or so old when the sun went. One problem was that Henry wasn't even sure that the tape really was what I just said, or maybe something else entirely. He convinced himself of it, though. And then he searched and searched until he dug up a computer program that they used to use for missile trajectories and spacecraft, and he started playing with it."

"Playing with it? What do you mean?"

"He never made it entirely clear to me. That was just about when he came to me and told me what he was doing. He wanted me to help him find some old books that would explain the physics of it for him, the underlying theory. He trusted me," he said softly. "I was his cousin and his boyhood friend. He always trusted me with his secrets. Always."

Jonathan shifted on the couch, making as much noise as he could.

"Well, look," his grandfather said, "I'll *show* you the

Martinsons." He went into his bedroom and opened the top drawer of a wooden chest. He had owned the chest for twenty years; it was the first piece of wooden furniture he had been able to buy. "Here it is!" he called out to Jonathan. He brought back a small framed photograph.

Three young people smiled out of it, closer in age to Jonathan than to Andrew, even though Andrew was one of the three. "That's me," Andrew said, pointing at one of the happy young faces and smiling himself, both in response to his smile of four decades earlier and as a sort of apology to his grandson for asking him to believe that Andrew had ever really been that young man. "I was only twenty-three when that was taken. Forty-one years ago. The three of us were on vacation."

But Jonathan was interested in the other two faces: the Martinsons, Henry and Cathy. Henry was a strongly built young man with a high forehead and a determined expression. Cathy was slender and blonde, clear skinned and pretty, with eyes that seemed to look out of the photograph, directly at Jonathan, directly into his soul. "She's beautiful," he whispered.

His grandfather didn't hear him. "My friends," he said, going back in time to those days. "She married him about a year later." After forty years, that thought no longer hurt, but it did induce a feeling of melancholy, of bright possibilities not grasped.

"Grampa," Jonathan said hesitantly, "can I have this picture?"

"Oh, Jonathan!" Andrew shook his head. "I'm sorry, Johnnie, but this is the only copy I have. It means too much to me."

Jonathan sighed. "Okay. So go on about Henry Martinson."

"One day," Andrew said, "he told me he had managed to figure out how to use the tape and the old program. He had made a run in which he removed the gravitational effect of the sun and then extrapolated the planets' trajectories forward. That's why he didn't agree with what we'd been told. He said his run showed that the gas giants—or maybe it was just Jupiter and Saturn, if those are the right ones—would have drawn together and the Earth would have gone into orbit around the resulting giant planet. He said he was sure his results were right, but he wanted me to help him figure out if the mass of the combined gas giants would be enough to start fusion. It would become a star in that case, you see, and the Earth's surface would possibly become livable again in only a matter of years.

"But neither of us knew enough to even start to calculate that sort of thing. Didn't matter to Henry, though. Inside, he was convinced that fusion must already be underway, and he just wanted help finding the equations he could use to prove it. He had the result in mind before he started. That's the point: he wasn't investigating anything; he was trying to find evidence he could use to convince others that he was right. We had already survived the worst of it down here, he said, with our air regeneration and heat and power from the Earth's core, from the magma. Now he wanted us to start sending expeditions to the surface so that we could prepare to move back outside."

Outside! Andrew shivered at the thought. At least Henry's atoms were now part of the core, doing their minuscule part to help provide the heat that powered and lit the caverns and made them livable, thus helping to preserve all that remained of America, of civilization, of mankind.

"That was it? That was his treason?" Jonathan's confusion was so evident that Andrew almost laughed. The boy would have to learn to conceal his feelings more effectively. Andrew hoped he would learn that lesson soon. He looked like a buck, with his eyes popping like that.

"That was almost the extent of it, but not quite," Andrew explained. "First, he tried the chain of command. The lower level supervisors tried to laugh him off, so he went still higher. Somewhere along the line, he was told firmly to give it all up, if he knew what was good for him. However, even that didn't stop him. Instead, he spoke to me and his other friends, urging us to organize into an expedition to go to the surface, of all things. Well, of course word of it got to the Department of Security eventually, and he received formal orders to stop his activities. And *that* was when he and Cathy really became traitors: when they ignored Security's orders and kept on proselytizing for their crazy idea. That was their treason—not so much their idea itself, as the fact that they defied government orders, kept on with something the government wanted stopped. That was why we lost them both."

Henry might be part of the core now, but not Cathy. Old as Andrew was, and growing older so rapidly, Cathy still lay up there far above him, still young and lovely, unchanging and unchangeable in her bed, her encasement, of ice and snow and vacuum.

Or had she even reached the surface? This thought struck him for the very first time, a horrifying idea. Had she died in the ventilation duct, and did her skeleton, the flesh long rotted from it, lie in a disordered heap of disconnected bones in some turning of the ancient pipes?

"Maybe he was right to try," Jonathan said dreamily, and his grandfather saw with fear that the boy's face was shining with the high adventure of the idea. "If the old computer tape and the program were right, then he had to try what he did." He paused in momentary thought, while his grandfather struggled for the right words. "In fact," Jonathan said, "if he knew enough about the computer and how to use the stuff he found, then he *had* to be right! Just think of it!"

"No! Nonsense! He was a fool." Andrew tried to force the frantic tone from his voice and speak firmly and authoritatively, but he knew he wasn't succeeding. "Henry had no idea what he was doing or what he was getting himself into. The government was protecting *him* as well as national security. If he tried to reach the surface through the old ventilation tunnels, he was sure to die somewhere in them on his way to the surface—or on the surface, for sure, if he somehow managed to reach it.

"When he . . . when he told me he planned to go ahead with it by himself, since none of his friends would help him, I reported him to the Department of Security for his own sake. Cathy had agreed to stay behind because she was pregnant. She was safe, but I wanted him safe, too. I saved his life! Or so I thought." His voice fell to a whisper that his grandson could scarcely hear. "I thought they'd put him in detention for a few months, maybe even a year or two. I—my God, I didn't know they'd kill him."

"*You* killed him!" the boy snarled. "At least he could have died trying." He threw his history book to the floor in fury and ran from the room, oblivious to Andrew's weak voice calling after him.

Tears coursed down the old man's cheeks. "They were my

friends," he sobbed. "I wanted to save them both. I loved them both." Equally, he told himself, and in the same way. He cried aloud and called after his grandson, but the sound of an old man's weeping could not penetrate the thick stone walls of America.

The rift between grandfather and grandson was not really healed during the months that followed, but it was patched over sufficiently for them to be civil toward each other. To Andrew's mind, the more serious injury was his grandson's obviously increasing fascination with the beliefs of the Martinsons. More and more, the boy seemed to withdraw from those around him, both the adults and his peers. When he did speak to Andrew— which was not as often as his grandfather wished—his conversation revolved around one subject: Henry Martinson's ideas about the solar system. Their conversations were more inquisitions than dialogues, with Jonathan quarrying for elusive scraps of information in his grandfather's inadequate memory.

Once, Andrew brought the issue into the open. "Jonathan, you can't keep this up. You can't end up the way Henry did!"

Jonathan looked at him without a spark of affection and replied coldly, "I won't, if no one reports me to the Department of Security."

Sometimes Andrew would try to talk his grandson into a more normal attitude. "Did you know," he once asked Jonathan, "that I knew Walter Geneen personally? He was a few years older than me, but I remember that when I was a kid, I used to consider him my friend. He was a wonderful fellow, even then."

"He was a hero, and he died for what he believed in," Jonathan said. His point was made, and the conversation on that subject languished.

If I hadn't told him anything about Henry's crazy ideas, Andrew told himself, maybe this wouldn't have happened. Perhaps he'll grow out of it. Andrew already bore more than a normal lifetime's worth of guilt; he didn't think he could stand the addition of any more to his burden.

But Jonathan gave no sign of growing out of his obsession. If anything, his fixation intensified throughout high school, as did his withdrawn seriousness. Like the ones before it since the great retreat underground, Jonathan's generation aged too fast and sickened too readily. But there was a flame within Jonathan, visible to his grandfather if not to anyone else, that seemed to compensate for whatever it was that other Americans lacked. Whether it was poor nutrition or poor air (and both had been suggested), or simply a physiological manifestation of the psychological effects of the lack of sunshine and scenery, open space and wildlife and wilderness, that caused the ills that made those around him languish, Jonathan avoided the degeneracy of other Americans; the thing which drove him, energized him. At eighteen, unlike his peers, he looked eighteen and not thirty.

It was the day after Jonathan's graduation from high school that Andrew decided he had to force matters into the open. He boldly asked his grandson what came next. "Your grades are so good. Are they going to let you go on for further training, or are they putting you to work?"

At first, Jonathan wouldn't meet his grandfather's eye. Then he did so, as if steeling himself, and said, "College. Starting next week."

"Wonderful!" Andrew's enthusiasm was forced; a chilling premonition of something awful had swept over him. Silly! he told himself. College is the first step into gentleman class. "Have they assigned you a major?"

Jonathan nodded. "They gave me my preference." He hesitated for only a moment, then added, "Computer science."

Before his grandfather could say anything, Jonathan turned on his heel and strode off down the long corridor, his body seeming to blink on and off, into and out of existence, as he passed from lighted sections into those where the lights had failed and then back into the light again.

This time, Andrew did not call after him. He watched him go in terror, his mouth open, his voice paralyzed. Computer science! He knew what that really meant: that Jonathan would learn all he needed to know to duplicate Henry Martinson's work; that it was for that reason that Jonathan had chosen that major.

The paralysis in Andrew's throat turned into a wave of numbing cold that spread lightning fast to encompass his entire left side. He felt as if he were floating, dimly aware of the floor rushing up toward him and the sound of Jonathan running back along the tunnel. The cold washed over him, engulfing his body. He knew it at last: it was the vast snow sea that covered the surface, the frozen atmosphere of Earth. "Cathy!" he whispered. "I've reached you at last."

When his mother begged Jonathan to take as much of his grandfather's willed belongings as he could to his new college dormitory, because "We don' have room in this damn 'partment for any o' this crap," Jonathan refused to take a single thing. "It's just a small dormitory room, Mother," he explained. "*I* won't have the room, either."

But at that moment, he noticed, atop the pile of stuff filling his parents' tiny living room, the framed photograph of the three young friends he had coveted since childhood. "I'll take this," he said, and quickly left the apartment.

Jonathan suppressed any guilt at his grandfather's death and pushed himself on. His estrangement from his parents and his peers freed him for work; only his love-hate relationship with his grandfather had remained to enmesh him in the normal, crippling web of human feelings. He was unaware of the ironic parallel between his situation after his grandfather's death and his grandfather's emotional condition after the deaths of the Martinsons. In both cases, the loss of an emotional commitment which had some of the qualities of entanglement had freed the man to concentrate on his career. And in both cases, the results were salubrious for that career.

Salubrious, indeed. Jonathan graduated in 2077. He had only a four-year degree, but he was quietly assured that his college degree qualified him for an important position in America's premier computer center. He jumped at the offer and soon was taking a major role in the husbanding of the limited computer resources still available to America. He was also given an immediately effective ranking of O1, the lowest of the gentleman ranks, but a gentleman nonetheless. Six months later, based on his outstanding work, he was advanced to O3, jumping over O2. "Why you'll be a general some day," the government representative told him happily, as though he were responsible for Jonathan's abilities and hard work.

It took more than two years of diligent, surreptitious searching in the dusty, abandoned, echoing vaults which held the decades of computer tapes. He had to squeeze his searches in whenever he could be certain no one was watching him. Jonathan was twenty-four when his diligence was rewarded.

Henry Martinson had been destroyed, but the Department of Security had either not thought or not bothered to track down the source of Martinson's fixation. What seemed most curious to Jonathan, at the end of his search, was how clearly the tape was marked after all. He had looked everywhere else, it seemed to him, plowed through piles of dust, pored over the disintegrating pages of old tape logbooks, and now here, in a far corner of a huge vault, gathering dust for all those years, a tape hung quietly from its hook, and the label just below it, still legible though peeling up at the corners, read EPHEMERIS—6/1/2000, and beneath that, MEAN OF 50 COORDS.

He could not yet interpret that jargon, but that would come, he was sure. In the meantime, the words were potent magic, conjuring up all the infinite spaces beyond the imprisoning kilometers of rock.

Another tape hung beside the first one, unlabelled. Empty spaces on both sides served to set the two apart physically from the other tapes as much as their possible significance set them apart in Jonathan's imagination. The unlabelled tape—how could it be anything but Henry Martinson's modified trajectory program? And the handprints still visible in the thick dust covering the tape—how could those be anything but the last marks left by Martinson himself?

Jonathan grasped the two tapes with trembling, sweating hands and told himself that even though it might take still more years before he knew how to use the two tapes properly, how to duplicate Martinson's work, he would manage it. And then, with indisputable proof, he would force the government to listen, force them to begin moving people back to the surface.

Henry Martinson, my spiritual father, rest easy. Your work was not in vain.

11

There were only five people working at the computer center. They were all overworked, but America had to make do with the resources available. The workers insisted on, and got, considerable autonomy. They were the cream of America's crop, and the government was wise enough to leave them to their own devices. The computer center was one of the very few places in America without signs exhorting citizens to work hard, be patriotic, love God, and multiply. Nor were the center's workers subjected to daily prayer meetings and circulating, uniformed chaplains.

Jonathan, due to his aptitudes and his request, was given complete charge of both of America's Rockway 3000's. These machines, two of the fewer than a dozen that had been built, were designed for heavy number-crunching: for scientific and engineering work. Their official function involved monitoring the heat flow and volume movements of the magma and feeding these measurements into various models, which were then evaluated to yield predictions of future heat and light flux. When Jonathan was in control, they had another function as well: to simulate the movements of the planets of the solar system with the gravitational influence of the sun removed.

It wasn't easy, after all, this matter of duplicating Henry Martinson's accomplishment. Had Jonathan been forced to start from scratch, as had Martinson, it might have taken him many years, he realized. As it was, he had Martinson's work to start with, in the form of a heavily modified trajectory program stored on the second tape. Over the next year, Jonathan struggled to understand Martinson's work, and his respect for the dead traitor increased greatly.

The mathematics of orbits and gravitational interaction was neglected in modern American education. After all, it had no application in Jonathan's world and no foreseeable application in the future. This had been just as true in Martinson's America, and he had had to search out old physics texts and educate himself. That he had succeeded awed Jonathan as much as it inspired him.

Unfortunately, those old texts were nowhere to be found. Whether this was due to accident or governmental design, Jonathan had no idea. At first, he tried to reconstruct the equations from Martinson's version of the trajectory program; he made virtually no headway. In the end, he decided that this was unnecessary, that he could do without the knowledge Martinson had managed to acquire. After all, Martinson had already done the work, so there was no need to repeat it. What he did need was a visual interpretation of it.

Where Martinson must have had a natural talent for the physics and mathematics involved, Jonathan had both a natural talent and an intensive education in computer science. Martinson's mind must have been of the symbolic sort, what one of Jonathan's mathematics professors had once classified as "a natural algebraist." Jonathan, by contrast, was a natural geometer: his mind worked most easily in pictures and images. He would take the validity of Martinson's mathematics on faith, but he would modify Martinson's program to give him its results in pictures rather than in lists of numbers.

It took Jonathan another two months of work before he was satisfied with what he had done. As the weeks went by, he began to see ever more meaningful pictures. The format of Martinson's output was repetitive, with only the values of the numbers changing from page to page. Finally, Jonathan reached the point where he was convinced that, now that he could produce meaningful displays from part of the data, his program would give him a worthwhile display from all of it. He was tempted to stay late that evening and run through all of the data right away; it shouldn't take more than an hour for his program to do that. However, it occurred to him that now was not the time to arouse any kind of suspicion: he had made for himself a reputation of punctuality and precision, and that included leaving work on time every day just as much as arriving on time.

He gave a sigh of mingled fatigue and satisfaction and closed down for the day. He was behind in his assigned work because of the time he had taken for his private investigation, and if he couldn't catch up by the end of the week, he might find himself in a difficult and exposed position. But he knew that none of that would matter anymore if he saw what he expected to see the next day.

But he didn't.

The first thing Jonathan did the next morning was start his graphics program running, then sit back and watch what happened. Over a period of months, in the time frame of the simulation, Jupiter and Saturn drew together and coalesced. "Well done, Henry Martinson!" Jonathan muttered. Mars drew into a tight orbit around them. Jonathan felt still more buoyed up.

The Earth drifted toward the new gas giant, but then suddenly it began to move ever more swiftly. At the end, it plunged into the gas giant, emerging on the other side and flying off beyond the screen. "Oh, Jesus!" Jonathan said aloud. He sat back, stunned, staring at the calm little system moving like clockwork on his screen: Jupiter/Saturn at the center, Mars in orbit around them, Earth nowhere to be seen.

For a long time, he stared at the new solar system, his mind a blank. At last, something occurred to him that gave him slight renewed hope.

There were assumed initial conditions built into Henry Martinson's original data, primarily the date and exact time of the disappearance of the sun. Jonathan visualized the Earth's orbit around the sun. Of course, he thought. The Earth's velocity vector was changing direction at the rate of a degree a day, roughly. A day's error would make quite a difference. Maybe even an hour would.

With renewed hope, he began patiently repeating the run, each time varying the starting time by an hour, until he had moved it forward two days, and backward the same amount, from the original value. Now the picture changed, but he never ended up with what he wanted to see, which was a stable new system with the gas giant in the center and the Earth in a circular orbit around it. Instead, in some cases the Earth escaped completely from the system without even coming close to the gas giant. In others, it did end up in orbit, but the orbit was highly elliptical, with the Earth approaching the gas giant dangerously close at one extreme and then heading out to a vast distance, spending decades so far away that, even if fusion were underway in the gas giant, the Earth would still remain frozen.

How could Martinson possibly not have seen this? Even if he only generated pages of numbers and never graphed them, he should have been able to see what was happening! Had he been so blinded by what he *wanted* to see that he refused to acknowledge what he really *did* see? Had he, after all, doomed his wife to death on an airless, frozen surface? Jonathan could feel his faith in his hero crumbling.

But there was another possibility, he realized: the gray hole, as it had been called. In school, they had been shown a film of the sun's final moments, as the gray hole covered it and then both disappeared. He had been struck then by how precisely equal in size the two bodies had seemed to be. What about mass? He couldn't recall ever being taught anything about the gray hole's mass, but that didn't mean anything: he had no doubt there were many important things in history that he and his generation had never been taught. So what if the gray hole had had the same mass as the sun, to start with a random guess? And then what about its trajectory? Even with only a solar mass, it must have had an effect on the planets of the solar system—unless it had come down at an angle of ninety degrees to the ecliptic.

So that gave him another set of runs to try. He added a body of solar mass moving in a straight line toward the sun at various speeds and at various angles to the ecliptic, from zero to ninety, and approaching from various directions. After that, he decided, he would try varying the foreign body's mass from, say, one-tenth solar mass to ten times solar mass. However, that set of runs did not prove necessary.

Varying velocity and angle gave him a range of resulting configurations, anywhere from the planets all heading into interstellar space, each on its own tangent, just as the American government insisted had happened, to very appealing new solar systems that looked remarkably like the old one, with the exception that what was at the center was the new gas giant instead of the sun.

Jonathan leaned back in his chair, exhausted. He had been at this for many hours, and the working day was long over. And so, he told himself, it all really became a matter of faith, after all. In fact, he had no idea what the situation above the caverns really was. It might be what the government had always said it was, or it might be what he had fiercely believed for so many years it must be. "Must be": that was the operative phrase. If the government was right, then he was truly trapped down here for the rest of his life. If his mental picture of what he wanted the solar system to look like now was correct, then there was no reason at all for him to remain—for anyone to remain. He could leave at any time, and he would survive on the surface.

Had Henry Martinson gone through a similar chain of reasoning? he wondered. Had Martinson decided that he should try to escape because the surface *should*, *must* be habitable, and not because it was demonstrably, provably so? Had he intended to risk his life for his faith? And if so, could Jonathan do less?

Late that night, as Jonathan was finishing his solitary meal in his apartment and longing for bed and sleep, feeling emotionally and physically drained, there was a light knock at his door. He hadn't had a visitor since the death of both of his parents from cancer the year before, he had no friends, and he had managed to effectively discourage those few of his neighbors who had tried to confuse physical proximity with social compatibility. And it was very late. Puzzled, he wiped his mouth and went to the door.

A short, slender, extremely plain young woman he had never seen before stood there. She was about his own age—which is to say, she looked the way an ancestress of hers on the surface would have looked at forty, and so that put her in her mid-twenties.

"Yes?" Jonathan was about to say, but the girl put her finger to her lips quickly and stepped into his apartment, pushing him ahead of her.

She held up a book-sized portable computer for him to see, pressed a button on its keyboard, and a message filled its screen. Jonathan took the computer from her and read the message.

"You donn know me," he said. "Im with the Dep of Security, Im asighnd to woch you, Im in thc ap next door, I know wat yor doing, I wan you to stop so I donn hav to report you." The screen went blank.

Jonathan stared at the screen for a long, frozen moment. He felt paralyzed with fear. Then he forced himself to move. He took the computer over to his table, pushed aside his dinner plate, put the machine down on the cleared space, and typed in a message of his own: "Why are you helping me?"

He handed it back to the girl, who was looking around nervously—looking toward certain specific points in the room, had Jonathan been alert enough to notice. He had to touch her shoulder to make her aware of the computer he was holding out to her. She jumped at his touch and blushed. She took the computer and read the message.

She hesitated for a while, her hand hovering above the keyboard, but she kept turning away toward the door and then turning back toward Jonathan. Finally, she made up her mind and touched a button, and another prestored message appeared on the screen. She held it up so that Jonathan could read it, but only for a moment. Then she grabbed the machine back, erased the message, and fled. "I lov you," it had said.

Loves me? Jonathan thought, staring after her with his mouth open. Loves me? That's crazy! She doesn't even know me!

But of course she did. He realized what she had meant by being assigned "to watch him," and belatedly he became aware of the way she had been looking around the room, as if thinking about cameras planted at various spots.

Were there cameras here, hidden so that he couldn't even see them? Were they equipped to see in the dark? Had she been watching him sleep, eat, masturbate, go to the toilet? The thought revolted him. He had never had a girl in his room, in fact had never yet made love to a girl. But if he had, would the Security woman next door have been watching that, too? He felt suddenly trapped, frantic, and impotent.

My God, she's just a buck! he told himself. How can a buck be assigned to spy on a gentleman?

And something else occurred to him, something that Jonathan told himself was far more important than any distress at a stranger having watched him during what he had assumed were private moments. It was this: presumably, everything he had done for the last year was known to this woman. Perhaps there weren't cameras everywhere, so perhaps it wasn't quite everything that she knew. But surely she must by now know enough that he would be condemned if she passed her information along. From her own words, he knew she had not informed on him yet. "Yet": that was the word that mattered. She could still do so. She had implied as much in her message. Or she might be reassigned and someone else placed in charge of observing him, someone else who wouldn't . . . fall in love with him.

Love! he thought. How could voyeurism lead to love? What she thought was love was something sick and repellent. But be that as it may, he told himself, it was apparently all that stood between him and disaster, all that had saved him so far.

Shaking, Jonathan went through his usual evening ritual of washing up and preparing for bed, trying as he did so to appear outwardly nonchalant. He couldn't pull it off, of course: he was aware every moment of being watched. But didn't she sleep, too? Was she on duty twenty-four hours a day? Was she relieved at night? Did she sleep when he slept, waking when he did by means of some sort of ingenious electronic alarm, or perhaps by some weird telepathic prompt? Were he and she linked together in some awful way for the rest of his now-shortened life? He tried to dismiss such nightmarish thoughts as foolish.

Nonetheless, impossible as he knew this to be, the walls seemed closer tonight, as if the caverns that housed America were shrinking. And the air, which was demonstrably cleaner than the unrecycled air of the surface had ever been, seemed thick and heavy, difficult to breathe, and loaded with strange, sickening smells. He was dying in this dying place.

Jonathan turned off the lights and lay still on his back in bed, trying to calm his hammering heart, trying not to gasp for breath, trying to achieve relaxation and sleep.

What if she could tell from watching him how he felt about her, how he hated her, despised her, wished her dead and gone? Would her sick love survive that? Or would she report him instantly? He must act right away; he dared not wait. Tomorrow: he would start tomorrow morning, right away. But in the meantime, would he be allowed to survive the night?

He smiled into the darkness, his face filled with tenderness. Hating himself as he did so, he formed his mouth into a kiss.

12

It was a different world than the one he had seen in old photographs. And different from what he had hoped for.

At his first breath of the bitterly cold air, first sight of the somber, reddish-white landscape and the fine snow drifting steadily down, powdery and silent, Jonathan leaned against the side of the tunnel entrance, filled with despair and a sense of betrayal. The government had been right after all, and Henry Martinson wrong. This was indeed the dead, frozen world of his school lessons. Now there was nothing left for him but inevitable death.

But no, he corrected himself, that was nonsense. Had the government been correct, he would already be dead, killed long since by lack of air and a temperature near absolute zero. There would have been no air or heat in the shaft, beyond the last seal. There would certainly be no light.

Jonathan squinted up at the red-white diffused light glowing through the overcast. The sun. *A* sun? But it was May, and the reading he'd done in preparation had told him that that meant it should be spring.

But the correspondence between calendar date and season had been a function of the Earth's orbit around the sun and its axial tilt. In his work with Martinson's tapes, he hadn't even bothered trying to predict what the new relative axial tilt would be, and so he hadn't known what season he would encounter. Therefore, Jonathan had prepared for his escape by gathering multiple layers of the lightweight clothing that was standard in the warm, changeless caverns. As he had moved up the ancient ventilation duct toward emergence and the temperature had dropped, he had put on more and more of those clothes, until finally he was wearing all of them.

It was completely inadequate covering in the face of this bone-chilling cold. But this was truly the outside, the surface, the goal for which he had sacrificed so many years, so much of his youth, and now it seemed he couldn't survive here. Good God, I can't go back underground!

Or could he? Had anyone seen him leave? He thought no more than three or four days had passed. It had been almost impossible to tell in the unlighted ventilation duct, his only guide and anchor the small circle cast by his stolen flashlight. He had left his watch behind and quickly lost track of the time. Life had become an endless process of crawling through tunnels and pulling himself up endless shafts. He had nibbled the tasteless food he'd brought with him whenever hunger became too great to ignore. He'd slept when fatigue overwhelmed him. He'd urinated and defecated along the tunnels whenever he had to, knowing he was leaving a trail for the Department of Security if they were chasing him, but not caring.

And now he was breathing the air of the surface of Earth and regaining his sanity. He had to assume this was winter. Winters had always been severe in many parts of the old United States; he knew that. Perhaps the sensible plan would be to return underground, tell the government what he had found, and urge the establishment of an observation post up here, at the exit to the tunnel. Then they could find out what the new year was like— the length of it and its seasons. If spring and summer came, they could all emerge then and begin the recolonization.

And the government will simply listen to you? he asked himself. Idiot! He would end up as Henry Martinson had. Well, he *had* proved Martinson correct—Martinson and himself. The skeptics and the government (and his grandfather) had all been wrong. Perhaps that was worth dying for—as he would if he either returned below or stayed here.

Curiously, the idea of dying appealed to him for the first time. He had once read that dying of cold was quite peaceful and painless, a matter of growing sleepiness, of going calmly to sleep and not waking up. He might as well step out into the cold and lie down on the snow and drift away. Jonathan could tell that his own thought processes weren't clear anymore, that he couldn't reason clearly. He wondered whether that was due to the cold or to his days in the ventilation system. He stood in the tunnel exit pondering this question in a vague sort of way, making no move either to leave the tunnel or retreat back into it.

A sound grew above him. It started as a faint hum; then it became a drone, and suddenly a roar. At last the source broke through the low-lying clouds. At first, Jonathan thought it was one of the flying insects from the hydroponics caverns, but grown monstrously huge and distorted: a bulbous body, long tail, and wings above it whirling in circles.

Then Jonathan's mind cleared and he recognized it as a man-made flying machine. The wings were called propellers, he thought. He couldn't remember its name, but he was sure he had seen one of these machines before in old pictures.

The flying machine landed only a few meters away from Jonathan, and a door sprang open in its side. Inside, a hooded figure was sitting in a chair, holding some sort of control wheel that emerged from the panel in front of him and beckoning urgently to Jonathan to enter.

With the cold penetrating ever deeper into him, Jonathan needed no prolonged urging. He shuffled across the snow, staggering as his feet sank deep into the powdery surface, and clambered clumsily into the vehicle. He sank gratefully into the seat next to the pilot's. The door shut behind him, and, with an abrupt lurch that made Jonathan grab frantically at the edges of his armless seat, the vehicle roared into the sky.

The pilot was bundled up in heavy, fur-lined clothing with a hood that completely hid his head and gloves that covered his hands. Jonathan, shivering more and more as the cold worked into him, envied the man no end. After a moment, however, the pilot gestured at a pile of clothing behind the chairs that Jonathan hadn't noticed before and said, "Put those on before you freeze to death. Don't play with the controls. You won't need them; it'll get pretty warm inside here soon."

Jonathan's shivering subsided slowly as he warmed up inside the protective clothing. Controls? He couldn't imagine what the man had meant, but he dismissed the problem, revelling in the warmth of the clothing and the growing warmth of the air inside the cabin. The profusion of fur lining was a wonder to him. Animal fur? It must be. Did they have that many animals to spare up here, live animals, not just pictures and models? Well, why not? Surely, up here, they could indulge themselves in having as many animals as they wanted. And not just domesticated, but even wild ones, as in the old days on Earth, before the sun's disappearance. The existence of this man and this machine was all the proof that Jonathan needed that there were summer and warmth on this Earth as there had been in the old days, and therefore there must be all the wildlife of the old days as well. Jonathan almost gasped aloud at the thought: herds of animals, like those in the old books, wandering across the surface of this strangely, familiarly alien world.

He realized that he must have gasped aloud after all, for the pilot laughed at him, apparently taking the sound for fear rather than wonder. With undisguised deliberation, the man put the vehicle through a series of maneuvers that had Jonathan fighting to suppress yells of terror. But suppress them he did, and the pilot, with a nod to show his admiration of Jonathan's seeming courage, levelled the craft below the cloud cover and flew steadily. He typed a few instructions into the keyboard in front of him, nodded again, this time in satisfaction as the computer took over control of the vehicle, and turned his attention to his passenger.

By now, the vehicle's heaters had completely banished the numbing cold air Jonathan had brought with him into the cockpit. The pilot said, "Thank God! I can get rid of this junk." He stripped his gloves off and threw back his hood.

Jonathan looked at him in amazement. "You're . . ." He paused, trying to remember the word from the history books. Brown? No, that wasn't the word, even though it would have been accurate. "Black!" he said at last, triumphantly. "You're black!"

The pilot grinned at him. "As the ace of spades, son."

Son! In fact, the pilot looked a couple of years younger than Jonathan. "I've never seen one of you before. In the flesh, I mean."

"I know. You're all dead white down there."

There was an undercurrent of anger in the pilot's voice that Jonathan didn't notice. "Dead," Jonathan muttered. "That's the word, all right."

The pause lengthened, the atmosphere becoming strained, until the pilot broke it. "This should be ready by now." He reached into a compartment in the panel in front of him and drew out two mugs filled with a steaming, pale brown liquid. "I know you don't have *this* brown stuff down there, either," he said mockingly, but smiling to ease the sting. "Try it."

Jonathan sipped at it cautiously, the heat burning his tongue. It was utterly foreign but just as utterly delicious. He gulped it down as soon as his mouth had grown accustomed to the heat. "Wonderful!"

"Brings you back to life, doesn't it?" the pilot said, sipping his own drink appreciatively.

"It does that," Jonathan agreed. "Speaking of which, I'm very grateful you happened along when you did. I couldn't have survived much longer, and I feel very lucky."

"Lucky!" The pilot snorted. "That's what you think, huh? There's no such thing as luck. Kyron gnothie, my grandma used to tell me. Hell, we've got sensors planted all over those old ventilation exits, and just about every other hole in the ground—anyplace where one of you guys might conceivably come out. You always show up without enough warm clothing. I guess you just can't imagine what it's like in most places nowadays, especially in the winter. We've lost some people, I hear. They came out even further north than you did, and we couldn't get to them in time because of a blizzard. I don't know what they used to do in the very beginning, before they even had all those sensors in place."

Jonathan was oppressed by a dull, heavy feeling of disappointment. "You mean . . ." He paused, then tried again. "You mean, I'm not just the second one to get out?"

The pilot roared with laughter. "Two people! Son, there's a whole department whose only job is to pick you guys up and take care of you. That's who I work for. We must get maybe a couple of you a month, on the average."

Jonathan shook his head. "Twenty-four a year! I don't

understand. How's that possible? I'd know if that many people had left America, even in *ten* years."

The pilot laughed again. "Thirty-six a year, that would be. You've got a few things to learn. You're the first from, uh, *America*, in a long, long time. The others came from other underground colonies. They're not always singlets, either. Often, it's a pair of people, usually a man and a woman. Sometimes they have kids with them, too. Once, we picked up a group of six adults and two kids. That was in France."

It was all too much for Jonathan to absorb at once. The conversation between the two men lapsed completely. This seemed to suit the pilot quite well, for about an hour later, he became very busy with his controls and with his radio, muttering cryptic phrases to someone who was apparently guiding him to a landing through the blinding snow.

Tension grew in the cockpit until at last Jonathan felt a slight bump and the pilot began methodically flicking switches on the panel in front of him. The roaring of the engines, which had been a constant background, slid downward in pitch and then disappeared abruptly. The pilot sighed and then stretched in his seat. "We're here," he said cheerfully. There were voices outside the vehicle. "They'll take care of you on the next leg," he told Jonathan.

The door on Jonathan's side opened, letting in a flood of air just as breathtakingly cold as he remembered from the ventilation shaft's exit. Two figures were silhouetted in the opening, both heavily covered with the same kind of fur-lined clothing the pilot—and now Jonathan—wore. One of them beckoned to Jonathan to get out and follow them.

"One last word of advice, son," the pilot said. "For the next few days, don't talk. Just listen."

The assumption of superiority by a man younger than him infuriated Jonathan, the more so since he felt so bewildered and ignorant and knew that the pilot really was his superior in this already confusing world of the surface—and even doubly so because the pilot was a member of a race American history books described as inferior. That, after all, was why none of them had been qualified to go underground and survive. With an effort, Jonathan suppressed his anger and said stiffly, "Thank you very much for all your help." He clasped the pilot's proferred hand briefly and then climbed quickly out to join the two men waiting in the snow.

Jonathan followed the two men faithfully, almost blinded by the snow, which seemed to be falling much more heavily here than where he had emerged. What had been a breeze where he'd escaped, was here a howling wind. That was a sound Jonathan had never heard before. He was thankful that at least now he had the warm clothing given him by the pilot.

They led him to a vague shape that loomed out of the shifting white curtain that filled the air. He could see only a brown, curved wall with small, circular windows cut into it, stretching away to left and right until it disappeared into the falling snow. His eyes kept filling with tears in the wind, so that he could hardly see anything. He blinked over and over again, squeezing his eyes shut, trying to clear them of tears. He could feel the tears freezing on his cheeks. Directly in front of him, a short flight of steps led up to the side of the wall. The two men motioned him to climb the steps. He obeyed unquestioningly. He was no longer in any sense in control of what happened to him.

As Jonathan struggled up the steps, which were slippery from snow that had melted on the warm metal and then refrozen, a rectangular portion of the wall at the top of the steps slid to one side, revealing what appeared to be a well lighted room beyond. A woman appeared in the opening, stout, middle-aged, graying, and obviously impatient, and snapped at Jonathan to hurry up. "I want to get this door closed before we all freeze in here. Come on!"

He muttered a quick apology that she surely could not have heard over the wind and, grasping the railing beside the steps firmly, tried to pull himself up the steps. However, his feet slid away from under him, and he hit the steps facedown. The only ice in America was man-made and came in small cubes.

"Oh, for Heaven's sake!" the woman said, but there was maternal concern beneath the annoyance. "Here." She stepped out of the doorway and reached down to him, grabbing his free arm and hauling him the rest of the way with a strength that astonished Jonathan. She pulled him through the doorway and slid the door quickly back into place, slamming a large lever set into its surface across to her left, a position marked LOCK in red letters painted on the door. Thumps and vibrations came through the floor.

The woman, who had loomed so large at the top of the stairs, was tiny, Jonathan now saw, scarcely reaching his chin. "There!" she said, nodding in satisfaction and gripping Jonathan's arm with a hand like a vise. "You're as light as a feather and as thin as a stick," she told him severely. "You're all like that when you come up. They must not feed you down there."

"No, ma'am," Jonathan mumbled.

"What? Speak up! You'll have to learn to do that, too."

"Yes, ma'am." One last spark of patriotism flared in Jonathan, fanned by resentment at his treatment and the easy assumption of superiority by these surface dwellers. "They feed us—uh, *down there*. We eat pretty well, considering the conditions."

"Humph. I suppose that's why so many of you risk your lives to get out."

To that, Jonathan had no answer. It wasn't lack of food that had driven him to climb to the surface. But he didn't feel like making a speech, and he doubted if she wanted to listen to one. So he submitted, moving along docilely, letting himself be led.

He became aware of his surroundings at last, and saw that the room he was in was strangely long and narrow and filled with seats arranged in rows. The seats were occupied by men and women of various ages and colors, many of them reading, others chatting quietly with each other. The warmth was almost as great as in America. He quickly shook off the fur-lined clothes the pilot had given him, and the outer layers of the clothes he had brought with him. The other people in the room wore clothing of many brilliant colors; each man or woman was a jarring rainbow. The contrast with the monotone grays, blacks, and browns of America made Jonathan uneasy. But then he sank down into one of the soft, padded chairs, and his fatigue overcame him, and he sighed with happiness.

Only then did Jonathan notice that one of the small, round windows he had noticed from outside was set into the wall beside him. Of course! he thought. This wasn't a building at all: it was yet another type of flying vehicle, one he had also seen in old pictures. He sat forward and craned his neck, looking at the rows of occupied seats. Rather like the trains in America, he thought, the ones that took workers through the kilometers of tunnels to their jobs and then back home, except that this one flew instead.

He pressed his face against the window, trying to see through the blank white of the storm. For an instant, he thought he could make out the two men who had led him from the first flying craft, standing on the ground and watching calmly, but then the white wall solidified again and he couldn't be sure if he had imagined it. So many new people, so many new things, so many new places and ideas! His head swam with it. How nice it was to be safe from the cold and snow and the howling wind.

"This is *real* food. You obviously need it."

It was the woman who had helped him in, this time carrying a tray loaded with dishes of steaming food. She held the tray easily balanced on one hand while with the other she pressed a button on the arm of Jonathan's chair. A shelf emerged from the wall beside him. She set the tray down deftly on this shelf and said, "Now, eat! I'll be back, and I want to see those plates clean."

Jonathan stared at the huge amount of food in dismay. "This is all for me?" he asked weakly.

"All of it. Eat up." She glared fiercely at him for a moment, then turned and stalked away.

The vibrations Jonathan had been only subliminally aware of for the past few minutes suddenly grew in intensity, forcing themselves into his awareness. He felt himself pressed backward into his seat and then suddenly downward. Instinctively, he grabbed at the tray of food to prevent it from sliding into his lap. The motion brought a wave of strange and fascinating smells to him, and he suddenly realized that he had not eaten a full meal since leaving America, so many days before.

He picked up the knife and fork on the tray and began gobbling the food almost frantically, scarcely stopping to wonder what the strange dishes were. There were pieces of what he guessed was meat, fibrous stuff with an exotic texture and flavor, swimming in sauces that seemed to burst into flavor on his tongue, as if jolting awake taste buds whose existence he had never before suspected. There were what he knew must be fruits and vegetables, but it seemed impossible that they could be related to the pallid, tasteless products of the hydro tanks in America. There were a bowl of a marvellous clear soup and a cup of the same hot beverage the pilot of the first vehicle had given him.

As suddenly as his hunger had assailed him, it disappeared. Jonathan leaned back in his seat, not sure whether he felt extraordinarily satisifed or close to bursting. He turned to the window, but it was still a blank circle of white. He became aware of the hum of conversation from his fellow passengers, and he leaned his head back and closed his eyes to help himself concentrate, trying to make out individual words. In seconds, he was sleep, drifting downward, sinking into a warm, dark place at whose center a red-yellow spark glowed with mingled invitation and threat.

When the woman who had taken charge of him at the entrance returned to check on him somewhat later, she nodded approvingly at the state of the food tray. "Managed almost half of it," she remarked to a passenger in the row behind Jonathan. "That's better than most of them do." She picked up the tray and pushed the shelf back into the wall until it clicked into locked position, moving carefully so as not to awaken her charge, and left. Jonathan slept on, in his dream orbiting about a new sun that was the naked core of the earth.

Then changing pitch of the engines awakened Jonathan. The airplane had left the vast snowstorm far behind, and outside the windows was clear sky above and land stretching to the horizon below.

He had never imagined such expanse, such openness. His gaze roamed far across the land to the horizon and then upward, to the dark blue sky. And there was the sun, the most amazing sight of all in this new world.

It was a huge ball hanging low in the sky, seeming at first glance to stretch almost a quarter of the way from horizon to zenith. It was yellow-red in color, hovering on the edge of pain, just barely so bright that he couldn't look at it for more than a second. He had seen the magma through its protective force screens; the color of the sun reminded him of that. When Jonathan looked at the sky far enough away from the sun, he could see the stars.

A voice spoke from behind him. "In the old days you couldn't see the stars when the sun was shining." It was the woman who had served him his food, now back to watch the landscape over his shoulder. "The old sun was much too bright. This one is still very dim. That's supposed to change. The sooner the better, I say." She sat down in the empty seat next to Jonathan's, shifting about for a moment to find a comfortable position, and then settling down with a satisfied grunt.

"You'll be able to see the green better as we get lower. That's crops, farmland, even some forest they're trying to reestablish. All the plants and animals are derived from what was brought back, of course. Thank God for the Moon." Jonathan didn't understand the reference, but he heard reverence, religious awe, behind it.

"At this latitude," the woman continued, "it used to be covered with plant life. Not that many people lived here. The latitude where you came out of the tunnel used to be just about the most heavily populated and farmed land in the world." She laughed at the thought. "That's hard to believe, isn't it? Nothing but snow and ice now. Most of us live here, now. Look down there."

Details were now appearing in the scene far below the aircraft that had not been visible before. Jonathan realized that they were dropping lower, heading for a landing. The landscape had been blurred by the atmosphere. Now it began to resolve itself into green areas amid what had seemed unrelieved brown. The green places were strikingly geometric; some of them were long, rectangular strips, and others were startingly perfect circles.

Still lower, and lines began to show, some running close alongside the green rectangles, others striking off across the brown expanses to connect one small population center with another.

Looking directly out the window, at a right angle to the airplane's flight, he could see the land rising in the distance, hazy from the atmosphere. The rising land paralleled their course, extending out of sight both forwards and to the rear. It was brown, unvegetated and cut by deep ravines.

"You're looking at where the land slopes upward?" the woman said. "That's the side of the Valley. We're flying down what we call the Long Valley. It's what used to be the Amazon Basin. There was the world's biggest river in the middle of it, and everything else was covered by jungle. Out there, where the land rises, you can see what happened when the sun began to warm up and the gases began to melt. Canyons were formed by the runoff all along the way. Then the original water, which was underneath the frozen gases, melted as well. It's wonderful farmland and grazing land, nowadays, and one of the biggest habitable stretches of land available in the world.

"We still have some small rivers in the Valley. That's because there's still snow in the Andes, which melts in the spring, and there's still rain in the highlands to either side of the Valley, which runs down into it. But there's not very much water available for precipitation, compared with before the Taking, so it's a very dry climate everywhere, generally speaking."

Jonathan didn't understand very much of this, but he listened intently nonetheless. It was fascinating and exotic, like a description of some other world circling some distant star, and he hung on every word, including those that meant nothing to him. Suddenly, ahead of the airplane, he saw a white object ascending from the ground, trailing smoke and fire behind it. It moved faster and faster, disappearing into the glare of the sun, leaving a pillar of smoke to mark its trail. It was his guide, Jonathan thought; a pillar of smoke to guide him by the sun's light. He pointed to it. "What was that?"

The woman glanced at the time displayed in the front of the

cabin. "Fourteen o'clock shuttle," she said. "Going up to orbit," she explained. "The shuttle port's only a few kilometers from Lander, so we're almost home. Lander's the capital."

The note of pride was unmistakable. Jonathan turned back to the window with even greater interest.

He could see now that many of the lines converged at one point far ahead, like the spokes of a wheel heading inward. This was surely the capital the woman had mentioned. But before anything definite resolved itself, the landscape slid to one side and the convergence point drifted out of sight, hidden by the body of the aircraft.

On takeoff, nothing had been visible outside the window because of the snow, and therefore there had been little sensation of movement other than the pressure of his body against the seat. The previous aircraft had taken off and landed vertically, and so there had been a sensation of movement but not one of speed relative to the ground. But this landing was different.

The surface below drew nearer and nearer, sliding away beneath him and to the rear with increasing and disturbing speed. Suddenly he was only meters above it. He could see the paved surface rushing up toward them, cracks in it and lines painted on it speeding backward. In the distance, off to the side, a row of buildings also moved steadily backward.

Only after the slight bump of wheels against ground and the long, slowing roll to a stop did Jonathan realize that almost every muscle in his body was tensed, his heart was pounding, and he was holding his breath. He relaxed with a *whoosh* of expelled air and willed his muscles to relax. He turned to see the woman smiling at him approvingly. "You did better than most escapees do the first time," she told him, and he felt absurdly pleased with himself.

"We *do* have vehicles in America, you know," he told her, aware of the defensiveness in his voice. "Fast ones."

She snorted. "Those trains you people ride in from one end of your world to another? I've seen the tapes. Snails on rails." The other passengers rose from their seats, stretched, and began moving slowly down the aisle between the seats, toward the rear, where Jonathan could hear thumps and metallic clangs, and the unasked questions evaporated from his mind.

The woman pushed herself up and beckoned him to follow. "Come along, young man. You've got a long and busy time ahead of you. It's high time you joined the rest of the human race. We've got to get you numbered and clothed and assigned a room, and all the rest of it."

"Gee. Sounds just like America."

For an instant, her maternal friendliness disappeared. Then her face softened again, but her voice held an angry snap. "Don't ever say that to anyone else."

"Sorry," Jonathan mumbled, not really sure why he was apologizing but cowed by her. "Uh, one thing I really don't understand."

"There are lots of things you don't understand," she said brusquely. "What, in particular?"

"Who *are* all you people? There shouldn't be anyone here! Where did you all come from?"

She grinned at him. "Why, from the moon, of course!"

13

During the months that followed, Jonathan had frequent cause to remember the cautionary words of the first pilot: "Don't talk. Just listen."

There was a plethora of new people and new ideas to deal with. For all of his life, Jonathan had dealt with a closed and limited world, a world in which he rarely met anyone he hadn't known for years and in which all the places were familiar and the ideas were old, and in which the sky was the ceiling above and the horizon was the walls to either side.

First he was told he would have to go to school. The speaker was an old woman named Hester; she didn't give him a last name. "We need to talk about your immediate future."

"Well, I know I'll need a while to get used to things, but I think that once I do, I'll have a lot to contribute."

Hester snorted. "You won't be able to contribute a damned thing. At the very least, you're going to be put through some ahbyoocheneyeh ee ahrentatsiya."

"Some what?"

"Um, training and orientation. And then after that, you'll be given some tests, so that we can see if you're suited for some existing omplwah."

"What?" What were these words she was using? Was something wrong with his ears?

"Sorry. Forgot for a moment. You escapees are like that. I meant, some sort of . . . work, or profession. Arbeit, you know? No, of course you don't. Something you can do for us."

"Hester, why aren't you speaking properly?"

"I am, Jonathan," she said gently. "This is the way all of us speak. You'll just have to get used to it. Other escapees have. It's because of our ancestors from the moon. You see, they came from all over the Earth, and even though English was the language of Mendeleev and of course the NASA bases, with so many non-

native oratoors . . . shprechern—damn it! Speakers, I mean."
She took a deep breath and tried again. "With so many people on
the moon who didn't grow up speaking English, they ended up,
um, incorporating a lot of words from other languages."

Jonathan would have said, "Words from foreign languages."
When he imagined life on the surface of the Earth, he had
visualized the people as Americans. He had anticipated a surface
society formed by colonists emerging from America to create a
newer and far vaster America above. How would he ever get used
to this mongrel language, this bastardized English, this diluted
and polluted tongue?

"All right," he sighed. "Training and orientation it is." He had
already managed to get lost once trying to find his way around
Lander without a guide. If by "orientation" Hester meant a quick
course in the city's layout, Jonathan was all for it. "How many
escapees are in a class?"

"Not exactly escapees," Hester said apologetically. "You
people are fershtroyt—scattered—all over the planet. There aren't
enough of you in Lander right now at the same degray of
ignorance to form a class. Or even to be in the same class. You'll
be with dityans. Children."

"Training and orientation" might be what Hester called it, but
to Jonathan it was more like a complete education. The sessions
were long and exhausting. He felt like a baby, utterly bewildered
by a thoroughly confusing world. Worst of all were his classmates:
children of ten and eleven who grasped all the new facts far faster
than he could and who even seemed to be physically stronger than
he was.

And they were healthier. Occasionally one of them would get a
cold that lasted for a day or two. Jonathan immediately caught
whatever it was and suffered cramps and chills and indigestion and
diarrhea for days. Puzzled and worried, he went to the school
clinic for help. "None of you escapees ever have immune systems
to speak of," the unconcerned middle-aged nurse told him.
"You're all like that. Give it a year or two. Your immune system
will probably get up to normal by then."

"*Probably*?" Jonathan repeated. "And if it doesn't?"

She shrugged. "You'll die. I'm very busy. Good-bye."

He felt inferior to surface people—and their children—in other ways, too. It took him months to conquer the fear that something was creeping up on him from behind whenever he was out in the open. Nor could he learn to properly judge distances beyond a few meters. It was as if there were important nerve pathways in his brain that had not been formed in childhood and now simply would not form, no matter how much he might will them to do so.

Everything he knew, and many things he had unconsciously viewed as eternal, were false or inadequate or obsolete. It was more than a whole new history; he could accept that—intellectually, at least. It was the background changes that did him in. The calendar, for example.

America, cut off from all outside contact, had preserved the old world as though it were sacred. Despite the unchanging lighting in the caverns, the nation preserved the twenty-four-hour day, the seven-day week, and the three-hundred-and-sixty-five-and-a-quarter-day year. The people on the surface had not hesitated to start with a new calendar to match their new world. The year here on the surface was also three hundred and sixty-five and a quarter days long; this seemed so proper and natural to Jonathan that he accepted it without question. Similarly, the day was still twenty-four hours long. From that point on, however, everything was different.

The year was now divided into eighteen months of four five-day weeks each. The days of the week were named, straightforwardly enough, Oneday, Twoday, Threeday, Fourday, and Fiveday. This disturbed Jonathan only for a short time; eventually, he decided it made a kind of sense. However, the month names were another matter. None of the eighteen months had familiar names; instead, they were named after the moons of the solar system, in descending order of size. Thus, instead of the ancient January through December, the months were, in order, Ganymede, Titan, Callisto, Triton, Luna, Io (quite properly pronounced "Yo," to Jonathan's consternation), Europa, Rhea, Titania, Oberon, Iapetus

("Yapetus," again a pronunciation that annoyed Jonathan), Ariel, Dione, Tethys, Umbriel, Enceladus, Mimas, and Hyperion.

This system resulted in a five-day week being left over at the end of the year. The entire week was a public holiday (or holidays)—the only one. It was called Landing Week, commemorating the landing of the first men from the moon who had dared to return to the warming Earth. This was considered to be the most important event in surface history since the disappearance of the sun, and when the commemorative week ended, the new year began. Other than that one-week holiday, everyone got one day off each week.

"Only one?" Jonathan asked in astonishment. "Not two?"

"And be thankful for that much!" he was told by an angry instructor. "When the lunar colony returned to Earth, there was so much work to do that no one got *any* time off, except to eat and sleep—a little bit. Someday, perhaps we'll be able to afford the two-day weekend, three-workday week, but that's a long way off. Why, where would we be now if the lunar colonists had worked that kind of schedule?" And then to the class at large, "Just imagine them, landing on a ruined world and then building it again from nothing! From *nothing,* using only their sweat and their hands and their brains. . . ."

Jonathan tuned him out at that point. Their holy hands and their sacred sweat, he thought. He had already learned that when the ancestral lunar colonists were invoked, all rational discussion was at an end. In America, the canonized ancestors were those in the first generation to retreat underground. Jonathan had known only a few people from that generation, such as his grandfather, and they had been children when the sun had been swallowed. On the surface, early conditions had been far harsher and life expectancy consequently less. As a result, the last survivor of the landing generation had died years before Jonathan had escaped from America. What the landing generation had in common with Andrew Holroyd and his peers and their parents was their status as saints: the surface dwellers invoked their heroic struggle in the early days as an answer to almost any argument on almost any subject. Just like America, Jonathan thought, but he had at last learned to keep such thoughts to himself.

Much of the time in school was taken up with descriptions of the Cold and movies of the life-style of explorers venturing into it. The Cold covered eighty-five percent of the surface on the Earth. It was everything outside the narrow habitable band along the equator. Almost all of the just over one hundred thousand inhabitants of the surface of the Earth lived entirely within that band. The only exceptions were the social misfits and the adventurous souls who chose to live in the Cold, and the researchers and explorers who were carrying out scientific work there (which in practice almost always meant archaeology in search of pre-Taking science). And of course those who entered the Cold to rescue escapees: the black helicopter pilot, for example.

It was in effect the worst ice age Earth had ever experienced. So much water was bound up in the ice and snow of the Cold that the Long Valley, where three quarters of the world's population lived, was a fairly dry place. Extensive irrigation was required to support the large areas under cultivation. The same was true along what had been the Congo River Basin, where most of the remaining one quarter of the population lived. The strange atmospheric and ocean currents caused by the Cold and its steep temperature gradients made the coastlines of Africa and South America inhospitable places, and hence both population centers were far inland. The Cold dominated everything. If the Taking had determined human history from that point on, the Cold determined the shape of human society on Earth.

Fishermen lived along the coasts: the primitive life-forms in the sea that had survived the Taking were proliferating now, with no competition and with huge amounts of organic matter constantly being washed into the seas as the Cold retreated.

There was no strict demarcation where the warm climate ended and the Cold began. Rather, the average temperature declined slowly as one moved either north or south away from the equator. There was still weather, even though its patterns would have seemed bizarre to anyone from before the Taking. There were still summer and winter, and precisely where the Cold began changed with the seasons. But at any time of year, it was never necessary to go very far from the equator in either direction before special clothing and shelter were required for survival, before the brown of the land gave way to the endless stretches of white, of glaring snow and ice many meters thick, and the clear skies of the equator became instead ever-present cold mist and blowing, drifting snow.

Jonathan told himself bravely that he would be able to adjust to the calendar eventually and that in fact he rather liked the idea of working for only four days in a row, instead of five, before getting a break. The question was, he told himself, what real work would he be given to do for those four days out of each five? The skills and competence of which he had been so proud in America seemed almost worthless here.

He had assumed at first that computers were one field in which his competence would still be respected. But these surface dwellers sneered at the technology he knew. They told him it was a century out of date, and so was his training. And sure enough, the children he was forced to attend school with were already ahead of him, and the computers used on the surface were based on new technologies and new scientific understandings that America had never even heard of.

Technology had not grown or evolved significantly in America since the first underground generation. Conditions in America were relatively benign. The surface dwellers, of course, had not had things so easy (as their descendants loved to remind him and each other, with a smug assumption of virtue for their ancestors' sufferings and achievements). The state-of-the-art technology brought back by the returning colonists had been stretched to its limit and beyond during their struggle to survive on Earth.

That struggle was far from over, and technology was still being stretched, forced along an accelerating path of change. The surface population lacked the manpower and material resources for any large-scale research efforts, but new ideas were always welcomed and, if possible, quickly tried, and the number of such new ideas listed in the standard schoolbook history amazed Jonathan.

Not only was Jonathan technologically backward compared to these people; he began to doubt that he could ever catch up.

What would there be for him to do? What was left, he wondered, other than manual labor? Based on his experiences in America, he might have expected that he would at least be suited for that. In America, he had been much healthier and stronger than his peers, who were on the whole a sickly lot as well as prematurely aged. And his climb to the surface had increased his respect for his own body's strength.

But even that small satisfaction, that tiny superiority, was denied him.

By the standards of the surface dwellers, Jonathan Holroyd was a weakling. He didn't know whether the difference lay in the food these people had eaten all of their lives, or in the air they breathed, or in the physical labor and hard-fought games almost all of them participated in. Whatever the cause, though, the result was clear-cut and dispiriting.

Jonathan, who had been tall for his generation underground (which was on average shorter than the generation preceding it), now found himself below average height on the surface. That bothered him only slightly, for he had never cared much about the fact that he was taller than his peers. But to find that everyone on the surface was tougher than he was—more resilient, healthier, more adaptable to temperature extremes—was almost more than he could bear.

Children had been a rarity in America. They were a plague, an infestation, on the surface. They were as noisy as they were numerous. They were intelligent, as quick mentally as they were physically, and the ones he was forced to associate with seemed to delight in proving their intellectual superiority over him whenever the opportunity offered.

Some of Jonathan's teachers were scarcely older than he was, and he tried often to associate with them during break periods, but they rejected him. To these surface dwellers, he was less than the children who surrounded him. They, at least, were future full itizens of the surface world; Jonathan would always be stigmatized by his inferior origins, and would never be fully accepted.

Sometimes he told himself he was being unfair, that no one on the surface really considered him innately inferior. But try as he might to feel charitable toward these people with whom he was doomed to spend the rest of his life, he couldn't delude himself for long about their feelings toward him. Over and over again, they proved to him just what those feelings were. Why did I leave America? he asked himself. Sometimes he thought, I wish I were back there. Sometimes he thought that if there were a safe way back underground, he would take it and never leave home again.

On the day his mandatory twenty months of orientation and training were up, Jonathan received a message to come to the office of Tom Hendrickson, the director of the school.

Hendrickson was tall from Jonathan's perspective, powerfully built, and healthy and handsome. He induced in Jonathan the same annoying feeling of inferiority as most of the surface dwellers did—a feeling Jonathan fought against manfully but could not defeat.

The director stood up when Jonathan entered and offered him a firm handshake, then motioned him to a chair and sat again behind his desk. "John?" he asked. "Johnny?"

"Jonathan." Or Mr. Holroyd, he thought but did not say.

Hendrickson looked surprised but said, "Whatever you prefer." He put his hands together on the desk, looked down at a paper framed by his forearms, cleared his throat, and then looked up at Jonathan and said rather formally, "Well, Jonathan, you've completed the orientation and training we require of all the escapees, and you've done quite well, from the reports reaching me. Now it's time for you to leave the school and begin contributing to the rebuilding of the Earth. You'll have to choose a specialty, of course, something we need. Lists of available jobs are sent to us regularly, and I'll be happy to provide you with a copy of the lists, but before you decide what to apply for, I urge you to take the aptitude tests we offer here. Remember, you might be committing yourself for a lifetime to whatever you choose now and so it's very important—"

"Historian," Jonathan cut in. "I want to be an historian."

"A . . . what?" Hendrickson said blankly. "Historian? don't remember seeing any requests for *historians*."

Jonathan nodded. "That doesn't surprise me at all, Tom Historians are just what the world needs, but no one seems t realize it."

"Well, I'm afraid I have to disagree, Jonathan. What the worl needs most is more hands. Willing, eager, strong, capable hand to do the rebuilding. As you know, we're trying to reclaim an repopulate thousands of square kilometers in South America Africa, Sumatra, Borneo, and Malaya. And as the warmin continues, the area will grow. We have to plant crops and rebuil industries. We have to build and maintain—"

"The legacy brought back from the moon," Jonathan finishe for him by rote. "Yes, Tom, I know that. But you see, ther you've put your finger precisely on the problem." Hendrickso preened unconsciously. "We have to ask ourselves exactly wha that legacy is." He held up his hand to keep Hendrickson fror reflexively reciting any of the usual textbook paragraphs. "Yo see, all we really know for sure are the details of what happene on the moon after the sun was taken by the aliens, and then ho the men and women from the moon returned to Earth once the saw that the surface could support life again. And then"—he too a deep breath and plunged ahead—"how they struggled an worked and suffered and sacrificed to build and maintain the legacy." For a moment, he almost expected Hendrickson to eithe stand and salute or else to bow his head in prayer, but the momer passed.

"But what we don't really know," Jonathan continued, "i what was going on behind the scenes."

"Behind the scenes?" Hendrickson said vaguely.

"Exactly. Was there disagreement on the moon about the pla to return to Earth? If so, who said what? What discussions c debates were there?" Hendrickson looked offended at the ver idea of such dissension among the godlike forebears on such subject, so Jonathan said quickly, "They *were* only human, Tom, after all. And don't you see, that's part of our legacy, too! How they felt, what they said—in opposition to the final plan, as much as what they said in support."

Jonathan realized he was leaning forward in his seat and raising his voice. He forced himself to calm down and sat back. "And of course, there's all the vast history of mankind before the aliens were even discovered. All the art and all the science: *that's* part of our legacy, too. And it's all out there, preserved for us, just waiting for us. Every country that used to exist on Earth before the Taking, every culture—they all left records. Libraries, universities, museums, data bases. Everything frozen and preserved, just for us. How can we rebuild the Earth if we don't understand what it was? All we've been taking from the Cold so far is whatever old technology we can use. But what about the history buried there? Think of it all!"

Hendrickson seemed snowed under by Jonathan's torrent of words, which was just what Jonathan had hoped for. Hendrickson, like all of his fellow surface dwellers, had been brought up to think that history began with the Taking, and that everything that had gone before was of minor importance. His mental picture of history, Jonathan suspected, depicted the thousands of years of human endeavor before the Taking as a brief, telescoped episode, while everything that had taken place since then was of enormous import and gigantic scope.

Even that short period had been mythologized. What should have been sober history, the doings of human beings of a previous generation, was always presented in modern schoolbooks in terms reminiscent of the hero epics of the ancient world. Jonathan was consumed with the need to know what had *really* happened, what words had been spoken and by whom. He wanted to be able to see the men and women of the period of the Taking *as* men and women and not as deities. Perhaps Earth didn't really need the study of history, but Jonathan Holroyd did.

Hendrickson tried to regain the superior position in the conversation by saying with pompous thoughtfulness, "It's an interesting idea. I'll have to take it up with the appropriate people and let you know if anything comes of it. Perhaps in a year or two, it might be possible to let you spend some time on historical work, but in the meantime, we'll have to try to find something—"

"No, sir," Jonathan cut in quickly. "I'm afraid we can't do it that way. Consider this: the Cold is retreating as the sun continues to warm up, isn't that so?"

Hendrickson nodded, uneasy at not knowing where he was being led.

"That means," Jonathan continued, "that all the pre-Taking records that have been preserved for us by the temperature in the Cold are in danger now. As the Earth continues to warm up and the Cold shrinks, more and more old museums and universities are being exposed to warm temperatures. It's imperative that we get to those records *before* the old cities warm up, so that we can remove the records to safe storage places."

This argument was hogwash, Jonathan was sure. The majority of the old records had surely been stored on computer tapes and disks and on microfiche, just as in America. He was betting that neither Hendrickson nor his superiors would know that.

"Let me—" Hendrickson began, but he broke off and looked puzzled. "Look, Holroyd, I'll have to contact you later about this. Go back to your quarters and wait."

Jonathan did so gladly, sensing he had already won.

It took two days before Jonathan got his reply, and then it didn't come from Hendrickson but in the form of a letter on the stationery of the Ministry of Manpower Resources.

While there were many schools for children and adolescents, such as the one in which Jonathan had been immured for the previous twenty months, Earth could not afford to tie up its recources in anything beyond what would once have been called high school. Schooling was intense up to around age seventeen; beyond that, training was accomplished on the job. Nonetheless, there had been a recognition from the start of the necessity of keeping scientific research alive, and so there was one small institution in Lander that was designated a university. The government provided funds, and the university was able to support a small staff of scholars and researchers. It was called the University of Lander, but no one ever referred to it as anything but "the University."

In the informal style which Jonathan found so refreshing in comparison with the way letters from government agencies in America were written, the Ministry of Manpower Resources told him that he was being assigned to the University to commence his historical research.

"Since you will be the first historian the University has ever had," the letter said ingenuously, "you'll have to invent the rules of the game as you go. We haven't yet decided whom you'll report to. The Ministry of Research doesn't want you, since what you'll be doing doesn't fit in with the kind of technical research they do. Therefore, in the meantime, you'll be paid through this office and will be expected to submit monthly reports of your progress to us." That part, at least, sounded familiar from Jonathan's years of working in America. "Report to Jerza Norgaard in Room 34, Building 5, at the University on Oneday morning, eleventh Tethys."

That left him with two days free. Jonathan enjoyed the two days, wandering around Lander and in a leisurely way packing the few belongings he had acquired during the last twenty months. The University was less than five kilometers from his quarters, but he assumed he'd be reassigned and his quarters given to some new student. On some level, he knew, despite his having escaped from America in search of freedom, his upbringing still controlled him; he still accepted unquestioningly the idea of assigned work and orders to change quarters.

But he shrugged that off. Jerza Norgaard would turn out to be a beautiful, blonde Scandinavian type who would fall madly in love with him. He would soon be poring over diaries and other personal records of the men and women who had survived the Taking on the moon. And the air in Lander was cool and fresh, with a steady breeze from the ice-capped mountains to the north. He was young, and life was as pleasant and full of promise as it should always have been, and Oneday would be the beginning of a new life for him.

14

But Jerza Norgaard was short, overweight, plain, and ten years older than Jonathan, and demonstrated not the slightest interest in falling in love with him. Nor would it have mattered if she had, for Jonathan would have been unable to respond. To him, a greater handicap than her age or her looks was her color: she was as black as the helicopter pilot who had picked him up after his escape from America, and Jonathan was still a long way from escaping from the prejudices America had preserved so carefully.

She was an abrupt, businesslike woman with a desk covered with papers. She took a grudging moment to dig out the forms connected with him, read them, and then consulted a chart for a few minutes. "All right," she said at last. "We can put you up in the graduate student building. There's a room becoming available there this afternoon. Someone moving out to start doing some *real* work." Jonathan understood the insult in just the way it was intended but said nothing. "And I think we can dig up an office for you to use. Goodbye."

"Uh, just a moment. I'm going to need access to documents and data bases. And I'm going to have to be able to keep in touch with the people who're going into the Cold. Most of my sources will come from the old cities as they're explored. Who should I see about all of that?"

"Damn," Jerza Norgaard said. She scribbled a note on a pad of paper before her. "All right. I'll take care of it. Anything *else*?"

"Well, yes. I said that *most* of my sources will come from the old cities in the Cold. But the other important source of data for my work will be from the moon, from the period between the Taking and the return to Earth. I don't know what's available— personal diaries, letters, notes, that sort of thing—but whatever there is, that's the stuff I want."

Jerza stared at him in amazement. "Christ, Holroyd, haven't

they taught you anything since you came up out of your hole in the ground? Anything like that is stored on the moon, exclusively. There aren't any copies of it down here. Mendeleev keeps all of that, where it'll be safe. No one's going to let you get *your* hands on it."

Or in other words, Jonathan realized, he was still a second-class citizen, and in the eyes of these surface dwellers would perhaps always be one. Inferior hands like his, which could not claim descent from the divine digits of the lunar survivors, would never be allowed to profane with their touch the sacred texts.

But those were the crucial sources for his understanding of history. He tried again. "I can understand that all of those documents are being saved for posterity, for history, but that's just what I am! I'm undertaking to write the history of that era, something that no one has done before. I'm the man who's going to preserve and interpret what happened. That's my job, now."

Norgaard said through gritted teeth, "We already *know* what happened, and we don't need someone like you to tell us what happened. But since it's your *job*, I'll look into it and see what I can do for you."

Absolutely nothing, in other words. "By the way, I'm puzzled by your name. How did you get it? Both your names, I mean."

Norgaard stared at him as if he were as stupid as he was inquisitive. "I inherited it, of course, just like everyone else. There was a Jerza Norgaard on the moon; one of my ancestors. Now, I'm busy. Some of us have *work* to do. Come back in a couple of hours, and I'll have the room and office assignment worked out for you. *Goodbye*."

With nothing else to do, Jonathan decided to kill the time with a stroll around the university grounds. He was disturbed by what Jerza Norgaard had said about her ancestor. Had the original Jerza Norgaard indeed been Scandinavian, perhaps looking the way he had imagined this one would look? If so, then there must have been intermarriage since then. He knew there were blacks living and working on the surface; but he had automatically assumed that the races kept their distance from each other after working hours. This new revelation made Jonathan feel queasy. What kind of world had he emerged into? America had its faults: obviously Jonathan knew that. But why couldn't these surface people copy at least some of the ways of the underground world?

The first day in his new office, Jonathan sat at his empty desk, twiddled his thumbs, and stared at the blank walls. He hoped some of his neighbors, whom he could see walking busily past his open door and whom he imagined working industriously in their offices up and down the corridor, would stop in and introduce themselves and welcome him into the academic community, but none of them did. He went back to his dormitory room deeply discouraged and depressed; the contempt with which he was openly regarded by the graduate students with whom he shared the dormitory didn't help at all. He caught himself wondering again why he had ever left home.

The second day, the efficiency and organization and high degree of computerization of the surface world began to have their effect. Boxes of books and crates of papers began arriving at his office. It turned out to be a random selection of historical material brought back by expeditions to cities in the Cold. The normal goal of such expeditions was reusable technology and resources, but occasionally other things were picked up, too, out of curiosity. Jonathan was now benefiting from that curiosity.

He unpacked and unwrapped, skimming as he went. The volume of information was dauntingly huge and maddeningly unselective. By the end of the day, his office was no longer empty: it was crammed full, and there was hardly room for him. More boxes were piled in the hallway outside his door, and more were still arriving. Very suddenly, matters had gotten completely out of hand. Where can I store all of this? Jonathan asked himself. How am I ever going to read all of it?

Storing it, though, was the first priority. He walked down the hallway, looking for someone who hadn't already left for the day. He found only one researcher, a man sitting hunched over his desk with his back to his open door.

Jonathán stood in the doorway and cleared his throat. "Excuse me." There was no response. "Excuse me!" Jonathan repeated, louder this time.

This time the man turned around. He proved to be young, and he wore a goatee and an annoyed expression. He was also white, which pleased Jonathan. Behind him was a small screen covered with formulae; he held a keyboard in his lap. "Yes? Yes?" he said.

"Hello. I'm Jonathan Holroyd from down the hall. I'm—"

"The historian. I've heard. Well?"

Jonathan couldn't tell if his unfriendliness was due to Jonathan's profession or just the man's nature, but it was too definite to be ignored. "I'm very sorry to have interrupted you, but I wonder if you could tell me something. I've got quite a few boxes of books and so on in my office and out in the hall—"

"Yes, I've noticed them. And I hope you plan to get rid of them soon. They're a hazard."

They wouldn't be if everyone learned to walk a bit more slowly. "Well, I realize that, and that's what I wanted to ask you. Is there any kind of storeroom around here I could use? This stuff is going to keep arriving. In fact, there's going to be a lot more of it, and I'd like to start putting it in order as soon as it comes in."

"Ask Jerza." The goatee turned away again to face the screen. The man's hands moved over the keyboard, and the rows of equations scrolled slowly up the screen.

"Thanks." But Jonathan's unneighborly neighbor had already forgotten him.

The next morning, which was Threeday, he steeled himself and went to Jerza Norgaard's office. His reluctance made every step an effort. Everything he did here, he realized, was an unpleasant effort. The only exception was reading the old books from the boxes. That had brought him real pleasure the previous day, and he was already looking forward to getting back to it. It provided escape from this hostile world he was now part of.

"You said you wanted everything we could get you from the Cold, and now you're complaining it's too much," Jerza Norgaard said in disgust. "You escapees are all alike. Give you a hand and you want the whole arm. All right, so I'll try to find you a storeroom to put your boxes in."

"There's more to it than that, though. What I'll really need is a room big enough to be a library. You know, with shelves so that I can put everything on them in some sort of order. The stuff's no good if it's not accessible, which it wouldn't be if I left it in the boxes. I guess I'll need the shelving, too."

Norgaard stared at him in wordless, stunned anger. At last she managed to say, "A *library*? A God damned *library*? Just who do you think you are? Everyone else here uses the computers we give them, and that's how they store their data. Why can't you?"

"It's not quite the same thing, is it?" Jonathan said patiently. "For one thing, their data is numeric, not textual, so it's much more information-dense. For another thing, they get their measurements and so forth already on computer media, so it's just a matter of transferring it electronically from one place to another. My data starts out in books and old documents. It would take me the rest of my life to type it all in. I'd need a whole staff if I wanted to do it in a reasonable time. Also, for the other researchers here, a number has the same value no matter what form it's stored in. With the data I work with, the original form is crucial. Information can be gleaned in the future by someone reexamining an original document. Basically, I'm the first historian since the Taking. I'm going to miss a lot, and it'll be up to future historians to reexamine the same sources and catch what I missed. Or reinterpret it. That sort of thing."

"The way you talk about it," Norgaard said scornfully, "you'd think it was a real science, and not just a way to keep you out of everyone's hair for a few years."

Jonathan gave up trying to control his anger. He leaned over the desk, and was pleased to see Norgaard withdraw as he loomed over her. "Now listen to me, you half-wit. What I'm doing isn't just make-work. You can believe what you want, but your superiors and mine obviously think it's very worthwhile. I'll be submitting quarterly reports to them, and if I have to say in those reports that I'm not accomplishing anything, I'm not going to take all of the blame by myself. I'll make it very clear that you've been obstructing me."

She blustered for a while, but it began to sound hollow. In the end, Jonathan got his library.

The library really wasn't much more than a long, narrow room unused for some years (which was surprising, Jonathan thought, in view of the space shortage at the University), and therefore filled with dust. It took him two days to get the room cleaned to his satisfaction, and then another two days to install the prefabricated shelving Jerza had managed to find for him. Much as he disliked her—for herself as much as for her skin color—and as nasty and uncooperative as she always was toward him, he had to admit that, when she decided to do something, she was competent.

He didn't finish installing the shelves until Fourday evening, and since he was exhausted, he gave up and went home. He could have used the day off which Fiveday normally was, but he told himself that would be a silly self-indulgence. After all, he reflected, he had no friends in this world, so what would he use a day off for? He might as well come back to the University and get something accomplished that would give him pleasure.

The next morning, Fiveday, Jonathan was back in his library bright and early. The task of shelving the materials from the Cold was hot and tedious, and he quickly realized that it would take far more than one day. Still, he was enjoying it so much that he soon found himself whistling.

"Could you stop that, please?" a voice said irritably.

"What?" Jonathan turned around to look. At the door was a young man he had noticed before, a slender, nervous Oriental with glasses that seemed half as big as his face. Jonathan's stomach tensed. Orientals! Negroes were inferior, but that wasn't really their fault. Orientals, however, had all been communists in the old days, the enemy.

"I said, could you please stop that? I've got a major problem with my terminal, and it's driving me crazy, and I can't think with that noise going on."

That was something Jonathan could sympathize with, no matter what race the person was who was having the problem. "I'm—"

"You're Jonathan Holroyd, the historian. Yes, I know. I'm Francis K'ai-Tao, and I've got to get back to work."

"I was going to say," Jonathan said, "that I'm sorry about the whistling. Maybe I can help you. What sort of problem is it?"

Francis snorted. "There's no one who can help me. The experts all died generations ago. It's the Goddamned Rockway operating system."

Jonathan's ears pricked up. "Rockway? I used to work on a Rockway 3000. I know that machine inside and out."

"No kidding?" Francis said excitedly, pushing his glasses back up on his nose. "No one else seems to know it even outside, not even the guys on the moon. That's where both the Rockways are—and they *are* both 3000's. Could you . . . come to my terminal and maybe just have a look?"

"I'd be delighted to!" Jonathan said sincerely. Only at that moment did he realize what he had been unconsciously missing most about America: the Rockway 3000 he had always considered his private property. Not really the people or even the way of life, in spite of his frequent silent complaints about the surface lifestyle, but rather a machine. But a great machine, he told himself in self-defense.

For Jonathan, Francis K'ai-Tao's problem was a simple one to solve. After showing Francis what he had been doing incorrectly, he spent some time giving him a quick course in the Rockway's unique operating system. "It may not be much compared to what they have here nowadays," he told Francis, "but in its day, it was the best for scientific work." He grew more enthusiastic as he talked about what had been one of his favorite pastimes. "Oh, I had some good times with this machine, back in America. Intellectually speaking, of course." He smiled. "Although, if it *were* possible to make love to a computer, this is the one I'd choose."

Francis grimaced. "Ugh! A hole in the wall would be better. At least it wouldn't be out to get you. Mendeleev authorized me an access code and a password for this things, and all I want from it is to use it to do my work."

Jonathan laughed. "Typical user attitude!" He felt relaxed, he realized. More accurately, he felt as if something of which he hadn't been aware, a tension inside himself, had just relaxed. Maybe a prejudice just snapped, he told himself silently. "I've got to get back to work, too," he told Francis. "Feel free to call on me anytime you have a problem with my sweetheart here."

"Thanks. I'm sure I'll be calling on you regularly."

That turned out to be the truth, and as a result, the two developed an easygoing office friendship. They never socialized outside work, but they both worked long hours and often were at the University on Fivedays. During those times they spent a lot of time talking to each other about their pasts. Jonathan taught Francis a lot about the Rockway, and Francis tried unsuccessfully to teach Jonathan something about botany. Friendless as they both were, the association was important to both of them.

Finally, even the room that was Jonathan's library became filled. In only a matter of weeks, he was back to storing boxes in the corridor, boxes he had not even unpacked because he had no place to put their contents. Much as he disliked the thought, he knew that there was no alternative but to pay Jerza Norgaard another visit.

She was furious—a genuine fury, he thought, wilting before it, rather than the partially feigned variety that was part of her everyday manner. Jonathan had assumed a black face couldn't grow red; now he discovered that it could, however, darken. "More library space?" she screamed at him. "Who the Hell do you think you are? The situation is completely out of hand. There are lots of other people who've had requests for space in for months, and they're being ignored because there's nothing to give them. And now you . . ." She paused for a few seconds for breath before continuing. "Now you," she continued in an artificially calm voice, "you come in here and demand even more space after I freed up that room for you. Forget it, Holroyd. At this rate, we'd have to build you your own building, and maybe even that wouldn't be the end of it! What do you want, a whole new University just for yourself?"

Jonathan nodded. "That's not a bad idea at all. However"—he held up his hand to prevent the imminent explosion—"I have a better idea, a reasonable alternative. What if I were to go with some of the expeditions into the Cold? That way, you see, I could make a catalogue of what's in the various places, microfiche everything, and only bring the most important stuff back with me. The materials will keep out there for now, at least until something can be done about the space problem. Something *will* have to be done eventually, you know. But in the meantime, this would be a temporary solution."

Jerza sneered. "An escapee in the Cold! I can just see it! Then I'd be in trouble for sending someone out who got lost and wandered away and froze to death. No thank you."

"We're really not children, you know. Escaping from America isn't exactly child's play."

"Tell me this," Norgaard said. "Why don't we just have the expeditions in the Cold microfiche your precious junk in the first place and send *that* to you. That would take up a lot less room."

Because I want to go out there myself, that's why! "Because they don't have the time or the expertise to decide what's important and what isn't. They'd just microfiche everything, and I'd have the same mess I have now, just a lot smaller. In fact, that's really a big part of the problem now, that they're just packing up everything and shipping it here. There's no selection. I'm the expert, after all. I could do that on the spot."

"I guess that makes a kind of sense," Jerza said grudgingly.

No, it doesn't, Jonathan thought. But as long as you think it does, that's what counts.

"I'll see what I can do," she said. "Get out of my office."

Two months passed without word. Jonathan had already learned that getting things done in Lander required a lot of patient waiting; in fact, trying to push things along was counterproductive as often as not, for it produced resentment and therefore delays. Finally he received a comm call from Jerza Norgaard. On the small screen, her face was as sour as ever—perhaps more so, because she had lost a round to him. "Next week," she said abruptly. "Threeday. Be ready to go."

"Where? The moon?"

Jerza laughed nastily. "Fat chance! No, the Cold. There's an expedition getting together for Montevideo. You're part of it if you don't forget to get up on Threeday morning and rendezvous at the airport."

"Wonderful! When? And what clothes do I need?"

"Nine o'clock. You can wear your birthday suit, if you want to, except that it would make everyone sick. Normal clothes. They'll give you what you need." With a click, the screen went blank.

The Cold! Jonathan's heart was hammering. He wasn't after old books and papers—not really, not primarily. He was after adventure and change and exotic, far places. Other than the moon, what could be further from Lander or more exotic than the Cold?

15

To Jonathan's pleasant surprise, the field workers were a considerably friendlier bunch than the people he had had to endure at the University. He was even more pleasantly surprised to discover that his being an escapee lent him a certain status. And when he admitted that he knew nothing about the Cold, his new companions were eager to teach him what he needed to know for survival. When he was comfortable with his gear, the team boarded the airplane that would take them to the Cold.

The airplane droned southward for hour after hour. They had started before noon, and as sunset approached, they were still flying. Jonathan didn't mind at all. He had quickly grabbed a window seat, and now he mechanically ate the meals he was served and kept his attention on the land beneath.

Farmland began right outside Lander. The two large habitable areas of modern Earth were probably the most intensively cultivated land in human history. Fortunately, the soil of modern Earth was very rich, indeed; it had been littered with vast numbers of frozen human and animal bodies, which had then thawed out as heat returned, richly fertilizing it. Microscopic life had survived the freezing in fine fettle as well.

Jonathan thought about the sights and smells that must have greeted the men and women returning from the moon, and he wondered whether they had wrinkled their noble nostrils. He laughed aloud at the thought and realized just how much his going on the expedition had raised his spirits.

But it wasn't all that far south of Lander that the farmland ended. Here, on the fringes of the Cold, the weather was warm enough in the summer for crops, but the growing season was too short for any crop varieties yet available. The Cold was retreating, but for the two steps it took backward in the summer, it managed to take at least one step forward again in the winter.

There were a few thousand hardy souls living on the fringes of the Cold, in the narrow area where the retreating ice and snow met the warmer air of the equator. The weather was fierce there, and even the climate was uncertain, with the boundary of the Cold oscillating back and forth unpredictably, as though the Cold were a living thing and reluctant to give up, to retreat, to yield its control of the world it had held in thrall. The men and women who lived along the harsh edges of the Cold were the misanthropes and loners every society in history has had; as the Cold retreated and more sociable humans invaded their wilderness, the solitary types retreated with the Cold, moving ever further from the equator. Someday, Jonathan supposed, when the Earth's climate had stabilized and there were once again two polar ice caps, these people would still live along the fringes of what was left of the Cold; they would be the spiritual descendants of the Eskimos of old Earth. By then, he expected, there'd be a special name for them, and they would grow culturally ever more distant from their more warm-blooded brothers and sisters. Someday, Jonathan thought, there might even be nations and wars again.

More than a year had passed, and yet Jonathan found he hadn't forgotten the low temperatures and the mist and the whiteness. From pictures he'd seen of the Cold, he knew that it was often clear and sunny, with the sky a brilliant blue and the ground an even more brilliant white, but that wasn't the case when they landed.

They came down through a haze that hid the ground. Through the window next to his seat, Jonathan could see nothing but the mist through which the airplane was descending. He began to worry about what the pilot could see when Charlie Yang, who was sitting next to him, said, "Not to worry. It's all done by instruments. Safer than if the pilot uses his own eyes."

Perhaps Charlie was right. The landing was smooth and comfortable; Jonathan couldn't tell when the skids touched down, and the mist was so thick outside that he couldn't tell when the airplane had finally stopped moving. The engines cut off, plunging them into sudden silence, and they had arrived in what had once been Montevideo.

Shadowy figures were waiting outside to lead them to shelter. The group of arrivees hurried along after their guides, eager to get out of the bitter wind. Jonathan pulled down the flap on the front of his coat and began fumbling with the controls. "Don't bother." It was Charlie Yang's voice, coming from a hooded figure beside him. Charlie, a squat, powerfully built young man, was in charge of the expedition, and he had made an extra effort to be helpful to Jonathan before the group left Lander. He sported a thick, black beard. Most of the male field workers were bearded. Charlie said it was for warmth, but Jonathan suspected that the beards also served to set the field workers apart as members of a tough and adventuresome breed. "It's not worth the trouble," Charlie said. "We'll be inside soon." Noises of machinery and motors came from the mist. Jonathan realized that the airplane was being serviced and their supplies unloaded, all by men working from the protection of ground vehicles.

The only shelter was a cramped, one-room building, its walls lined with cabinets and bunks. With the newcomers' coats and sweaters piled up on every available surface, the place seemed even smaller. "I thought they used to live in larger buildings than this, before the Taking," Jonathan mused aloud.

"Oh, this isn't one of the old buildings." It was Charlie again. He had two steaming mugs, one of which he held out to Jonathan. "One of our advance parties put this one up. They also smoothed out the snow and packed it down to form a landing strip. All the original buildings are buried beneath the snow, of course—a hundred meters below us. That's why we can't even work too far into the Cold: the further in you go, the deeper the snow is. The depth here is about the limit. When we want to explore a building, we have to dig down to it, and then it's a real fight to keep it from getting covered up again. If it wasn't for that, we'd just use the original airport to land in. But then, if it wasn't for the Taking and the Cold . . ." He shrugged. "Well, things would be very different, wouldn't they?"

"I suppose so," Jonathan replied vaguely, not really paying

attention. Something had struck him: Charlie Yang was awfully constant in his presence and helpfulness. Jonathan was unpleasantly reminded of the girl in America, the spy from the Department of Security who lived next door to him and was assigned to watch him. He had thought he had left all of that behind him when he escaped from the buried nation. Was it just as present here, only more clumsily done? The thought infuriated him. Bluntly he asked, "Charlie, were you told to keep an eye on me?"

Charlie looked surprised and then embarrassed. "Well," he mumbled, "you're our only historian, so far. We wouldn't want you to wander off into the Cold and get lost."

"That's all? That's the only reason you're hanging around me this way?"

Charlie's innocent surprise could not have been feigned, Jonathan thought. "Why else?" Suddenly his puzzlement disappeared. "Oh, I get it! I've seen the tapes. You think I'm some kind of spy, like they have in some of the underground places. Hell, no. I didn't have anything to do right now, since I'm between assignments, and Jerza asked me to help you out and make sure you don't get hurt or lost. That can happen really easily out here. People don't realize just *how* easily, when they come to the Cold for the first time. Also, I'm interested in what you're doing. I might want to switch my specialty sometime, myself."

"The tapes" again. The woman on Jonathan's very first airplane had said something about them, too. Before he could question Charlie further about the phrase, Jonathan's group was ordered to start choosing bunks for the night, and in the bustle and commotion of doing that and then of going out to the storage sheds to check on their equipment and prepare it for the upcoming trek to the research sites, he forgot all about his question.

An earlier expedition, working from old maps of Montevideo, had located the city's largest university and had dug down to the roof of the university library.

Jonathan and Charlie Yang and two others of the group from the airplane, a young woman named Greta and a young man named

Shiro, were driven from their base shack across kilometers of
snow to the entrance to the shaft that led down into the library.
They travelled in huge vehicles with caterpillar treads. Their cabin
was well sealed and insulated and heated, and the four of them set
their clothing for coolness and relaxed. To Jonathan there was
something both otherworldly and familiar about the situation. It
was exotic, divorced from reality, to be sitting in such comfort and
warmth with mugs of hot beverages being passed around, while
just beyond the windows were the mist and the bitter temperatures—the Cold. And yet the situation was hauntingly reminiscent
of America, where he had grown up thinking that only the sealed
walls and the magma heat source stood between the warmth and
light and life within and the vacuum and heatlessness outside.

Their destination was another shack, scarcely visible through
the mist. Fortunately, their driver knew the way and halted their
vehicle almost against the doorway to the shack. "Shack,"
though, was a misnomer, as Jonathan realized after the four of
them had entered it. The buildings here in the Cold were all of
heavy-duty construction. They looked flimsy at first glance, but
the walls were built of some substance that, though thin, was
extremely sturdy.

While they had been driving, a wind had risen, and during their
short walk from the vehicle to the shack, they had had to find their
way through a sudden ground blizzard. Inside the shack, even
with the door closed, they could hear the wind howling outside,
rising in intensity and pitch. Faintly through that noise they could
hear their vehicle rumbling away, its sound fading and then
becoming lost in the wind.

"Gonna be a bad one," Charlie said. "We got inside just in
time. We may be stuck here for a few hours." Then he grinned.
"But you'll see—the time will fly."

"I guess these buildings have to withstand a lot of wind, then?"
Jonathan asked.

"Snow, even more than wind. Did you see the way the stuff was
drifting when we came in? At that rate, in a few days, it can cover
up a building like this one entirely. You can either keep putting up
new cabins on top of the old ones, in layers, or keep shovelling the

stuff away. If you spend a lot of time inside here, all wrapped up in what you're doing, without paying attention to what's going on outside, you try to emerge but discover that you can't, because you're now a few meters beneath the surface of the snow."

Greta shivered. Charlie said quickly, "Oh, don't worry about it. This storm won't go on for that long. Not according to the forecast. It's just that the Cold doesn't like to let people in without getting in a few licks. It doesn't give up easily."

The young woman who had shivered said, "Thank God it's warm in here, at least." She began to take off her coat.

"Uh-uh," Charlie said. "If you're down there, and your clothes are up here, and something happens to the heating, you might not be able to make it back up in time. Especially if the lights go off as well."

She shivered again and zipped her coat up.

"Down there," Jonathan realized, meant the old university library far beneath them. In the center of the hut a circular railing with one opening marked the top of the wide shaft leading downward. Sounds drifted up the shaft—metallic clangs and occasional faint human voices. Once there was what seemed to be a short snatch of song, and after that a faraway laugh.

"Okay, now," Charlie said, "down we go. If any of you have claustrophobia or a weak heart, you shouldn't have been cleared for this expedition, so I'll assume you're all sufficiently healthy to manage the climb. I'll go first. Turn down your suit temperatures now, because you'll be getting pretty hot."

Charlie climbed onto the metal ladder that projected above the shaft opening and began climbing down it, looking like some strange, bulky creature native to the Cold.

Jonathan felt a reluctance he couldn't fully understand to begin that climb—which was especially strange, considering how long he had been waiting for the chance to be on one of these explorations. He waited until the other two had followed Charlie before he forced himself to put his booted feet on the rungs of the ladder. He stood at the top, looking down at them as they laboriously moved away from him, and then he took one last look around the hut.

"Hey!" a voice called from below. "You coming, Jonathan?"

Jonathan set his teeth and began climbing downward. He had only gone about two meters when he stopped, struck at last by the source of his discomfort. His companions were out of sight below, and the top of the shaft was far enough above him that he could easily imagine he was alone. Hanging on the ladder, his hands and feet frozen in place, he experienced a frightening feeling of *déjà vu*: he was in the tunnels leading up from America again, and if he continued moving downward, he would end up back in there.

He forced himself to start moving again. It was only another meter or so before he reached a sort of landing, a flat resting place extending into the side of the tunnel where his companions were waiting for him, and he spent the time it took to traverse the short distance lecturing himself.

There was space to sit, but not to stand. For one man, there would have been room to lie down; with four of them, the little area was cramped and uncomfortable. Jonathan realized suddenly that he'd rather be climbing again than trying to rest here. During his escape from America, he had spent many hours sleeping fitfully in similar tiny spaces—escape slots or tool cabinets, he hadn't known which—and waking frequently in terror that he would roll over in his sleep and fall into the shaft and drop forever and forever, or not forever but instead into the white-hot, eager magma. . . .

Charlie said, "Let's get moving, or we'll never get down there."

The university library wasn't what Jonathan had anticipated.

Unconsciously, he had expected something much like America. He had assumed that excavating a building buried under the snow was simply a matter of digging out the many cubic meters of snow and ice and dragging them up to the surface. Then the original corridors and rooms would be accessible—probably looking much the way they had before the Taking. He would walk through hallways that would look much like those of America, and climb stairs to rooms on higher floors.

Instead, the ladder ended in a narrow corridor, lined with the same brown stuff as the tunnel and the floor of the hut on the surface, and after a long walk they came out of the corridor to find themselves in a brightly lighted, vast, open space under the snow. The walls of this, too, were covered with the now familiar brown insulating cover.

In the middle of the great open space was an enormous pile of ice and snow. Here and there, the broken ends of wooden planks projected from it, and Jonathan could see bricks and stones dotting its surface. The mound of rubble almost filled the space, reaching to the brown covering of the ceiling and leaving only a narrow walkway of a meter and a half between itself and the walls. Here, the floor was not covered; it was solidly compacted snow, which had long ago turned to ice.

The lighting in the cavern came from powerful spotlights mounted high on the walls all around the cavern and trained on the shapeless pile. Their light reflected from it dazzlingly, casting a crazy quilt of light and shadow everywhere. Along the margin of the pile, small pools of water stood on the icy surface of the cavern; more of it ran down the sides of the mound and dripped to the floor. The spotlights were melting the huge pile of ice, but with glacial slowness.

Human figures surrounded the pile, working cautiously at it with some sort of hand-held devices. They looked like guns, but the effect when they were pointed at the ice was that it melted in small areas, to a depth that could have been measured in centimeters. The workers then reached into the shallow holes they had made and tugged at the exposed rubble until pieces of it came loose. These pieces they piled behind them, along the walls of the cavern.

This was where the noises and voices they had heard earlier had come from. The air was misty with condensing steam from the hand-held melters and from the breath of the workers. Vapor moved in curtains past the spotlights, and there was a chill dampness to the air. The work must have been hot, though, for most of the workers had discarded their heavy coats. Charlie Yang's earlier warning to Greta didn't seem to bother these people.

The jumbled pile loomed over the people working around

it; Jonathan estimated the height of the pile at ten meters. And suddenly he realized what it was.

"My God," he said. "That's the library!"

"What's left of it," Charlie agreed.

"But it must have collapsed! I don't understand."

"You mean, you thought it would still be standing?" Charlie said in amazement. "Hell, no. Just think about it. First there was the war, right at the very end. Big cities like this one were hit hard. We're lucky there wasn't a strike anywhere near the university, or there'd be nothing left unvaporized here. Nothing safe to come near, anyway. And then most of the buildings that weren't knocked over by the blasts or the ground waves collapsed later under the weight of the snow. Especially the older, lower buildings with flat roofs like this one. There are a few buildings that made it through intact, because they weren't too deep in the Cold or because of their shape, but not too many."

Shiro groaned. "I guess this means that we have to help pull all that junk away and spread it around before we can even find the books."

Charlie grinned at him. "You guessed it. This is where you guys start earning your keep. Stay right here."

He made his way along the narrow walkway, squeezing past the men and women working away at the encased library ruins, and disappeared around the curve of the cavern. After a quarter-hour, he returned, carrying four of the hand-held melters. "You can see what the others are doing," he said. "Do the same thing. But if you uncover a book, a diskette, a tape, a wafer—any kind of recorded information, in other words—sing out and I'll come running. That's what we're all really after."

Jonathan discarded his coat before he even began working, despite Charlie's stern warnings not to, although, forewarned by the example of those around him, he kept his gloves on. And despite his lack of strength compared to those around him, Jonathan worked with a will.

16

Jonathan arrived back at his apartment in Lander late at night, exhausted. He had uncovered a fair number of old records—books, original documents, computer disks and wafers—that he thought from his quick scanning of them in Montevideo would be of great value to him. Tomorrow, he would have an argument with Jerza Norgaard.

He stripped off his clothing and was about to collapse into bed when he noticed the amber message light glowing on his comm unit. He was tempted to leave it for the next day but finally decided to see what the message was.

It was a voice he didn't recognize, a woman's voice. The message was a request that he call a certain number as soon as he returned. Jonathan shrugged and decided that it could certainly wait until morning. For now, sleep was more important than anything else.

The next morning, Jonathan had breakfast at the University cafeteria and went immediately to Jerza Norgaard's office, hoping to score a moral victory by getting there before she did. However, she was already behind her desk, hard at work. Hard at work making life difficult for me, Jonathan told himself.

She greeted him with insincere affability and asked how he had enjoyed his stay in the Cold.

Jonathan smiled pleasantly at her. "It was exhausting and uncomfortable," he said. "Outside, the air was so cold you could hardly breathe, and inside it stank so much you didn't want to. I spent too much of my time doing unskilled work that someone else could have done at least as well, and which wasted time I could have used more profitably otherwise."

"Glad to hear it." She maintained the false air of bonhomie. "Did you want something? *I'm* busy."

149

"What makes you so hostile to me? Just wondering."

For the first time, Jerza looked directly at him, instead of over his shoulder. "You're an escapee. People like you waste our time and resources. You don't contribute anything, and you get in the way. In my opinion, you all ought to be put together in some wilderness area and left to make it or starve. I'm not the only one who feels that way. Instead, we spend—" She broke off, looking annoyed. "I don't have time for this. Anything else?"

Jonathan nodded. "Mm-hmm. Once before, I talked to you about a library, a special building to store the materials from the Cold. Now that I've been out there, I can see that we need it even more than I realized."

Jerza said with finality, "Microfiche your rubbish. The originals can be left in the Cold, where they're found. The temperature will preserve them."

"And the damp will destroy them. The buildings they were housed in are all collapsed on top of them. Everything gets soaked when it's recovered, because the ice and snow has to be melted off. It could be dried out and stored in special buildings out there, but if we're going to have to go to all that trouble and expense anyway, doesn't it make more sense to do it here in Lander, where it would be cheaper and easier, and where all the people who'd want to refer to the materials are already located? It makes more sense to me."

"Nothing you've said since you showed up has made any sense at all to me!" Jerza snapped. "It's out of the question. We can't spare the manpower or the materials for extra buildings, either here or in the Cold, so I don't want to be bothered by you with this anymore. Now, *let me get back to my work*!"

Somehow, Jonathan had thought he'd win this argument. He was too depressed by his defeat to go to his office immediately and do any real work of his own, so instead he found a public comm unit, contacted the unit in his apartment, and replayed the message he had found waiting for him the previous evening.

He still didn't recognize the voice or the name, Elena Simkin. However, he reflected, he really knew very few people on the surface, even after all this time, so that was hardly surprising. What did surprise him, though, was the hostility he thought he detected in the unknown Elena's voice. If there was one thing he didn't need that morning, it was meeting another woman who hated him for no reason.

He spoke the ID number the woman had left in her message into the comm unit and waited while strange electronic noises came faintly from it. At last she answered. "Hello. This is Elena." The voice was the same, instantly recognizable, rather low and hoarse and a bit timid. Jonathan suddenly felt intrigued.

"Yes, this is Jonathan Holroyd. You left a message on my comm unit for me to call you."

Even before she spoke, he could sense the hostility on the other end. What is she, he wondered in disgust, a friend of Jerza Norgaard's?

"Jonathan Holroyd. Yes. I'm glad you returned my call at last. I'd like to see you. I have a place not too far from the University. When do you think you could come over?"

Jonathan was getting angry again. What was wrong with these people? He was just as good as they were, even if he was an escapee—maybe even better. Jerza Norgaard's voice would never have intrigued him, so in a way her hostility didn't really matter (or so he tried to convince himself), but this Elena was a different matter. Perhaps she held the same political beliefs about escapees as Jerza. Maybe, he told himself, she was part of some fringe group of crazies that intended to kidnap him and any other escapees they could find and abandon them all out in the wilderness. Well, let them try. He was no longer the weakling he had been a year ago. "Give me the address," he demanded. He liked the decisiveness he heard in his own voice.

Just as much as America, Lander had its wealthier and poorer sections. And the area Elena Simkin lived in was one of the most elegant parts of the city.

About half an hour after speaking to Elena via comm, Jonathan was walking along a wide, pleasant street lined with stunted trees

that fairly glowed in the reddish sunlight. He decided that it was
much easier to tell where the money was in Lander than it had
been in America. There, the clues were such things as how clean
the corridors were kept and whether the strictly functional metal
doors set into the rock walls had been replaced with rare wooden
ones by the owners of the apartments.

Here, by contrast, virtually all the doors were wooden. Even
after all this time, that alone still struck Jonathan as a more than
slightly obscene waste, a luxury indulged in for the sake of
opulence, of decadence, of Sybaritism.

Most people in Lander still lived in apartment buildings or
government-run boarding houses. The houses that had been built
were concentrated in areas such as the one Jonathan now found
himself in, and the apartment buildings here were smaller. Both
kinds of buildings were set in more spacious grounds than the ones
around the University. Of course, even that was hard for him to
judge: there was just so much room available on the surface that
no one needed to be cramped. For all he knew, the larger spaces
here, the wider lawns and sidewalks, might be due to individual
tastes rather than more money. Nonetheless, he had the sense that
this neighborhood represented more money than he had encountered before—and more power.

The address Elena had given him turned out to be a house, not
an apartment building. That disarmed him, or rather it robbed him
of the cockiness and aggressiveness with which he had started out.
The woman who answered the door disarmed him even more.

She was blonde and blue-eyed and very pretty—the American
ideal!—and happily she was shorter than Jonathan. She had an air
of fragility to her that would have made most men want to put
their arms about her and protect her from the world. But what
struck him most of all was her remarkable resemblance to Cathy
Martinson.

"Elena Simkin? I'm Jonathan Holroyd."

"Yes, I know. Come in." Once again, Jonathan sensed the
hostility in her face and voice. Following her and watching with
interest her slender form walking down a long hallway, he tried

hard to muster hostility in response, but failed. It annoyed him that he was attracted to her. More than merely attracted to her: he had known from the first instant, when she'd answered the door, that this was the girl he had been waiting for since puberty, if not before—certainly since he had first seen that old photograph of Cathy Martinson.

They ended up in a large, sunny room sparsely furnished with elegant furniture. An American would have demonstrated his wealth with a profusion of wood, with deliberately massive furniture. Here, though, everything was light and graceful, from the slender legs of the two small end tables to the arms of the chair Elena indicated Jonathan was to sit in. And there was no abundance of wood; instead, most of what he saw was plastic or metal.

Elena took a chair opposite his. Sitting, she looked even smaller and more fragile, and, if anything, even more like Cathy Martinson. She tried to smile in a sociable manner, but it was not a successful smile. "I suppose you like to be called Jonathan? I mean, not John or anything like that."

"That's right."

She nodded. "You Americans are like that, I've noticed. Standoffish. The men, at least."

"Oh, I don't know. It's more that we're kept at arm's length up here."

Elena looked surprised. "Do you feel that way? I didn't realize that." She shook her head. "Well, that doesn't matter. I guess I ought to explain why I contacted you."

"Yes, I think you ought to."

"Curiosity. My grandmother was an escapee, too, just like you. And from America, too. I was looking at a list of the past year's escapees, and I noticed your last name and the fact that you were from America."

"My last name?"

"Yes. You see, I was very close to my grandmother before she died. That was when I was nineteen. She used to tell me about her life in America. We talked about it a lot. The government murdered her husband, my grandfather. They were betrayed by a man named Holroyd."

Jonathan felt dizzy and short of breath. "You're—" He gasped for air. "You're Cathy Martinson's granddaughter?"

Elena sat back, withdrawing from him. "Yes, that's right. That was her name. How did you know?"

"How did I know? Are you joking?" Jonathan stood up and walked around the room, too full of energy and emotion to sit still. "You look just like her when she was young! God, this is wonderful! She survived and reached the surface and had her baby. My grandfather was always sure she had died. Of course, that was because of the way he thought the surface was, and I thought he was wrong about that, and the government was wrong, but even so I just assumed she was dead, too, without really thinking much about it."

Elena had sat motionless, not saying a word, during his outburst, watching him expressionlessly. Now Jonathan suddenly became aware that she was holding in a great deal of pain and bewilderment. Overcome by a feeling of sympathy for her, guessing what she was feeling, he said gently, "Was that why you wanted to meet me? Because of what my grandfather did?"

"Yes." Her voice was tense and quiet. "Yes. I grew up hearing about the terrible thing he did to my grandparents. My grandmother taught me to hate him, and then when I saw your name and guessed that you might be related to him, I decided I ought to hate you, too, and I wanted to see what you looked like, what such people, the Holroyds, could look like."

"Cathy—I'm sorry, I mean, Elena. Listen. My grandfather never forgave himself for what happened. He told me he didn't want things to work out the way they did. He only turned your grandparents in to save them, because he thought that if they climbed to the surface, they'd die, because the government had told everyone that there was no air on the surface, and no heat. He turned them in to save their lives. He thought they'd be punished and then released, and that would still be better than suffocating and freezing to death."

She looked at him (his heart skipped a beat) and asked, "Why did you leave, then?"

Jonathan returned to his seat. "Because I was convinced your grandfather was right and the government was wrong." Then he told her about his long and painstaking work, first the search for the old tapes Henry Martinson had used and then the duplication of his work. "I always considered him my spiritual father." But he omitted the discovery that Henry Martinson had either been wrong in his predictions or had chosen to believe on faith that the surface was habitable—and had risked his wife's life on that tenuous basis.

"But you talked so understandingly about your grandfather just now."

"Yes." Jonathan paused, remembering his last meeting with his grandfather. "Yes. I didn't really understand him then, when I was still living in America. When I first learned about your grandparents and what he had done to them, I hated him for it. And I let him know it. It was only after I had come here, to the surface, that I began to think about him again and I remembered what he had said to defend himself. Also how worried he was that I would follow in Henry Martinson's footsteps and also be lost to him. I think I understand the old man now. I wish I had then. He loved both your grandparents, but especially Cathy. He had an old photograph of the three of them together, on vacation, when they were all young. About our age, I'd say. He showed it to me once. I wanted him to give it to me, but he wouldn't. It was all he had left of them."

"The poor man!" Elena said suddenly. Then she smiled. "My grandmother would have been horrified to hear me say that about Andrew Holroyd! Why did you want the picture?"

"Because I admired Henry so much and . . . and because I was in love with Cathy." He grinned. "I was a teenager, after all!" They both laughed. Jonathan added, "Do you realize that we're third cousins?"

Elena smiled happily at him, a wide, unrestrained smile that dazzled Jonathan. "I know. Isn't that nice? Welcome to Lander,

Cousin. It sounded like you haven't been happy here until now. Maybe things will start improving."

Oh, they will, Jonathan thought. They already have. It seemed to him that an impossible dream from adolescence had suddenly started coming true.

17

Meeting Elena, and the friendship that developed between them, made a great difference in Jonathan's life. Not that his circumstances were changed. He still spent his days reading and organizing the material that flowed in steadily from the Cold, and the ever-increasing number of crates of books and papers still seemed like a mountain that would someday topple over and crush him, intellectually if not physically. Except for Elena and, to a lesser extent, Francis K'ai-Tao, he still had no real friends. He still argued constantly (and usually unsuccessfully) with Jerza Norgaard, and he still felt discriminated against because he was an escapee. The difference was that now none of this bothered him very much.

Jonathan wasn't naïve. He understood perfectly well his own mental workings. He was in love, and love always makes the world new, bright, and shiny, with all problems minimized.

He was also a competent enough judge of the emotions of others to see that Elena was not in love with him. All he could do, he supposed, was spend as much time with her as possible, in hopes that constant exposure would make her friendly feelings deepen into something more passionate.

However, it proved difficult to spend as much time with Elena as he wanted to.

He would see her occasionally after work, by arrangement, and sometimes on weekends. Occasionally, she would show up at the University and persuade him to leave his work behind him and go to a park with her, or for a short hike in the countryside outside the city, or perhaps to an open-air concert or a theater performance. She seemed able to take time off whenever she wished from whatever it was she did; he never found out what that was. And she often had tickets even to events that had been long sold out. Jonathan didn't question his good fortune, though; he accepted the time with Elena as a precious gift from the God he still believed in.

The problem, though, was that she would disappear for weeks at a time, without warning or explanation, and with no message or forwarding code on her comm unit. He'd leave messages for her—one or two per day, artificially cheerful, disciplining himself not to call more often. And he never gave in so far as to go to her house in hopes that she'd be there. Suddenly she'd be back and would contact him again, still with no explanation, and certainly not with an apology. Jonathan knew better than to presume on their friendship—and endanger it—by demanding either.

Lander offered little in the way of entertainment. It was a small city, to begin with, and the population tended to an earnestness, a narrowness of purpose, a dedication to goals and work, which precluded much time being devoted to urban pleasures. Jonathan's pre-Taking ancestors would have dismissed Lander as provincial and dreary.

From Jonathan's point of view, though, what little the city offered was exciting and exotic, and he enjoyed sampling these delights in Elena's company. But eventually, as his agoraphobia wore off, it was the open spaces outside the city that intrigued and delighted him most of all. In this, he was becoming a true native: the citizens of Lander generally preferred being out of the city, enjoying landscapes and spacious views or exerting themselves on hikes or climbing mountains.

For Jonathan, there was an extra dimension to this preference.

Inside, whether in a theater or a restaurant, he might as well have been back in America. Outside, that depressing illusion was impossible. This was especially true outside the city, where the fields stretched away to the horizon, and overhead, instead of a rock ceiling only a meter or so above his head, were the infinite depths of the sky, blue with a lovely reddish tinge in the daytime, black and filled with stars at night. During the day, there was the huge, red ball of the sun. And, day or night, going through its phases, the moon.

Jonathan loved watching the moon most of all. It was the only object in the sky that was so clearly another world, a mottled, pockmarked sphere hanging in the sky. He would stare at it for long, endless minutes, time suspended, revelling in its beauty, its distance, its solidity, and most of all its attainability. There were men up there! Invisible to the eye, there were bases on the face of the moon, and men and women from Earth rocketed up there and back again. The idea inspired wonder and envy and deep satisfaction.

Elena found his fascination with the moon amusing. "It's just a place," she told him once. "Not all that different from here, you know. In fact, it's inferior in one way, because you can't just go outside and enjoy the breeze and the view, the way you can here. You have to suit up and everything. And inside, it's just like being inside a building here, except for the lower gravity. That's one thing I *do* like."

"You've been there?" Jonathan demanded. Elena had never hinted at that before.

"A few times," she said reluctantly. "My work takes me there. Come on, let's start walking again. I want to make some real distance before we turn back, and I don't want to be out after dark."

"Sure." It was an odd request, coming from her. Unlike everyone else he knew, Elena had less stamina than he did. Their walks in the countryside were usually cut short by her inability to go far. It was frustrating to him at times.

They went on. It was a mild and pleasant day. Jonathan felt invigorated, but he could tell that Elena was having increasing trouble. She was gasping audibly for breath. He thought of suggesting they turn back or at least stop for a rest, but he was hesitant, fearing she'd be insulted.

At last Elena stopped. "I'm sorry, Jonathan. I just can't go any further. Let's stop here."

They sat on the ground under the shade of a cottonwood tree, sitting side by side and leaning back against its wide trunk. They were both wearing hiking shorts. Jonathan stared with undisguised delight at Elena's pale, slender legs stretched out next to his. For a moment he contemplated doing or saying something to change the basis of their relationship—using this Heaven-sent opportunity to tell her how drawn he was to her. He imagined himself putting his arms around her small, slender body and drawing her gently to him, her arms sliding about his neck, her face turning toward his, her lips opening under his. . . .

"It's definitely getting warmer, these days," Elena said with a note of satisfaction. "I don't like the heat, but we're obviously doing the right thing with the sun. The climate's improving."

Jonathan could tell that the time was no longer ripe. "Doing the right thing with the sun? What do you mean?"

Elena's fatigue seemed to vanish. "You haven't been told about that? What do they teach you kids these days?"

Jonathan wasn't amused. "Not whatever it is you're talking about, at any rate."

Elena was full of enthusiasm. "You know all about T-band, don't you?"

Jonathan nodded. "That's how the gray hole was first detected, and supposedly the aliens used some sort of method of transporting mass based on the T-band idea to get it here."

"Very good!" Elena laughed at Jonathan's sour expression and pushed him playfully. "After the Taking, the people on the moon watched patiently while Jupiter and Saturn came together and coalesced into one gas giant. The new planet gave out some heat because of gravitational collapse, but not enough for all this." She gestured at the sunlit fields around them. Wildflowers bloomed off to their left; Jonathan could hear the hum of bees from that direction.

"Yes, they taught us all of that. There was disagreement among the astronomers on the moon about whether the new planet had sufficient mass for fusion to start. Gosh, just think," he said with relish, "the holy ancestors actually argued about something. I wonder if they ever came to blows?"

Elena's playfulness had vanished. She looked disturbed and uncomfortable. "Please don't talk like that, Jonathan."

It was the closing of another door, the foreclosing of a movement toward greater intimacy. Jonathan realized he'd best

not insult the lunar ancestors when talking with Elena, any more
than he would with any other surface resident.

He continued the conversation breezily, hoping to smooth over
the troubled moment. "But then fusion did start after all, and the
lunar colonists returned to Earth, and here we are. So what?"

Elena shook her head. "But it didn't just start—not by itself.
We had to help it along."

"A large undertaking," Jonathan said. Truly worthy of Zeus
and the other Olympians, he added silently.

"Yes, it was, of course," Elena said with returned enthusiasm.
"But that's just the sort of terrific thing they did in those days. We
had T-band radio, and we knew the aliens had some way of using
the same principle to transport mass. Well, we didn't know how to
do that. If we had, we'd have had interstellar travel, and we could
all have just migrated to some other solar system. What we were
able to do, though, was use T-band techniques to increase the
temperature and pressure in the core of the new gas giant and start
fusion going. We're still doing it, from the moon. That's what I
meant about the climate improving steadily. Someday, the Cold
will be no bigger than the Arctic and Antarctic regions used to be,
and the Earth will be just about the way it was, before the
Taking."

"Well, this time, let's not tell the aliens about ourselves, or they
may decide to take away the sun we have now." What Elena had
just described was an enormous achievement—worthy of Olym-
pian Zeus, indeed. Jonathan reluctantly admitted as much to
himself. Elena's ancestors and his had started off at the same level,
technologically, and yet his people had stagnated, while hers had
leapt to such breathtaking heights. Of course, the people on the
moon had in effect been selected for extremely high intelligence
and scientific and technological talent. But on the other hand, so
had the staff of the underground military establishment that had
become America. So, given that, why had the lunar settlers done
so much better than America had? Resources? Could that be the
whole explanation? Or was there some kind of innate superiority
involved—as with the schoolchildren who had outdone him in
everything?

Another thought struck him. "Elena, if your ancestors had been able to emigrate to another star system, maybe the world would still be frozen. I'd have died when I got out of America. So would your grandmother. And America would have been truly doomed."

"Hm?"

He realized that Elena had been dozing quietly in the pleasant, mild afternoon air. He repeated what he had said.

Elena sat up and stretched. Jonathan turned away because he was sure his yearning showed in his face. "America's doomed anyway," Elena said. "It can't go on much longer. I've seen the tapes."

The same phrase he had heard right after his rescue, from the woman on the airplane, and from Charlie Yang during the expedition to Montevideo! "Someone said something like that to me before. What tapes are you talking about?"

"Why, the recordings, I mean. The recordings from the cameras the American government has all over the place."

Jonathan knew about those cameras. "You have access to all of that?"

"Of course. You mean you didn't know? I thought everyone did."

Jonathan clenched his teeth. "Everyone except escapees, maybe. People don't like to tell *us* very much."

Elena patted his shoulder. "I know. It isn't really fair. Anyway, we like to keep track of what's going on in the underground countries, if we can. They all end up with the kind of government America has, even if they don't start out that way, so sooner or later most of them install spy cameras to keep watch on their citizens. All we have to do is locate any part of the communications system the cameras use and tap into it. The ones that are so badly off that they don't even have the cameras or the technical expertise to use them—well, those places go dark so quickly, we don't really have to bother with them."

"Go dark": it was a phrase whose meaning she did not have to explain to him.

"So I could possibly see myself on those tapes," he said

thoughtfully. "Or my grandfather. Or maybe even the Martinsons."

"No. I don't think the Americans had the cameras installed that long ago. I think they only go back about twenty-five or thirty years."

"I'd like to see them, anyway."

"Why? It would just depress you. Why bother with it?"

"I'm not sure. Maybe just to bring my family and friends back to life." Maybe to see myself, ten years ago, being shown the old photograph of Cathy Martinson for the first time.

Elena frowned. "Only a few authorized people normally see those things. And I don't know about letting you see America. How about something different, like Russia?"

"You mean, look at tapes from a bunch of Russians living underground? They survived, too?"

"That's right. Just like America."

Jonathan wore an expression of distaste. "Don't say that! Russians!"

Elena laughed. "Oh, that's right. I forgot about the kind of paranoia and nationalism they train into you, underground. I've seen—"

"The tapes. Right."

"Well, I *have*. They taught you that the Russians were responsible for what happened to the sun, didn't they?"

"Yes, that's right."

"But you know better now, don't you? You know about the aliens and what really happened. All that nonsense, you know, Jonathan—all that hatred of other countries and super patriotism and so on—all of that has no place up here. You should be beyond it by now."

"I think I am, by and large. But *Russians*!"

"Seems to me," Elena said, getting to her feet, "that you would benefit from seeing how the Russians really live underground. I'm going to look into this as soon as I get back."

Two days later, Jonathan received a message summoning him to a building in Lander to watch tapes from surveillance cameras in Russia. He didn't understand how Elena had managed to put her whim into action so quickly, or what the nature was of her official pull which this had revealed, but he knew he had to comply promptly with this order so thinly disguised as a request.

There was no overall plan to Lander, no thought-out system to its traffic flows or uniformity to its architecture. The city had grown randomly outward in all directions from the original landing spot of the first returning Lunarians. The landing point was thus roughly in the middle of the city, surrounded by grass and fences; it was perhaps the holiest place on Earth, as was attested to by the ever-present line of pilgrims from all over, waiting their turn to step on the steel plate marking the actual point of touchdown of the first pod. Steel tablets set in stone around it detailed the event and gave the date: 1ST GANYMEDE (28TH JULY), 2015.

Most of the buildings surrounding this park were government buildings. Jonathan's destination was a small, dingy building distinguished in no way from those around it. Inside, he found the air of purpose and efficiency and industry that seemed to characterize everyone in this world. He was greeted, registered, and quickly guided to a small room containing a chair, a control panel with a few buttons, a screen covering one wall, and a set of headphones.

The technician who had led him to the room was about to leave when Jonathan said, "Wait a minute! How do I work all of this?"

The technician stared at him for a moment, clearly astonished at his ineptitude. Then he said, "Real simple. I'll show you. You're cleared for the Russian tapes. Type in a date and a time, like this." He showed Jonathan how to do that on the console. "If there's anything within an hour of that, the computer will dig it out. If not, it'll tell you so with a message up there. Like this." He typed in the next day's date, and the large screen on the wall lit up with the message NOT AVAILABLE, in five-centimeter-high, blinking amber letters. "There's a default location—a camera from which the tape you get was recorded. And other defaults behind that, in case there's nothing from that camera near the time you asked for. Here's how you get a map of the Russian complex, with all the camera locations numbered on it." He entered a command, and the screen lit up with a complex gridwork, three dimensions cleverly represented in two, with different colors representing the different levels of underground Russia, and red dots to indicate the surveillance cameras from which recordings had been made.

"You can change to a tape from another camera by entering the camera's code, which is on the map right next to it, like this." The technician showed Jonathan the command. "And there's a manual in the drawer right in front of you, in case you want to experiment or you can't remember what I showed you. Also, wear the headphones for sound. I've set the computer to translate for you. I assumed you'd want the Russian translated into English?"

"Uh, yes." Jonathan was sure that the technician's bland expression hid contempt for this escapee inadequacy. Hell, I bet there aren't that many people on the surface who understand Russian, Jonathan told himself. But he suspected that he was wrong. "Well, I guess that's everything," Jonathan said with forced heartiness. "If I need any more help, I'll call out."

"Don't bother," the technician said. "I won't be available. If you need more help, read the manual." He left, closing the door behind him, and leaving Jonathan in the dead silence of the soundproofed room.

Jonathan shrugged, put on the headphones, and stared for a moment at the console. On a whim, he typed in 7 MAY 80, the date he had climbed into the ventilation shaft in Chicago. Then he caught his mistake, backspaced, and changed it to 4 UMB 80, and pressed the RETURN key.

The screen before him switched instantly from featureless gray to equally featureless black. Problems already, Jonathan told himself disgustedly, and pulled open the drawer containing the manual. But then a red glow began to grow in the center of the screen; it was pulsating or moving somehow. Jonathan stared at it, intrigued and disturbed: how he feared things that glowed red in the dark!

The glow continued to brighten, and as it did so, details became clear. And after a while, Jonathan realized what he was watching. It was an image of a heat pattern, perhaps taken with an infrared camera, and the moving glow was a couple making love in what they must have thought was the privacy of their darkened bedroom.

Jonathan looked away, embarrassed—not so much by what he was watching as by the fact that he was intruding *by* watching. But it all happened over a year ago, he told himself. It's not as if it's happening right now. That rationalization didn't help. He was still spying on someone else's intimacy, doing to these people exactly what had been done to him in America.

But they're Russians, he argued with himself. That struck him as ludicrous, and he laughed.

They finished making love, and only then did they talk to each other, in low, satisfied voices, and only then did Jonathan permit himself to look at the screen again.

He noticed a light switch on the wall next to the door. He stood up, stretched, and flipped the lights off. Then he sat down again and concentrated fully on the screen. In the dark, he could see the couple much more clearly. Even though the image must have been obtained in infrared, it was surprisingly clear, and it was even in color, a tribute (an annoying one, to Jonathan) to Russian engineering and computer science. The Russian couple was young—younger than Jonathan—and both blond, with a frail, wispy beauty. They called each other Petya and Julie. Jonathan watched them, suddenly entranced, drawn instantly into their lives.

18

Through the headphones, Petya and Julie spoke the mongrelized English of the surface. Unconsciously, as he did when speaking with Elena Simkin or anyone else on the surface, Jonathan mentally translated their words further into idiomatic American English— a habit which made it easy for him to forget that Julie and Petya were Russians. Only an occasional glimpse of Cyrillic script brought back to him what these people were.

The spy cameras weren't angled to let him read what Julie and Petya were reading. However, there were words and phrases painted on walls and doors everywhere. Jonathan could tell the signs were important by the lighting: the hallways were generally dim, while each sign had a spotlight shining on it. He wondered if the Russians weren't just as much in the habit of ignoring the signs as Americans were with the signs in their country.

Trying to follow Petya and Julie through their days, Jonathan quickly learned how to switch from camera to camera, calling up the map of Russia to get the reference numbers by which he specified which camera he wanted. Sometimes, a few lines of Cyrillic letters would appear on the bottom of the screen, stay there for a while, and then disapper. Only then would Jonathan remember that what he was watching was available to Russian government observers as well. The thought, when it occurred, disturbed him: it distressed him to think of Julie and Petya being subject to constant surveillance, and it made him feel uneasy to think that he was in any sense like those Soviet censors.

Of course, Petya and Julie didn't know they were being watched. They thought that what they did in the privacy of either's apartment really was done in privacy. From what they said to each other, Jonathan understood that theirs was a puritanical government, and that unmarried sex, in particular, was strictly forbidden.

But obviously the government *did* know what the young couple was doing. So why weren't Julie and Petya in prison? Or dead?

Jonathan finally concluded that the population of Russia was too low for the government to imprison or eliminate anyone with a valuable skill—at least, not for relatively minor crimes. Some principles, then, remained in the realm of lip service. In which case, the government of Russia was rather more flexible than that of America.

He was getting little sleep and often not remembering to eat. Toward midnight the cleaning crew would arrive and find him still at the console, switching cameras to follow Julie or Petya, or jumping forward to skip the time when they were at work or sleeping. The crew would remind him that everyone else in the building had gone hours ago, and Jonathan would rise from his chair still in a dream of other lives and walk slowly home through the dark streets.

He also neglected his work. But even though he knew that the boxes from the Cold were piling up outside his office door, he no longer felt any urgency about his historical work. Now he felt that the real answer—to a question he couldn't yet formulate—lay in vicariously living the lives of the two young Russians and not in studying the lives of people who had died before the Taking.

Uniforms were common in Russia, just as they were in America. It made Jonathan realize just how rare uniforms were on the surface—so rare that he wasn't sure he had ever seen one.

Julie and Petya wore uniforms themselves. At first, the Russian uniforms all looked alike to Jonathan, but after a couple of weeks he began to be able to tell them apart. Eventually, he realized, he would be as familiar with Russia as its own citizens were. He would be able to pass for a Russian, were he by some accident to find himself there. He didn't care for this thought.

Jonathan was surprised at how much entertainment seemed to be available to the two young Russians. The images of Russia Jonathan had been fed in school were of a land where it snowed all the time, where one third or more of the land surface was given over to vast prison camps for those who dared to complain or to question official policy, where weary old women with scarves on their heads painfully polished the escalator railings in the absurd Moscow subway, a nation whose people were afraid to talk to each other and who had nothing to do after their hours of backbreaking, inefficient work but drink vodka or deadly brandies. Food was notoriously inadequate in old Russia, but drink, so Jonathan had been told, was plentiful. Well, that was understandable: alcohol was the opiate of the people.

Underground Russia didn't quite jibe with that image.

He didn't see very many fat people; most of them had the sort of frail slenderness that had struck him immediately in the case of Petya and Julie. But Americans were rather like that, too.

Jonathan spent almost a full day searching through the map and trying all of the available cameras, looking for the prison camps, but he didn't find any. Must be a separate camera system, he reasoned. I just don't have access to those recordings.

Not that his old ideas were entirely wrong. It *was* snowing all the time now in old Russia. Jonathan laughed to himself.

In America, whole sections were dark because the lights had burned out and not been replaced. In Russia, there were no dark areas, which implied a work force constantly on patrol and equipped with replacements, which in turn implied either massive stores brought underground at the beginning or factories dedicated to producing such items. On the other hand, the lights in Russia were all dim, except for those aimed at the exhortatory signs. This implied to Jonathan that the Russian power source was less reliable or less constant than America's magma bubble.

Just what the Russian power source was, he began to suspect from the large number of Russians with strange, dark lumps on their faces, or those who walked slowly, weakly, and looked even paler and more fragile than their fellow citizens.

Julie and Petya didn't seem reluctant to talk to their friends, and their evenings were quite full. Some days after work they attended orchestra concerts. On other days, it might be a movie or a play, or they would spend a quiet evening together in his or her apartment reading and later making love (periods over which Jonathan would skip quickly). Very often, though, they would meet friends at a restaurant—and talk treason.

Clearly, they had not the faintest idea that anyone was watching them and listening to their conversations. They and their friends chatted, oblivious to Jonathan's phantom presence, and he felt insecure and jumpy for them, felt the fear they should have been feeling, the half awareness of someone watching over his shoulder. He had forgotten that feeling until now.

Their best friends seemed to be another young couple named Daniel Davidovich and Tashie. They were both taller than Petya and Julie, and they shared the other couple's fragile paleness. Tashie had black hair and pale skin, while Daniel was blond. (So many Russians *were* blond. Jonathan had been led to believe they were all short, dark, and ugly.)

Tashie was a romantic; Daniel Davidovich (he insisted on the second name, the significance of which escaped Jonathan) was a skeptic. Perhaps the word was "cynic": no matter what the other three might propose, Daniel Davidovich was ready to puncture their balloon. He went along on their adventures into distant parts of the Russian caverns, but always with a cynical smile on his face, as if to say, "This is all a foolish waste of time, but someone grown-up ought to go with you just to keep you out of trouble."

One day, Julie suggested escaping from Russia. Petya nodded his agreement; this was an idea they had discussed a couple of times before, in bed with their apartment. "We hate it here," Julie said fiercely. "We have to get out! We're going crazy down here."

Tashie gasped and said, "How exciting! Yes, we could all go!"

But Daniel Davidovich smiled his little smile and said one word: "How?"

"Ah! We've figured that out," Petya told him. "Or rather, Julie has."

"I certainly have," Julie said. "Look. When they first came down here, whenever it was—"

"Seventy-two years ago," Daniel Davidovich said promptly.

"Yes, all right. Anyway, we know they had enormous door-ways and ramps back then, because that was how they got all sorts of supplies and equipment down here, and also how they transported the people in."

"So?"

"So," Petya said excitedly, "it's all still there! It has to be. Yes, I know, you're going to say it's all sealed shut. But with so many different entrances as they must have had—"

"It must be possible to reopen some of them," Julie finished. Daniel Davidovich shook his head. "False assumption. Moreover, you can be sure that entire area is heavily guarded, just to make sure some idiots like you don't try to reopen the old doors. And a good thing, too."

Petya said, "Huh! I thought you were the one who was so anti-government!"

"It's nothing to do with being pro- or anti-government," Daniel Davidovich said with a shrug, "although if it comes to that, you know I'd prefer Ivan the Terrible to the men we have in power now. No, what I meant was that if anyone *did* succeed in opening one of the old doors, the rest of us would die along with him."

"Oh, I wish you wouldn't say things like that," Tashie said. "I think their idea is very beautiful, and you shouldn't say such things to spoil it."

"I'm not saying it just to spoil their idea, Tashie," Daniel Davidovich said, and for once, his mask of cynicism seemed to have disappeared. "We all learned in school what it's like outside, up on the surface of the Earth. There's no sun, so there's no heat, and the atmosphere is all frozen. It's too cold for life, and anyway, there's no air. If we didn't have our reactors for heat and electricity, and if our caves weren't entirely airtight, we wouldn't be able to live down here, either."

Without thinking, Jonathan leaned forward and said urgently, "No, no! Listen to Julie and Petya! They're right: you *can* escape, and you *can* live on the surface!"

Completely ignoring Jonathan's attempts to interrupt him, Daniel Davidovich concluded, "So you see, even if you could get past the guards and open one of the doors, all you'd accomplish would be to kill yourselves and, a few minutes later, everyone else in Russia."

For the moment, at least, that put an end to the discussion. The four of them talked about other things, but without any real enthusiasm. Suddenly, in the middle of a word, Tashie's voice cut off and the screen went blank.

Jonathan, thrown so rudely and suddenly from their lives, punched buttons angrily, trying to get the next recording. But then something penetrated his absorption. When Julie had not remembered how long it had been since the Russians had retreated underground, Daniel Davidovich had supplied the number: seventy-two years. But that was the case right now: it was 2081, seventy-two years since the Taking.

Jonathan reran the tape of the conversation in the restaurant, this time paying close attention to the Lander date and time displayed in the lower right-hand corner of the screen. At the moment the conversation cut off, the date was today's, and the time corresponded to the time on Jonathan's watch. And this time there was slightly more to the conversation. He had been spending so many hours skipping forward through the lives of the young Russians that he had at last caught up with himself: he was now watching the recording from the camera in the restaurant almost as it was being made. That conversation—and the laying of those vague plans to escape on the part of Petya and Julie—all of that was happening right now!

Jonathan raced from the viewing room. He had to find Elena right away.

Outside, it was noon. The change from the dimly lit corridors of Russia was startling. Jonathan stood in momentary confusion, staring at the stars shining brightly near the horizon, at the larger lights of the other planets near the zenith, and at the glowing ball overhead. The sun, he thought, and rebelled at the thought. But it isn't the sun! It was an inferior substitute, a minor, insulting, accidental gift from the aliens to the people whose civilization they had destroyed, whom they had doomed to a swift death on the surface of their world or a lingering one beneath it. They didn't mean to do even this much for us. It just happened.

He usually enjoyed the walk to Elena's house, but this time

Jonathan felt too obsessed with a sense of urgency regarding the young Russians to take the extra time. He hopped aboard one of the public trams when it stopped briefly near him and hastily made his way to a seat.

The tram accelerated suddenly, rising in the air and heading toward the central depot. There, Jonathan transferred to another one which would pass within a couple of blocks of Elena's house. It didn't occur to him how much at ease he had become with this transportation system—and how very much a citizen of Lander that implied he had become.

Doors were always unlocked in Lander, and Jonathan entered without knocking, too absorbed in his mission to think of such things. He found Elena seated before her comm unit. On the screen in front of her was the face of a heavy-browed, black-haired, middle-aged man with an enormous black beard. He was talking quietly, and Elena was nodding and making notes on a tablet in her lap.

Jonathan had never seen such a beard before. He came up behind Elena quietly and stood staring at the screen in fascination. Elena wasn't aware of his presence, but the man she was talking to looked over her shoulder at Jonathan. An annoyed expression crossed his face. He said, "Take care of your friend. Zavtra!" The screen went blank.

Elena turned around. "Jonathan! I didn't hear you knock."

"Um, I didn't. I'm sorry."

She looked annoyed, her expression like that of the man on the screen. "Do, in the future." When she was angry, she no longer seemed frail and in need of protection.

"I *am* sorry, Elena. But never mind about that, please. I've been watching the recordings from Russia for . . . I don't know how long. Weeks. Anyway, I just realized something about those people. They need our help." He paced about the room, while Elena watched him silently. "Christ, they're even worse off than we were in America. Their technology's falling apart faster, and it was probably inferior to begin with. They're practically living in the dark. You can see just from watching them that a lot of them have medical problems that their society can't treat. They're probably out of medicine or don't have the equipment anymore. And radiation poisoning! Jesus!" He thought of a man with a purple growth on his cheek and shivered.

"It's ridiculous—all those people down there, and we're up here, and all we do is study recordings of them instead of helping them! I even watched one young man and woman in Russia who were talking about escaping."

Elena nodded. "Good for them."

"No, it isn't! A friend of theirs pointed out that all the exits are probably heavily guarded. They could get themselves shot, or sent to . . . to whatever substitute they have for Siberia."

Elena frowned. "Siberia?"

"Never mind that." He waved his hand. "It's not important." I guess they'd have to escape from Russia to get to Siberia. The thought amused him, and he felt guilty at being amused. "The point is, there are all those people in Russia and America and whatever other underground refuges you people know about, and they're all in trouble, they're all suffering, and some of them are risking death to escape, and yet here we are up here on the surface, warm and safe, and we don't do anything to help them."

"What do you think we should do?"

"Rescue them," Jonathan said promptly. "Get them out, bring them up. The Russians and the Americans both have good communications systems inside their caves. We're already plugged into them, right? So we can just use that to communicate with them first, so that it wouldn't be such a shock—prepare them, in other words—and then we can start ferrying them out."

"You know the American government because you grew up under it," Elena said. "And by now you should know quite a bit about the Russian government. They both have their little empires. Do you really think either one of them would let its citizens go without a fight? How would you handle that?"

Jonathan shrugged. "Force, if necessary. It's the citizens that matter, not the government or its opinion. We outnumber them by five to one, right? We can get them out."

"Why?"

"Why? Are you joking? Because they're all in trouble, that's why! Because they're going to die if we don't. They're stuck down there under the ground because they think they can't survive up here, but we know they're wrong. They're only living underground because of a mistake, that's why."

Elena shook her head. "No, Jonathan. That's not a good enough reason. There are a few people on the surface who might agree with you and your misguided humanitarianism, but only a small minority. What you have to understand is that the people underground are there because they *chose* to be."

"Sure, at the time. At the time of the Taking, there wasn't any *other* choice. They either went underground or they died."

Elena nodded. "Seventy-two years ago. But what about since then? Why are they still there?"

"I already *told* you why!" Jonathan shouted. "They don't know any better! They assume things haven't changed on the surface. And it's a reasonable assumption given what they know. That's why we have to explain—"

"But you know better."

"No, I didn't. Henry Martinson figured it out. I just picked up on what he'd done. But anyway, I had special access to the old data. The ordinary man down there—"

"Is not the kind of man we want up here. We only want the extraordinary ones, the ones like you, the ones with the intelligence to realize what conditions are really like on the surface and the courage to escape. If that Russian couple you mentioned manage to get out, we'll welcome them with open arms."

Jonathan, remembering his own early treatment on the surface, thought, Like Hell you will. "What would you have done if you had been born in America, Elena? Your grandmother escaped, and you're living on the surface now because of *her* courage, not because of anything you did yourself."

Elena looked away. "She's proof that I have the right kind of genes."

"Jesus!" Jonathan muttered.

"Please go away now, Jonathan. I'd like to think about what you've said. And I need to comm a few people. I'll call you later."

Jonathan walked home. Rather suddenly, it seemed to him, he was no longer bothered by Elena's coldness. Without his being aware of it, he was at last being freed from his years-long worship of Cathy Martinson and his more recent subjection to her granddaughter. It wasn't that he was escaping by an act of will or desire; rather, a process was underway within him that asked neither his permission nor his cooperation.

Jonathan worked nonstop for the next week. The boxes shipped in from the Cold had indeed been piling up. But that was just as well: he needed something to occupy him fully, some task at which he could work to exhaustion, late every night, and beginning early again the next morning; it kept his mind off Julie and Petya and all the others like them—all those who would have to find their own salvation, with no help from the surface. He stayed away from the building where he had observed the Russians because he didn't think he could stand to watch them anymore, knowing that he could do nothing to help them.

But why not? he asked himself. Why should he wait for the surface government to decide officially to help the Russians or the Americans? He hadn't waited for the government to change its mind when he escaped from America. If he could find out where in the Cold the entrance to the Russian caves was, or find again where he had emerged from America, and if he could get his hands on an airplane with a sympathetic pilot, he could mount his own rescue mission. He knew it was a large undertaking, but he told himself that he was no ordinary man: he was an escapee. As Elena herself had said, that proved that he had extraordinary genes.

Jonathan had just reached this decision when Elena called. She was smiling and happy and friendly this time. "It's all arranged," she said. "We've got an expedition all set up to go down into a refuge in Asia. Japan, I think. Yes or no? I've got to have your decision immediately."

"Yes! Yes, of course! I—" But Elena, with a final grin, had blanked the screen.

This changed everything. He could forget his foolish plans for rescue missions. Clearly, the surface government had come around to his way of thinking.

And also clearly, Elena had important contacts within that government. If he wanted to influence the government, all he had to do was argue her around to his point of view. It was no longer a matter of his feelings toward her: Jonathan had to keep alive his friendship with her.

19

"You look different," Elena said.

"Travel is broadening."

"What?"

"That's an old saying. I came across it in one of the books from before the Taking. It means that if you travel all over the world, you encounter different cultures, and your outlook broadens and matures."

Elena frowned at him. "I don't understand."

"Well, now, first you have to understand that the world used to be covered with different cultures. Many, many different languages and religions and cuisines and so on. So those who travelled were exposed to all of this variety, and it had an effect on them. But where I come from, it isn't that way. It isn't that way in Russia, either. And it isn't that way on the surface, nowadays, is it? I mean, you all speak the same mangled English and you all dress the same and eat the same, and you all have the very same government, everywhere, no matter where you go, on Earth or on the moon. You *do* have racial differences, but those don't seem to bother anymore. You people don't give a shit about that. You all sleep with anyone."

"What's wrong with you?" Hurt had replaced the puzzlement.

"I've been travelling the world, as I said. I've been to the Cold, and I've been to Japan. Sort of, anyway. Hokkaido."

"Oh." Elena turned away from him and stared at the distant hills. Behind them, higher peaks were visible, snow covered, gleaming red in the noon sun.

"Yes, Japan. Romantic Japan, home of geishas and samurai and . . . whatever else. And lots of dead bodies."

Elena sighed and turned to face him. "I'm sorry if it was a shock to you, Jonathan. But you know how we feel about the people underground. Those Japanese refugees could have come to the surface, too, just as you did. Just as my ancestress did."

"I went to Sumatra, too," Jonathan said. "That was the staging point for the flight into the Cold, you see. It should have been exotic and Oriental, but the town we were in looked just like Lander, except smaller. Then we flew to Hokkaido and went down into what used to be a coal mine belonging to the Yamada Iron and Steel Company. The first thing we found was a body. The man had killed himself ritually by slitting his stomach right there near the exit. His face looked very composed. His name was Nikoya, which we know because he left a farewell statement in the computer. He was the last one to die in there. He was a very honorable man, I think. A hero, I'd say. I was told that we were monitoring their computer from the surface, and the expedition was delayed until we knew they were all dead. I thought it was a rescue mission, but the real purpose was just to loot the place. I wanted to be a rescuer, and I turned out to be a grave robber."

"Don't be melodramatic, Jonathan. It's all over now."

"It didn't have to be. We could have saved the last few of them, you know. Nikoya, at least."

"Like it or not, Jonathan," Elena said angrily, "that's the way things are. Your Nikoya didn't escape on his own, so that's the end of it."

"I think we've had this, um, discussion before."

"*I* think we should eat our sandwiches and head back to town."

They munched their picnic lunch for a while in a less than companionable silence. Jonathan was the first to speak.

"I suppose what really upsets me," he said thoughtfully, "is that it's all a *diktat,* not a vote."

"What are you talking about now?"

"You talk about the kind of people *we* want on the surface. But who decides that? Was there ever an election to decide what kind of people are wanted, or whether or not there should be rescue missions? Which brings up the next question: when was the government elected, and when's the next election? They never explained any of that during my training period, even though I asked a couple of times. I'm eager to vote."

Elena said harshly, "Don't try your fake ingenuousness on me. You understand the situation just as well as I do. The government we have isn't voted into office. We can't afford that luxury. Someday, when the Cold is gone and Earth is hospitable to mankind again, maybe then we can experiment a bit. Right now, though, we have to have a strong authority that can run things quickly and efficiently, without delays."

"Government by heroes," Jonathan said. "It's interesting: that's exactly the argument used by the government in America to explain why *they* don't have democracy, either. Someday, they always say."

Elena snapped, "We're not like your damned America! Not in any way!"

Jonathan stared at her wordlessly for a moment. "There were five hundred people in that Japanese refuge," he said. "I looked up the records. The American government condemns people to death, people like your grandfather, and executes them by dropping them through the force field into the magma, but I doubt that they've killed as many as five hundred people in all the seventy-two years America has existed. You people let five hundred Japanese die underground, when you could have rescued them. And you're willing to let thousands of Americans and Russians die the same way. And the others! The Chinese, the British, the French . . . ! My God, how many other refuges are there?"

Elena stood up. "I think it's time to go back to Lander."

Jonathan stood up too and caught her arm. "Wait a minute. I wanted to tell you something else." That I love you and I can't sleep for thinking about you. For a moment, he felt that his feeling for her was governed by laws as ineluctable as those which govern the movements of the planets.

"I mean I wanted to talk about something else," he amended, releasing her arm. They collected their belongings and began walking back toward town.

"The sun," Jonathan said, pointing upward at the glowing red ball that filled so much of the sky.

"That's what that is," Elena said, her voice filled with sarcasm.

"That's what it isn't. It's an inferior substitute. But that's not the point. The aliens took the sun in 2009. Okay. Then Jupiter and Saturn were drawn together by gravitational attraction, and the Earth was attracted to the combined planet and took up a new orbit around it. So here we are in an almost circular orbit with a radius of just about ten million miles and a year of three hundred and sixty five and a quarter days. Isn't that something?"

"No," Elena said with mixed annoyance and puzzlement, "that's the way things are. So what?"

"Only that that's the same as the orbital period before the Taking. I did a lot of calculations involving the Earth's orbit before I escaped from America. I was worried about how much effect there would be on my trajectory results if the history books were wrong about the date of the gray hole. I found out some interesting things. For example, in one year, the Earth's velocity vector moves through a full circle."

"That's obvious. So what?"

"Patience. For convenience, let's say a year used to be three hundred and sixty days. Now, that means that the direction of the velocity vector used to change by one degree each day. One degree! Back then, the closest Earth and Jupiter even came to each other was about three hundred and ninety million miles. At that distance, one degree translates to 6.8 million miles." The road they were walking down was sandy and unused. Dust hung in the air and drifted with the breeze. They were both sweating, and a fine layer of dust coated their skins. Elena looked exhausted, but Jonathan didn't notice.

"What I mean by that is that an angle of one degree subtends a distance of 6.8 million miles at a distance of three hundred and ninety million miles. Or another way of putting it is that if you try to aim at something three hundred and ninety million miles away, and you're off by one degree, you'll be off by 6.8 million miles in your aim. That's more than two thirds of the radius of our present orbit around the . . . sun. What you call the sun."

"This is really very boring, Jonathan," Elena said impatiently.

"It is?" Jonathan said. "I'm surprised you feel that way. *I* think it's fascinating. Don't you see? The gray hole *had* to come exactly when it did—and I mean virtually down to the second—for us to end up here. I don't know what its mass was, but if it had any significant mass, then it must have perturbed the orbits of the planets. And don't forget that the velocity vectors of Jupiter and Saturn had to be just right relative to each other, as well. It looks to me like the way the solar system looks now is the result of careful planning. Or incredible luck; too much luck for me to believe in it. What were the odds against the gray hole coming at just the right time and having the correct perturbation effect purely by chance?"

"What were the odds against the gray hole coming at all?" Elena said impatiently. "Things just worked out that way, that's all. Listen, Jonathan. I'm hot and I'm tired, and I don't feel like discussing any of this anymore."

They walked on in silence until they reached a transportation terminal, where Elena left for her house without saying goodbye. Jonathan watched the small capsule containing Elena and three others rise in the air, turn, and *wssh* away toward the center of Lander. *But there's so much more I wanted to say!* Jonathan cried out mentally. He commed her house the next day but only got a recording.

It took two days before Elena returned his call. During that time, Jonathan made half a dozen trips to Elena's house, but it always looked empty. Finally, on a Twoday, she called him.

"There's a concert tomorrow in Chicago that I really wanted to see. Would you like to go?"

"Chicago?" Jonathan experienced a moment of disorientation. Chicago was where his grandfather and the Martinsons had taken their vacation decades ago, in the threesome's youth; that was where the photograph of Cathy Martinson had been taken. But of course Elena was referring to the small city about five hundred kilometers from Lander.

"Are you there?" Elena said. "Where's your mind?"

"Travelling again. I'm sorry. Yes, I'd love to go."

How could he wait any longer? He had to tell Elena how he felt. Tonight, with the two of them travelling together in a two-man vehicle, would be a Heaven-sent opportunity. Jonathan could visualize the scene quite easily. He would slide his arm along the back of the seat. He would lean over Elena, his face moving toward hers. She would gasp faintly in surprise, then smile, then close her eyes in preparation, awaiting rapture. He would lower his mouth onto hers, gently parting her lips with his, and begin to make love to her while she moaned with pleasure.

It didn't turn out quite that way.

The floater in which Elena picked him up was tiny. Jonathan saw right away that making love in the confined space would be impossible for anyone who was normal-jointed. Even a kiss— casual or passionate—would be difficult. He decided to wait.

The concert was mildly interesting: a string quartet performing a composition called "A Death in the Cold," by one of the more respected current composers. Jonathan thought the title depressing if sociologically significant, and the music innocuous. The violinist, a young woman with hip-length, gleaming blond hair, fascinated him. His attraction to her made him feel guilty.

On the way back to Lander, while Elena rattled on excitedly about the evening's performance and the delights of the music, Jonathan studied her profile while she drove. The beautiful violinist was forgotten. How lovely Elena's profile was! Had Cathy Martinson looked as good from this angle?

"Don't you agree?" Elena said, grinning her enthusiasm at him.

"Absolutely," Jonathan said, utterly ignorant of what she had been referring to. *Whatever you say. For the rest of my life.*

She grounded the floater in front of Jonathan's apartment building. "Thanks for coming with me. I hate going to those things alone, but I didn't want to miss it. Wasn't it wonderful?"

"Wonderful's the word," Jonathan agreed, putting his left hand out to stroke her hair and leaning toward her.

"Jonathan! What are you doing?"

And I thought I was naïve! "Kissing you. Trying to."

"My God, we're cousins! Are you crazy?"

He drew back. "I don't think I see the connection. We're

cousins, and I want to kiss you. I want to make love to you. I want to spend my life with you."

Elena sank back against her side of the cabin. "Oh, no, Jonathan! How can you say such terrible things?"

"Terrible? What's terrible about it? I'm completely in love with you, Elena. You're the woman I dreamed about all my life. I found you, and now I want to marry you. What's crazy about that?"

"But, Jonathan, we're *cousins*!"

"So what? My parents were brother and sister. Who cares? I don't. Let's not waste any more time, Elena."

"Oh, God!" Elena moaned. There was horror on her face. "Get out, right now!"

Numbly, Jonathan obeyed. He stood on the cool, springy moss and watched Elena's floater hum off the ground and flee down the street. I repelled her, he kept thinking. Why? He could understand none of it.

The next morning, Jonathan tried to contact Elena. There was no reply from her house, and since he had no idea where she worked (or, for that matter, what she did), he knew no other comm code he could try in an attempt to reach her. He left a message for her to call him and tried to turn his attention back to his work. Fifteen minutes later, he commed again, but there was still no reply. He kept trying throughout the day. Every time he called, there was no reply. Each time, he left a message, aware as he did so of the increasingly pleading tone in his voice.

A week passed without a word from Elena, without a hint of her existence. Jonathan realized belatedly that they had no common friends, so that he couldn't even try to find her through that route. For Jonathan, Elena Simkin had vanished from the face of the Earth.

As offhandedly as he could, Jonathan asked Francis if he had ever been romantically attracted to a cousin or other female relative. Francis reacted with horror to the suggestion. "Are you joking? What an awful thing to say to me! Of course not! Why do you assume I'm a pervert?"

Hastily, Jonathan explained the moral code of America.

"Your parents are *brother* and *sister*?" Francis repeated in disbelief, pushing his glasses back up on his nose. "That's *awful*!"

"So it's not acceptable here, in other words."

"Not acc— That's putting it mildly! Why do you think we maintain such careful genealogies here? It could happen without your knowing it, since the population is still so small and we're all descended from the two thousand people or so on the moon, so before you even so much as approach a girl, you check into both your ancestries, just to make sure you're no closer than sixth cousins."

"Must cut down on your options a lot."

"It's tricky," Francis admitted. "But it's worth the trouble, isn't it? I mean, to ensure against . . . against incest." He looked slightly ill at the word. "Anything's better than that."

The next day, Jonathan received a call from Jerza Norgaard.

Just what I need, he moaned to himself as Norgaard's perpetually angry face appeared on the screen on his desk. "Yes, Jerza?" he said sweetly. "Feeling hostile and in need of a punching bag?"

Norgaard scowled and muttered something unintelligible.

"I've missed you too, Jerza."

Norgaard's scowl deepened. "I've got a new, temporary assignment for you. It just came through from Mendeleev, so there's no arguing with it. We've got three new escapees coming here this afternoon, and instead of sending them through the usual orientation and training, we're assigning them to you for a few weeks. You're going to show them around and educate them in the way things are here. Teach them everything you know, which should take care of the first day. Any questions? Good. Be here at fourteen."

Mendeleev: the magic word. An order from the moon base was like an edict from God. Perhaps Elena could get him released from this pointless obligation, if he could find her. He put in a quick comm to her house, but still with no success. Jonathan shrugged and tried to get back to his work.

*   *   *

He reached Jerza's office a few minutes before fourteen o'clock.
It was empty. He strolled about looking at the framed photographs
on the walls. Most of them were beautiful landscape scenes, many
from the Cold. There were also a few close-up shots of flowers,
and one ancient painting, possibly pre-Taking, depicting imposs-
ibly furry baby rabbits with sweet expressions and enormous eyes.
He had never noticed these wall decorations before. They were
jarringly at odds with his perception of Jerza's character.

Jonathan had just reached that conclusion when Jerza Norgaard
herself entered the office. She saw Jonathan already there and
looked surprised. "Didn't think you'd show up," she muttered.
She turned and waved the three people behind her into the office.
They entered uncertainly, watching her fearfully, as if they didn't
know what to expect from her. They saw Jonathan and looked
even more nervous.

At the sight of them, Jonathan gasped in surprise, then grinned
delightedly and stepped forward, his hand out. "Julie! You made
it! And you brought Tashie and Daniel Davidovich with you!"

The three young Russians looked up at him openmouthed.

"But where's Petya?" At his question, Julie burst into tears,
and the other two put their arms around her comfortingly and
glared at Jonathan.

"How did—" Jerza said. "Oh, yes, that's right. I remember
seeing the records. Were these the people you were spying on?"

"Observing," Jonathan corrected her. "There's supposed to be
a fourth one with them, a young man."

Jerza nodded. "Yeah, I know. The girls speak a little English,
and I speak a little Russian. The boy doesn't talk at all. I bet you
don't know a word of Russian, right?"

"Right, I don't."

Jerza said, with the contempt Jonathan was used to hearing in
her voice, "Of course not. Anyway, if I understood it all correctly,
that kid's boyfriend was shot while they were getting away, and he
died before they could reach the surface."

"Oh, no!" Jonathan felt as if he had lost a dear friend.

"It's your problem now, Holroyd. Get them out of here. Wait.

Take this. It's their authorization for quarters." She held out a computer wafer.

Jonathan managed to get the three of them across Lander to the rooms that had been assigned to them. They travelled by public tram, and all the way, Jonathan kept up a rattle of nervous chatter, telling himself he was trying to calm them with all the words they couldn't understand, but in reality trying to calm himself.

It was the strangest experience he had had since his escape. He kept thinking the three young Russians knew him. In his memories of them, he was a part of their group. He had to consciously remind himself that he had been watching them on a screen, and they had had no awareness of his presence.

In the flesh, they were all both smaller and frailer than they had seemed on the screen. Julie, in particular, shrunken in grief, seemed almost like a child. And he was struck by her resemblance to Elena. This was something he had not even noticed while watching her on the screen.

While Jonathan kept up his stream of nervous talk, Daniel Davidovich muttered something to the other two. Even though Jonathan didn't understand what he said, he did catch the word *Amerikanyetz*. This was followed by hostile glares from both Daniel and Tashie. Julie seemed still too sunk in grief to pay much attention to her fellow Russians or to Jonathan.

Jonathan wondered if these three had been brought up to hate Americans just as much as he had been brought up to hate Russians. Watching them live their daily lives had helped him overcome those atavistic feelings. Not so with them: whatever myths they had been fed, they probably still believed.

How often, while watching them, he had wanted to say something to them, to become a part of their conversation! And now they were here with him, in the flesh, and he couldn't talk to them because of their xenophobia and because of a language barrier that hadn't existed when he'd watched them on the screen.

Give them time, he cautioned himself. It had taken him long enough to get used to this new world. And Julie had her tragedy to overcome. Jonathan hadn't had to cope with leaving behind a dead lover. He wondered if he'd ever have one on the surface.

20

One morning, Jonathan commed Jerza Norgaard and told her he thought the three Russians were finished with their orientation and training and were ready to begin working. "Especially the girl, Julie."

"She's the one whose boyfriend was killed?" For once, Norgaard was almost civil.

"She's the one. She's right on the edge, but I think that we can save her with the right kind of work. It's the only thing that makes her react normally—when I ask her a question in her field. History of science."

Nogaard nodded. "Okay, I'll see what I can do about it. Good job, Holroyd." She disconnected.

"Son of a bitch," Jonathan muttered. Next he commed Daniel Davidovich's room. Tashie answered, and he told her they had the day off. "I'll pick you up tomorrow morning," he told her. "There's a park I want to show you. Today . . . I have to do some other things today."

Tashie smiled at him. "Okay, Jonathan."

And in fact, Jonathan did go to his office at the University. He hadn't been there for weeks—ever since the three Russians had been assigned to him—and he wanted to deal with the inevitable backlog of boxes. Jonathan worked with a fierce determination. He skipped lunch, working into the afternoon, getting dusty and sweaty.

Early in the afternoon, he was interrupted by a comm call. It was from Elena, at last.

"Elena!" Jonathan said as soon as her face formed on his screen. "Where are you?"

"At work, of course."

With the man with the black beard? Jonathan felt consumed with jealousy. Was that the real problem? Was he competing with that older man, not with Elena's fears of incest? "Yes, but where—"

"Just listen, Jonathan. I don't have much time. I've just heard what a good job you've done with the three Russians. I knew you'd pull it off. Isn't Julie beautiful?"

"So you *did* have something to do with this assignment! I was wondering. Julie's beautiful, yes. You know about Petya, her boyfriend, don't you? I suppose you know everything about them."

"I know quite a bit about them," Elena said. "It's a very sad story. I feel terribly sorry for her. What she needs now is someone else to love, to try to take her mind off what happened."

"Yes, I know, I've thought about that, too. Listen, Elena, where are you, exactly?"

"I may be able to come down there next week for a day or two. I'd like to meet her."

"Who?"

"Julie, of course. I'm glad you've been thinking about what she needs. She's so beautiful, it would be such a shame if she never found anyone else."

"I don't know what her being beautiful has to do with that, but I agree it would be a terrible shame." Jonathan had the feeling there were two separate conversations underway, his and Elena's—that they only seemed to be talking to each other. "Elena, I don't think we're communicating properly."

"It's hard by comm," Elena agreed. "If I can get down there next week, we'll be able to talk more easily. I'm looking forward to meeting Julie. Take good care of her, and be especially kind to her. I'll see you both soon."

She disconnected before Jonathan could say anything more. The call had left him feeling more frustrated then ever.

It was Julie who made the connection for Jonathan.

He was strolling through the holy grounds of the park at the center of Lander with them and telling them about the ancestor worship of the world they all found themselves in. "But they aren't quite as superior as they like to think," he confided. This, he thought, was not the sort of lecture they would have received in the standard course of orientation and training! "For example, they're still behind in chemistry. In the other sciences and in technology, yes, they do well. Of course, a lot of that's due to old technology they've uncovered in the Cold and refurbished. But chemistry is the exception. I suppose it's because that's one science that needs specific materials, and most of the deposits where the stuff used to come from are still covered with ice."

"And," Daniel Davidovich added smugly, "there aren't enough Russians up here. Chemistry is a Russian science."

"What?" Jonathan said angrily. "What are you talking about? It's American. All modern science is."

"Mendeleev," Tashie said. "Periodic law. Periodic table of elements. Basis of everything."

"Men—" Jonathan no longer noticed the smugness on either face. "Mendeleev?" he repeated.

Tashie nodded. "Famous Russian scientist."

Julie spoke up, her interest aroused by her favorite subject. "Big crater on back of moon named Mendeleev, after Dimitri Ivanovich Mendeleev. Same man."

"Yes, of course," Daniel said. "That's where the big international observatory was, before the Taking."

"Where you said the orders come from," Julie said.

"Damn it," Jonathan muttered, "why didn't I make the connection? Excuse me." Jonathan started running, leaving the three Russians standing in the park and staring after him in surprise. Mendeleev: where else could Elena work? That was why she seemed to have so much influence. And she had mentioned having been on the moon. There were other little things, too, that all suddenly seemed to click into place.

It isn't always true, Jonathan felt, that absence makes the heart grow fonder. Sometimes absence makes the heart forget. He had missed Elena terribly for the first week or two, but by now he was aware that the ache was fading, that he had to consciously massage it back to proper painfulness every now and then. People had to see each other regularly in order to maintain a relationship, he thought. That was a problem in this world, where it was possible to meet someone once and then never see her again for the rest of one's life. How different from America, where one saw the same people over and over and over, until one could scream with irrational fury at the sight of them.

There was a public comm set not far from the boundaries of the park. When he reached it, he had to stand hanging on to it for a few minutes, gasping, until he could breathe more normally again. Finally he punched the assistance code and waited impatiently for the computer-generated helpful face to materialize on the screen.

It was a female face this time, a young woman with a mass of curly black hair framing her head and, to Jonathan's distaste, dark brown skin. He reminded himself that this was only a fictitious person created by a computer, or perhaps a recording of someone real who might by now be retired or even dead of old age. And he admitted grudgingly to himself that he found the black woman attractive, but that didn't help quell his reaction; perhaps it made it worse. "I'd like to comm Mendeleev, please," he said with cool politeness.

"Certainly, sir. Your access code, please?"

"My what?"

There shouldn't have been suspicion on a fictive face, but there was. "Your access code, sir. Mendeleev is restricted, and you cannot place a call there without a proper access code."

Now what? "Um, Simkin. Try Simkin." He spelled it out.

"Thank you, sir." The face froze into immobility as the computer turned its attention elsewhere.

Testing the woman's reality, Jonathan said casually, "You certainly are pretty. How about dinner with me sometime?"

A surprised smile crossed the face on the screen. "Why, thank you, sir. But we're not allowed to date customers. I think your call's going through now, sir." Her face vanished, leaving Jonathan no wiser than before. Was the computer playing a game with him, or going to extreme lengths to maintain the illusion of a human operator? And if she was real, did that mean that he had really just asked a black woman for a date? He felt a tingle of excitement.

Then another face formed on the screen. It was that of the black-bearded man Jonathan had seen Elena comming. The man stared at him in surprise. "You! How did you get through to me?"

Despite himself, Jonathan felt cowed by the man's heavy brows, fierce eyes, heavy face, and deep, powerful voice. "Uh, I was actually trying to reach Elena."

The bearded man suddenly drew back from the screen and laughed. "Tyen!" he shouted. He leaned forward and aimed his intimidating gaze at Jonathan again (but he was smiling this time) and said, "You surprise and impress me, young man. I'll put you through."

His face disappeared, and after an interminable wait, Elena's face formed in front of Jonathan. She stared at him wordlessly for a long moment. At last she said, "Dad said it was you. What do you want, Jonathan?" Her voice was cool, her expression closed.

Elena's father! Jonathan managed to cover up his surprise. Thank God he liked me. "I've missed you, Elena."

Elena's face softened. "I've missed our picnics, too, Jonathan. I've been working very hard up here. No time for breaks. I certainly haven't had any time for male companionship."

"Do you still plan to be here next week?"

"I don't know. I may have been a bit hasty when I said that. What I'm doing now is open-ended. It could be next year."

"Next year! I—"

Elena interrupted. "How are your three Russians coming along?"

"They're fine. They don't need me anymore. All they need is more practice with English. The two women, anyway. Daniel's English is very good, for a Russian. They've got good training, good schooling. We can probably find useful jobs for them."

"How's Julie doing? Have you been following my advice?"

"Julie. She's . . . recovering slowly. Give her time. They were very deeply in love. It's very tragic." Watching Elena's lovely face, Jonathan felt all his feelings for her grip him again at full strength, and his pity for Julie knew no bounds. How awful, he thought, to irretrievably lose the one you love, with no hope of regaining her! "I wouldn't call her beautiful, but she *is* pretty.

Maybe eventually she'll find someone here, and then she'll be able to recover." Can you replace a lost, true love with someone else? he wondered. Not easily, and never fully.

Elena was looking at him intently. "She's some sort of historian, isn't she? Maybe she should be assigned to work under you. Someone she knows and trusts—that should help her even more, as she learns to fit into our world."

"History of science. Not quite the same thing. Still, it's not a bad idea. I've already spoken to Jerza the Cow about it."

Elena giggled. "Jonathan! Jerza gets the job done; that's what counts. Anyway, don't bother. Just hold on." She looked down, and Jonathan could tell she was typing something on the keyboard below his vision. She looked up, seemingly past his left shoulder, frowned, looked down, and typed again. Then she looked up again, over his shoulder, and nodded in satisfaction. She looked at him. "All taken care of. Julie's all yours, as of tomorrow morning. Do what you want with her."

Was she leering at him? "Oh, by the way," he said casually, "I've got a problem with my work. Maybe you can help. I can't bridge the gap between the period just before the Taking and the recolonization of Earth. I need to know what happened on the moon during that time."

"It's in all the history books."

Jonathan snorted. "Mythology, Elena! I don't want that. I need to know what really happened. I need the original sources."

"I don't see how I can help you."

Jonathan hesitated only a moment before he said, "The original sources aren't available anywhere on Earth. I've already checked. There aren't many places such things are stored, down here. If the sources exist at all, they must still be up where you are, at Mendeleev."

Elena was shocked. "You want to come here? To do *history* research?"

Jonathan suppressed his anger. "If that's the only place I can do my work properly, why shouldn't I go there?"

Elena said doubtfully, "No one's ever come up here for that

kind of reason before. I'll have to think about it and call you back. This evening. Where will you be? Your own place?"

Now Jonathan's suspicion became a certainty. "*Yes*," he said firmly. "At my own place. No one else's."

Elena looked disappointed. "I'll leave a message, if you're not." The screen became a featureless gray again.

When Jonathan told Julie she was assigned to work under his direction and would be starting the next moring, she reacted with her usual apathy.

Daniel Davidovich listened to Jonathan's announcement and look suspicious. He asked, "What about the two of us? We're ready to work, too."

Jonathan hesitated. He couldn't put Daniel off by saying he needed to learn more English—or even by saying that Tashie did, because in that case, what about Julie? "You're right," he said at last. "Tomorrow afternoon we'll go see Jerza Norgaard. Remember her? You'll get along well. She loves escapees."

That evening, Elena called Jonathan at his apartment. He had eaten a light supper and was relaxing with a novel retrieved from the Cold. Fiction scarcely existed in America, and what there was tended either toward the childish or the didactic. This book was quite different. It involved furious action and love and space travel and time travel and political assassinations. Jonathan had tried to rationalize the reading of novels as part of his work: fiction provided a picture of how people had lived in pre-Taking days. But how could he pretend that the outlandish action in the novel he was reading had anything at all to do with the real past? It was a moral dilemma, which Jonathan resolved by losing himself in the story. When the comm set beeped at him, he felt annoyed at the interruption.

But when he saw Elena's face on the screen, his annoyance vanished.

"Hello, Jonathan," she said. "I've managed to do it for you. Three weeks from now, you can come up to Mendeleev. I'm sending you the authorization and travel vouchers; all the dates are on those. You'll have a full two weeks up here."

"Two weeks! I'll probably need a few months!"

"Be thankful you got even this much," Elena said, looking hurt. "You don't have any idea what I had to go through even to get this. Your reasons for coming are completely outside the normal bounds."

Jonathan broke the rule he had been successfully imposing on himself for quite some time. He said, "Sounds more like America all the time."

Elena, instead of getting angry, grinned at him. "You really like to think that, don't you? I'll see you when you get here. I'm too busy to spend much time comming nowadays. Take care of Julie. She needs your help." Once again, as her face faded from Jonathan's screen, he could have sworn Elena was leering.

21

The paperwork arrived the following Oneday, and the next three weeks seemed interminable. During that long wait, Jonathan tried manfully to help Julie, but he was constantly distracted, his mind a quarter of a million miles away. He found himself apologizing frequently to Julie for his inattentiveness, for having to ask her to repeat her questions, for not having gotten some information he had promised to find for her. Her hurt expression bothered him, but her obvious sudden romantic interest in him bothered him even more.

At last the third of Ariel arrived. Jonathan sent a very brief message to Elena: "See you in a few days. I love you. Let's get married." Then he left short and cheerful good-bye messages for Julie and Francis K'ai-Tao and his few other acquaintances and took a public tram heading west up the Long Valley toward the shuttle port. It was a ten-minute trip from Lander, but even that seemed to take forever; the closer Jonathan got to Mendeleev, the longer the delays seemed to be.

He tried to make himself enjoy the beautiful weather. On the eastern horizon, the giant red sun glowed in a ruddy blue sky. Ahead of Jonathan, stars twinkled brilliantly. The city and the rising land beyond it, to his right, glowed red in the sunrise.

The tram rounded a small hill, and the port came in sight. Standing on the runway, gleaming in the sunlight, was one of the sleek, triple-bodied shuttles. Blue vapor clouds rose from the tail of the lowest and largest of the craft's three fuselages. Jonathan's heart hammered madly; he could hardly breathe. This was it! This must be the spaceship he would ride upward, away from Earth, into space for the first time in his life!

The tram came to a stop. Jonathan dragged his single suitcase from beneath his seat and stumbled off the tram to the ground. He was scarcely aware of what he was doing, oblivious to his surroundings except for the waiting shuttle. His eyes fixed on the beautiful spacecraft, Jonathan began walking across the ground toward it.

Someone grabbed his arm and held it in a painful grip. Jonathan looked around and found himself staring up at the annoyed face of a huge, uniformed black man. Jonathan disengaged his arm. "Yes?"

"Your papers," the black man said impatiently.

"Oh. Right." He fumbled in his shirt pocket and brought out the small packet he had received. "Hurry, please. I don't want to miss the shuttle." A cool breeze had sprung up, blowing down the Valley from the west. A cloud drifted across the face of the sun, throwing the entire shuttle port into shadow.

The black man smiled faintly. "Varte noor, varte noor. Shuttle won't leave without you, if you're authorized."

Speak English! Jonathan wanted to shout. He felt at that moment that he had endured these people's pretentious quirks up to and beyond the limits of his patience.

The uniformed black man passed a small wand over Jonathan's papers. The instrument produced a harsh squawk. The black man frowned and tried again. Again there was the squawk. He looked up at Jonathan and shook his head. "I'm sorry, but these aren't acceptable."

"What are you *talking* about?" Jonathan cried. After all this waiting, was he to be thwarted by this primitive flunky? "Those were just sent to me a few weeks ago, straight from Mendeleev. How can anything be wrong with them?"

At Jonathan's mention of Mendeleev, the black man's manner changed abruptly. "I'm very sorry, sir," he said respectfully, "but the computer just isn't accepting your papers. This gadget"—he held up the narrow, pencillike wand—"doesn't give me any more information than that. If you'd like, you could go across the field to the flight office. They can probably call up a detailed display for you there."

"Jesus!" Jonathan muttered. "All right, all right. Just make sure that shuttle doesn't leave without me." He started walking toward the building the black man had indicated. The air seemed colder than ever, but he began to sweat and his suitcase grew heavier as he walked.

Just as he reached the door of the flight office, there was a rumbling thunder behind him. He spun around. The shuttle was moving across the great open space, slowly at first and then ever faster.

The rumble became a deafening roar. The shuttle's rear end, pointed toward Jonathan, was a glowing red star surrounded by clouds of smoke and dust. Suddenly the vehicle leapt into the air and accelerated still more. The sound faded slowly. The red star dwindled to a point of light above the horizon.

Then the star split into two, one of them dropping toward the ground, the other moving upward, even faster. It was no longer visible when the third stage separated and ignited and the second dropped back to Earth.

Jonathan watched until he could see and hear nothing. At last, filled with an aching loss, he turned away from the field and pushed into the flight office.

The short, dusky-skinned woman behind the counter wore a uniform similar to that of the black man who had stopped Jonathan at the shuttle, but she was much more sympathetic. She invited Jonathan to come around the counter and watch the screen of her console himself while she entered some of the numbers from his flight authorization. The screen filled with various numbers and abbreviations, but one line, in the very middle and highlighted, caught Jonathan's eye immediately: CANCELLED BY ORDER OF E. SIMKIN, it read.

The face of the woman who was helping him filled with awe. "Sorry, sir. We can't do anything when it's *that* name."

Numbly and slowly, Jonathan left the flight office and caught a tram back to Lander.

By the time he got off the tram in the city, Jonathan knew what to do.

He went to his office as usual and pretended to work. Long after most of the others on his floor had left for the day, Jonathan was still there. Well after dark, Francis K'ai-Tao stopped at Jonathan's office to exchange a few pleasantries. Finally, Francis left.

Jonathan waited an extra half hour, and then he rose slowly from his chair and stretched to combat the stiffness and walked down the hallway, checking carefully. All of the offices were empty. He entered Francis's cramped office, closed the door quietly behind him, sat down at Francis's terminal, and turned it on.

He entered Francis's access code and user number and was rewarded with a line across the top of the screen which read LOAM OPERATING SYSTEM, VERSION 2.6, JAN. 2006. Jonathan smiled happily and set to work.

He spent the rest of the night writing and testing a sequence of short programs. It was almost daylight before he was satisfied with what he had done. Then he started the first program running in batch mode on the old Rockway computer at Mendeleev, logged off, turned off Francis's terminal, and went home.

Jonathan's comm set awoke him just before noon. The caller was a woman of around Jonathan's age; her face and voice were unfamiliar, but Jonathan found both charming. "Mr. Holroyd? Jonathan Holroyd?"

"That's right."

"My name is Connie Allendorf. I'm calling from Mendeleev. We're having a real problem with one of the old computers we have up here, and we don't have anyone qualified to look at it. The Admin. People at Lander gave us your name as something of an expert on these old machines. If you have the time, we'd really appreciate some help."

"Tell me the details."

"I'm afraid I don't really know any of them. All I've been told is that something's looping, and we can't reboot."

"Did you try simply turning the machine off?"

"We did power down, but then when we started everything up again, it still behaved the same way."

Jonathan managed not to grin. "That's a weird one, all right. Looks like I'd have to come up there and take a close look."

Allendorf hesitated for a moment. "I might have a bit of trouble arranging that."

"Well, I just don't see how much good I can do from a quarter of a million miles away."

"I'll have to call you back." She disconnected.

Jonathan had a shower, whistling all the while, and went to the nearest cafeteria to have a lunch that would serve as his breakfast. Shortly after he returned, his comm set chimed again. It was Connie Allendorf once more.

"All arranged," she said cheerfully, with an engaging smile. "How much time do you need to get ready for the trip?"

Jonathan frowned as though in deep thought. "Let's see," he said abstractedly. "Packing, winding up projects, arranging for someone else to take over something for me. Oh, I'd say I can be at the shuttle port in an hour."

Connie's mouth opened, then closed. Then she said, "If you say so. They'll be expecting you. I'll meet you when you arrive at the base and take you to Mendeleev."

"I look forward to seeing you in person, Connie. Good-bye."

She smiled at him. "Good-bye . . . Mr. Holroyd."

It was an invigorating challenge. Suddenly Jonathan felt as if nothing could stand in his way.

22

"The moon," Jonathan breathed. "My God, I'm on the moon!"

"Watch it, sir."

Jonathan turned around, the motion making him rise in the air. Two men were guiding a wheeled cart loaded with luggage across the open space, and he was in their way. "Sorry." He stepped aside.

The motion, however, sent him skimming two meters over the dirt floor. He landed, surprised and off-balance, and began to topple over slowly, sideways. He tried to twist himself, during his slow-motion fall, so that he could gracefully get his feet under him before reaching the ground, but he managed only to land on his face instead of his side. He picked himself up with enormous care, regaining his feet successfully at last, and began to slap the fine dust from his clothes and face.

He discovered that the two men with the wheeled cart had stopped to watch him, and both were grinning. "Welcome to low-g!" one of them called out. They both laughed, and so did various other people Jonathan now realized had been watching him.

"Mr. Holroyd!" It was Connie Allendorf.

"Thank God," Jonathan said. "Get me out of here."

"I'm afraid it's the same all over the moon," Connie said. "Same gravity everywhere. The only way around it is to wear weighted clothes and shoes to bring your weight up to its Earth value. Some people do that."

"Sounds like a good idea."

She shook her head. "No, it isn't, because they never adjust. They become completely dependent on the added weight. They can spend years here without ever learning to handle themselves under lunar gravity. Don't do that to yourself. Low-g can be fun. You shouldn't deprive yourself of it."

Jonathan looked her over carefully. She had pale skin and

201

almost black hair, cut very short and very thick and glossy. She was a small, wiry woman, considerably shorter than Jonathan—which was always a relief to him, these days. She was considerably more attractive than she had seemed on the comm screen. She had a surprisingly large mouth, filled with large, strong teeth. Her friendly, we-share-a-secret grin strongly implied what some of the pleasures associated with low-g were, and Jonathan found his mood brightening immediately.

"Tell you what, Connie," he said, "I'll reserve judgment on low-g. I'll give you a chance to show me how it can be fun, before I make up my mind."

"Well, we'll just see," she said. She took his arm. "Right now, we've got to get you signed in and registered and so on. And then we have to get over to the Mendeleev tram. If we miss this one, it's a three-hour wait for the next one."

They walked together across the dirt floor of the covered space toward an exit. Looking at the way the floor rose on all sides, Jonathan realized the space was a covered crater. All he had been able to see from the lem as it descended toward the moon's surface was the top of the roof, looking like a flattened bubble.

The lem had landed next to the bubble and then been attached to it by a flexible tube. Small trams, much like those in America, had transported the passengers down the tube and into the crater, where everyone else had moved off rapidly and purposefully. Jonathan had stood staring about until he was asked to move and had begun the low-g acrobatics which had provided such amusement to the natives.

"They didn't give you a course in low-g on the station?" Connie asked.

"The station? Oh, the space station. No, I wasn't there for long enough. They were offering one, but the Earth-Moon shuttle was leaving a few hours after I got there, and I was scheduled to be on it, and I had to get some sleep. So I spent my hours on the—on the station in regular Earth gravity, sleeping. And then I blundered around in zero-g on the shuttle on the way here. So this is the first true low-g I've experienced."

"You'll get used to it," Connie assured him. "Was it a nice

trip?" She pressed his arm against her side and looked up at him, a direct look Jonathan found physically disturbing.

"God, it was beautiful! I never imagined anything like the stars from space! And the sun, of course—very impressive. The night sky is amazing enough from Earth, but that's nothing compared to what you see outside the atmosphere. So many stars and so many colors—"

"I know," Connie interrupted a bit impatiently. "I've seen it. When you go outside on the surface here in a suit, it looks the same. Believe it or not, some people get bored with it. Some people never go outside at all; they say that's not what they're here for."

They didn't grow up where I did, Jonathan thought.

"It's too bad we have to rush right back to Mendeleev, Mr. Holroyd," Connie said. "There are so many interesting things to see here at the base. Maybe after you take care of this crisis at Mendeleev, we can come back."

"I'd like that. Especially if you'll start calling me Jonathan."

Connie grinned up at him. "You'll have to give me a good reason to do that."

I'll do my best, he thought.

They had arrived at the exit. There was a small desk with an attendant there. Jonathan let Connie do the talking. After a few minutes, she returned to Jonathan. "All done. Now we go through this exit and right onto the tram."

This was a reverse of the process by which Jonathan had come from the lem to the interior of the covered crater. Before they sat down on the small sled which would take them down the tube and into the Mendeleev tram, Jonathan looked around again. "This is the old NASA base?" he asked. "Just this big crater with a few landing sites? It's nothing but an interchange point."

"Oh, no. The old base is next door to us. You get to it through another exit, which you probably didn't notice. Anyway, you have to have the right kind of permission to go through there, and you don't have it."

Jonathan called up the image of the lunar surface during the lem's descent and frowned. "I didn't see any buildings. All I saw was this crater where we are now."

Connie laughed. "It's underground, of course. Didn't you know that? Most of the human habitation on the moon is underground—something like seventy percent, I think. Places like this are above, because it's more practical. And parts of Mendeleev, of course, because it started out as an observatory. But otherwise, everything's under the surface. With the technology they had in the old days, that was the easiest way to keep the heat in and make things airtight."

Jonathan thought of people coming all the way to the moon and then ending up living in tunnels underground.

Connie felt the quivering of his body and looked up at him in alarm. "Something wrong, Mr. Holroyd?"

"I'll survive. Let's get into the tram."

Considerately, Connie had reserved their seats so that one was next to a window, and she motioned Jonathan into that one. He spent the nearly seven-and-a-half-hour trip with his face glued to the glass, stopping only to eat the two light meals provided and to make one trip to the bathroom.

"You like the vacuum?" Connie asked at one point, after having vainly tried to keep a conversation going.

"It's wonderful," he breathed.

As the tram sped along at almost eight hundred kilometers per hour, the Earth and the sun slipped down toward the horizon. Jonathan had to press his face against the glass to see them, for they were almost directly behind the tram. The Earth was half full, glowing a beautiful reddish blue against the black sky. The sun was a huge, yellow-red ball. Everywhere, there were stars, as numerous and colorful as from the Earth-moon shuttle, just as Connie had promised.

Jonathan looked down again at the surface of the moon, at the rilles and craters and soft, rounded slopes of hills, the shadows spreading on them as the sun fell toward the horizon. Absolutely airless, he thought. He was safe inside the tram's pressurized, heated cabin, but down there a man without a special suit would die almost instantly. He would freeze and suffocate and desiccate all at the same time. Jonathan felt short of breath at the thought; his heart hammered. How curious to think that this lunar reality below him was what he had been taught since childhood was the true nature of the surface of the Earth!

Jonathan had expected the arrival at Mendeleev to mimic the departure from Frontside Base, but in reverse. Instead, there was no bubble at all, but only the raised rim of a crater looming up ahead like a low, broken range of mountains. The tram had passed into nighttime hours before, and the crater rim was visible only as a silhouette against the stars. As the tram moved, other silhouettes above the rim formed spiderweb patterns in the sky. He blinked, unsure he had really seen the strange shadows, and turned to Connie to ask her if there was really something there, but then brilliant lights sprang into being ahead and below, and he forgot about his question.

A great swath of perfectly levelled lunar surface was illuminated. Ahead, the surface tilted up, rising almost to the vertical. White, suited figures were visible in the lights, moving equipment around. Rows of colored lights came on, outlining a square space. The tram slowed rapidly and moved toward the outlined square, hovering over it and then descending onto it.

The figures outside pushed sleds and drove wheeled vehicles across the surface toward the tram. The dust raised by the wheels cascaded forward like sheets of gray water; there was no hovering cloud. No air for the dust to hang in, Jonathan thought, feeling the airlessness of the lunar surface as something physical for the first time.

Around him, everyone was standing and stretching. "Come on," Connie said. "Time to go underground."

As they lined up to exit and then stepped from the tram into a capsule fastened to its door, she explained, "Nothing is allowed to land inside Mendeleev or take off from it. We'll go in this vehicle the rest of the way." This was a slightly smaller version of the tram's passenger cabin, with seats and window arranged in the same way.

The capsule was carried on one of the wheeled vehicles

Jonathan had seen through the window. They were taken from the tram up to the vertical wall of rock Jonathan had noticed before and deposited on a broad platform. The capsule quivered and then began to move toward the wall of rock. At the last moment, a door, invisible until that moment, slid up ahead of them and the capsule moved into a black tunnel. Jonathan caught his breath.

Behind them, the door slid down again, and the capsule began to move more and more swiftly. Lights came on, showing the gray rock walls speeding by, flowing to the rear. Jonathan breathed again.

"We're under the floor of the crater now," Connie told him. "We're getting there. Not too long, now."

Thank God, Jonathan thought. He didn't say it, for he sensed it would lower Connie's opinion of him, and it was important to him that that opinion be high. But his heart was pounding, and he felt that if this underground trip didn't end soon, he would either faint or have to get out of the capsule and claw his way through the soil to the surface, even though he had no surface suit and would die.

When they reached the end of the trip at last, the capsule slid sideways onto a small platform. Jonathan could see now that they had been sitting atop a kind of cradle that rode on wheels on rails which stretched back in the direction they had come from. The lights in the tunnel they had come through were now off, and the rails, gleaming gray in the light, plunged into utter blackness and vanished. Jonathan closed his eyes for a moment and offered up a silent prayer.

The platform they now sat on began rising. They moved upward through a lighted shaft with walls of rock. First the birth canal, and then a reenactment of my escape from America, Jonathan thought. Every symbol I would rather avoid is waiting for me on the moon. Under the moon.

They ended up in a sort of small hangar, where they finally were able to climb down from their capsule. There were no windows, to Jonathan's disappointment.

Connie led the way to the rear of the capsule, where luggage was being unloaded. They picked up Jonathan's two small suitcases, which felt surprisingly light to Jonathan even though he had expected this, and set out down one of the hallways radiating away from the hangar. He tried to imitate her shuffling walk, little steps which resulted in a stride of normal length.

She held his arm firmly all the way and carried one of his suitcases. She talked cheerfully as they went, pointing out side corridors and telling where they led, explaining the design of Mendeleev, greeting people they passed and occasionally introducing them to Jonathan, feeding him a stream of names he instantly forgot.

In fact, he heard little that she said. He was searching the faces they passed, constantly hoping to see the one he had come here to find. But he didn't see Elena. He interrupted Connie's explanation of something or other to ask her, "How many people *are* there in this place?"

She glanced up at him curiously before replying. "Afraid I can't tell you that. Learn not to ask such questions. Which brings me to another point. You'll be given a badge tomorrow morning which has numbered codes on it. Those show which parts of Mendeleev you're authorized for. Please don't try to enter any other sections; it's really not worth the repercussions."

He had noticed the badges, with pictures, on the people he passed but hadn't thought much about it. Connie, however, was the exception. "You don't have a badge."

She nodded. "That's right. I don't need one. I can go anywhere I want to. I'm very special."

That opening line dangled in the air for a few moments before Jonathan gathered his wits and responded with something appropriately flirtatious.

"And here we are," Connie said suddenly, stopping before a door that looked like all the others they had passed. "Your home away from home for however long it takes you to do what you were brought here to do. I'm sure you're ready for a good night's sleep. If you get hungry, there's a comm set in your room, and you can have sandwiches delivered to your door. They're not very good, but don't go wandering around trying to find a cafeteria; you'd just get lost and in trouble for not having a badge. Someone will be here in the morning to take you to the admissions office for issuance of your badge and to get you started. The door's already set for your palm. Good night, Mr. Holroyd."

"Wait a minute! Aren't you going to come inside?"

Connie grinned at him. "Really, now."

"So when will I see you again?"

"I'll comm you when I'm told you've finished your task. So make it quick."

"Okay. Tomorrow afternoon. How's that?"

"Oh? The best experts here work unsuccessfully at it for days, and you can take care of it in less than a day?"

"We breed superior men in America. Keep your schedule clear tomorrow afternoon."

Connie laughed. "Good night again, Mr. Holroyd." She walked down the hallway still chuckling and disappeared around a corner.

Jonathan congratulated himself on his suaveness, opened his door, shoved both suitcases, still packed, into a closet, lay down on the double bed in the center of the room, and fell instantly asleep.

The next morning, Jonathan was awakened by a steady pounding at his door. Still half asleep, he looked around for a robe to put on, but everything he had brought with him was still packed in his suitcases. Then he realized he had slept in his clothes. Getting out of bed propelled him halfway across the room. He took a deep breath and stood still for a moment, determined not to have the same sort of trouble he had had when he'd first arrived on the moon. Moving very carefully, trying consciously with each step not to exert much force against the floor, he made it to the door and, after fumbling with it for a few seconds, managed to get it open.

A young woman stood outside, looking impatient. She was taller than Jonathan, plain, with nondescript brown hair and a forgettable face, and she aroused his instant hostility. "It's seven o'clock already, Holroyd. I have work to do. Get yourself ready and let's get moving."

"All right. Hold on." He closed the door in her face and went back to bed.

He was dozing pleasantly when the pounding began again. "Still here?" he said to her. She was still impatient, and now she was angry as well.

"Hell, yes, I'm still here! Why aren't you ready yet?"

"Two minutes." He closed the door on her again and stripped off his clothing. He put the two suitcases on the bed, opened them, and dumped their contents onto the bed. His clothes floated down to the surface of the bed with a lazy, curiously graceful motion. Jonathan picked out what he wanted to wear for the day, then stripped and glided over to the bathroom. There he stepped into the shower, turned it on, and stood for a while under the stream of water, enjoying the sensation.

He gave himself the gift of a leisurely shower, spending much time staring in fascination at the behavior of the water droplets in low gravity. He thought he could hear, faint and faraway through the rushing sound of the water, a pounding from the other room. It stopped at last, and Jonathan, grinning, continued with his shower. I've come a long way, he assured himself. From an escapee who did what he was told and kept his mouth shut, to a citizen who stands up to authority. He finished his shower, dried himself off, and dressed in the fresh clothing he had picked out earlier.

The young woman was still standing outside the door, her face impassive. Jonathan stepped out into the hallway and pulled his door shut behind him. "Please call me Jonathan," he said in a friendly tone; she didn't respond to the overture.

"This way." She led off down the hallway, and when Jonathan tried to catch up to her, she increased her pace so as to keep a step or two in the lead. He was too unskilled at walking in low gravity to fight this tactic, and after a few minutes of undignified jockeying, Jonathan gave in and walked behind her.

They ended up in front of an office door marked PERSONNEL. Jonathan estimated they had walked two kilometers, all apparently underground. He knew he would never be able to find his way back to his room unaided, let alone to a cafeteria or to the computer he was to work on. This made him almost sorry for his treatment of his guide, but when he tried to start a conversation with her, she ignored him, opened the door in front of them, and preceded him into the office.

Ahead of them was a receptionist's desk. His guide pointed at it and, still without a word, turned and left. Jonathan shrugged. There were other women on the moon—Connie Allendorf, for example.

His records had arrived well ahead of him. He was processed quickly through the required procedures, had a badge with photograph issued to him, and was given a map. The latter was given to him by a tall, severely overweight, chestnut-skinned man with numerous wrinkles and white hair. He had introduced himself as Fin Lucero. He spread the map out on his desk and gestured Jonathan closer. "See the way it's divided into numbered sections?" Jonathan nodded. "The numbers on your badge show you which sections you're allowed into. You'll see them posted on the walls, too, especially where one section ends and another begins." Jonathan hadn't noticed anything of the sort on his way here. The signs must be discreet indeed, unlike the exhortatory ones in America, and he had learned to ignore even those. "Your badge will let you know if you go where you aren't supposed to. It'll beep, and the deeper you get into the illegal section, the louder the beep. It'll also let us know, as well as the Security people, so watch where you go, please.

"I've marked the room you were assigned to, right here," Lucero continued. "Cafeterias and rec rooms are accessible by everyone, of course. Rest rooms are all over the place. Here's where you'll be working." He pointed to a spot on the map. "It's not far from here. Turn left when you leave this office, and from then on you'll have to follow the map. If you haven't had breakfast yet, there's a good cafeteria in the other direction. Turn right when you leave the office and follow your nose. Any questions?"

"I don't know enough to ask any yet," Jonathan said.

The personnel man laughed. "Too bad. This is your last chance. Oh, yes, I mustn't forget this. Isaac Simkin wants to see you this evening." His face took on a look of reverence as he spoke the name. "Try to be back here at about eighteen o'clock. That's when we close up. I'll escort you myself."

"An escort again? I thought my badge eliminated the need for one."

"Not when it comes to that particular section of the base. You don't have the number for it on your badge. Neither do I, normally. In fact, hardly anyone is cleared for that area. They only gave me a clearance for it because of you."

"So why didn't they just give me a temporary clearance?"

"Because I have a friend in a high place, and that's the way I managed to arrange it. I'm not going to miss the chance to visit where the Simkins live."

The words electrified Jonathan. He managed to behave normally and left, clutching his map and trying to find his way to the cafeteria, but the thought that he might at last get to see Elena—or at least where she lived, or *really* lived—crowded everything else from his mind.

When Jonathan found the cafeteria and ordered his breakfast and began eating it, it occurred to him to wonder if Fin Lucero's taste in food was very bad. This was what Lucero considered good food? Or did it mean that this *was* good food, by lunar standards? If the latter, then he had a good reason to get back to Earth as soon as he could. Of course, he also had very good reasons, better reasons, to stay on the moon as long as he could.

It was almost eleven o'clock when Jonathan finally arrived at the computer center. Plenty of time, he thought, to get done and get back to his room to wait for Connie's call, and then to arrange something with her and still get to the personnel office before it closed.

The Mendeleev computer center was an amazingly busy place, with harried men and women rushing in and out of it constantly. The size of the place and the number of people he saw astonished and intimidated Jonathan. In America, the computer center had had three machines still working, and five employees, of whom Jonathan had been one. But his name turned out to be magic, once he had been directed to the right person. This was a frantic,

middle-aged woman who greeted Jonathan like a long-lost son—
or lover—and ushered him into a back room.

"Here it is," she told him. "I hope to God you can do
something with it. I hate this antique hardware. Don't you? But
we're too dependent on it all over the place to scrap it. Is there
anything you need, anything at all?"

"Peace and quiet," Jonathan said promptly. "And solitude,
absolute solitude."

"Whatever you say. No one will disturb you. Absolutely no
one. But if you do need anything else, ask for me. My name's
Cora."

"I know," Jonathan told her. "When that other fellow brought
me to you, he told me your name, remember?"

"Why, that's right!" She laughed. "Well, ask for Cora. Good
luck with that monstrosity." She left, and Jonathan closed the door
behind her. He was alone in a small room with a Rockway 3000.
He laughed in delight.

The Rockway 3000 was a special-purpose machine, considered
immensely powerful in its day. It had been produced from 2006
until the Taking had put an end to everything on the surface of the
Earth. Its unique architecture and operating system had been
designed to meet specifications issued by the United States Army.
Of the handful produced, two had been installed in the underground shelter that later became all that was left of America. One
had been acquired by the increasingly military-dominated NASA,
shipped to the moon in pieces, and reassembled at Frontside Base;
after the Taking, it was moved to Mendeleev as total authority
over the humans who survived on the moon shifted there.
Jonathan stroked its surface lovingly and then sat down in front of
its console.

The screen was full of asterisks. The bottom line of them
blinked, showing that the screen image was actually scrolling up
rapidly one line at a time, with a new line of asterisks springing
into being at the bottom as the one on top scrolled off the screen.
Oh, I'm so clever, Jonathan thought.

He typed in a long series of letters, numbers, and punctuation
marks. Instantly the screen went blank, and then in the middle of

it appeared the message, "Thanks, Jonathan. I feel much better."
Jonathan chuckled, blanked the screen again, and then set about
eliminating the patches he had added to the Rockway's operating
system. The whole process took him less than an hour. He spent a
bit of time testing the result to be sure it worked as it had before
his modifications, and then he spent three more hours playing a
game of chess against the Rockway.

It was the same chess program, provided by the machine's
manufacturer, that he had played against the machine so often in
America, and it caused an attack of nostalgia.

At fifteen-thirty o'clock, Jonathan emerged from his room and
went to Cora's desk.

"Giving up for the day?" she asked, looking disappointed.

Jonathan shook his head. "I'm done. I'm going to have
something to eat, since I missed lunch, and then I'm going back to
my room."

Cora's mouth dropped open. "Done? You mean, completely?
It's *working*?"

"Humming along, so to speak."

"But that's amazing! How did you do it so quickly?"

Jonathan smiled. "Old computers like me. Good-bye. Try not
to break it again."

"Wait a minute! What was wrong with it? You didn't even bring
any hardware in with you."

"Oh, no." Jonathan shook his head. "There wasn't anything
wrong with the hardware. The machine just needed someone to
talk its troubles over with, that's all, and I'm a good listener." If
he had wanted to establish a reputation on Mendeleev as a genius,
Jonathan thought, looking at the awestruck expression on Cora's
face, then he had done it.

Not that I really give a shit about that, he thought as he walked
back to his room, glancing occasionally at the map. I'm here for
one reason, and that's not to fix a Rockway 3000 or get a chance to
play with it or even to play with Connie Allendorf. Although
playing with Connie would be fun, he was sure, and he was
looking forward to it with much eagerness; but he was here to find

and speak to Elena Simkin, and everything else was of secondary importance.

How much like America this is! he thought as he walked through the seemingly endless corridors. He passed more people than he would have in America, and they were far healthier looking and dressed so much more colorfully, and unlike the situation in America, here there seemed to be no hallways permanently sealed off and abandoned, no stretches where the lights didn't work or the air was dead and unmoving. Despite those differences, though, this place had in common with America the unrelenting sameness of corridors, the lack of a view of an outside world—the feeling, above all, that there *was* no outside world, that this was all there was to the Universe, and that anything else was a dream, a fable, a wish for something that, by natural law, could never be.

And yet there was the one-sixth gravity, and Jonathan was grateful for that, for it was a constant reminder that he was on the moon and not buried beneath the Earth. By the time he reached his room, he had managed to achieve a fair approximation of the economical, gliding shuffle of the people he passed.

He might have assured himself that the chance to play certain games with Connie Allendorf was not among his reasons for being on the moon, but nonetheless, when he had waited for as long as he could before he had to leave if he were to reach the personnel office by eighteen o'clock, and Connie had still not commed, he felt enormously disappointed and depressed. By accomplishing so quickly the task for which he had officially been brought to the moon, he had deprived himself of any reason to stay there longer, and so there would probably be no further chances to see Connie: he assumed he'd be sent back to Earth the next day.

At least he would be seeing Elena that evening. That was something to look forward to. Perhaps there would be some progress there, some resolution.

23

Fin Lucero was waiting for Jonathan when he arrived. Lucero looked freshly shaved and showered, too, and he was also wearing fresh clothes, different from those he had worn when Jonathan had seen him that morning, and far more colorful. This visit seemed to be as important to him as it was to Jonathan.

"Mr. Holroyd," Lucero said happily. "Let's go!"

"Jonathan, please." There was something he liked about this man; perhaps it was only that someone of his age was so openly pleased, almost childishly excited, about an expedition.

"Fine! Call me Fin."

"Fin," Jonathan repeated as they walked down the hallway together. "Is that short for something?"

"Nope. Sounds like it should be, doesn't it? It's a permanent symbol of my parents' imaginative ways. You should hear what they named my brothers and sisters. Amazing names!" Fin laughed at the thought. He continued talking about himself and his siblings and his own children as they walked, laughing often, eliciting laughter from Jonathan.

What a cheerful man! Jonathan thought admiringly. He thought that Fin was the type of person nothing could depress, and he wished he could become that way himself. Was this what Lunar Man was like? Or was Fin Lucero as much an exception here as his type was on the surface of Earth—or under it?

Lucero had produced two special badges, one for each of them. These had photographs on them, like all the others Jonathan had seen, but no numbers. Jonathan asked about that.

"Special purpose," Fin explained. "Since these admit us to the section we're going to, they also admit us anywhere else. There's a hierarchy to these numbers. I didn't bother explaining that this morning, but that's the way it works. If you have a . . . oh, let's

215

see, a two-fifty-three on your badge, for example, you can also go into sections one-forty-three and ninety-two."

"And every other section is subordinate to this one we're heading for?"

"That's right."

"I don't understand all of this. Just who *is* Isaac Simkin?"

Fin stopped walking and turned to Jonathan, staring at him in amazement. "You don't know?"

"No. That's why I asked."

"You're joking! No, never mind, you're not joking. Well!" He resumed walking. "I'm just surprised, that's all. Isaac Simkin is the Director of the Mendeleev Observatory."

"That's it? Director of an astronomical observatory?"

Fin laughed somewhat nervously. "That's not quite the idea. I said he's the Director of the Mendeleev Observatory. That means he's Director of this base—of everything here, not just the telescope and the astronomers."

"But . . . Aah." Suddenly Jonathan understood. On Earth, everything deferred to Mendeleev. All permissions came from here, all directions, all policy setting; in short, all orders originated here. That was to say that all power was centered here: Mendeleev was the true capitol of the human race, despite the offical designation of Lander as the Earth's capital city. Isaac Simkin, therefore, was the unelected ruler of the human race. That explained Elena's ability to get things done quickly and easily! "I see."

Conversation languished somewhat after that. They entered an elevator that took them up an unknown number of floors. Jonathan wondered if the elevator also checked their badges.

When they exited from the elevator, Jonathan's eye was caught by a brilliant photograph of the sky, the star field as seen from space, that covered much of the wall across from the elevator. "Beautiful!" he said. Then he stepped forward for a closer look and realized the photograph was actually a window. Along the bottom of the view, the stars were cut off by an uneven, curved black silhouette.

"Too bad it's not daytime," Fin said from behind him. "Lunar day, I mean. Then we'd be able to see the surface."

Jonathan turned to look at him, struck by something in his tone of voice. Lucero was staring around him with open hunger and awe in his face. "Isaac Simkin lives here!" he whispered. "Just think of it!"

A familiar voice called out, "Here you are at last! Welcome."

It was Connie Allendorf, dressed in something rainbowlike, floor length, and, from the way it clung to her skin, as substantial as spiderweb. Jonathan caught his breath, stunned by a wave of physical desire stronger than anything of the kind he had ever felt before.

"Hello, Jonathan." Connie took his arm as she had the day before.

"Mr. Lucero." She held out her hand to him, and Fin took it eagerly, bowing slightly and looking quite overcome with emotion. "Thank you so much for escorting Jonathan up here," Connie said with all the gracious condescension of a monarch. "The Director is very grateful. I'm sure he'll feel free to call upon you for any similar service in the future."

It was a dismissal. Fin looked at her, stunned, and then looked up and down the corridor. His face bore a look of immeasurable loss. Jonathan was filled with pity for him.

Fin backed into the elevator, which had waited all this time, doors open, behind him. The elevator doors closed on his wounded look. There was a *whoosh*, and Fin Lucero was swept back down to his normal level.

Jonathan turned to Connie, intending to intercede for Fin, to ask if the man couldn't possibly be invited to come back up to this level and meet Simkin. But Connie was grinning up at him, and Jonathan was shaken again by sexual desire, and Fin Lucero's problems vanished from his mind. "You called me Jonathan. What did I do to deserve that?"

Connie pressed his arm against her side. His forearm was against the side of her breast. "Just what you said you'd do: finished up your work in a matter of hours."

"That appeals to you?"

She nodded. "Competence does something for me."

"So now you're calling me Jonathan. That's my reward for competence?"

"That's part of it."

"I was waiting for you to comm me. You said you would."

"No, I think I said I'd contact you when I heard you were finished. That's what I'm doing now." She squeezed his arm more tightly against her breast. "Why? Were you waiting really eagerly?"

Jonathan laughed. He remembered with absolute clarity her promising she would comm him. "Very eagerly." He understood perfectly well the game she was playing with him, and to his surprise he found he enjoyed it.

They took another elevator the rest of the way. "Why not use the elevator I arrived in?" Jonathan asked.

"Security," Connie said. "That one doesn't go any higher than the floor I met you on."

They were approaching a set of massive double doors made of some dark, reddish wood. This must be it, Jonathan thought. His heart was pounding with the combination of Connie's body brushing against his as they walked and the feeling of his arm against her, and the thought that Elena was waiting for him beyond those doors.

The doors opened to Connie's palm, which didn't entirely surprise Jonathan. But Elena wasn't waiting beyond them; Isaac Simkin was.

He looked exactly as he had on the comm screen the two times Jonathan had seen him on it, but his comm image hadn't prepared Jonathan for the man's impact in person. On the comm, Simkin had a strong, almost intimidating presence. In the flesh, he had all that, and even more. He was quite tall, which made him a giant from Jonathan's point of view. In addition, he was powerfully built, with broad, heavy shoulders and big arms, the obvious result of much hard work—deliberate exercise, Jonathan assumed, since the ruler of the human race surely had no need to do manual labor. Simkin was overweight, with an impressive belly, but he carried himself lightly and gracefully, thanks both to his underlying muscle and the low gravity of the moon. In contrast to the usual colorful clothing of his society, he wore plain dark trousers and a white shirt. All in all, he looked like a buck worker in America.

He didn't need color in his clothes, though. The drabness of what he wore served to emphasize the force of his personality. This, Jonathan realized, was a born leader. His thick black hair and beard caught one's attention, and his eyes were large, bright, and penetrating. It was a large room, but Simkin filled it.

Jonathan had momentarily forgotten Connie, despite her closeness and his earlier excitement. He glanced down at her quickly and discovered that she was staring greedily at Isaac Simkin, her mouth slightly open. The sight made Jonathan uncomfortable.

Simkin broke the short silence. "Jonathan Holroyd," he said. Even his voice was big and powerful. It was deep and resonant, a trained speaker's voice, demanding attention no matter whether what Simkin was saying was profound or trivial. "Welcome to the moon, Jonathan." He held out a large hand and enveloped Jonathan's with it. "I hope you haven't eaten yet. I don't know if Connie explained, but I've arranged for a light supper for us. This way." He led the way into an adjoining room, where there was a long dinner table, made of the same reddish wood as the double doors. Three places had been set, one at the head of the table and the other two on either side.

At the far end of the table, the wall consisted mostly of another large window. Jonathan walked over to it immediately and stared out, mesmerized. It was still lunar night, but floodlights on the exterior wall below the window lit up the ground for many square meters. Unfortunately, this wasn't unspoiled lunar landscape: it had been graded long ago, all nearby craters and craterlets filled in and smoothed over, and the surface was covered by footprints and tire tracks—virtually immortal tracks, Jonathan realized, because of the lack of weather. A trio of figures in bulky white suits with glass-fronted helmets passed into view, their suits glaring in the powerful lights, and skimmed past, disappearing into the shadows. "Come and sit down, Jonathan," Simkin said. To disobey was unthinkable.

Simkin took the place at the head of the table, of course, so that Jonathan and Connie sat facing each other across the table. Jonathan noticed with a bleak feeling that there was no fourth setting. Immediately, formally dressed servants began appearing carrying trays and dishes. The table became increasingly loaded with an astonishing meal, food that looked tantalizing and smelled wonderful. The quantity amazed Jonathan; he wondered what Simkin considered a heavy supper. He realized he was ravenously hungry. "Go ahead," Simkin said. "No formality here, especially not for family."

Connie's related to him? Jonathan wondered. That would explain her ability to come and go wherever she wanted. He put the question aside for later consideration and began eating. The food was as delicious as it had looked and smelled. The variety surprised him. There were vegetables and poultry and fish that must have been brought up from Earth but which he had never even encountered there.

Simkin watched him for a few moments with an amused expression. "Like it?"

"Mm-hmm," Jonathan replied with his mouth full.

"Elena sends her regrets. She's tied up and couldn't make it. We were all very impressed with the job you did on that old computer today. So old computers like you, eh?"

Jonathan forced down his mouthful of food. "Looks that way. Generally speaking, anyway."

"Hmm. You know, we have a lot of old computers up here, left over from before the Taking. Of course, since then, we've established our own technological directions, and what we produce now is far superior to the old stuff. But we can't produce our own machines fast enough for the work we have for them, and we have a lot of data and software on the old machines. The result of all this is that we have to keep them up and running, but we don't have many qualified people who know anything about them. Escapees have encountered them, of course, because that's normally the only kind of computer anyone has in the underground refuges—when they have computers at all. Problem is, you see, that it's rare to find an escapee who was trained to use and maintain the computers underground. You're a rare combination." He paused, staring at Jonathan as if weighing his soul. "We need you here far more than on Earth. How would you like to transfer up here?"

Jonathan stared down at his plate to hide his reaction. Stay here on the moon? Stay here where Elena was? She couldn't keep avoiding him if he was living and working on the moon—unless she then decided to move down to Earth. But how likely was that, with her father and therefore her avenue to authority, to power, up here? And Connie . . . He looked across the table at her. She was grinning happily at him, a clear promise of much joy and pleasure in the future. He turned to Simkin, who he was surprised to see was watching him anxiously. "I'd be delighted."

"Tchoodyesnih! Wonderful!" Simkin boomed. "I'm very glad. I think it's good to have family with you, and you're almost family, you know." He waved his hand. "By marriage, by ancient friendships. You knew, didn't you, that my late wife was the daughter of Cathy Martinson, who was married to Henry Martinson, your grandfather's cousin? That makes you and Elena . . . what?"

"Third cousins," Jonathan said. Connie looked bored.

Simkin nodded. "That's right. So you see, everything always works out for the best in the long run."

The rest of the meal went very well. Jonathan consumed a quantity of food that surprised him, and quite a few glasses of the excellent white wine that was served with it. Later, servants brought in small glasses half filled with a golden liquid that was thick, sweet, and, Jonathan realized too late, potent; he had already gulped his first glass down and was halfway through the second before he began to feel the effect. "Uh-oh," he muttered.

Simkin laughed. "Sorry. I should have warned you. You have to get used to this stuff. Did you have alcohol in, um, America?"

Jonathan shook his head. "The government outlawed it before I was born. Waste of scarce resources, they said. My grandfather told me about it, though."

Simkin chuckled but said nothing.

Connie yawned theatrically and said, "It's getting late, Isaac. I think I'd better guide Jonathan back to his room so he can get an early start on fixing up all our old junk all over the moon."

Simkin looked from her to Jonathan and back, and then he grinned. "Excellent idea." They all rose, and Jonathan and Simkin shook hands again. "Have a good night's sleep, Jonathan, if you're able to."

Later, as they walked hand in hand toward Jonathan's room, Connie said, "Good old Uncle Isaac. He never misses anything."

"Is he your uncle?"

"Only spiritually. My parents were friends of his and his wife's, and I've known him all my life. I'm . . . sort of his secretary."

Jonathan decided not to pursue the subject any further. "I'm feeling kind of drunk," he said hesitantly. "Maybe I should just go to sleep. I'm not sure I'm good for anything."

Connie chuckled and squeezed his hand. "I'll do the hard part. That's the way I prefer it, anyway. We'll manage."

And they did.

Jonathan was not given any work to do for the next week. It was an informal vacation, not applied for and not officially granted, but something he realized he had needed for some time. He spent every night with Connie (always in his own room; he had yet to see her living quarters), and most of every day, as well.

Twice during that time, he and Connie dined with Isaac Simkin again, at Simkin's invitation. Both times, only the three of them were there. Elena, according to what her father said, was always just too busy to attend but sent her regrets and best wishes. Connie seemed to prefer things that way: as far as Jonathan could tell, she liked having these two particular men to herself, paying attention to her and ready to be manipulated by her. That is, Jonathan was easily, even willingly, manipulated by Connie; he doubted that anyone could ever manipulate Isaac Simkin.

Nor could the man be pumped for information. During those dinners, Jonathan tried hard, but subtly, to find out where Elena was and when she would be back at Mendeleev. Simkin was openly amused by Jonathan's conversational ploys and never fell for them. Jonathan soon realized that Simkin's seeming hearty openness communicated absolutely nothing that the Director didn't want communicated.

He didn't notice, though, the increasingly respectful manner Simkin displayed toward him. Connie pointed it out after their second dinner with the Director. "He's very impressed with you," she told him. "So am I, of course, but Isaac hasn't even been to bed with you, and he's *still* impressed."

"What the Hell does that mean?"

"A joke. Laugh. You escapees are so humorless. I meant that I'm impressed with your prick, but Uncle Isaac likes you for your mind."

Jonathan always felt extremely uncomfortable when Connie used such language. There were some things about America that he knew would always stay with him.

"All you have to do," Connie went on, "is do the same sort of job on some of the other computers that you did on the one you fixed last week, and you'll be his fair-haired boy in no time. And that's not bad for anyone's career."

"Maybe he'll pass the word along to Elena," Jonathan muttered, thinking aloud.

Connie said nothing for a few minutes. Then she said, "Speaking of being eclipsed, how would you like to see one?"

"What?"

"An eclipse. There's one due in a couple of days. You can only see them from Frontside, of course. This one should be pretty good, because there'll be some transits right before it. We can spend tomorrow doing surface suit training and then tram over there first thing the next morning. We'll get there just in time. What do you say?"

"Yes! God, of course!"

Connie grinned and hugged him quickly. "Your enthusiasm for things like that—that's another thing I like about you."

The next morning, they made love hastily, showered and dressed quickly, and walked rapidly down the hallway toward the nearest cafeteria. "This might take a long time," Connie explained. "Got to allow as much of the day for this as we can."

After eating, they went to an air lock where two suits were waiting for them. "These are surface suits," Connie explained. "This one's mine. Special size." It was the smaller of the two. The letters CA were stencilled on the helmet's forehead, above the visor. It really was her suit, Jonathan realized, her personalized suit.

He felt envious. How wonderful it would be, how much a true spaceman it would make him feel, to have a suit of his own. He asked her about that.

"One of your own?" Connie said doubtfully. "Well, I don't know. They do that for people who have to do a lot of work outside, but you won't be in that category. Anyway, you're pretty much a standard size, so that shouldn't be a problem for you."

Connie helped him put his surface suit on and taught him how to check for airtightness and what the various displays inside his helmet, projected on his visor, meant. Then she took his helmet off again and pulled his head down for a kiss. "Now, look in here," she said. "See this lever? That's the radio channel selector. Tongue-controlled."

"*Tongue*!" Jonathan cried. "Are you joking?"

"Nope. Sorry, but I'm not. How else do you suppose you can manipulate things inside your helmet?"

"But that's disgusting! And it's not even my own personalized helmet!"

"You're right," Connie agreed. "It *is* disgusting. Countless other tongues have licked this rod," she said with relish. "And now yours gets added to the number. I think it's sexy."

"You think everything's sexy."

Connie thought about that for a moment. "*Almost* everything," she corrected. "Don't worry, the selector gets sterilized every time you bring a suit back inside. Same applies to all the other controls inside the helmet. They're almost all tongue controlled. Weren't you paying attention before when I was explaining all of that to you?" She explained how to use the lever to select radio channels. "One through Eight," she said. "That's enough for normal needs.

And if you're outside and your needs are abnormal, you're probably doomed, anyway. Never be confident about your survival; that's the first rule of survival on the surface."

"How many rules of survival are there?"

"One. There's no point in having any others. Okay, here's On and Off. And that's it. Now. Signals. If someone points to their helmet, that means they want you to turn your radio on. They tap their hand against their helmet the number of times for the channel they're using. Got that? It's very simple."

"Sounds like a really stupid pantomime show."

Connie nodded. "One that could save your life some day. It's already saved many others. Now, put your helmet back on and we'll practice."

"Do we have to, Mom?"

"We have to," Connie said firmly.

Jonathan grinned. "I love it when you take control."

That earned him another kiss. "And tonight I'll show you a lot of other new things," Connie promised. "Now, put your helmet on. We're going out to the practice area."

Fortunately, Jonathan found that after they had been outside for only a few minutes, he forgot entirely about the other tongues that had pushed against the various controls inside the helmet. He was too fascinated with the stars and the ground his helmet light illuminated and too preoccupied with trying to move properly in his bulky suit. It added about twenty-three kilograms to his weight, which meant less than four kilograms in the moon's low gravity, but that was enough to completely disrupt the control he had managed to learn over his motions in low-g. He tripped often at first. Fortunately, the suit acted like a balloon, and he bounced.

Connie laughed harder each time he tripped forward and bounced back to his feet like some sort of oversized children's toy. Her laughter boomed inside his helmet until he found the radio's volume control and tongued it down. "I'm glad I'm keeping you amused," he said angrily.

Connie stopped laughing. "It *is* funny," she said. "Just try not to fall against anything sharp. You could rip your suit open, and all the sticky patches I have with me are quite small."

Jonathan walked much more carefully after that.

After a few hours of practice in the suit, Jonathan was beginning to feel fairly competent. "You'll do," Connie told him. He was also drenched with sweat and trembling with exhaustion. "Poor baby," Connie said when he complained. "Mummy's going to have to put you to bed and massage you all over and think of something to perk you back up."

Jonathan had no doubt she *would* think of something.

24

The night was more exhausting than the day had been. Jonathan awoke to the sound of music from his comm set. He felt drained and listless. "Let me sleep," he moaned.

"It's upsy-daisy time!" Connie sang, bouncing up and down on the bed. She was still naked.

He smiled sleepily. "Another hour, okay?"

Connie shook her head.

"Thirty minutes? Ten? Just a few seconds!"

"Nope. We'll miss the Frontside tram. Well, all right," she relented. "I'll shower first, and you can sleep until I'm done, but then you'd better be ready to get up and moving."

"I promise," he promised, and fell back instantly into a deep sleep. He awoke to Connie sucking with astonishing vigor on his penis. "Jesus Christ!" Jonathan moaned.

Connie released him. "You're up now. Get in the shower, and be quick."

They made the Frontside tram with time to spare. As before, Jonathan spent the entire trip with his face glued to the window. Connie made a few attempts to engage him in conversation, but then shrugged and gave up.

When the sun rose over the horizon before them as they flew, the Earth was invisible. Jonathan had a moment of irrational fear that the aliens had struck again, taking the Earth itself this time. "Where's the Earth?" he whispered.

"New Earth," Connie said. "Just think about the geometry."

Jonathan did so, visualizing the three bodies in his mind. Of course, he told himself, feeling abysmally stupid. The Earth's moving between us and the sun, so we're facing its dark side now. His alarm may have been stupid, but he felt greatly relieved.

After they landed at Frontside, they put on surface suits— Connie had managed somehow to bring her personal suit along, although Jonathan had seen no sign of it until now—and went outside onto the surface. They joined a throng of hundreds of silent, suited figures on the bright, gray plain surrounding the base. Jonathan glanced behind at the base and could see no sign of exposed windows. He realized that the only way for these people to see the sky was to come outside.

"Look!" It was Connie's voice, calling his attention back to the sun. Inevitably, since the suits only had eight channels, quite a few other people were using the same channel and Connie's voice was quickly drowned out.

A string of four black dots was moving slowly across the red face of the sun, moving from left to right. They varied in size and the distances between them were uneven, but they were roughly in a straight line. Fear gripped Jonathan again. What was happening to the sun? "What is it?" he asked. A dozen voices answered him. Half of them said, "Hush!" as though the event were making a sound and he were keeping them from hearing it. But the other half, saying it in various ways, told him it was a transit. A few other people asked what that meant.

"Everyone shut up!" Connie Allendorf's voice echoed in his helmet. "One at a time!" The other voices died down, although not without a few resentful mutterings. Connie spoke again, at a more normal volume this time. "Jonathan, and everyone else, you're seeing some of the other moons moving between us and the sun. They're transiting. Let's see, those are Io, Europa, Ganymede, and Rhea. They're unusually close together this time, but transits are common, given all the moons orbiting the sun. Okay, keep an eye out. Here comes the Earth."

By now, the black dots had moved halfway across the sun. From the right side, something much bigger began to obscure the sun, moving to meet the smaller dots head-on. The new object was just as black, moving slowly, with ponderous inexorability. Jonathan found himself holding his breath.

He had seen an old picture of a total solar eclipse, taken at that classic moment when the moon's disk coincided with the old sun's and only the sun's corona was visible, flaring out around the black circle of the moon. But now of course he was seeing it in reverse, from the moon, and moreover he could see that the proportions were different nowadays: the disk of the Earth was considerably bigger than that of the new sun—three times as big, he would later calculate. The result was something ominous. What he was seeing could almost have been a new gray hole taking the sun. Perhaps he wasn't the only one to whom the parallel occurred: the others were just as silent as he was.

The Earth met the moving dots of the moons and swallowed them. Then it kept on moving and swallowed the sun. Instead of a corona, as in the old photograph, there were red flares, their tips just visible with the sun covered.

The lunar surface had disappeared into darkness. The hundreds of suited figures had also disappeared. Here and there, a helmet light came on as someone felt he had to fight the blackness. There were words of protest, and the helmet lights went off again.

The total part of the eclipse lasted for three and three quarters hours. When at last the bright red limb of the sun began to show again on the right, there were sighs and mutters of relief. Most of the crowd began to disperse, heading back for the air locks. Those, Jonathan decided, were the more experienced lunar citizens. A small group, however, including him and Connie, remained, waiting for the sun to appear entirely again, whole and safe. When it did, after another hour and twenty minutes, the small dots of the transiting moons had gone—as if swallowed permanently by the black disk of the Earth.

"Well?" Connie asked. "How did you like it?"

"Amazing," he breathed. "Amazing! Thank you."

"Oh, don't thank me. Thank the aliens."

"Now there's a Hell of a thought." There were nervous laughs from all around—others sharing their conversation. Jonathan gestured toward the air lock behind them without talking.

Connie said, "Hokey-dokey," and they went back inside.

The next day, they returned to Mendeleev. Jonathan was happy to leave Frontside. Once the eclipse was over, there was little more to do there. Not that Mendeleev was full of entertainment, either, but Frontside was far worse.

When they got back, Jonathan found three messages waiting for him. All were urgent requests for him to visit various outlying sites to help reactivate or repair old pre-Taking computers. He read the messages from the comm screen with a secret sense of relief.

Connie was more than exhausting: she was also emotionally frightening. He found her enormously exciting, and not just because he was twenty-seven and she was his first sexual experience, but also because of her nature—so sensual and uninhibited, so delighted with sexuality in all its varieties, so eager and competent. But his feelings for Connie didn't extend much beyond excitement, friendliness, and gratitude, and he could tell that her feelings were rapidly becoming far deeper and stronger than that. He didn't want to hurt her; going away from Mendeleev might be a cowardly solution, but it was the only one he could think of.

He spent most of the next three months travelling to one remote site after another. Often the task was almost as easy as his work on the Rockway machine at Mendeleev the day after his arrival. At other times, it took him days—three weeks, in one case—to track down and remedy the problem. And twice there was no solution: boards had gone bad in the old computers, and there were no replacements available anymore, and there never would be; the computers had to be retired, designated as collections of spare parts, and their users, with much gnashing of teeth, had no choice but to begin the tedious task of rewriting their software for newer machines and converting and reloading their data.

In spite of these occasional failures, Jonathan encountered nothing but friendship and respect from the lunar workers. His background as an escapee seemed far less important up here than it had on Earth. He wondered about that. Perhaps, he thought, since the men and women on the moon considered themselves the cream of the human crop—and rightly so, judging by those he had met so far—they felt that anyone who was permitted to work on the moon must be equally superior. And of course there was Isaac

Simkin's magic name, never mentioned to his face but no doubt known to everyone as the name of Jonathan's sponsor.

Jonathan was finding at last, on the moon, the kind of camaraderie and acceptance and feeling of self-worth he had yearned for for so long.

The work with the old computers and their users was, after all, far more satisfying to him than his short-lived job as an historian. Perhaps this was his true calling, he concluded somewhat reluctantly, and he put aside any thought of researching old documents ever again. He did his best not to think about the boxes of documents from the Cold that must be piling up outside his office at the University in Lander. He also put aside any thoughts of Julie, except to hope she had adjusted to her new world, was at home with her work, and had found someone to love and to love her.

Whenever he happened to be back at Mendeleev, Connie always seemed aware of it without his contacting her, and he would soon receive a comm call from her. Once or twice he tried to steel himself to tell her over the comm that they should stop seeing each other, but each time he saw her face on the screen, read the hunger and eagerness in it, and listened to her voice, his desire would flare up, as if it had been a banked fire hidden within him, hidden from his own view, and contact with Connie was the breath required to blow it into vigorous life again.

Sometimes he mentioned Elena to her; she would shrug and change the subject. Occasionally, he was invited to dine with Isaac Simkin again, and not always with Connie. But always without Elena. Always she sent her regrets *via* her father, along with the explanation that her mysterious work (never described) was keeping her too busy for a social life. What made this all the more frustrating was that Isaac often mentioned having seen his daughter recently. In other words, she was visiting Mendeleev, but it always happened—and obviously not by chance—that her visits and Jonathan's never overlapped.

Elena's deliberately avoiding him filled Jonathan with helpless resentment—and simultaneously made him more desperate to see her.

In spite of himself, he found he liked Isaac Simkin more each time he spent an evening in his company, and it was clear that Isaac was increasingly fond of him and trusted him more and more. Connie was pleased with Jonathan's progress in this regard, repeating occasionally her earlier proverb that he was doing his career no harm.

None of this mattered to Jonathan. He wanted Elena.

The inevitable end to Jonathan's relationship with Connie Allendorf was just as unpleasant as he had feared it would be.

Connie had been away from Mendeleev for a couple of days, and so had Jonathan. He returned and spent a day alone doing nothing of importance, and then the next evening Connie showed up at his quarters, as determindedly cheerful as ever. She had a bulky package under one arm.

"Hello, hello," she said, having let herself in. (The door had begun opening to her palm in addition to his shortly after their affair began. Jonathan and Connie had never discussed the question of access, but the change had taken place anyway.) "Got something for you."

Jonathan, sunk in his armchair, looked up from the old novel he was listlessly trying to read and forced a smile. "Oh? What is it?"

"Mr. Sunshine, aren't you?" Connie said, observantly and sharply.

"Sorry. I haven't been feeling too lively lately."

"Overworking?"

"Working hard at impressing people up here. Cementing my position."

She came over to him, took the book from him and put it on the small table beside the chair, placed her package on top of it, and sat in his lap and put her arms around his neck. "I just happen to know that you don't have to work at that anymore. Everyone at Mendeleev and the remote sites is so impressed with you that if you impress them any more, they'll all want to marry you. Or at least go to bed with you."

Connie's habit of putting everything in sexual terms was

beginning to annoy Jonathan. "I'll be satisfied with one person wanting to marry me."

Connie drew back and stared at him for a moment. "Will you settle for me just moving in instead? Not that I'm not flattered."

"Oh, I didn't—"

There was a long silence. Connie removed her arms from his neck and pushed herself to her feet. She stared at Jonathan, and Jonathan stared at the floor. "You didn't mean me," she said quietly. "Right?" When he didn't reply, she said, "Right, Jonathan? Look at me!"

He raised his eyes to her face. She was expressionless. Jonathan had to clear his throat in order to speak. "I'm sorry."

"You bastard," Connie said in a perfectly normal tone. Tears spilled from her eyes, but other than that, she gave no sign of grief. "Men always fall in love with *me,* not the other way around. I even spent the last two days digging this shit up for you"—she pointed to the package beside Jonathan's chair— "because I found out about your historical work and your request to see the documents kept up here. I really had to work hard to get this for you. You still want Elena, don't you?"

Jonathan looked away again, staring at the wall. He wanted to tell her again how sorry he was, and how miserable he felt, but he couldn't bring himself to talk at all. He felt that, somehow, everything would resolve itself if he simply kept quiet.

"Elena! That—No, I won't let you turn me against her. Jonathan!" Her voice turned suddenly pleading, a sound he had never heard before. It jerked his gaze back to her face. She leaned toward him, putting her hands on the arms of his chair. "Jonathan! What can I do to replace her for you?"

He shook his head, wanting to say "Nothing," but afraid to.

Connie sighed and straightened up. They stared wordlessly at each other for a moment. Suddenly Connie's face contorted. "You bastard!" she screamed. Jonathan jumped at the sound. "You son of a bitch! You . . . Fuck you!" She ran from the room, slamming the door behind her.

My God, Jonathan thought, dazed, that's the end of it. She won't ever be here again! With Connie, he somehow knew, there would never be reconciliations; the first break would always be the last.

Unable to sleep that night, Jonathan opened Connie's package and started to read what he found inside.

It was an unbound pile of pages, typed single-spaced with narrow margins. Skimming it first, he realized that he held excerpts from some sort of diary—or journal, rather, for the entries were short essays rather than descriptions of a day's events. Furthermore, each entry was preceded by a name or an initial, apparently that of the author of that entry: it seemed that the journal was the work of many individuals. He turned back to the beginning, and soon the scene with Connie was forgotten.

25

Monday, 9th February, 2009. A. Battani.

I have asked certain members of our staff to join me in maintaining a journal, a combination of historical and personal document. This will record permanently what happens here at the Mendeleev Observatory and what our reactions are to events. I have chosen English as the language of this journal since it is the official language of the observatory as well as that of the NASA base at Frontside. The crew at that base have elected to place themselves under our administration.

As to the future, there are only two possibilities: either we will survive, or we will not. (That reminds me of a wonderful joke about a physicist, a chemist, and a mathematician trapped in a hotel during a fire, but I must not use this space for frivolous purposes. Moreover, Moira tells me I cannot tell a joke properly.)

If we survive, this document will serve as a valuable historical datum for future generations. If we do not, it may be of interest to some alien race which visits our solar system in the future. Perhaps even the alien race. If this is the case, and yours are the eyes which read this, I request you to consider what you have done and the consequences to an entire sentient species, and many other species as well.

To proceed. I will begin this journal with a short précis of our current situation.

Yesterday morning, at 9:30 A.M., Greenwich Mean Time, our sun was somehow removed from us. How such a thing could have been done, we as yet have no idea. Why it was done and the race by which it was done are another matter entirely. To explain all of that would, it seems to me, be tedious and pointless. Pointless because all the relevant details are already on record here at the observatory, and it remains only to organize them in a form useful to future historians (of whatever species). I prefer that this journal should record events and reactions from the time of the taking of the sun onward.

Early this morning, our Director, Professor Larrieux, announced his intention to leave Mendeleev and go to NASA's base at Frontside. There he will join a small group returning to Earth. The venture is of course suicide. Very few chose to go with him, and those of us who are staying tried very hard to change the minds of all in Professor Larrieux's party. However, he was adamant. They left at 3 P.M. this afternoon, by the clock we still use.

He named me Acting Director before he left. Since there is no organization left on Earth to oversee the observatory's operations, all control is therefore now vested here on the moon. Also, since it is clear to me that the Director and his followers will never return from Earth, it appears that I am now Director de jure as well as de facto. I do not wish to appear cold-blooded, but I feel we must treat Professor Larrieux's death as already an accomplished fact and act in that light. However, I will wait until it is a confirmed fact before I organize our survivors. At that time, I will ask for an election to determine the permanent Director and, for that matter, the form of government our little republic will observe. Clemmons assures me I am already the choice of the majority.

For the immediate future, I have requested that life and work continue at Mendeleev as if nothing unusual had happened. Of course, that is extremely difficult, given the natural fear of the staff that we are all doomed. Even if we do survive, many of us are emotionally stunned by the complete loss of all the family and friends we left behind on Earth. Nonetheless, life must go on, as after any great catastrophe. The future will not take care of itself; we must do that ourselves.

Now, I must explain why I write of the future in this fashion, as though I expected to be alive to see it.

Some days ago, the aliens sent us a message telling what was about to happen and giving the precise time interval remaining before the taking of the sun was to occur. Using that datum, we deduced a trajectory for the gray hole. Indeed, that trajectory is extremely close to the one the gray hole then followed. Also, we *have a considerable body of observations on the path the gray hole followed through the solar system before that message was received. Finally, we have a good estimate of the gray hole's mass from the noticeable effect its passage has had on the gas giants as it passed.*

Combining all of these, my immediate staff and I concluded early that, upon the disappearance of the sun and its gravitational influence upon the bodies of the solar system, the following scenario will occur.

Jupiter and Saturn will be drawn together by mutual gravitational attraction. The Earth and the other planets of the solar system, along with their moons, will then be drawn into orbit around the new gas giant thus formed. Moreover, the Earth's new orbit will be at such a distance (in round numbers, 3.0×10^6 meters) that its new sidereal year will be identical to the old one of 365.256 days. This, it seemed to me, could not be a coincidence. All that was missing for the creation of a new solar system, one as habitable as the old, was for the new gas giant to undergo fusion and turn into a new sun. Unfortunately, the mass of the gas giant will not be sufficient for that to happen.

Nonetheless, my consideration of the above numbers convinced me that we on the moon, and the few men in space who had also survived the taking of the sun and the nuclear war on Earth immediately afterward, were not after all doomed. Too much effort had gone into planning the gray hole's trajectory for our extermination to be intended. Nor did I believe that the aliens had taken all of this trouble only to create a new system devoid of native life that they could then take over themselves, sometime in the future. If that were their plan, why bother to create a new system in which the length of the Earth's year would be exactly the same as it always had been in human memory, thus assuring a system in which human beings would be comfortable? No, it was obvious to me that our survival was included in their plans.

That conviction was the source of my optimism, my attempts to rally the personnel at the observatory. However, at the same time, I did not want to arouse unrealistic hopes by saying too much.

However, after the taking of the sun, we finally received

another message from the aliens, and this one confirmed all of my calculations and assumptions. Moreover, the aliens promised us a method of starting fusion in the new gas giant. They will transmit plans and specifications for the necessary devices in the near future. We will then have approximately three years to build and test the devices before conditions will be proper for starting fusion. More time will have to pass before the gas giant emits enough heat to revaporize the atmosphere of Earth, which will have long been frozen by then. How long it will then be before we can contemplate returning to Earth to resettle it, I do not know; years, perhaps. Eventually, however, we will do just that.

Rereading what I've just written, I find that it is not a personal comment, after all, but instead a rather objective narrative of recent events. Yet I specified when beginning this journal that it was to be a personal record, as well. Very well, then, I shall try.

I find it difficult in the extreme to bare inner feelings for the reading pleasure of strangers, and probably strangers not yet born or born to human parents. Perhaps as the years go by and I continue to contribute to this journal, it will become easier. For now, I will limit myself to a few comments concerning those I have lost.

As is the case with almost everyone else here (and no doubt at the NASA base, as well), I have lost family and friends on Earth. Worse than having lost them, I must endure the thought that they may be still alive, but dying in the cold and the dark on the surface of the Earth at this moment. Only when I drink enough can I drive such thoughts from me and pretend to cheerfulness. It was the torture of such thoughts that drove Professor Larrieux and some others to return to Earth to find their loved ones and die with them if they could not bring them here. Should I feel guilty that I did not make the same choice?

But what good would it do? The manpower and organization necessary to refuel a landed shuttle and then relaunch it—why, surely none of that still exists on Earth. Let alone the transportation systems required, in my case, to journey to my home in Milan from the landing/launch site and then journey back with my daughter and grandchild.

I tell myself these logical thoughts, which should absolve me from any sin, but I also know that I will be haunted for the rest of my life by the thought that I could have done something to save them. Or that I should have returned to die with them. But I want to live!

Monday, February 9, 2009. C. Horwith.

I've read what Al just wrote. I don't think I can write as fluently as he does, even though English is my native language, but I'll try. Four score and seven years ago, etc. That's the only eloquent speech I know.

I don't think Al should feel guilty, not at all. We've all had to make the same decision, and it looks like we all made the same choice he did. Except for the group of suicidal fools that went back down with Prof. L. From what I've been able to see, L. was never much of a director for this place. In fact, Al always did all the work for him, anyway, so he might as well have the title and salary as well as the work. Not that there is any salary anymore, of course. I mean that he might as well have the offical status, since he has to do the work.

Al has tried to explain to me just how and why we're all going to survive. I couldn't understand much of it, only the broad outlines. Sorry, Al. I want to be honest and open in this journal, so I hope your feelings don't get hurt. Anyway, I'm willing to take his word that everything will work out. Funny that not too long ago, I thought I was doomed and so was the entire human race. Now I find that I'm one of the lucky few, and that I can plan to have a long life and children and so on. Thank God I've got someone to plan such a future with.

What makes it easier for me is that I don't have anyone back home to feel torn up about. Both my parents died when I was in college, and the only sibling I have is a brother. Let's just say we're not friends. I shouldn't feel glad about what's happening to him, but we're supposed to be honest, and I do. I never had really close friends, not until I got to Mendeleev, which is a hell of a thing for a man of my age to have to admit, but that's the way it is. I feel I'm making up for lost time now. Especially now, because there's nothing like knowing you're the last surviving group of human beings in the Universe to make a bunch of people draw close together. The folks at Mendeleev have suddenly begun to feel like my family to me. I hope they all feel the same way.

I don't have any useful information to contribute to this, not like Al, so I guess my parts will be all personal feelings and emotional reactions. At least, as much of that kind of thing as I can write down. Like Al said, it's very hard to expose yourself to strangers you'll probably never even know—and maybe alien strangers to boot.

Wednesday, 11th February, 2009. Moira Thabanchu Horwith.

Dr. Battani tells me there is no need to provide biographical background material for this journal, since all of that is available already at the observatory, and those who read this document in the future can refer to those papers.

I see that both Dr. Battani and my husband have written about the pain or lack thereof of losing friends and relatives left behind on Earth. I concur fully with Clemmons's statement that Dr. Battani need feel no guilt at not returning to Earth. Professor Larrieux and his group, including many NASA people, will be landing late tomorrow night or early Friday morning, and then we will see what conditions they discover. I for one have no doubt that they will discover nothing but corpses—or at best the living who wish they were corpses already and will do their best to make corpses out of Professor Larrieux and the others.

I, too, have family and other dear ones on Earth. Had, I should say. Legally, I still have a husband, assuming Adrian du Plessis survives. Above, I mentioned my present husband, Clemmons Horwith. Since Adrian's death is a foregone conclusion (or if by some miracle he should survive, then our permanent separation), I decided last night that I can consider myself a widow. After some argument, I prevailed upon Dr. Battani to include the power to perform marriages in his new position, and Clemmons and I were married a few hours ago.

Adrian and I should never have married; we were utterly unsuited. Young as we were, we allowed ourselves to be ruled by our glands rather than our heads. He was no more to blame for the collapse of the marriage than I was, although at the time it happened, it was difficult for either of us to be so objective. Once the initial pain had died down, however, I found it easy to wish him the best. I wish I could feel grief at what must have happened to him, or be happening at this moment, but I confess that I feel only an abstract regret, something more intellectual than emotional. For my family, too, I feel far less than I know I ought to.

I think it's because, more than anyone else up here, even Dr. Battani, I've felt like a Lunarian (Dr. Battani insists upon that usage) since the day I arrived. I was happy to leave Earth, happy to be here. To a degree, I'm ashamed to admit that what has happened to Earth almost pleases me: now my cutting-off from Earth, my separation from my earlier life, is complete and final, and that without my having to do anything to finalize or complete it. The aliens have done me a service, although I doubt whether it would please them to know it.

There were other entries from other Mendeleev personnel of the time. At first, Jonathan read it all, fascinated, intrigued. But much of it was biographical detail, in spite of Battani's apparent request not to include such material, and too much of it was a detailing of grief and loss that Jonathan found utterly depressing and eventually repetitive. After a few pages, he began to skip ahead. He wanted especially to find the next references to the landing on Earth of the Larrieux party, if there were such references. He found one at last, written by Moira Horwith.

Friday, 13th February, 2009. Moira H.
A few hours ago, we received a lengthy transmission from Professor Larrieux, passed on through Frontside. They had just landed at the Kennedy Space Center, which Larrieux chose personally as the site most likely to support refueling and relaunching. However, the situation is even worse than we had guessed.
Their landing was a bad one. This was apparently due both to the condition of the runway and the lack of ground support, either

air-traffic control or lighting. The shuttle was severely damaged during landing—so damaged, Larrieux reported, that reuse would be unlikely even were the spaceport operating at what used to be normal; as it is, repairs are impossible.

They have found chaos. The temperatures in Florida are still quite bearable, but society has collapsed. As we already knew, America's major cities were bombed with nuclear weapons immediately after the disappearance of the sun. The combined effects of the war and the darkness mean that the shuttle will never fly again. The spaceport crew seems to have left, and in fact the landing party has found few people at all in that area.

With the collapse of all transportation systems, it appears that the landing party can't even make their way to their homes, so that their subsidiary purpose in returning to Earth—to at least die with their families, if they were unable to bring them up here—can't even be fulfilled. Those foolish people have left the safety of the moon only to end up dying of cold and hunger within meters of the shuttle.

What a grim joke today's date is! It could only be more appropriate if this had been the day on which the sun was taken from us.

I can't tell if Dr. Battani (who now wants me to call him Al, as Clemmons does, but I still can't) has been able at all to divest himself of his feelings of guilt, given this proof of the pointlessness of Professor Larrieux's actions. I hope he can do so. Strangely enough, I find my own guilt growing in inverse proportion to my conviction that I made the right decision in staying on the moon. That is, the clearer it becomes that I could have done nothing by returning to Earth, the guiltier I feel that I did not.

Nonetheless, I look forward to the future with growing hope. Now that I am convinced Earth will again become habitable and that we can manage to survive until then on the moon, thanks to the plants and animals that have long been kept at Frontside Base for biological and botanical experiments, I need have no more fears for my own physical survival. My emotional survival, which

*seemed in doubt long before the aliens took our sun, now also
seems assured, thanks to Clemmons Horwith.*

*I note that Clemmons wrote in this journal a few days ago about
our having children. Clemmons, it seems proper that we should
discuss this idea in person rather than through the medium of this
public forum! Nonetheless, I will say that I agree with you: we
should have children. And others on the moon should begin to
consider doing the same.*

Jonathan read for many hours more, unaware of the passage of
time. While many people had contributed to the Mendeleev
journal, the ones whose entries stayed with him and whose names
he sought most eagerly as he read through the unbound pages were
Alfredo Battani, Moira Horwith, and Clemmons Horwith. More
than any of the others, they commented on each other's contributions, maintaining a dialogue through their writing. It ranged from
caustic to gentle, and Jonathan could tell from their writing that
they had been close friends.

Each had a distinct personality. At least, the personalities
displayed by their writing were distinct and unique—and fascinating to Jonathan. Battani's writing was for the most part deliberately impersonal, filled with descriptions of events and technical data
but little that was internal. Moira tried to be less impersonal, but
the result was almost painfully analytical, a sort of grim and
purposeful self-exposure that lacked conviction. As she said
herself of her own feelings and reactions, she knew what she
ought to feel but felt it only on an intellectual level, almost as an
intellectual exercise, rather than emotionally. The exception was
her feelings for her new husband: those shone through even her
most stilted and formal prose.

And her husband, Clemmons Horwith, was to Jonathan's mind
the most likable of all. As opposed to his wife, he strove for
formality and eloquence in his prose but rarely achieved it.
Instead, his writing was relaxed and informal, often amusing, and
the true man showed clearly through it. Of all of them, he was the
one Jonathan most wished he could have known. Battani, he
admired for his intellect; he would have been thrilled to have that

man for a teacher. Thabanchu, seeing her through Horwith's eyes and glimpsing her elusive and complex soul through her own words, he could easily fantasize loving. When he realized what her race was, Jonathan was surprised to find that it made no difference to him.

But he would never know any of them. They had all been adults when his grandfather and the Martinsons were born, probably older than Jonathan himself was now. They were long dead and gone, returned to the dust. (Of the moon or the Earth? He had no idea. Part of him wanted to know; part of him wished never to find out.)

For the moment, at least, he had forgotten about Connie and the sudden end of their affair. He had even forgotten about Elena (for the moment!). All he could think of was the people who had lived on the moon at the time of the Taking. How different they were, he thought, from the people who lived on the moon now! Or those who lived on the surface of the Earth. Modern Lunarians could pride themselves on their descent from those heroic ancestors— and now Jonathan, too, considered them heroic—but they had descended far indeed.

He would never, except in dreams, know these people whose words he was reading. He was limited to knowing their descendants and listening to today's citizens' historical self-deceptions, their mythologizing of their past. It was almost enough to make him weep. If only he could travel into the past, or, better yet, bring those people forward to the present! He had an aching, empty feeling of a terrible loss of something wonderful he had never possessed.

At last Jonathan turned out the lights and went to sleep. As he drifted off, there were tears on his cheeks.

═══26═══

A few weeks later, Jonathan was asked to accompany a couple of environmental engineers to a remote site which was scheduled to be reoccupied.

One of the engineers was named Sessu Ndamena. He was short and wiry, with short, tightly curled black hair, a broad, flat nose, and the blackest skin Jonathan had ever seen. The other, John Lin, was tall, heavily muscled, and apparently of unmixed Oriental ancestry. Jonathan observed his own reactions with interest: he felt no distaste or dislike at all, and no hesitancy about spending however many days it would be isolated with them in an old base, far from Mendeleev. It seemed curious to Jonathan that he no longer felt any such revulsion; he would have felt it not that long ago.

Perhaps it was reading the diaries that had done the trick, he guessed; more specifically, perhaps it was identifying with Clemmons Horwith and his love for his wife. Whatever the reason, something had purged him of his old prejudice. And I'm glad it's gone, he thought. Life is so much easier this way.

"Afraid we're going to have to drive," John Lin said. "I tried to arrange for us to fly, but there weren't any crews or machines available."

"Exquisite, J. Lin," Sessu said in his high, thin, soft voice. He sighed melodramatically. "Days on end sitting cramped in one of those rovers, breathing my own air and drinking my own fluids, fearing death because of your driving."

"Why do you always complain so much?" Lin said testily. "I swear to you," he said to Jonathan, "this man does nothing but complain. If he wasn't one of the best at what he does, I'd refuse to work with him anymore."

"*One* of the best!" Sessu said in mock indignation. He winked at Jonathan while Lin raved on.

"Anyway," John Lin said after he had vented his feelings, "you won't have to endure my driving, this time. I'm bringing along extra equipment, so there'll be no room in my rover for any passengers. I'm not sure I'd want you along anyway. You and Jonathan can drive together."

"You know how to drive a rover, don't you?" Sessu asked Jonathan hopefully.

"Sorry. In fact, I don't know how to drive anything."

"Exquisite," Sessu said. Jonathan was to learn that that was his favorite word, and he always used it when he thought something was very bad, indeed. "The only thing I hate more than J. Lin's driving is my own."

The rovers were the same skeletal vehicles Clemmons Horwith had known, very little changed since those days except for being faster and much more reliable. They weren't capable of very high speeds by Earth standards—not, for example, compared to the public trams in Lander—but Sessu managed to coax out of theirs a velocity that terrified Jonathan.

There were well marked trails for them to follow, and deviating from them except in urgent situations was against regulations. That scarcely mattered to Sessu. As he veered from the trail, Sessu said to Jonathan, "The trails are flat. Graded. That's what I don't like about them."

"What?"

Sessu didn't reply. He demonstrated. The multitude of tiny craters, from half a meter down to microscopic, he simply drove over, ignoring them. This produced a bumpy ride that varied from vibratory to bone-rattling. The larger craters—anywhere up to five or ten meters across—he headed straight for, accelerating and shouting with laughter. Jonathan clutched the railing beside him with his right hand and the seat edge with his left and closed his eyes. The rover would sail into the air, land skidding in the dust halfway down the crater slope, and then roar across the crater floor and up the far side, bouncing over the rim at the top and then back onto the surface of the plain. "I love these rovers!" Sessu shouted. "Having fun?"

A few times on their long trip, they encountered huge craters, with depths of many meters. These were Sessu's favorite. He would head the rover down their inside walls at a shallow angle, straighten out so that he was moving parallel to the rim, and accelerate all the way around the crater, using its inner rim as a racetrack. Dust rose around them in a blinding cloud, picked up by the rover's cleated wheels and thrown up and dumped over its passengers. On the moon, dust didn't hang in the air, Jonathan found, because there wasn't any air: it fell down rapidly, each dust particle following its own ballistic trajectory. Most of those trajectories seemed to end on Jonathan.

"What about the equipment?" he asked Sessu. "Won't all this dust damage it?"

Sessu jerked the steering wheel to the right and the rover climbed up the crater wall, its wheels spinning in the dust and throwing up even more of it. The vehicle leapt over the crater rim and crashed slow motion to the ground beyond it. Jonathan rose in the air and floated back to his seat. "We'll let J. Lin clean it off!" Sessu yelled. Lin, far behind, could hear the conversation just as well as Jonathan. He cursed at his colleague. Sessu laughed.

"No cobwebs. That's one of the advantages of vacuum." Sessu swept his flashlight around the interior of the station. "No spiders, and no drifting dust."

He was right, but there was plenty of dust lying on every surface, and especially on the dirt floor. Jonathan remarked on it.

"Someone left a door open," Sessu said. "Or a few doors. This site hasn't been used since long before the Taking. It was abandoned back when the retrenchment from space was under way, in the late nineties. I've heard there was a lot of resentment over that, and some workers on the moon deliberately sabotaged things."

"So they left the doors open."

"That's it. So let's try to find them. We have to close all the locks and make this place airtight again and then get the heat and lights on."

John Lin arrived almost two hours later, by which time Jonathan and Sessu had the small station airtight and pressurized.

They greeted him with their helmets off. "We've got air and light, J. Lin," Sessu greeted him. "Not much heat, yet. It's been cold for too long. Take off your suit and stay for a while."

Lin grunted a surly hello and doffed his surface suit, and then he and Sessu set to work. Jonathan was impressed, watching them, at their efficiency and cooperation, at how well they worked together, despite Sessu's constant jibes and Lin's constant angry responses. His own work was so solitary. What would it be like, he wondered, to have a partner, and moreover one who was able to virtually read one's thoughts? He shrugged and went into the small room which contained the site's minicomputer.

It was a very fortunate thing that records had been so scrupulously kept before the Taking and so reverently preserved after it. As it was, Jonathan had known precisely what this machine was before he left Mendeleev, and he had brought with him enough parts, salvaged from the Cold or stored on the moon, to rebuild it almost from scratch. Surgery that drastic wasn't necessary; by the next day, Jonathan had the machine running and executing simple test programs to his satisfaction.

The next step was to link the old computer to one of the powerful mainframes at Mendeleev and allow the newer, faster, and far more powerful machine at the observatory to subject the old minicomputer to a large battery of tests with far greater speed and accuracy than Jonathan could achieve himself. He went through the process of setting the link up and starting the tests, but he did so mechanically. His mind was on other matters. He left the minicomputer blinking happily to itself as it chatted with the mainframe at Mendeleev and wandered over to where the two engineers were working.

Dressed in shorts and shirtless, the two of them were wrestling an old refrigerator up a dirt ramp. It was an enormous gadget; even in the moon's one-sixth gravity, it must have weighed over a hundred kilograms. Both were sweating. John Lin, who was in the rear and carrying most of the weight, was cursing. Sessu was grinning; his grin widened with every one of Lin's curses. They put the refrigerator down and stopped to rest.

"I could have been a doctor," Lin said. "Like my father."

"The quack," Sessu said. "This is more socially valuable work, J. Lin. This refrigerator"—he slapped the side of it—"will be used to keep beers cold when the astronomers are working here again. We're contributing to someone's inspiration, some new Herschel, mayhap."

"Herschel?"

"Philistine. Up."

They heaved the refrigerator off the ground again, Jonathan stepped forward to help, and John Lin lost his footing on the soft surface. Lunar dirt crumpled away beneath his shoe, and his feet slid backward, down the slope.

Jonathan lunged and managed to get his fingers under the refrigerator just in time to guide its slow descent to the ground. John Lin was still falling facedown toward the floor, with his hands under the refrigerator. Jonathan had a vision of the edge of the refrigerator grinding remorselessly down, slow motion, on them, crushing the bones. He was able to push it to one side so that it missed Lin's hands; he barely managed to yank his own fingers away in time.

Jonathan straightened up, gasping. "Thank God everything happens so slowly here!"

"Thank Newton, you mean," Sessu said, and for once his flippancy sounded forced. "And you. God had nothing to do with it."

"Yeah," John Lin said. "Thanks." His few words carried even more sincerity.

"I guess that's why they told me never to work alone on the moon," Jonathan said thoughtfully. "So that if an accident happens, you won't find yourself hurt without anyone to help and no one knowing where you are."

John Lin shook his head. "They always know where you are."

"That's right," Sessu said. "It's all on the Admin. computer at Mendeleev. Maybe you'd better help us with this."

"Gladly." He helped them heave the huge old machine the rest of the way up the ramp and then across the base to the new location they had chosen for it, but his mind was elsewhere. Was the location of everyone on the Admin. computer at Mendeleev, even that of the daughter of the Director?

While Sessu Ndamena and John Lin slept their well earned sleep that night, Jonathan worked at the computer.

Acessing the Admin. computer at Mendeleev was simple enough, since it was one of the machines available to him for his tests. Finding and reading the database containing personnel locations on the moon was a different matter and would have been a laborious and virtually endless task had he tried to do it manually. Instead, he spent the hours he should have been sleeping, modifying some of the test programs on the minicomputer. Then he set up a batch runstream on the Mendeleev Admin. computer to run the remote mini through its test paces and went to his own cot to try to sleep. The mini would do his work for him.

He dozed fitfully for an hour. At that point, Sessu and Lin both began stirring, and Jonathan feigned sleep. He heard Sessu make a low, good-natured joke about his sleeping late and Lin answering abruptly by saying that Jonathan had still been up and working when he went to bed. Sessu laughed and headed for the tiny portable shower stall.

Jonathan must have fallen genuinely asleep after that, for he woke to find Sessu and Lin already back at work with all signs of their breakfast cleaned away.

He roused himself, showered, and ate breakfast. Then he checked the minicomputer. It was still running through its series of tests, and according to its console display was little more than halfway done with it. This surprised Jonathan. Then he realized that the Admin. computer was so heavily used by the Mendeleev staff that it was probably accessing the mini only rarely. If that had been true during the night and early morning, it must be even more so now, with more people at their desks at Mendeleev. In that case, it might be many more hours yet before he had his answer.

He spent the rest of the day doing minor odd jobs and helping the two engineers as much as he could. There really wasn't much he could do for them, since he had no training at all in their multidisciplinary field, but he was able to fetch tools and help them lift things. He also fetched Sessu his numerous bottles of beer. It turned out that Sessu had brought an enormous supply of beer with him on the rover, although Jonathan hadn't noticed it, and the heavy refrigerator the three of them had moved the day before was now working well and filled with the beer, which Sessu drank by the liter despite Lin's dour disapproval.

After supper, the two engineers both showered, sat talking for a short while, their eyelids drooping, and then tumbled into their beds and fell into instant sleep.

Jonathan waited for a few minutes to be sure they were both soundly asleep. Then he stood up and walked around, making a fair amount of noise. There was no response at all from the two sleeping figures. Their hours of hard work were a definite advantage to him. Jonathan fairly ran to the minicomputer.

The computer was still working on the test programs. But judging by what the console showed him, it was well past the point where it had tried to access the personnel location database. Impatiently, Jonathan killed the run and displayed the small file he had had the test program build. It was only one record long. The first field was the employee name, and it contained the characters SIMKIN ELENA. The next two fields were numbers—lunar latitude and longitude.

Jonathan put on his surface suit and went out to the rover, where Sessu had a map he had used occasionally during the trip from Mendeleev. When he came back inside, the inner door of the air lock made a disturbingly loud noise as it *whooshed* shut. John Lin stirred in his sleep and mumbled something. Jonathan froze. When the engineer seemed to be sleeping peacefully again, Jonathan moved carefully across the open space to the main room, hoping the map, which he was carrying opened out, wouldn't crackle or rustle.

He made it to the small computer room without disturbing them, doffed his helmet, and set about finding Elena's location on the map.

According to the map, at least, there was nothing there—no noteworthy geological structure and no man-made structure.

Jonathan shrugged. For whatever reason she was there, that was where he would be, too.

Sessu had marked the base they were in with a red circle, which helped matters. Peering at the map, Jonathan estimated it shouldn't take him more than three hours to travel by rover from the old base to Elena's location. Sessu and Lin would be all right, because they had the other rover, the one Lin had driven. And Jonathan would manage because he had watched carefully while Sessu drove them from Mendeleev, and he was sure he could operate the vehicle. The final question—what he would do when he reached Elena—he had no answer to, only a vague idea that he would, with eloquence and the force of his love and his personality, persuade her to change her mind and marry him. Or at the very least to stop refusing to communicate with him. For a moment, he wondered if his lack of sleep were affecting his judgment, but he dismissed the thought as irrelevant to what he had to do.

With the computer room door closed, Jonathan performed the noisy task of putting on his helmet and sealing it again and then folded the map. Then, quietly, he left the base, started up the rover he and Sessu had driven in, and started moving in a straight line toward Elena's latitude and longitude.

Driving the rover was easy, after all. He did everything he had seen Sessu do—except that he avoided large craters and slowed down for the small ones.

Isaac Simkin was one of those rare and enviable people who never sleep—or at least never seem to sleep. Presumably he didn't really stay awake every minute of every hour of every day, but no one who worked with him could honestly say they had ever seen him so much as nap.

That was one of the reasons Isaac loved the moon. He loved it half the time, at any rate: during the fourteen-day-long days. Then the sun-drenched landscape outside Mendeleev always matched his inner clock, and he used to say that his ancestors hadn't survived on the moon; they had evolved there. He made that joke to Elena quite often, and she always smiled dutifully. "Your mother was the opposite," he once told Elena in a rare moment of confidence about his marriage. "She liked to sleep all the time. She was always in bed, and I was always out of it. It didn't help matters."

His wakefulness was a convenient habit for Isaac Simkin. He sometimes wondered if all the great rulers of history had shared his peculiar biology. How else could one man keep his finger on the pulse of a vast number of subjects? How else could a man stay in control?

He did eat, though, and so that kept him away from his office on a fairly regular schedule. Thus he was in his private suite, digesting a light meal and staring, through the window that formed one wall, at the slanting shadows of late afternoon on the moon's surface, when his comm set beeped at him. It was a man from the base computer center. "We've had an unauthorized access into the personnel data base sir," the man said.

Isaac cursed. "When?"

"It just happened, sir. The Admin. computer just alerted me, and I called you right away."

"Where—Never mind. I'm heading back to my office. I'll call you from there in a few minutes."

Isaac hurried back to his office, debating with himself as he walked whether he ought to have his suite expanded and the data facilities of his office duplicated there. That way, I'd never be out of touch with things, no matter where I was, he thought. He had had that debate before but had never actually done anything more than argue with himself about it so far.

Once at his office, Isaac commed the computer center and had all the available information dumped to his desk. This sort of thing was supposed to be impossible—or so he had been assured five years earlier, after the last such success. With the safeguards that had been added, who was there, outside the computer center itself, with the knowledge and ability to pull off such a penetration? He knew the answer to his own question even as he asked it.

Confirming his suspicion, the access had been made from an old remote observing site, abandoned long before the Taking but currently being renovated for reuse. Three men were there now, he quickly determined, and one of them was Jonathan Holroyd. Isaac nodded to himself and typed in more commands.

The access had been an attempt to read the current status record of Elena Simkin, his daughter. Isaac nodded again. And where was Jonathan Holroyd now? Isaac accessed the personnel data base himself and requested that information. The latitude and longitude that resulted were different from those of the base where Jonathan was supposed to be working.

Isaac consulted a map and sighed. There was no reasonable doubt: Jonathan was making a beeline for Elena's position. Good thing he doesn't know about the transponder built into everyone's suit, Isaac thought. If he were to disable it somehow, I'd have no idea where he was or where he was heading. Not that Jonathan could have disabled the transponder, even if he had been aware of its presence: its design deliberately integrated the transponder with the electronics for the suit's air regenerator; thus the only way a man could move about untraced on the moon's surface would be if he could hold his breath for a very long time.

Isaac waited a measured few minutes, accessed the database for Jonathan's position again, and then calculated the younger man's speed and probable arrival time. He had perhaps three hours, yet, and possibly longer. His first impulse was to send out personnel to intercept Jonathan and bring him back to be placed in detention at Mendeleev. Unauthorized computer access alone was a sufficient charge. His second impulse was to pretend to ignore this trangression and see what happened. Why imprison Jonathan when Isaac saw such potential in him? Why destroy his usefulness and in all likelihood turn him into an enemy?

His third impulse was not to take too many chances. He ordered up a vehicle and crew and ordered that his personal (and transponderless) surface suit be delivered to the port from which the lunar tram would depart. And he unlocked a drawer in his desk which normally always stayed locked.

The great red sun was in his eyes, a problem despite the darker visor he had lowered over his faceplate. And the sun was low, so that the shadows were long and dangerous; Jonathan was constantly afraid he would hit a crater, invisible because of the shadows and the dark visor, and cripple the rover.

He knew he was near Elena's coordinates, but he could see nothing. She wouldn't be out in the open, would she? he asked himself. But if there *were* a building, then it must be very small indeed. Or perhaps within a crater. All the other buildings he had seen on the moon, including those sheltered inside craters, gave away their presence by their outbuildings and antennae.

Could it be just beyond the horizon? The horizon was much closer on the moon than on Earth, and the clarity of vacuum made everything seem much closer in addition, so that judgments based on familiarity with terrestrial landscapes were difficult—and doubly difficult for Jonathan.

She's hiding from me! That's why I can't find her. Well, damn her. I'll track her down.

He drove his rover slowly into a shallow crater and retracted its antenna. Now it was visible only from above or from the very edge of the crater. He climbed out of the crater and continued on foot, in the direction of Elena's surface position.

Jonathan avoided the distance-devouring floating skips of lunar surface travellers: he didn't want to come upon Elena too suddenly, before he had time to prepare. Instead he took careful, small steps, which turned into short kangaroo hops. His pace was laborious, but Elena would have no warning of his approach. What he was feeling toward her as he trudged along was far more like hate than love, and part of him was horrified at that, and yet another part of him welcomed the new feelings.

When he found a building at last, it was almost by accident. It was little more than a roof supported by a few poles driven into the rock. It was situated between two large boulders and, with the sun in his eyes, Jonathan almost blundered into it before he saw it.

What he noticed first was not the roof or the poles but the space-suited figure sitting within the shelter. Jonathan pressed himself against one of the sheltering boulders to hide from sight. Fortunately the seated figure wasn't facing toward him, but rather toward the right. Why, he wondered, was there such a strange structure out here? Why not either a completely airtight building, like the others on the moon, or else no shelter at all?

The glare of the sun made it hard to see properly. Moving slowly, Jonathan circled the place, passing behind the space-suited figure, and ending up hidden by the other of the two large boulders, this time with the sun behind him.

He leaned forward for a quick look and then ducked back into the shelter of the rock. He was able to tell that the other person's suit was hooked by cable to a large pile of electronic equipment. Something then, he reasoned, that needed to be protected from direct sunlight but needed vacuum to operate. Communications equipment, perhaps? That would explain the cable from the space suit. In that case, why not use the powerful equipment at the main base, rather than this strange assortment of unidentifiable gadgets? More than that, he asked himself, thoroughly intrigued: how could he manage to overhear the communication?

If it's experimental equipment and if it's powerful enough, Jonathan thought, then its signal is probably leaking over a wide range of frequencies. From a close range, I might be able to pick it up, if I'm lucky and one of those frequences is covered by this suit's radio.

Carefully, Jonathan edged forward again until his helmet antenna was exposed, and then he began to manipulate the tuning lever with his tongue, searching for the signal. What he found was faint and distorted. He could tell only that he was hearing Elena's voice, and that she was speaking an unfamiliar language.

Standing utterly still, Jonathan listened intently. He soon realized that it was only good fortune that had enabled him to hear Elena's voice when he did: she was spending much more time listening than talking. He couldn't pick up the signal to which she was listening, so he could hear nothing at all when she wasn't speaking. When she did speak, even paying much more careful attention than he had at first, Jonathan could not understand the language. His mind whirled. This was all so surreptitious, her being out here and talking to some distant conspirator in a foreign language. What is that language? he asked himself. And what's she saying? Who on Earth is she talking to?

It was just as he asked himself that that Jonathan became aware of a long shadow on the rock beside him. He whirled about. Another space-suited figure, silhouetted against the sun, stood watching him calmly. It was hard to make out details against the glare, but he could see that the figure was holding a gun aimed at him.

27

The figure before him gestured toward its helmet with the hand not holding the gun. The gun remained utterly steady, aimed at Jonathan's chest. Jonathan raised both hands slightly to the side, pretending not to understand. Despite the concealing suit, the figure projected impatience. It repeated the gesture, then tapped its helmet five times.

Jonathan decided his defiance was pointless and childish. He bent forward slightly within his suit and tongued his radio to channel five. He held up a hand to indicate he was ready. His helmet boomed with Isaac Simkin's voice. "Just wait where you are until she's finished."

The wait seemed eternal. During it, the two men exchanged not a word. At last Elena emerged from the shelter. "He was listening to you on the T-band," Simkin told his daughter.

Sudden understanding struck Jonathan. "The aliens?" he asked in astonishment. "You were speaking to the aliens?"

There was no response. Elena simply stared at him. The sun glared from her white surface suit and turned her visor into a blazing mirror; she was invisible inside her suit, anonymous.

Isaac said, "Go ahead. Tell him. Explain everything to him— and I do mean everything."

"How did you find me, Jonathan? How did you get here?"

"Suhkray!" Isaac exclaimed. He said sharply, "Never mind that now. I'll tell you all of that later. Right now, explain to Jonathan what you've been doing here."

"All right, all right! Jonathan, did they tell you in school about the last message the aliens sent, just before the gray hole arrived? The one that said that the gray hole was going to remove our sun and destroy us because we were so ethically offensive to them?"

Jonathan nodded, then caught himself. "Yes, they did."

"Well, it wasn't really the last one. In fact, we've been in fairly regular contact with them all along, although there was a long gap, while they waited to see what we would do." As she spoke, her father held his gun unwaveringly aimed at Jonathan.

"Right after the Taking," Elena went on, "we received another message. At this receiver. This is where all the messages from the aliens were received. This was the only working T-band receiver in existence, back then, and it's still the one we use for communicating with the aliens."

"Because it's hidden and far away and no one will find out."

Elena paused before replying. "Yes," she said at last. "But don't make it sound like something evil. We decided from the beginning to keep the continuing contact secret. There's never been more than a small circle of people at Mendeleev who know about it. But we do have a good reason. We have to avoid panic, for one thing. There's another reason, too. I'll get to that.

"Anyway, the message that was picked up right after the Taking explained that the gray hole wasn't really just an instrument of destruction."

"In other words, they were only kidding," Jonathan said. This had all been in Battani's journal, but he kept silent on that subject. He didn't want to implicate Connie Allendorf, for one thing. And for another, he sensed that he might hear more than had been recorded in the journal, if he kept his mouth shut.

"I didn't . . ." Elena paused, then started again. "Do you remember when you pointed out to me what an amazing coincidence it was the way everything turned out? How the timing of the gray hole was just right so that Jupiter and Saturn coalesced and we ended up in the orbit we did?"

"Yes, and you brushed me off."

"I'm sorry. I didn't want to be drawn into a discussion of it because I couldn't tell you anything then. I wouldn't even be telling you this now if Dad hadn't ordered me to.

"You said what had happened to the solar system was very unlikely. Well, it didn't happen by chance. The aliens worked everything out from their T-band astronomy. I mean, they observed the solar system for a while and then calculated the arrival and trajectory of the gray hole so we'd end up exactly as we have. They planned for us to be the way we are now."

"Why?" Jonathan asked. "What kind of stupid game are they playing with us? They destroy an entire solar system, killing billions of people, but only in order to recreate it as an inferior model of itself. Cat and mouse, or something? It doesn't make any sense to me."

"Nor entirely to us," Isaac admitted. "When the contact with the aliens continued, after the Taking, the people at Mendeleev who were communicating with them began to learn their language, so that we wouldn't have to rely on computer translation, as before, and be bound by the slowness and inadequacy of the machines. Elena and I are both quite fluent, by human standards. By the standards of the aliens, we both speak at the level of a very young child. We've both spent uncounted hours talking with them, and I've studied the recordings of conversations from before my own time. I've listened to them over and over, but I still can't answer your question."

"The most we can glean is this," Elena said. "We're not Proper Ones. We know that much. But what makes us not Proper Ones is the complicated part. It's not really any one thing, like bad table manners. It's a combination of things. In fact, the response of Mendeleev to the first contact, when they sent the aliens a sort of electronic encyclopedia describing the human race and its civilization, was probably about the worst thing they could have done. It's precisely something about the overall picture that offended the aliens so much—"

"But that's not entirely true, Elena," her father broke in. "And this is important, too, Jonathan. If there was any one thing about us they really hated, really despised us for, it seems to have been our hesitancy in the face of dangerous adventure—specifically, the way mankind was turning away from space exploration at the time of the first T-band contact. Space travel and exploration are very deeply bound up with their religion."

"So," Elena said, "although their first impulse *was* to destroy us, they ended up deciding to winnow us."

"To winnow us?" Jonathan repeated. He had read nothing like this in Battani's journal.

"Yes, that's right. They understood that many among us were still in favor of pushing out into new territory and gaining new knowledge, and that the people on the moon were almost entirely of that sort. So they decided to try to reshape the human race, to make us worthy of the Universe and to increase our potential for someday becoming Proper Ones by . . . um . . . eliminating the chaff."

"How very biblical of them," Jonathan said. "Are they gods, or do they just think they are?"

Isaac Simkin said, "You're beginning to make me wonder if *you're* worth saving, Jonathan. I don't care for your attitude at all."

"Please, Dad," Elena said. "It's too soon to judge him. Listen, Jonathan, I think you misjudge them. They could have destroyed us, or they could have enslaved us. You can tell they have the power to do that, just from what they did do. Instead they decided to *help* us—to help us grow and improve, to become something much closer to our own potential. The gray hole didn't create conditions utterly inimical to human survival. Instead it created the opportunity for survival, but only through strenuous efforts, great daring, and enormous courage. Especially through heroic work off the Earth, in space.

"In other words," she said proudly, "the aliens have been working to remake Man into something new, creature in their own image. It wasn't Earth Man they chose, because he had proved he was inadequate. It was Lunar Man. Lunar Man is a big step in the direction of the Proper One."

"Too bad about all the chaff on Earth," Jonathan said. "All those billions of people who died from starvation and cold and nuclear war—"

"You *can't* blame the aliens for the war!" Elena shouted.

"—and of course all the ones who survived all that by going underground, only to die later," Jonathan finished, ignoring her. "And *why* were they chaff? It's not true that they weren't living on the moon because of some inferiority on their part. They just happened to be on Earth, just as your ancestors just happened to be here. Half of your ancestors," he said to Elena. "Maybe a lot of them *wanted* to live on the moon or were in favor of space exploration. And maybe a lot of the scientists who were up here really didn't give a damn about space travel: they were just here because for astronomers and astrophysicists, this was the premier place to advance their careers."

Isaac Simkin bellowed, "*Rubbish*! My ancestors were the finest part of their race, the cream. Don't you think the aliens considered exactly the argument you just gave? Of course they did! And they rejected it. I'm perfectly willing to live with their conclusions. I trust their wisdom as well as their knowledge."

"I gather," Jonathan said, "they miscalculated something, though. The mass of Jupiter and Saturn was inadequate to start fusion spontaneously after the coalescence. If the aliens are so close to perfection, they should know enough physics to have predicted that. *We* may still not know everything about how stellar fusion works, but *they* should."

"What happened was deliberate," Isaac countered. "That was our first reason to turn to them for help. One of their messages immediately after the Taking invited us to turn to them for technical advice. They warned us not to even ask for the secret of T-band travel—what they had used to transport the gray hole from their system to ours. From that, we realized that we were to make this system livable again somehow and not plan to move to another. And also, we concluded that we still had to be careful about offending their code. If we did offend them again, we feared they might cut off all contact forever and leave the human race to sink or swim on its own.

"Mendeleev took the chance of asking for a way of starting fusion, once it was clear that it wasn't going to start on its own. The aliens responded right away—so quickly that it was clear they had been simply waiting for us to ask. They sent us specifications for a device based on T-band technology with which fusion could be encouraged."

"It gave us a way of tunnelling energy from the moon directly into the center of the new sun," Elena explained. "And we've been keeping it up, to keep improving it."

"You see," Isaac said, "ever since they helped us survive in that basic way—by giving us a sun to replace the one we lost"—Lost? Jonathan thought—"the Director of Mendeleev and his immediate subordinates have kept in close touch with the aliens. Their advice and technological hints have made the difference between life and death for all mankind."

Not quite all, Jonathan thought, but he didn't bother speaking aloud.

"You see, Jonathan," Isaac said, "that's the other reason for keeping all of this from the public. It's very important that human beings think they've accomplished all of this themselves. Because of the Taking, our collective self-confidence is very shaky, very fragile. I think it would destroy that self-confidence utterly if the people found out the truth."

So that, Jonathan thought, is the real reason for much of the surface world's technological lead over America. It's not because they're superior to us at all. The surface world, he saw, was led by sycophants who lied to their own people. The entire surface society was corrupted by its leaders' submission to the aliens. And so after all only America was deserving of his allegiance.

"Now that I know your secret," Jonathan asked Isaac, "what happens to me? Are you going to use that gun now?"

"Would I have wasted this much time talking, if I'd planned that? I want you to join me and Elena and the rest of the inner circle. We can get all the advice and help we need from the aliens, as long as we're careful to limit our questions properly, but we don't have all the manpower we need. And I don't have anyone close to me whom I can trust other than Elena."

"It's very hard to recruit," Elena explained. "It's so hard to know who's trustworthy."

"But since you stumbled on the secret on your own," Isaac said, "I thought it best to tell you everything and see how you reacted. Now you know the whole story. How do you feel?"

"Come in with us, Jonathan," Elena said, her voice warm and inviting. "It's wonderful work. It's the most wonderful thing anyone has ever been able to do for mankind."

"It's not wonderful at all," Jonathan said. "It's disgusting.

You're all traitors to humanity; you're all collaborators with the enemy. You aren't following their advice. You're transmitting their orders, doing their bidding. This must be exposed. The world must be told about this."

"That can't be allowed," Isaac said calmly. He allowed the implication to sink in. "Elena, will you please use Channel Three and say 'Ready for pickup'?"

"That's all I should say?"

"That's it. Do it now, please."

It was a prearranged signal that brought a lunar tram skimming over the horizon to a landing near the three of them. "This is how I came here from Mendeleev," Isaac said. "Much more comfortable than your trip, Jonathan. Elena, if you're finished here, you can come back with us. Unless you have more to do and have a pickup already arranged?"

"I did, but I can cancel it. I'd like to return with you . . . and Jonathan."

Jonathan stared at the bars. For the first day or so, the bars seemed to paralyze his ability to think.

His meals were delivered with unfailing regularity, and they were always plentiful and delicious. But the guard—not uniformed, but still clearly a guard—who delivered them had a pleasant smile for Jonathan but never a word, not even when Jonathan spoke to him.

There was, however, a comm set in his cell. At first, this surprised Jonathan. But he discovered that the unit was selective: no matter what code he entered, the screen always lit up with Isaac Simkin's face. Each time, Jonathan disconnected immediately. The fifth time, Isaac held up his hand quickly to prevent Jonathan's disconnecting and said, "You'll just keep getting me, Jonathan, no matter what you do. I'll be there when you change your mind. Call me when you have." And then he disconnected.

I could keep calling him day and night, Jonathan thought. Keep him from getting any sleep.

He could maintain his defiance and never agree to join Simkin's nner circle. In that case, sooner or later someone would no doubt decide that it was no longer worth providing him with meals and shelter. . . .

After a while, Jonathan stopped bothering to keep track of the time. The lighting never changed, and he had no way of knowing for sure if the meals followed the standard three-meal-a-day pattern he had been using to count the days. So all in all, it didn't seem worth the effort of counting.

And then one morning (as measured by his having just wakened from what had seemed a long sleep, having used the toilet, and having eaten a meal of cold cereal and egg), Isaac Simkin came to his cell to see him.

"Comm calls seem so impersonal sometimes, don't you think?" Isaac asked as the bars slid sideways out of sight into the wall and he entered the cell. They slid closed again immediately behind him. He closed the lid on the toilet and sat on it; the action would have made anyone else look foolish. When Jonathan stared at him wordlessly, Isaac went on, "I got tired of waiting for you to call. I decided to visit you in person to give you another chance to join us. Come on, Jonathan. You can't just waste your talent in a jail cell. Have you come around yet?"

"As soon as I can get myself out of here," Jonathan said coldly, "I intend to tell everyone I can the truth about your T-band contact with the aliens. And I'll agitate for a new form of government to replace yours—a democratic form."

A look of annoyance crossed Simkin's face and was replaced with an expression of affability that was entirely unconvincing. "You're consistent, anyway. I'll grant you that. Doesn't your adolescent idealism get a bit tiring even to you, after a while? Life isn't as simple as you pretend it is. You're old enough to know that. You've lived in our world for long enough to be able to understand why we do things the way we do. And I certainly expect you to understand why we stay in contact with the aliens and why we keep that fact a secret."

"What crap!" Jonathan said angrily. "This is a dictatorship no matter how you try to justify it." He searched for something that would wound. "This place is no better than America."

Isaac's face turned red and he leapt to his feet. He stared a
Jonathan for a moment, opening and closing his mouth but sayin,
nothing. Finally he stalked from the cell.

The bars had slid aside for Simkin and then back into place a
he left. Jonathan immediately approached them, but they didn'
move. Surveillance cameras, he thought. They're watching me al
the time. His taunt had been the truth.

Simkin had not yet given up. The next day, Jonathan ha-
another visitor. This time it was Elena.

"My father asked me to come here," she said frankly. "I didn'
want to see you at all while you were in here. I hate detentio:
cells." She looked at the three solid walls, all so close to her, an
the row of metal bars which formed the room's fourth wall, an
she shivered. "How are you holding up?"

Jonathan shrugged. "I suppose it's easier for me than it woul-
be for you, because of where I grew up. Why did your father as
you to come here?"

"To try to get you to change your mind, of course. Jonathar
he's worried about you!"

"I can tell. I always lock people up when I'm worried abou
them, too."

"Don't try to put me off with a stupid joke, Jonathan. Your lif
is at stake here."

That was no worse than he had expected. "Do you want me t
lie to save my life?"

"No. I want you to believe we're doing the right thing and offe
freely to join us. To save your life."

"Even if I did say I had changed my mind and wanted to joi
you," Jonathan pointed out, "wouldn't it be a bit suspec
Wouldn't you think I *was* lying because of the danger?"

"*I* wouldn't. I know you too well already. I know you cou
never lie or pretend or play a role, no matter how much dang
you were in. You're too honest and honorable for that."

Jonathan stared at her in amazement. "You think that about m
Good God, Elena, you sound like a wife in a Victorian novel.

"I've never read one. But . . . I do want you to know that I've been thinking about what you said to me a while ago."

"Oh? And you agree with me now about being in contact with the aliens?"

"Oh, Jonathan, I'm not talking about that!" Elena had been standing with her back against the bars ever since entering the cell. Now she stepped across the cell and sat down beside Jonathan on the bunk. "I meant when you said you loved me and wanted to marry me. I know I didn't react well at the time, but I've changed since then. I suppose it's mainly the kind of courage you've shown that's done it. I really admire men who display great enterprise, the way you did in tracking me down and driving out to where I was." She stared at the bars as she spoke. "That, plus the way you're sticking up for your convictions now, even at the risk of your life." She nodded, agreeing with herself, and then continued with painful earnestness, "I'm very attracted to bravery."

She turned to Jonathan. "Don't you understand what I'm saying? I'm willing to live with you—or even to get married, if that's really what you want."

Jonathan stared at her tense body and the fear she couldn't keep from her face. Her moral repugnance at what she considered incest was as strong as ever, he could see, and yet she was willing to make what would be a great sacrifice for her just to save his life. "I'm very touched by your offer, but I couldn't do that to you. I don't think it would be satisfactory to either of us in the long run, would it?"

Elena tried to look disappointed but instead looked relieved. Jonathan's feelings of smug nobility were undermined by the thought that perhaps she hadn't offered herself to save his life but to please her father, who still seemed to want Jonathan on his side—or perhaps even merely because her father had ordered her to.

Elena jumped to her feet buoyantly. "Well, then, I guess that's settled! I'll try to visit you again tomorrow, all right?"

"Why bother?"

She looked stricken. "I'm really worried about you, Jonathan."

"Oh, Jesus, I'm sorry I said that." He stood up, and they embraced. Jonathan could feel that it was a sisterly, or perhaps a friendly, embrace and nothing more than that. "I'm sorry. I'm grateful to you for your concern. And your visits."

But Elena didn't come the next day. Nor did she come the day after that, nor any day thereafter. After that brief touch of friendship, Jonathan's renewed solitariness was all the more devastating.

He knew that was deliberate, a psychological ploy of Isaac's to wear him down all the faster by first getting his hopes up, and he determined anew not to give in. If I know the game he's playing, he reasoned, I can fight it more easily. But not much more easily, as the passing days showed: knowing *how* Isaac was trying to wear him down didn't seem to prevent the technique *from* wearing him down.

After a time—many days, but how long Jonathan didn't know—his defiance began to seem to him a pale and weak thing, more and more an intellectual position and less and less a powerful emotional force. It lost its tangibility; he could no longer lean on it, depend on it, and certainly could no longer call it up, fan it into life to warm his soul and give him strength. That's it, he thought. My strength is fading. Perhaps it never had been very great, after all.

Eventually, Jonathan presented to himself the argument that he was accomplishing nothing in detention. His defiance was doing nothing to change the conditions of which he disapproved. And if he were eventually killed because his captors were tired of bothering to keep him alive to no end, then all chance of changing things would of course disappear. Seen in that light, it was clear that cooperation didn't really mean compromising his convictions.

When he guessed that enough time had passed to make a conversion seem more convincing, Jonathan called up Simkin and told him that he was willing at least to talk about their differences. "I'm not promising anything," he told the ruler of mankind, "but I *am* willing to discuss things."

*   *   *

As he turned away from the blank comm screen to face his daughter, Isaac Simkin said, "Are you happy now, darling? Your friend's on the road to survival through common sense."

Elena asked worriedly, "Do you really think he's come over?"

Isaac laughed. "Of course not! He's underestimating me if he thinks I'm that easily duped. You know, I had to be ruthless to get where I am. Also strong and intelligent. And I've required all those qualities to *stay* on top."

Elena smiled dutifully. It was a speech she'd heard before.

"But in addition," Isaac went on, adding something he had never said to her before, "I've had to develop the ability to judge character accurately and to penetrate subterfuge quickly. No, it's clear to me that Jonathan is insincere. No doubt he still thinks he can single-handedly push me out of power and change the way mankind handles its own affairs. But he's showing political sense, for the first time. It's not enough to make speeches. You have to be in a position where you can actually *do* something, if you really want to change history. He's realized that at last and now he wants to get into such a position.

"However, I've got a little surprise in store for him. He thinks we're fooled and will welcome him with open arms. Instead, I've got some tapes for him to watch, some old ones and some new ones."

"Not the Walter Geneen stuff!"

Isaac nodded. "And some other recordings, as well. We'll see what those do to Jonathan's idealism. I'm counting on that material to make his conversion real." He got up and put his arm around his daughter's shoulders. "Don't worry, darling. I think he's worth saving, no matter how much trouble it takes, and I think I'll be able to do it. He's going to lead a long, productive, and useful life."

28

"The earliest date you can get on these is the sixth of Ariel," Isaac Simkin had told him. That was two days before Jonathan's arrival on the moon, but Jonathan assumed there was no connection. The console facing him was identical to the one he had used while watching Petya, Julie, Tashie and Daniel Davidovich leading their lives in Russia, so he knew how to request the date he wanted. And he knew how to call up a map of the underground world from which the recordings came.

When he did so, the grid that formed on the wall before him had a puzzling familiarity. He stared at it for some moments, and then suddenly it became clear: it was a map of America.

It was different from the maps he had been familiar with when he'd lived there, designed for a different purpose: surveillance rather than route finding. Nonetheless, as he stared at it, its congruences with his mental picture of the corridors and levels of America became clear.

Where to look first? His own apartment? The office he had worked in? At the center of the map there was a rough circle representing the magma cell on which America utterly depended. That was also where the numbered red lights representing surveillance cameras were heaviest.

He selected one of those at random and punched the number in. He was rewarded with a scene of unattended consoles. According to what his grandfather had told him, each and every console must be under human watch every second of every day and night. The process couldn't have been computerized: Jonathan knew too well how inadequate America's computers were to such a task, and how those computers became less adequate to their tasks every year due to breakdown of irreplaceable parts. Why were these consoles unattended? Puzzled, he began to switch around from camera to camera in the vicinity of the magma cell.

Many of the cameras marked on the map were apparently no longer working. Those that were, showed scene after scene of empty consoles. At last, though, he found some people.

He came across two men murmuring to each other in a lonely hallway, outside one of the rooms where the magma operators' consoles were. He was struck by their drab, almost identical clothing, and even more by their unhealthy, doughy faces and slouched, weak bodies. They were looking around nervously while they talked, wary of informers; Jonathan knew the look and the gesture. The two men were no more aware than he had been of the hidden cameras and microphones picking up their conversation. During Jonathan's adolescence, it had sometimes happened that an acquaintance would let treasonous ideas slip and then would later disappear. Now he knew why that had happened.

Jonathan turned the sound up high to catch what the two were talking about.

"If we keep losing it like this," one of them said, "you know what's going to happen to us."

From his own class, Jonathan thought with pleasure. He felt close to these two already, even though he didn't recognize either of them.

The other man nodded. "If the withdrawal doesn't stop, it'll be a disaster for the country. But there's nothing we can do about it."

"No," his companion agreed in a bitter tone. "Just keep monitoring it. Watching the light and heat go away."

"I heard they've had to evacuate Chicago. Temporary measure, they said."

The other man grunted in disgust. "Sure, temporary! They keep saying that. But every time they close down a section, you know it's for good. Trying to save what little power there is left. You just watch: some day, we'll all be living in one room, just waiting for the lights to go out."

The second man grimaced. "However many of us are left by then."

Jonathan wanted to hear more, but at that point the two men said good-bye to each other and went their separate ways.

Jonathan wondered if they had both been picked up immediately afterward. He could have tried to follow them, but he was too interested in what they had been talking about. It could only be the magma.

He experimented with various camera codes and finally found a view of the magma cell itself. He drew back in horror from the giant, baleful red glow on the wall. He was sure that this was the same camera through which the execution of Henry Martinson had been recorded, the recording he had seen in school, the vision of death that had haunted his dreams.

Jonathan forced himself to look at the magma cell objectively. Surely it was duller than in that fifty-year-old recording. Was that it, then? Was the source of America's power withdrawing from the people who depended on it for survival, oozing back down into the Earth's interior?

Jonathan skipped ahead a week—then two more days to make it the old-style week. He stared intently at the image of the magma cell but couldn't tell if it was any dimmer than it had been seven days earlier. If it was changing, it was too slow for his eyes to detect over such a short period. Perhaps it would take the sensitive instruments whose readings the operators' consoles monitored to detect a change. But it wouldn't take much change, he realized, to be serious for America. The country had always lived on the edge of extinction.

He decided to check on his own apartment—salve for his conscience, even though the application was so belated. But none of the cameras in the section he had lived in was working. He skipped back a week—seven days—again, but there were still no images from Philadelphia.

Even without the retreat of the magma, Jonathan thought, America had always been a doomed world. He remembered the steady deterioration of everything underground, from minor repairs that couldn't be made, to computers that went down and couldn't be brought up again, to food that seemed continually less nourishing. It was a world of retrenchment and decay.

Jonathan set himself grimly to moving forward through time as far as the tapes would let him.

He saw the death of his world.

At first, it was only a matter of inward movement, of outer sections being closed down and citizens ordered to relocate closer to the magma cell. But the deterioration kept accelerating.

He saw American society's last gasps, a frightening end in political chaos and civil war. At the very end, there was no picture, only sound, as the fading catastrophe trailed away in darkened caverns and cold tunnels. There were screams and cries for help, flashes and echoing booms as guns were fired. He heard grunts and snarls from individual fights to the death; or were those the sounds of desperate sex, copulation in defiance of the end? Jonathan couldn't tell the difference.

Neglected equipment gave way. The only light was from the cameras aimed at the magma cell itself, now reduced to a pale glow, with barely enough energy left to power the force screen that kept America safe from it.

And what would happen when the screen finally gave out? Jonathan wondered. Perhaps the magma would have withdrawn enough by then not to be a danger. Someday, though, it would surely return, following the mysterious tides and shrinkings and swellings of the Earth's incandescent interior. Perhaps the machinery that had controlled the screen would still be working and, with the return of power from the magma, would reactivate the screen and America could come back to life, if anyone still survived. (Even that would require a miracle from the God he had been taught to worship. Jonathan had heard mass prayers cried out to that God in the dark tunnels, but he had seen no evidence of a reply.) It seemed more likely to him that if and when the magma returned, the force screen would not reappear and the magma would spill into the tunnels and vaporize whatever it encountered.

Would that include any living human beings? How could anyone have survived what he had seen and heard? It would require a miracle, as he had thought before. He wondered if miracles still happened. Had they ever happened?

The end of all power meant the end of the recordings. That had happened three weeks ago. Jonathan stared at the blank wall, thinking.

How long could people have lived after the power ended? There would be no air regeneration, but with so many cubic meters of air in the tunnels, if the number of survivors was small, they could live for three weeks on what was already there, couldn't they? There might be someone alive down there to rescue right now. But he remembered the underground refuge in Japan, and he knew how futile it would be to suggest a rescue mission to America. Perhaps there were people down there right now, even as he sat here, suffocating or starving. Perhaps his former coworkers had survived and were dying now, or perhaps the girl who had spied on him just before his escape was choking to death in the dark at that very moment.

If I had stayed, he told himself, I could have helped. I could have helped that girl. And I could have helped everyone else.

He knew better. Had he stayed, he would simply have died along with everyone else. The surface people, on the other hand . . . Yes: they could have saved everyone merely by breaking into the caverns and pulling the population out. Just as they could have done the same for those Japanese. And the Russians and everyone else. Isaac Simkin and Elena Simkin, who wanted his allegiance to the surface world—they were all guilty of the death of all the Americans who had died during the country's last days. Wasn't it a form of murder?

Behind it all were the aliens. Clearly their guilt was the greatest of all, because they had created the unnatural situation in the first place; their actions had forced men to live underground, to become moles and be doomed by that choice. Everything that had happened to America was really their fault. Who were they to set themselves up in moral judgment over an entire world?

Once, when he and Elena had been arguing about religion and the existence of God, she had said, "If God exists and is all powerful, then He has allowed evil to exist in the world. He allows good people to suffer for no reason. Therefore, if He exists and is all-powerful, He must be evil. How can you worship such a being?"

"The Devil is the source of evil," Jonathan had explained.

"In that case, God created the Devil the way he is and allow im to cause evil, so my previous argument still applies. Or if God is so weak that He's *unable* to prevent evil, there seems even less reason to worship him, let alone fear him."

Now at last Jonathan knew he had no more need or fear or love of God left, not after witnessing the death of his world and hearing its unanswered prayers. Now the aliens had taken the place of both God and the Devil in his mind, and he despised them. Why didn't Elena see that her arguments could be applied to the aliens? Why didn't she despise them, too?

When the guard came to escort him back to his cell an hour later, he found Jonathan still staring at the blank wall. He had to shake Jonathan's shoulder twice before he responded, and then he walked back to his cell as though in a trance. The guard noticed how pale Jonathan was and thought about reporting the matter to his superiors but decided not to bother.

The next morning, after Jonathan had been brought a breakfast he couldn't touch, Isaac Simkin came to visit him. Jonathan sat on his bunk and stared dully at his visitor. Simkin looked at him appraisingly and nodded as if unsurprised.

"Do you know," Simkin said conversationally, "that my mother-in-law couldn't have left America much earlier than she did, and survived? The thawing wouldn't have progressed far enough. And of course, First Landing wasn't until 2015, so there would have been no rescue for any escapees before that. They would have had to make it out of the Cold all by themselves, which I dare say would have been impossible.

"And as you now know, no one can escape from America now, because there's no one left alive. It's a very sad waste." Startlingly, to Jonathan, Simkin's expression indicated a genuine feeling of loss.

"So in other words," Simkin said after a thoughtful pause, "there was really a relatively brief period during which anyone could have escaped from America—or any of the other underground refuges we know about. And for virtually all of them, that time is now over. Fershtay? Bon. Come, now." He rose. Jonathan rose mechanically. "I want you to see some more tapes, although

this time, I shall be there to add a commentary. And so wil
Elena.''

They left the cell and walked down the corridor side by side
but Simkin in subtle fashion in the lead. "There actually was :
very early escapee from America," Simkin said quietly. "The ai
was there, but he froze to death as soon as he got outside. W
found his body years later. He brought some magnetic tapes witl
him. That's what you're going to see this time. A very brave man
He couldn't stand what he saw happening to his country. Or so w
assume. At any rate, the tapes are a valuable historical record
They come from a time before we were eavesdropping, so the
show us things we would never have known about. As it is
they're sketchy, but we think we've reconstructed America
history of that period by means of much thought and consideratio
and repeated viewing of the tapes the man brought out. His nam
was Walter Geneen. Heard of him?''

"Yes!" Surprise broke through Jonathan's withdrawal. "Yes, o
course. Walter Geneen was an early hero. He was a child whe
America went underground, the son of a cabinet secretary. Late
he was killed by the rebels during the coup attempt. We learned al
about him in school. He sacrificed himself to save his country.'

Isaac Simkin laughed. "Tchoodyesni! I'd call him a hero; yes,
would. But you see, he didn't die in the coup but on the surface
where he escaped some years later. The coup was the other wa
around. But you'll see what I mean.''

They continued in silence until they reached the room wher
Jonathan had watched the recordings of America's last days. A
Isaac had promised, Elena was there, waiting for them.

"Ready?" Isaac asked her. She nodded. "Get it started, then.
Elena sat down in front of the control panel, and Isaac an
Jonathan took seats beside her. All three stared at the blank wa
above the console.

A picture took shape. A beefy, middle-aged man was standin
on a platform making a speech to a roomful of cheering men an
women. "It's President Nelson!" Jonathan said. "And that's h
cabinet sitting behind him." He named them all. "And, let's se

hat's the Speaker of the House and the Senate Majority Leader nd—why, those are all the first-generation leadership!"

"They certainly indoctrinated you well, didn't they?" Elena aid in disgust.

Coldly Jonathan said, "You have your deified ancestors. I have nine."

Isaac laughed. "*Touché*! Jonathan, Elena's grandmother ssigned the same names to the same faces. It's good to have you onfirm that her memory was correct. As far as we can tell, the ntire first generation of American survivors is in that room istening to that somewhat bombastic speech. Everyone except the perators monitoring the magma and a few other essential ersonnel like that, I suppose."

Jonathan listened to the speech for a moment. "I've never seen film of this, but I've read it many times. This was right after the etreat—after the Taking, I mean. Right after they went under-round. President Nelson was telling them how they'd survive and ourish underground and how someday we'd figure out what the tussians had done and reclaim our world."

Isaac grunted. "Hope springs eternal. Awful lot of uniforms in iat crowd, aren't there?"

"That's because it was basically a military installation original-/," Jonathan said defensively. "The President and other govern-ient leaders, and essential civilian workers and all their families, ll went underground. But the rest was the military leadership. ut it was all under civilian control; that's the important point."

"Of course," Isaac said. "No doubt the surveillance in those ays was intended for security rather than suppression, although ie distinction between those two is often imperceptible. What appened to President Nelson, that forceful speech maker?"

"He was killed in the coup attempt," Jonathan said sadly. "A rrible loss. But fortunately the government was able to reestab-sh itself after the initial confusion."

"How wonderful to have a constitution!" Isaac agreed. He odded at Elena, who entered a date into the console. "After the oup," Isaac said, gesturing at the wall screen.

Jonathan looked eagerly, glad to see in the flesh the heroes about whom he had read so often in childhood. Instead, a line o defeated, spiritless men and women shuffled across the screen moving slowly down a corridor. The villains, he realized: the me and women who, in league with Russia, had tried to overthrow th constitutional authority and establish in its place a Marxist state Suddenly he jumped to his feet and yelled, "Wait a minute!"

Isaac gestured to Elena, who froze the picture.

"That's the Vice President!" Jonathan said. "My God, that' the rest of his family!" And many of the others he recognized too: they were government leaders and their wives or husbands and many of them had children with them. He sat down slowly. " don't understand this. What's going on?"

"This should explain," Elena said, her voice gentle. Sh switched to another camera, this one aimed downward from th ceiling at the fierce glare of the magma cell.

But the magma's glare was almost entirely obscured. Jonatha stared at the strange pattern of red light and dark and finall identified the shadow pattern as heaped human bodies lying on th force screen. To the left of the screen was the front of the line the had seen before, moving slowly forward. A man in uniform raise a pistol. He held its muzzle against the back of the head of the firs man in line and fired. The victim's forehead exploded in a re spray, and his body fell forward, twitching, onto the others pile above the magma cell. Jonathan could see some of the bodies sti moving slightly.

The uniformed man signalled to someone out of sight. A secon force screen came into existence above the bodies, pressing dow upon them. It was a replay of the execution of Henry Martinson but without the cat-and-mouse playing with the victim.

The lower screen collapsed, the magma surged, and the pile c dead men and women shrivelled, vaporized, and disappeared. Th uniformed man gestured the line of victims to start movin forward again, raised his pistol again, and the slaughter went on

"Why?" Jonathan whispered. "What is it?"

"It's the coup you were taught about," Isaac said matter-o factly. "Except that it was a military coup, not an uprising by small group of Marxist revolutionaries. It was an overthrow c civilian authority. Haven't you ever wondered about the terminology you were brought up with?" There was anger in his voice.

"Terminology?" Jonathan asked vaguely.

"Yes, you know. President-General at the head. Platoon leaders and so on at the bottom. And bucks and noncoms and warrants and gentlemen. Not civilian usage, is it?"

"It's just the way it is," Jonathan said slowly, his mind elsewhere.

"Dad," Elena said, "have some sympathy."

Isaac leaned back in his chair. "Yes, you're right. It must be quite a shock to him. But we have to go on with this thing. Skip forward, about a year at a time. And move around the complex. Jonathan, had you been in the right frame of mind to notice, you would have seen that all the women being executed were old. The young ones were preserved for, um, other uses. Walter Geneen survived the coup by professing loyalty to the new military rulers and publicly condemning his own family. But we'll get to that later."

Scenes of mass meetings alternated with private conversations. "If you were to study all of this as we have," Isaac said, "you would follow the ascension to power within the ruling military clique of a fanatical group of fundamentalist Christians."

"The Shield of the Lord," Jonathan said. "I know about them. But they never held any power."

Isaac smiled. "Correction: they were smart enough never to appear to hold power. Elena, switch back to the beginning, to President Nelson's 'Welcome to the Underworld' speech." When she had done so, Isaac continued. "Now, Jonathan, look at the audience. You can see quite a large section of it in this view. Doesn't anything strike you, something very different from the America you knew?"

Jonathan stared hard, trying to do what Isaac wanted him to. He had been subjected to too many shocks; his mind seemed unable to absorb anything new, unable to analyze things as Isaac was requesting. But then he saw what Isaac meant. "There are black men and women there! A lot of them. I never saw any in America."

"Exactly," Isaac said. "Elena, jump forward again, back to where we were. Jonathan, if there were identifying tags, you'd also see a lot of Jews and Catholics in that meeting, but I bet you never knew any yourself, did you? Or atheists?"

Jonathan shook his head. "Did they die out?"

"In a manner of speaking. Go ahead, Elena. Show it to him."

Once again, there was a scene of mass execution, of a crowd of defeated men and women, beyond resistance, shuffling down the corridor leading to the magma cell and then being shot and their bodies being vaporized. Perhaps every third victim was black.

"You see?" Isaac asked him. "They *did* die out, but not through their own choice. The white victims in that scene are the Jews and Catholics and atheists. The Shield of the Lord people seem to have had very strict ideas about who is acceptable to God and who isn't."

"But that's . . ." Jonathan felt incapable of speech.

"I think it's time for Walter Geneen," Elena said. Isaac nodded. She entered another command, and the screen filled with the ceiling-high face of a young man. He was no older than Jonathan, but he radiated remarkable strength and determination. He had a thick mop of black hair and dark brown eyes, and a heavy stubble covered his jaw and cheeks. His skin was pale. There was sweat along his upper lip and on his forehead. Jonathan could sense that Elena was sexually aroused by the huge face looming over them; he resented her reaction and felt a rush of anger.

"My name is Walter Geneen," the young man said. "This may be my last will and testament." He smiled crookedly. "I was born on the surface of the Earth on September 13, 1993. Three years ago, on July 4th, 2011, my entire family was murdered by forces under the command of General McIntyre." His face contorted with grief, and then that gave way again to determination. "I escaped only by declaring my loyalty to the general and condemning my father and all of his friends. I felt I could do more good alive than dead. I don't know why the general let me live. Perhaps he liked the idea of reforming a sinner's child. Or perhaps he thought of me as a pet.

"I managed to get myself into the Department of Security soon after it was formed. Eventually, I was assigned to monitor some of the surveillance cameras located throughout the caverns—or America, as we're supposed to call it now. I copied the tapes detailing the history of the coup. I intend to climb back to the surface taking those tapes with me, along with one containing this statement. Originally, I hoped I'd be able to undermine the military's control over the caverns and help return civilian rule. A countercoup, in other words. However, I've found that I can't do anything like that. I have no way of doing it by myself, and everyone else is afraid to even discuss antigovernment ideas, so it's impossible to form any kind of group. Executions continue at the rate of two or three a week.

"If I stayed in America, I'm sure they'd get around to me eventually. I've spoken my mind to too many people. No doubt it's impossible to live on the surface without some sort of space suit. But maybe there'll be an overland expedition someday from somewhere else, because there must be other groups surviving underground, just like us. If there are, I hope they'll find my body and the tapes and watch them before they try to make contact with the American government. It's not much of a contribution, but it's the only one I can make—the only one I can dream up, anyway."

Geneen paused and looked off into space for a while. At last he looked back at the camera. "I must admit I don't like the idea of dying, but I guess I don't have the choice of dying or not dying, but only of *how* I die—by freezing and suffocating on the surface or by being vaporized in the magma." He grinned suddenly. "Hell of a choice, isn't it? This is Walter Geneen, saying good-bye. And if I don't make it and Hank McIntyre ends up watching this tape, here's something for you, Hank." He held his fist up to the camera and slowly, deliberately extended his middle finger. The screen went blank again.

Isaac chuckled. "Defiant to the end. How I admire that! Well, Jonathan, now you've seen some genuine American history. I'd like you to consider something. In our world, various races and nationalities live together in harmony. Each man truly is judged on his own merits. In America, before the Taking, that was also true in theory. However, if it really had been true, do you think your underground world could have gone the way it did? The germ of the genocides you saw on Walter Geneen's tapes must have been present all along in the society, long before the Taking. Going underground and living under those restricted and hopeless conditions just exacerbated something that was already there. How can you grieve for that?

"Now it's time for you to make your decision. Jonathan, are you with us now?"

Jonathan felt as though he had been beaten. He felt as though his inner self were covered with bruises and cuts; it was nothing anyone could see, but he could feel it. Tears were running down his face—tears as much of weariness and weakness as of grief or loss. Elena put her arm about his shoulder.

"Not now," she told her father. "Let him recover. Give him a few days."

But Isaac shook his head. "Yes, now, while he still feels the impact fully. What we'll get now are his true feelings."

Jonathan put his face in his hands. "Yes," he whispered. "I'm with you. Completely."

But it was a lie.

He was with Isaac and Elena now, but only *almost* completely, *almost* without reservation, with *most* of his heart. That tiny, burning core of him that had never before committed utterly to anything except escaping from America and which had been searching ever since then for something to be dedicated to, had found a new goal, something worth pursuing, something worth total commitment.

2108

$$\begin{array}{r} 2108 \\ \underline{53} \\ \overline{2055} \end{array}$$

29

Lovely music played softly in the background—the meditation from *Thaïs*. Jonathan drifted slowly up from the depths of sleep, from dreams of burning cores and dangerous stars, through strata of unconsciousness toward the pale, red light of day. The shutters were opening slowly, lighting up the room. The music was swelling ever louder, forcing him to wake and turn it off. Even a piece so beautiful as Massenet's lost some charm as the volume increased. As a child he had always waked so easily. Yesterday had been his fifty-third birthday. How hard would it be to face reality after his sixty-third birthday? Or his seventy-third if he got that far? Yesterday had also been his twenty-fifth wedding anniversary. Then he remembered what was scheduled for that day, and he awoke completely and suddenly, with a smile on his face.

Elena murmured and moved restlessly next to him. Jonathan stretched and pressed a button. The music ceased, replaced by a quiet voice reading the news. The lead story, of course, was the landing by the aliens. Jonathan tuned the voice out mentally and thought about other things. After all, what could a newscast have to tell him about the alien landing that he hadn't known long before the news organization did? And couldn't he have told them a few things, if he were so minded!

The daily lives of dictators, Jonathan reflected, are no different from those of other men. The details of what they do have far more importance, but the details are still the same.

As if to prove his point, Elena turned over to face him and started talking in her drowsy, soft morning voice about the children. "Andy commed yesterday. He's still having trouble with physics. He was hoping you could put some pressure on his professor."

Jonathan snorted. "What did you tell him?"

Elena smiled. "I told him I didn't think you'd like that idea at all, and you'd probably make a speech about him standing on his own two feet."

Jonathan laughed. "Consider it made. You know me too well."

"Very well. But it'll never be well enough." She raised herself on one elbow, leaned over him, and kissed him warmly. "You did pretty well last night, for a man of your advanced age. Thank God for birth control. Just imagine what it must have been like before the Taking, when they didn't have it."

"They had birth control before the Taking. It wasn't invented by your ancestors at Mendeleev or given to us by the aliens." He pulled Elena down onto him and stroked her hair with one hand, her back with the other. "Heard anything from Cathy lately?"

"Oh, that feels good. She called yesterday, too. I forgot to tell you."

Jonathan stopped stroking for a moment, then resumed. "And?"

"She's coming up at the end of the week. And bringing a boy with her to meet us."

"Oh, Jesus! She's too young to get serious about anyone yet!" And far more important, he wanted his daughter's mental and emotional attention free so he could groom her for eventual power. She was his favorite and his hope for the future, for mankind's future. He couldn't bear the thought of her settling into a rut of wifehood and motherhood. He needed her too much; the human race needed her too much. He didn't feel that his attitude exaggerated the situation at all.

Jonathan kicked the covers away and levered himself out of bed. Years ago, he would have been able to push himself halfway across the room with that motion. He hadn't been back to Earth for . . . He thought for a moment. More than twelve years; now close to thirteen. On the spot, he decided that he never would bother going back again. He knew he would be unable to bear weighing seventy kilos again. However, there were more important things to think about today. "Got any plans for this morning?"

"No," Elena said. She sat up in bed. "I'm going to spend the whole day getting ready for the landing."

Jonathan stepped into the tiny shower and turned on the water. "What does that mean?" he called over the sound. "Going to pick out your best dress for them?"

Elena laughed. "Would they know the difference? No, I'm planning to spend the time reviewing a few rules of grammar so that I won't make some embarrassing mistake. I wouldn't want them to think we're not aspiring to be Proper Ones after all."

"How could anyone think you're not a Proper One?" Jonathan said. He finished his shower in silence, stepped out, and began towelling himself. "You know, as I told you before, you don't have to bother coming today. You can take the day off. I can handle their language well enough."

Elena looked offended, as she had the day before when Jonathan had made the same suggestion. "I want to be there, darling. I want to do the translating for you. Most of all, I want to see them when they step off their ship. After all these years, I want to see what they look like."

That's the problem, Jonathan thought. "Suit yourself, dear. At least the kids won't be here until after the initial fuss is over."

"My father would have loved to be here to see this," Elena said wistfully.

Jonathan grunted noncommittally. Isaac Simkin had died fifteen years earlier, at the age of sixty-three. He had been on one of his sight-seeing rambles beyond the Mendeleev crater rim, out of sight of everyone in violation of one of his own safety rules, when his suit's seals had undergone a sudden and catastrophic failure. Isaac had tried to make it back to the base, unable to radio for help because his suit was evacuated and he had had to hold his breath. He had run two hundred meters, according to his footprints, before collapsing: an impressive feat for a man of his age and health, but not impressive enough. Two hours had passed before he was found, by which time, of course, it was far too late to help him.

His will had named Elena the heir to his office and his power. Cathy was four years old at the time, Andy three. Elena was three months pregnant. The fetus was a boy, and Jonathan had decided to name the child Henry, a clean completion of the triangle, but

Elena had miscarried upon news of her father's accident. She had spent months in the hospital and had emerged far weaker in body and personality. During her hospitalization, Jonathan had taken over Isaac's job. When she returned home, Elena had been content to leave matters that way; she had said she lacked the strength to run anything.

I would have been the one even without that, Jonathan thought. I would have ended up in control. But of course he would never know the truth about that.

Elena, knowing how little Jonathan liked it when she referred to her father's accident, changed the subject. "How much ahead of time are you going to be there?" She walked past him into the shower, closed the door, and turned on the water.

"Couple of hours," Jonathan said loudly. He glided into the kitchen and turned on the intercom to the bathroom and started the process of producing scrambled eggs and sausage for both of them. Even after so many years since his escape from America such food still held wonder and romance for him. Real meat, eggs, and milk were magical.

"Why so early?"

"Don't want to risk missing mankind's big moment," Jonathan said, hoping the distortion of the intercom would mask the sarcasm he could hear in his voice. "I have to check on the arrangements. I want to be sure there's not a single mistake." We can't afford a single mistake, not the slightest foul-up.

"Well, I'll be there a few minutes ahead of time. We know how accurate they are. Just think about the Taking."

Yes, just think about it. There was silence while Elena finished her shower and Jonathan set out two servings of breakfast. Had it all been worth it, after all? A question he only rarely asked himself. Elena was happy, had had a happy life, he was quite sure. She would have had a very different life if Jonathan hadn't shown up, or if she hadn't given in to various pressures and married him. But she had learned to love him soon after that. She had become utterly devoted to him, so deeply in his emotional thrall that he had come to dominate her body and soul without wanting to and despite his conviction that that was not what the nature of the

elationship between husband and wife should be. They should be
quals, Jonathan felt; but he and Elena certainly were not.

He ruled mankind, and he ruled his wife: the former power he
ad wanted; the latter, he had not. The former had come about as a
natural result of the latter and Elena's offical position. The latter,
e supposed, was the product of his and Elena's natures—or at
east, of Elena's nature as it had become after Isaac Simkin's death
and her subsequent miscarriage. No point in continually chewing
t over, he told himself. Protest against the situation as he might,
e knew that he liked the way matters had come about.

Naked, they sat across the small, circular glass table from each
ther and ate their eggs and sausage. They spoke little, smiled at
ach other often. My God, how I love her! Jonathan thought
uddenly, staring in wonder at her face, still beautiful and showing
ew signs of age. Unconsciously, he lowered his knife and fork to
he table and stared at Elena. He was seized by a powerful feeling,
y a longing for the past, for the Elena that had been, the strong
nd elusive woman he had first known.

Later, while Elena disposed of dishes and cutlery, Jonathan
ressed himself carefully in front of a mirror. Despite his jibe at
lena earlier, and despite her joke that the aliens wouldn't
cognize her best dress even if she did wear it, he *was* dressing
imself in his best. The aliens wouldn't know the difference, but
e would, and so would the humans gathered with him at the
anding place. Actually, that wasn't quite true, either: he'd be
earing a surface suit, of course; it would cover up his formal suit
nd he'd look like anyone else outside, on the exposed lunar
urface. But before that, on the way, flying there in a pressurized
ip, and afterwards, back in the ship with the aliens—then the
ther humans would see him at his best. Then, in fact, it would be
articularly important that they be impressed by him, even cowed,
ust in case anyone had any belated second thoughts. As someone
ould, he was sure; it was inevitable.

Just for a moment, before he began pulling on his pants, he
ared at himself naked. Back in America, he had always been
oud of his physical condition, so much better than that of most

of his peers. Now he understood that it wasn't a result of some
superiority on his part, or even of hard work. Largely it was that
he had, as the old joke had it, chosen his parents well. Now the
signs of aging were there. Nothing major, nothing terrible or
repulsive. But despite the years under low-g, his chest muscles
were flattening and sagging, and so were the insides of his thighs.
His buttocks, too, he supposed, but he didn't make any effort to
look at them. It comes to everyone, he assured himself. Yes, but I
always thought I'd be immune! And everyone else probably thinks
the same.

Who cares? Today was what he had been living for, waiting for,
for years. This was the moment that counted—the moment, the
event, and not the state of his body. I'm in good health, anyway.
I'll live to see the fruits of today's work. It had taken years to talk
the aliens into sending an embassy to mankind. This was the
culmination of that effort. And then there would be years filled
with desperate, frantic work to bring about the final victory.
Jonathan's chest felt tight with excitement.

He breathed deeply and slowly, and eventually he felt calm
again. He grinned at himself in the mirror and resumed dressing.
"You're glowing," he told his reflection. "You're burning up.
But you'll make it."

"What?" Elena called from the bedroom.

"Nothing, dear. Just talking to myself."

Hours later, Jonathan stood alone in red sunlight on the surface
of the moon. A flat space was before him, cleared of rocks and
with all small craters filled in. Behind him stood the spiderlike
craft that had brought him to this spot. Great numbers of men and
women had preceded him to this spot, but they were all invisible.

Another suited figure leaped from the craft behind Jonathan,
landed lightly, and began moving toward him with long, slow,
gliding steps. It was Elena. She reached Jonathan and said,
"Mendeleev has them in sight now. They're right on schedule."

"Naturally. They're always right on schedule. After all, they're
Proper Ones. Just ask them."

Elena paused, puzzled by his tone. Then she said, "There

something I don't understand. The captain of my guards was talking about the soldiers being ready and in place here. He seemed to think I knew what he was talking about, but I didn't." She stopped, waiting for an explanation.

Jonathan felt a wash of warm concern for her, of protectiveness for Elena and their two children, and for all the hundreds of thousands of human beings on Earth, the moon, and the growing settlements on the other moons and planets and in space. "Crack troops," he said. "Thousands of 'em. A Goddamned army.

"You know," he said, staring upward at the stars, knowing he couldn't yet see the alien ship with the naked eye but trying anyway, "I never really considered them Proper Ones. Not by my standards, anyway. If I were to invent a definition for a creature who deserved to be called a Proper One, I'm not sure what I'd include, but I *am* sure that what they did to us when they took the sun disqualifies them. Arrogant bastards. Don't you think they deserve something in return after all these years of our suffering?"

"But . . . Jonathan, I don't understand! You've always seemed so reconciled to the situation. You always seemed to admire the aliens and want to learn from them."

"Ever since your father pointed a gun at me and gave me the choice of feeling that way or dying," Jonathan agreed. "But you see, 'seemed' is the important word. People who grow up in the underground societies learn to seem to be whatever they have to seem to be to survive. Track down Julie and Tashie and Daniel Davidovich and ask them; they'll tell you the same thing."

Elena paused, then decided to try a different tack. "Why are the soldiers here?"

She could hear the grin in Jonathan's voice. "Wait and see."

They stood together in silence and waited. A small point of red light became visible above them. It enlarged, becoming a dull, metallic sphere, reddish in the sunlight. It was a miniature of the gray hole that had played such a monstrous role in human history.

It drifted down toward the lunar surface and touched lightly only a few meters in front of Jonathan and Elena. It was immense; Elena could not estimate its diameter. A vertical slit appeared on its lower curve, like a cat's pupil. The bright lights within the alien ship turned the lunar surface white. A tall, slender figure moved through the slit, downward toward the surface, and then toward Jonathan, floating just slightly above the ground. As it came closer, Elena could see that it was half again the height of a man, but it was enclosed in a glowing field of some sort that made the details impossible to discern.

Jonathan spoke a formal greeting in the alien language. And then he stepped forward, his right hand extended. "Shake, Ambassador," he said in English.

Elena gasped. The alien recoiled and suddenly began to move back toward his ship.

But at Jonathan's words, the ground had erupted into clouds of dust in a circle all around the three figures and the ship. Surface-suited figures emerged from the dust clouds, hurtling so fast toward the doorway in the alien ship that they appeared to be flying. Suddenly Elena realized that they were: they were propelled by rockets on their backs.

The opening began to close, but it wasn't in time. The suited soldiers rocketed through it, there were flashes inside the doorway, and then it opened wide again. A seemingly endless stream of men poured into the alien ship. A separate group of them had surrounded the ambassador and were now carrying him away. Words of outrage and protest in the alien language came over Elena's suit radio. Minutes later, a parade of soldiers emerged from the alien ship bearing more aliens surrounded by the same glowing fields. The clouds of dust had vanished, revealing gaping holes in the lunar surface.

"Jonathan!" Elena said at last. "Jonathan! What—?"

For a while, Jonathan ignored her. At last, all the furious activity was over, and the two of them were alone with the alien ship, its entrance gaping open. Now Jonathan spoke to her. "By now, we have a pretty good idea of what sensors they have. We took the chance that they wouldn't be able to detect our men hidden below the surface. We were right. They're so blind because of their hauteur and technological supremacy and because they're such Goddamned Proper Ones, that they didn't even suspect I'd dare trick them."

"But why?" Elena asked in utter bewilderment.

Jonathan laughed. "I love you. Do you really understand that? Have you ever really believed me when I've told you that?"

Elena breathed silent thanks for private, coded suit-to-suit channels. "I used to at first, but maybe not for the last few years."

Jonathan's voice was sober again, lacking any trace of laughter or hint of a smile on his face. "I know. But it's more true now than it ever was. For myself, I don't know if I'd be doing any of this. Or any of the other things I've had to do since Isaac died. We're going to take that ship apart and put it back together. I've got an army of scientists and engineers waiting, too. And biologists; they'll take the ambassador and his staff apart for the sake of curiosity. Can't put *them* back together, of course. Pity. Of course, we'll preserve some of them—the technical experts they promised to send us along with the ambassador. From them, we want every single fact their brains contain."

"Good God, Jonathan! This is an act of war!"

"Really? And what was taking our sun and murdering billions of Earthmen?"

Elena searched desperately for the right thing to say. "Won't their home world realize something's gone wrong? And retaliate?"

"What could they do? Take the sun again?" He laughed. "I guess they could, couldn't they? Anyway, the ambassador's boys didn't even have time to send a message home saying they're under attack. Especially since we're jamming any T-band transmissions; we know how to do that, now. I suppose they'll realize that something's gone wrong, but they won't know we did anything hostile. We'll have the knowledge we want before they take any kind of action against us. All we need is a few months—a year at most."

"How about our people? The whole world's waiting to see the alien ambassador."

"And they will. After all, no one knows what the aliens look like, do they? I have an actor ready for the part. Tomorrow, I'll present him to the world. He'll circulate in society, but very carefully. He'll be distant and unapproachable."

"That's ridiculous!" Elena said. "Sooner or later, he'll slip up. How long do you think you can carry that off?"

"Long enough."

"But what's the point, Jonathan?" Elena pleaded. "*Why* do this? They'd teach us all of this science and technology eventually, anyway."

"*Teach* it to us!" Jonathan yelled. "Hell, yes, they'd hand it out in little dollops, while we wagged our tails! You and your father and his predecessors sacrificed our pride long ago. Now we'll get it back. No more begging, no more grateful acceptance of little gifts and pats on the head. We'll approach them as their equals. And they'll know it when we show up at their home world in our own fleet of ships. That's when . . ." He paused. "What's done *can* be undone," he said softly.

"That's when what?"

"It won't hurt to tell you, I suppose. Their sun is virtually identical in mass and spectral type to ours. I mean the one we used to have, the one they took from us. Don't you think it's time we restored our world and our solar system to the way they used to be? And after we're done, the aliens won't be a threat to us. They winnowed us; that's not what we have in store for them."

Elena stepped back, drifting away from Jonathan. He didn't notice. His attention was all on the alien ship before him. He made no move toward it; he seemed satisfied just to watch it.

Elena watched him standing alone on the brilliant red-gray surface of the moon. He was alone but not lonely, solitary but embodying all of mankind within his isolated figure. He stood upright, proud, radiating strength she could feel, archetypal. How well the aliens had succeeded in their winnowing! she thought. It was an irony she suspected they would not appreciate. She stared wordlessly at him, compelled despite herself to something approaching a sense of worship.

Jonathan stood calmly, patiently, his inner fires banked at last, well prepared for his destiny: Man at the brink of his conquest of the Universe.

AWARD-WINNING
Science Fiction!

The following works are winners of the prestigious Nebula or Hugo Award for excellence in Science Fiction. A must for lovers of good science fiction everywhere!

☐ 0-441-77422-9	**SOLDIER ASK NOT,** Gordon R. Dickson	$3.50
☐ 0-441-47812-3	**THE LEFT HAND OF DARKNESS,** Ursula K. Le Guin	$3.95
☐ 0-441-16708-X	**THE DREAM MASTER,** Roger Zelazny	$2.95
☐ 0-441-56959-5	**NEUROMANCER,** William Gibson	$3.50
☐ 0-441-23777-0	**THE FINAL ENCYCLOPEDIA,** Gordon R. Dickson	$5.25
☐ 0-441-06797-2	**BLOOD MUSIC,** Greg Bear	$2.95
☐ 0-441-79034-8	**STRANGER IN A STRANGE LAND,** Robert A. Heinlein	$4.50

BESTSELLING
Science Fiction
and
Fantasy